**"[Holly] creates tantalizing tales."**
***—Rendezvous***

## Fantasy: An Anthology

"Emma Holly's Luisa del Fiore takes sexual allure to new heights . . . A five-star winner . . . Will keep you reading under those covers late into the night." —*Affaire de Coeur*

## Beyond Seduction

"Holly brings a level of sensuality to her storytelling that may shock the uninitiated . . . [A] combination of heady sexuality and intriguing characterization."

—*Publishers Weekly*

"Emma Holly once again pens an unforgettably erotic love story . . . A wonderful tale of creative genius and unbridled passion." —*Affaire de Coeur*

## Beyond Innocence

"An excellent mixture of eroticism and romance."

—*All About Romance*

"A complex plot, a dark and brooding hero, and [a] charming heroine . . . a winner in every way. Go out and grab a copy—it's a fabulous read . . . A treat."

—*Romance Reviews Today*

"Truly beautiful." —*Sensual Romance*

## *Books by Emma Holly*

### *Upyr Novels*

### *The Fitz Clare Chronicles*

SAVING MIDNIGHT
BREAKING MIDNIGHT
KISSING MIDNIGHT

COURTING MIDNIGHT
HOT BLOODED
*(with Christine Feehan, Maggie Shayne, and Angela Knight)*
HUNTING MIDNIGHT
CATCHING MIDNIGHT
FANTASY
*(with Christine Feehan, Sabrina Jeffries, and Elda Minger)*

### *Tales of the Demon World*

DEMON'S FIRE
BEYOND THE DARK
*(with Angela Knight, Lora Leigh, and Diane Whiteside)*
DEMON'S DELIGHT
*(with MaryJanice Davidson, Vickie Taylor, and Catherine Spangler)*
PRINCE OF ICE
HOT SPELL
*(with Lora Leigh, Shiloh Walker, and Meljean Brook)*
THE DEMON'S DAUGHTER

BEYOND SEDUCTION
BEYOND INNOCENCE

ALL U CAN EAT
FAIRYVILLE
STRANGE ATTRACTIONS
PERSONAL ASSETS

### *Anthologies*

HEAT OF THE NIGHT
MIDNIGHT DESIRE
BEYOND DESIRE

# Demon's Fire

EMMA HOLLY

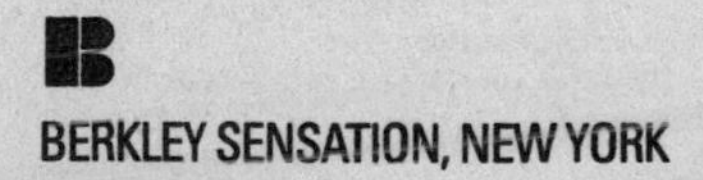

BERKLEY SENSATION, NEW YORK

**THE BERKLEY PUBLISHING GROUP**
**Published by the Penguin Group**
**Penguin Group (USA) Inc.**
**375 Hudson Street, New York, New York 10014, USA**
Penguin Group (Canada), 90 Eglinton Avenue East, Suite 700, Toronto, Ontario M4P 2Y3, Canada
(a division of Pearson Penguin Canada Inc.)
Penguin Books Ltd., 80 Strand, London WC2R 0RL, England
Penguin Group Ireland, 25 St. Stephen's Green, Dublin 2, Ireland (a division of Penguin Books Ltd.)
Penguin Group (Australia), 250 Camberwell Road, Camberwell, Victoria 3124, Australia
(a division of Pearson Australia Group Pty. Ltd.)
Penguin Books India Pvt. Ltd., 11 Community Centre, Panchsheel Park, New Delhi—110 017, India
Penguin Group (NZ), 67 Apollo Drive, Rosedale, North Shore 0632, New Zealand
(a division of Pearson New Zealand Ltd.)
Penguin Books (South Africa) (Pty.) Ltd., 24 Sturdee Avenue, Rosebank, Johannesburg 2196,
South Africa

Penguin Books Ltd., Registered Offices: 80 Strand, London WC2R 0RL, England



DEMON'S FIRE

A Berkley Sensation Book / published by arrangement with the author

PRINTING HISTORY
Berkley Sensation trade edition / April 2008
Berkley Sensation mass-market edition / October 2010


Cover art by Phil Heffernan.
Cover design by George Long.
Interior text design by Kristin del Rosario.


For information, address: The Berkley Publishing Group,
a division of Penguin Group (USA) Inc.,
375 Hudson Street, New York, New York 10014.

ISBN: 978-0-425-23749-6

BERKLEY® SENSATION
Berkley Sensation Books are published by The Berkley Publishing Group,
a division of Penguin Group (USA) Inc.,
375 Hudson Street, New York, New York 10014.
BERKLEY® SENSATION and the "B" design are trademarks of Penguin Group (USA) Inc.

PRINTED IN THE UNITED STATES OF AMERICA

10 9 8 7 6 5 4 3 2 1

*To my fans,*
*because you make it*
*that much sweeter.*

# PROLOGUE

Eavesdropping hadn't been Prince Pahndir's intent.

He hadn't known what was happening when the guards slipped into his rooms at the Purple Crane. Breaking into a pillow house was no great feat, but these men were professionals. Silent as the grave, they'd worn no livery, their all-black outfits bearing no identifying marks. Prince Pahndir's first thought was that his family had finally decided to make good on their pretense that he was dead.

His second was whether he minded.

But it wasn't his day to die. The guards informed him he was coming with them, then led him—without explanation—to an aircar that had been fitted out to look like a food delivery airvan. It set down on the roof of Midarri Palace, a place he'd only ever seen from outside. His family hadn't been as high on the royal ladder as that of Buttercup's prince.

The thought of her tightened the muscles above his breastbone. Buttercup must have had something to do with his rescue from the pillow house, and he was far from sure that was a good thing. He'd heard her fellow students talking about her arrest, but had only gotten pieces of the story. Madame Fagin had been uncustomarily nervous since the event, snapping at her students and working girls alike. It was as if she were hoping her former pupil would be executed, and—for some unfathomable reason—feared the consequences if she were not. Pahndir supposed his liberation from the madame's care meant the trial had gone Buttercup's way.

Somehow, he doubted the silent guards would confirm this if he asked.

Before he could attempt it, they were transferring him from the delivery van to a private aircar, which was emblazoned with the Midarri crest. Normally, it would have seated eight in luxury, but the seats had been removed to make room for a pile of plastic packing crates. The guards withdrew once he was inside, with the exception of the youngest one.

"We'll move you to another flyer for liftoff," he said. "Some of the other cars were compromised during an incident this afternoon, but the security systems in this one are fine. You'll be safe as long as you don't unlock the door."

*Safe from what?* Pahndir thought as the door slid shut behind his last companion. *And safe* for *what?*

He could have cursed Buttercup for involving herself in his affairs. What happened to him hadn't mattered in a long time. His body's reactions to her were nothing more than a stirring of physical urges that hadn't had the decency to die with his wife. He cared about Buttercup just enough to wish her far away from him.

That long-ago night in Madame Fagin's parlor, watching through the hidden portrait hole as the girls lined up, he'd seen Prince Corum's eyes go black. Pahndir hadn't been certain Cor and Buttercup would be mates, but he had sensed their relationship would be rare. He'd wanted Buttercup to have that. Only she, of all of Madame Fagin's students, had treated him like a man. She shouldn't be jeopardizing her future by championing his cause. If he'd wanted it championed, he'd have fought for himself. As it was, he'd discouraged her as cuttingly as he could from giving him a second thought after she left.

It had been the only act he'd been proud of in years. And now it seemed it hadn't worked.

He pressed his temples between the heels of his palms. Couldn't she see his family had been right to fake his death and send him into servitude? Thallah's suicide had exposed his fatal weakness, making it obvious to anyone who met him that he'd never survive the cutthroat world of royal life. He was damaged: He grieved, while others buried their hurt in decent Yamish ice. Pahndir couldn't lead his own second-tier family, much less take over a powerful one like the Fengs.

If Buttercup had ruined her chance for happiness by helping him, he'd never forgive himself.

He didn't know how long he stood there, wondering what in creation he could do that wouldn't make matters worse. As much as an hour might have passed. Though the aircar's cabin windows were opaqued for privacy, the change in the light told him winter's early dusk had arrived.

It occurred to him that the guards had not come back to move him to another car. Had something happened to rob them of the chance? They'd seemed too professional to forget, but maybe his disappearance had been noticed, and they didn't want to risk discovery with more contact. He hoped they'd warned whoever's vehicle this was that he was here . . . unless they'd decided to give the owners deniability about their stowaway.

With that possibility uppermost in his mind, he heard footsteps coming up the outside ramp.

He moved with the quickness any royal prince could call upon. Mere seconds were required to lift the stretchy web that secured the crates and make a cave for himself between them. He was well concealed, if not comfortable, by the time Prince Corum and Buttercup walked in.

It was immediately obvious they had no idea he was there. The sound of their openmouthed kisses was a plague he could have done without. Robes were torn off and thrown, endearments exchanged, then overtaken by sighs and moans. He knew the instant the prince slid inside his partner. That groan of relieved entry was one he'd made himself countless times.

When one was a solitary, with only one mate in all the world, the word *relief* took on a new meaning.

To judge by the ensuing, breathless conversation, Cor and Buttercup were mates after all—and joyous ones. Though Pahndir had wanted a future like this for his friend, knowing she had it hurt all the same.

He remembered being that much in love, remembered needing so deeply to connect that it was agony. Thallah had been more than his genetic match; she'd been the perfect playmate for his erotic adventuring, a lover and confidante. He'd thought he'd known her better than any living creature until she killed herself.

That had been a breach of trust he still didn't understand.

His body woke at the memories, but even more at Buttercup's extremely aroused nearness. He knew she was part human; that bit of news had reached him. He supposed this was why her chi was so intoxicating, why it had made him feel he could almost come when she stroked him. Her energy teased him now. His heat was days away, but—as had happened so many times at the pillow school—he felt her presence spur it on early.

He lifted within his clothing, thickening, stretching, growing heavy with blood and lust. Images clawed unbidden through his mind: tearing Prince Corum off his beloved, taking his place between her legs, plunging into Buttercup so hard she screamed.

In the end, the desperate pounding of his cock was too much to bear. He'd been deprived of true release for too long—through every heat since Thallah died, through every class of students who tried to devise new ways to "get a rise" from him. No matter that the drive for sex wasn't that different from the drive for life; some dark and bestial corner of his soul was perfectly ready to betray his one great love. His soul was exhausted with just surviving. It wanted to mate again.

He shoved his hand into his trousers and gripped himself. Up and down he rubbed his aching erection, his fist so tight the pressure burned his skin. He didn't care. The moans outside the boxes increased in volume, the eager slapping of flesh to flesh. If he couldn't join them, by Infinity, he could lose himself in their lust. At the least, he knew his orgasm would be good. All living beings radiated extra etheric force at climax, and from what he'd tasted of it already, Buttercup's was sure to be sweet.

He timed his strokes to match their excitement—faster, tighter, and then their mutual peak was there. The prince and Buttercup cried out hoarsely, the energy of their orgasm rolling over him like a hot, moist wind—a palpable shock wave of ecstasy.

He was not prepared for the intensity of the effect. His sensations peaked beyond any he could recall, his balls contracting as if a large, strong hand had slapped them to his root.

He tensed, throttling back a scream. This couldn't be happening. This was too much. Too good.

His body overruled his mind's objections. Deep in his groin, gates that had been tightly shut fibrillated wildly and flew open. His own sexual essences flooded him too quickly for him to muster the least defense. Heat rushed through his cock and burst violently over his hand. For the first time in seven years, Prince Pahndir spilled his semen.

When it was over, he gulped for air as quietly as he could, his relief as momentous as his shock. However this miracle had happened, he knew what it meant: His curse was broken. He was alive again.

And he didn't have the faintest concept what to do about that.

# ONE

Sex rode the air in Bhamjran as thickly as the scent of coffee or sand or spice. Not for nothing did humans call this the "city of laissez-faire." Whatever your erotic wish, however twisted or exotic, you could satisfy it here.

Or you could if you weren't a solitary demon royal. Prince Pahndir, former captive and teaching tool at the Purple Crane, had discovered—to his intense physical dismay—that for him, satisfaction was elusive at any price.

He leaned back in his gaudy, gilded booth in Bhamjran's busy market square. It was the height of the desert city's morning rush, with shoppers seeking everything from fruit to chickens to new brass pots. It was a challenge to compete with the color and flair of the locals' stalls, but the eye-catching wooden structure beneath which he sat—his calling card, as it were—had been carved into a lacework of creatively copulating statuettes; ironic, considering his own long-standing sexual predicament.

The acid humor he experienced at the reminder showed itself as no more than a deepening of the shadows around his mouth. He was resigned to living in exile among the humans, even to profiting from them. But smile as they did? Demonstrate that his control over his emotions was as poor as theirs?

He tutted silently in his head.

That, despite two years of hope denied, he still had too much pride to do.

He wouldn't have been in this *chowk* at all if it weren't for pride, hawking other people's flesh to keep from having to sell his own. Oh, he could have let Prince Cor continue to support him. Deep as his pockets were, the Midarri prince wouldn't have complained. But Pahndir couldn't tolerate taking charity from a man who'd married the one woman he'd . . . connected with since his own wife's death.

He nodded slightly to himself beneath his yellow awning's shade. *Connected* was a word he could allow himself. He didn't love Buttercup—or *Xishi*, as he forced himself to call her now that she was no longer a pillow girl. He wouldn't love her—couldn't—despite his body's prompting to the contrary. Xishi was Cor's mate, physically bound to him by the tyranny of her genes, just as Pahndir had been bound to Thallah. For that matter, Xishi's love for Cor would have been enough to keep Pahndir at a distance. Her happiness was everything.

Or so Pahndir told himself.

He shifted in his low folding leather seat, the mere thought of Xishi enough to thicken his male organ. What he wouldn't have given for another true release from her. Or from anyone, for that matter. He wasn't even near his heat. His last bout of torture had ended a week ago. This time, he hadn't given in to the temptation to seek a partner; that particular brand of disappointment was exhausting him. Nonetheless, the idea of ejaculating, of emptying his seed without a Yamish doctor's aid, was an obsession he could not shake.

In a way, that obsession had led him to his current occupation as the owner of The Prince's Flame. In his quest to find a human who could do for him what Xishi had, he'd visited every brothel the city had, most of them more than once. Sexual longing, and the lengths to which a person would go to gratify it, was a phenomenon he understood extremely well.

That being so, why shouldn't he be the first man in Bhamjran to run a bawdy house?

Never mind this was a matriarchal city. Never mind many of the local males were expected to keep to the *zenana* and be cosseted. Bhamjran was an Ohramese possession now, and the Ohramese were used to men running things. More important, thanks to their prissy virgin queen Victoria, the Ohramese weren't as comfortable with their desires as their Bhamjrishi subjects. They didn't want to explain their supposedly inappropriate cravings to a human madam. Explaining them to a demon like himself, a being they considered too depraved to be capable of judging them, was easier.

Add to that the fact that no human would ever best his kind in business, and it was no wonder The Prince's Flame was quietly becoming a commercial force.

A shadow fell across Pahndir's feet where he had stretched his pointed slippers into the sun. He shook himself from his musings and looked up.

His shills for the day, a pretty human girl named Alia and an even prettier human boy named Tomas, stood side by side before him on the dusty ground, their expressions wavering between caution and sulkiness. They worked for Pahndir because he gave them a larger cut than his rivals, and because he more readily allowed them to draw the line of what they would not do. His house was cleaner than the ancient city's other brothels, and safer, too. He supplied his workers with finer clothing, more varied food, and all the Yamish amenities Prince Cor's connections had enabled him to install: electric lights and running water, to name two.

Considering how much more advanced Yama were, they had to be careful what technology they allowed into human hands, but all the necessities of health and civility Pahndir's house supplied.

Despite these advantages, his employees hadn't lost their fear of him. Pahndir was forever Other to the humans, a member of a race they'd called "demon" since discovering them accidentally forty years ago. Now Pahndir's alabaster skin, his ink-black hair, his height, his rim-to-rim silver eyes declared his alien nature. He didn't even have to maintain his trademark Yamish stoniness; no matter how kind he thought himself, these young humans wouldn't warm up to their master.

A sensation he didn't choose to name constricted his vocal cords. His employees' affection couldn't have mattered less to him. In a country whose lower class was as large and poor as Bhamjran's, there would always be those who wanted or needed to sell themselves. Feared or loved, Pahndir's more favorable fiscal arrangements ensured that The Prince's Flame would always get the cream of the crop.

In spite of which, Pahndir preferred not to institute a rule of terror.

"What is it?" he asked as gently as he could—though for all he knew his voice sounded as cool as ever to their human ears.

"We're tired," Alia announced. "We worked all last night."

Less bold than his companion, Tomas nodded shyly in agreement. Both their shoulders were drooping.

"It's your turn in the market," Pahndir reminded them. "You being here, embodying what The Prince's Flame has to offer, drums up business for everyone."

"But we're *really* tired," Alia blurted. "No one wants to take our cards this early in the day."

This was patently untrue. Pahndir could see she held no more than half the stack he'd given her to pass out, and Tomas held less than a third. Alia bit her lip and flushed when she saw his gaze had fallen to her hand. Pahndir almost smiled but caught himself. Humans were so easy to read sometimes that he truly couldn't help but be amused.

"Beauty such as yours will always stir interest," he assured them, "no matter what the hour. But perhaps you would benefit from a coffee break." He dropped a clinking rain of silver *denars* into Tomas's palm, a show of favor that had the young man flushing as deeply as his companion. Bhamjrishi males weren't often trusted with money.

"Thank you, sir," the boy whispered. "We'll bring back the change."

"A black espresso will be good enough."

Tomas jerked his head in agreement, and the pair ran off with the exuberance of prisoners freed from hard labor.

Once he'd shrugged off the unflattering eagerness of their departure, it was not unpleasant to be left alone. Pahndir didn't mind the blazing summer heat the way humans did. Millennia of genetic manipulation had given his kind the ability to adjust to extremes. Now, with his body slouched in the chair and his limbs relaxed, he felt very much the snake basking in the sun that so many humans would have seen.

Nor was his ease the heat's doing alone. The square held such a crowd of humans, all jostling and striving and *feeling* the way humans did, that it was impossible not to imbibe a bit of their etheric force, even without touching them. The unavoidable transfer of energy went to his head like brandy spiked with caffeine. His world, frustrations notwithstanding, took on a golden glow. Maybe he should come to the *chowk* every morning, instead of his usual once-a-week visit. Live with the edges blurred for a while. Let himself pretend he was at peace.

Lacing his hands across his flat, hard belly, he narrowed his eyes in search of potential customers.

A low, bushy palm tree obscured his leftward view, but to the right, where Shiva's Way fed into the square beneath a sandstone arch, Pahndir's gaze encompassed all. A handsome lady of her house in a sapphire tunic, her arms agleam with gold bangles, seemed worth sending Tomas after when he returned. Sadly, at the moment, the rest of the crowd appeared too poor for his rates.

And then he saw them: a man and a woman walking shoulder to shoulder past a line of citrus stalls. They were human, Ohramese by their dress, smiling with enjoyment for the young, new day. The woman wore a crisp white shirtwaist with a long navy skirt, the man a close-cut suit in sand-colored cloth. Neither looked far into their twenties, and both were tall for their race—the man a hair over six feet and the woman a shade below.

They weren't aristocrats; their clothes weren't fine enough for that, but neither were they poor. Upper working class, Pahndir deduced. Flush enough to holiday in Bhamjran, but not much more. Definitely not flush enough for The Prince's Flame, and still he couldn't look away. Something about them caught his attention: some intensity within them, some repressed passion.

As Pahndir watched, the woman picked up an orange and held it to her nose, closing her eyes as she breathed in the scent. Her cheeks were sun browned, her hair a gleaming fall of chestnut caught in a simple tail. Her lush, full lips were dark as cinnamon. When she wet the upper, Pahndir's heart jolted in his chest, his nerves quickening to a degree he couldn't remember feeling for some time. The fans of her lashes lifted as the hand that held the orange fell. Clear across the market, Pahndir saw her eyes were honey-gold.

Oblivious to his attention, she elbowed her companion in a friendly way, a gesture that shook her breasts behind the white shirtwaist.

Pahndir cursed softly to himself. She couldn't have known how the sun shone through that starched white cotton, how it turned every curve of her lithe, young torso to a clear shadow. She wore no corset, and he could see the slightly swollen peaks of her nipples, the high, conelike projection of her small, firm breasts. She was built like a gazelle, all racing lines and smooth, hard strength.

Generally speaking, Pahndir preferred more plumpness in a human female—most likely because his own kind was lean—but her looks were just different enough to call to him. His body tightened as he imagined her naked beneath him: her struggle against his strength, his inexorable penetration; the taste of salt on her human skin . . .

Barely aware that he was doing it, his tongue came out to wet his mouth, just as hers had moments earlier. Unlike her, in him the gesture bared a dark forked marking, a natural coloration that had once terrified her kind. Seeing it, the vendor in the next stall over turned away nervously.

*Demon* he was then, a demon who longed to ravish and plunder.

The woman's companion bent to her to say something—some human tease, apparently, because she threw back her head and laughed. To Pahndir's secret delight, the sound was no ladylike tinkle, but a true guffaw.

"Charles!" Pahndir heard her humorous outrage ring out. "You're impossible!"

The woman shoved his arm as she said it, as if she were a boy herself and he her schoolmate.

*They're not lovers then,* Pahndir thought, without stopping to worry that the idea flooded him with hot relief.

Her companion laughed more quietly back at her, tossed a coin to the vendor, and began peeling her orange. Pahndir could feel the pair's high spirits as they continued to stroll in his direction around the square: two healthy young Ohramese come to shop with the natives. They'd take this story back with them when they went home—how quaint and foreign everything was, how deliciously risqué. The man tossed bits of orange pith at his friend, causing her to laugh again. Her eyes were glowing, her color high. Within her narrow-waisted skirt, her long, sure strides swung like a man's.

*Tomboy,* Pahndir thought, retrieving the human word.

The trait didn't squelch his fascination. She looked alive laughing with the man; carefree and innocent. With an odd little ache pinching in his chest, Pahndir realized only a human could wear a look like that. Among his own kind, with their byzantine sophistication and endless scheming, innocence was stamped out young.

Just then, as the male fed an orange section into the woman's laughing mouth, a long-tailed desert falcon wheeled overhead. The bird screamed a challenge, perhaps offended by the noise below. In unison, the humans turned their eyes to the sky.

Pahndir's first clear sight of the man's face was his second gut-punch of the morning.

The male was fair in every sense of the word, his hair a straight silvery blond, his eyes a dreamy seaswept blue. His features were so exquisitely cut and balanced they could have belonged to one of Pahndir's race. Oh, the human's coloring would have been unusual for a Yama but not impossible. His was a beauty that transcended genes, a throat-squeezing, breath-stealing symmetry. The yearning he betrayed as he watched that hawk circling overhead only heightened his appeal.

Anyone who saw his expression, whatever their culture, would know he hungered for freedom.

Freedom from what, Pahndir could not guess. The man turned from the hawk before the woman did. As luck would have it, his gaze clicked precisely into Pahndir's. A prickle swept Pahndir's nape, lifting the little hairs that grew there, but he didn't lower his eyes. The man's look of yearning had blown away with the hot, dry wind. In its place, Pahndir read a flash of recognition, followed by a sardonic self-consciousness.

This man, stranger though he was to Pahndir, knew who he was. This man knew what he was hawking from his golden stall.

More to the point, this man was interested in his wares—against his will, perhaps, but interested all the same.

Pahndir nodded to him, man to man, then gave his head the subtle tilt that was a universal signal to come near. The man went still, then glanced at his companion, guilt in the gesture if ever there were. He didn't, however, seem alarmed to have been addressed by a demon. Pahndir's heart pulsed hard in his throat as he waited to see what the man would do.

What he did was squeeze his companion's arm, speak softly in her ear, and draw away. She watched him walk toward Pahndir's stall but didn't follow him.

The man stopped just within the shadow of Pahndir's awning and removed his brimmed straw hat. Something about the way he held it before his heart, as if unconsciously shielding that organ, made Pahndir tread carefully.

For more reasons than the usual, this was a customer he wanted to reel in.

"I see you know who I am," Pahndir said when the man remained silent. "So the question is, how may I serve you?"

The man's face was quiet but not as quiet as a Yama's would have been. Thoughts moved behind it, temptations he might have struggled with for years. And here Pahndir was, doing his best to nudge the stranger over the brink.

"I was wondering . . ." The man swallowed, nervous despite the dignity he was trying to project. "I was wondering if you offer the services of other races."

Pahndir felt his brows draw together above his nose. Sometimes humans from one country referred to humans from another as a different race, but Pahndir sensed this was not the man's meaning. Then comprehension dawned, and along with it another quickening of his pulse. He had to pull in a breath to speak smoothly.

"You mean, do I pander the unfortunates of my own race to my customers?"

The man gave a jerking nod, a vein now beating harder in his strong brown neck. That neck led into the open collar of his cambric shirt, the edges of which had been stained past scrubbing by the dusty golden sands of the Vharzovhin. Perhaps he was one of Herrington's crew out on the dig. That was one demon every Yama had heard of, a famous diplomat who lived with the humans in their capital. Lord Herrington had fathered a half-demon bastard on an opera singer, and then had the cheek to acknowledge her publicly. Archaeology was Herrington's hobby. His luck at it, or maybe it was brilliance, had made him something of a hero to both races.

Intrigued by the possibility that this young man worked for him—though not as much as by their conversation—Pahndir filed the thought away. He could see the object of his interest fighting to breathe normally.

Suddenly enjoying this very much, Pahndir smoothed his eminently *un*stained pale blue tunic down his thighs. "As it happens, I have two beautiful demons who work for me. One male. One female. You could take your pick."

His potential customer dropped his eyes but, evidently, not because he'd been offered both genders.

"They're *rohn*?" the human asked in a soft, harsh voice.

"They are," Pahndir confirmed, refraining from pointing out that members of the upper class, *his* class, would hardly condescend to sell their bodies as a career; as a lark, perhaps—*daimyo* were decadent enough for anything—but not to earn their daily bread.

"Do they . . ." The young man swallowed as the words broke in his throat. "Do they have to be hired for sex?"

Pahndir had been leaning forward, caught up in the drama of their exchange, but this query sent him lounging back in the folding chair. He steepled graceful fingers before his chin. "You mean you'd like them to take your energy."

The man said nothing, but the unhappiness in his eyes confirmed the guess well enough. Somehow, somewhere, this beautiful Ohramese boy had developed a fixation with being fed on by demons. To witness such shame over what was, to Pahndir, an understandable enough desire nearly shamed him as well . . . nearly, but not quite.

After all, if humans viewed what Pahndir was selling as a step on the road to hell, that was their concern. *He* didn't have to consider himself the devil whispering in their ear.

"It can be done as carefully as you wish," he said, "with whatever safeguards you desire to prevent undue fatigue. For that matter . . ." Pahndir hesitated half a moment, an impulse he didn't understand spurring him. "If you preferred it, I would take your energy myself."

The young man held Pahndir in his considering sea-blue gaze, not accepting, but also not repelled. Ohramese though he was, this man knew something of what two males could do together. Pahndir's body heated deep and low, like opium smoke curling in his groin. In his desire to find a human to help him spill his seed, he had not considered a male might do, but this one certainly made him think *maybe.* Pahndir had been with his own sex before, now and then. Royal Yama were naturally adventurous. Given the stringent limits within which their biology operated, they'd have been fools not to experiment. Pahndir knew that to drink this human's etheric force would be a pleasure in itself—a dangerous pleasure, but he was not averse to that. What would it matter if he absorbed the human's emotions along with his energy? Pahndir was a prince. Unlike the *rohn* in his employ, whose self-control was proportional to their class, Pahndir would get over it.

"At least take my card," Pahndir said, offering him one. "You can decide at your leisure."

The young man looked at the small cream-colored square, then back over his shoulder at the woman he'd come to the market with.

Pahndir had almost forgotten her during their exchange, but the reminder had his flesh humming anew, electricity flowing like a zephyr across his skin. *Her* energy seemed able to reach him across the *chowk*, like heat waves shimmering over sunbaked dunes. The effect was extraordinary. Sensual. Teasing. And that to a man whose erotic interest, by nature and circumstance, needed little encouragement to rise.

Had he ever seen anyone, human or Yama, shine this vibrantly? She stood in a sari stall, lifting a length of scarlet silk into the sun to examine it. The garment fluttered against her breasts like water, painting her in the color of sex itself. He wasn't the only one who thought so. Again, Pahndir saw that yearning in her companion's face, this time for a prize he seemed to think as far beyond his deserving as an emperor's crown.

It was a yearning he was clearly used to tamping down. When the Ohramese's attention returned to Pahndir, his expression was like carved granite. The faintest flush on his cheekbones was all that exposed his imperfect human control.

*Infinity help me,* Pahndir thought, struggling to keep his reaction to this sight concealed. What he wouldn't give to bed both of them!

"I don't need a card to find The Prince's Flame," the young man said.

The comment begged a rejoinder, preferably a flirtatious one. Seeing the young man's self-derision, Pahndir restrained himself.

"I hope you *do* find it," was all he said, obliged to content himself with but a shade of hope as the Ohramese turned and walked off.

From the first, Beth had been aware of the demon's gaze. The attention intrigued her but also made her self-conscious. People simply didn't stare at her when she was with Charles.

Charles was . . . well, not quite a cousin, though he liked to treat her as if he were. Charles was the former ward of Beth's older brother's wife, a woman who had rescued Charles and his younger brother from starving on the street. Beth didn't think of herself as vain, but Charles was the only person she knew who made her feel homely. He had the face of a fallen angel, his bitter humor as beautiful as others' cheer.

Despite which, the demon had stared at her.

Her cheeks felt hot as she pretended the scarlet sari

she'd picked up was engaging her whole interest. What were Charles and the Yama talking about? Not her, surely. That was too great a stretch. Charles had called the demon "an acquaintance," had claimed he "ought to say hello," but when he'd said it, his eyes had evaded hers. Obviously, this association was one of his secrets, the deep, dark who-knew-whats he thought she was too decent a girl to hear about. The attitude drove her mad. Beth might not have grown up like he did, might never have gone hungry or done unmentionable things to survive, but she was far from being as nice a girl as Charles insisted on believing.

If she had been, she wouldn't have pestered her parents for literally years to let her travel here with Lord Herrington.

Beth's parents—bless their well-meaning souls—wanted her to settle down and marry like her older sisters, wanted her to pop out babies and stay home. Beth understood why they felt that way. They'd worked hard for most of their lives. The fact that they'd raised daughters who didn't have to meant a lot to them, and Beth being the baby made it twice as hard for them to let go. But Beth had never desired an ordinary life. With all her being, she craved an extraordinary one. She thanked all the stars in heaven that her family had finally given up their hopes for her

"Excuse me," Beth whispered to the patiently waiting sari vendor. "What is the business of that man in the golden booth?"

Fortunately, like most Bhamjrishi, this vendor spoke her conquerors' tongue. "That is Mr. Pahndir," she said in the lilting local accent. "He runs The Prince's Flame."

"The Prince's Flame?"

The older woman's earthy amusement might have been invented by her countrywomen. Certainly, they'd perfected it. "The Prince's Flame is a pleasure house. It is expensive but very clean. I've heard he runs it honestly."

Beth's mouth abruptly felt glued shut, unable to say a word. *A pleasure house.* And Charles had called the demon an acquaintance. Beth was embarrassed to find she could be shocked. But it was none of her business what Charles did along those lines. No matter what her silly private daydreams—which a female would have to be dead and blind not to entertain—she and Charles were not romantically involved. She was twenty-four, for heaven's sake, old enough to know what went on in a pleasure house, old enough to be married, had she been inclined. People her age had sex, and those people included Charles.

The vendor must have sensed her inner battle, because she smiled and spoke again. "You do know that pleasure houses in Bhamjran serve women as well as men?"

"Of course I do," Beth said too quickly, having forgotten that entirely.

The vendor laughed softly. "Perhaps The Prince's Flame would be worth the price for you."

Beth blushed as hotly as if her cheeks had been steamed, but she had to ask. "You don't suppose that demon . . ."

The vendor joined her in regarding the man Charles was talking to. "I haven't heard whether Mr. Pahndir takes customers. We don't get many Yama in Bhamjran, but it cannot be denied they are a handsome lot. And they're stronger than humans. More self-controlled. I've heard their males can go all night."

Beth had a reasonable understanding of what they could "go all night" at, though this was not a phrase she'd heard before. Her legs felt weak of a sudden, her upper thighs prickly and warm. The demon sprawled in his chair as arrogant as a prince, his long legs stretched, his hair a cloak of raven silk spilling down his arms. Beautiful blue highlights gleamed in it. He *was* handsome, in a strange, foreign way—exotically attractive, like the curving silver daggers desert tribes employed. That she couldn't read his expression sent a pleasant shiver coursing down her spine. Lord Herrington, the only demon she knew personally, had lived among humans for so many years he'd gone a bit native. This one was the genuine, undiluted article. This one wasn't even sweating in the desert heat.

*I'd like to make him sweat,* Beth thought out of the blue.

The impulse startled her. However not-nice she thought she was, she knew she couldn't begin to fathom the forbidden thrills that being alone with this Yama would entail.

The vendor drew her attention by touching her wrist. "Your young man returns," she warned.

*He's not my young man,* Beth began to say, but considering the conversation they'd just had, it seemed easier not to explain.

Charles's face was serious as he wended back between the market's slowly moving crowd. Beth was sorry to see the change in him. She enjoyed his playful side, something only she and his younger brother, Max, seemed able to bring out in him.

Mind you, Charles wasn't like a demon. He had deep feelings. He adored his adoptive family; respected Beth's older brother, Adrian, probably more than Adrian's blood relatives; and treated his job as a chef like a religious calling. Easy, however, was not a path he knew how to walk. On that score, an icy, emotionless demon had a considerable advantage over him.

"Ready to leave?" he asked as soon as he reached her.

Beth put the scarlet sari back on its table. "If you wish."

Charles's expression flickered. "Forgive me. You'd like to do more shopping."

"I don't need to." Concerned, she laid her hand on the rumpled linen of his coat sleeve. She wished she dared ask what the demon had said to him. "Charles, are you all right? You look rather grim."

"I'm fine." He shook his head as if to fling out unwelcome thoughts. "Everything is fine. We can stay or go, as you please."

"I think I'd rather go." She turned to the helpful vendor. "Thank you for your time. I hope I may return another day."

As the vendor nodded, Charles offered Beth his elbow. The gesture was politeness rather than care. Preferring the latter, Beth curled her fingers over his, grateful for the heat that drove more gently born females than she to go without gloves.

At the touch, he looked at her, a sweep of stubble glinting on his lean, sharp jaw. The prickles were one shade darker than his sun-bleached hair. "I'm fine, Beth. Truly. I have work at camp."

Beth made herself smile at him, unconvinced but understanding he was doing his best not to subject her to his darkened mood. "I do as well," she said as lightly as she could. "I expect there's a thousand notebook sheets to scan by now."

"At the least," he agreed, the fondness in his eyes catching at her breath.

*It is enough,* she told herself. Charles might not be the easiest soul to be friends with, but as much as he cared for anyone, he cared for her.

Contrary to her intent, the thought saddened her. She had chased her ordinary beaus away—their numbers greater even than her family knew—because the kind of life they represented didn't interest her. Her relationship with Charles was probably the closest she would ever have with a male, and she knew better than to think he'd want to marry her. Why, in ten long years, they hadn't shared so much as a peck on the cheek!

*There must be more than this,* she thought, her unfamiliar surroundings giving the old desires new clarity. *These can't be all the choices a woman has. Married or a spinster. Fallen or alone.*

*I wish I were different,* she thought. *I wish I were as bold as a Bhamjrishi.*

Charles led her beneath the market's arching sandstone gate, his hold on her protective and secure. She had a sudden urge to throw off his hand, to run like a wild thing into the ancient city and disappear.

*I wish,* she thought, her third of the day, *that I were as strong and icy as that demon.*

If she had been, she'd be bold enough for anything.

Pahndir waited until the Ohramese had left to rise from his chair. He made no pretense where he was headed, though the sari vendor watched every step with a knowing smile.

He considered slipping her a coin to get the answers he desired, then decided she might take insult.

"I'd like to know where those two were from," he said.

"Ohram," said the woman, her head turned down to hide her amusement.

Pahndir fought an urge to grind his teeth. "I meant, where are they staying here? Do you know if they're part of the dig?"

"They didn't tell me," the woman said—honestly enough, he judged. Her expression turned humorous again. "Couldn't you go after them and ask?"

He could, but such directness wasn't the Yamish way.

"Thank you," he said instead. "I appreciate your time."

# TWO

All that day, Charles thought about the Yama's offer to feed from him. People came in and out of the cook tent buzzing with excitement, but he did his job of overseeing the excavation's meals like an automaton.

Hhamoun, as this site had been dubbed, was a big operation. Two hundred local diggers were employed by Herrington, plus a number of archaeological experts from Ohrâm. All of them had to eat, preferably well—which was Charles's responsibility. Most days he thrived under the pressure, but today his head was caught up in its own demons.

As far as he could tell, no one had noticed his distraction. Whatever he forgot to do, the local undercooks remembered. They were as quick as he was, and more adept at curries.

All the workers here loved curries, regardless of their national origins.

His mouth slanted with humor at how little his culinary expertise had been missed. He might have been better off had his crew needed more guidance. With nothing to keep his mind from wandering, the thought of going to The Prince's Flame obsessed him more than ever—and the brothel had occupied his thoughts quite enough since he'd learned of its existence last summer.

Bhamjran had a pleasure house run by a demon, with demon luxuries and demon whores. Charles wondered if the Yama's human employees let him take their energy, if maybe they wanted the improvement in their looks the exchange could bring. Charles didn't want his looks improved; his looks had brought him sufficient grief as it was. He certainly *shouldn't* have wanted the act itself. On his own since the age of twelve, he'd spent a good portion of his youth doing things that shamed him in order to avoid becoming a "demon's boy." Other street children had sold their etheric force to the Yama in return for food. Charles had only sold himself to his own kind. He'd thought it the lesser of two evils, but he'd ended up here all the same.

He was obsessed with them. Aroused by them. Tossing in his bed each night and wishing he could physically peel off the taint. Yes, he wanted things besides to feed the demons, wanted clean, warm, normal things. Hell, he wanted Beth enough to ache. He simply couldn't exorcize that old dark desire. It was embedded, like coal dust, deep in his erotic nature, and had been since he'd known what it was to feel any arousal at all.

Those three years, before Roxanne rescued him at fifteen, had scarred him for life.

"Boss?" said his head dishwasher, finding him staring blankly at the now cold grill in the dig's cook tent. "It's time to close up."

It was time. Battered tin plates stood in tall, clean stacks ready for tomorrow, the utensils no one but Northerners used shining now in bins. The dishwasher was holding the tent's flap open. He had pulled on his outer robes in preparation for leaving, and—to Charles's eyes—the garment turned his polite gesture into a regal thing. The idea of

Southland being conquered occasionally amused him. Charles's people were simply the latest who'd convinced themselves that they'd mastered this country.

Charles liked knowing they were wrong, liked the stubborn *differences* of this place. He'd been coming to Hhamoun every season for the last six years, grateful for the job at first, and then grateful for the escape. He felt less of a freak in Bhamjran, less of a broken, twisted misfit trying to fit in.

*Wolf,* he thought, blinking at the waiting dishwasher. *I'm a bloody wolf who wants the sheep to love him.*

"I'll be along," he said out loud. "You can go."

"Miss Philips leaves her tent around this time," the Bhamjrishi remarked slyly. "Maybe she'll want to ride back to the *haveli* in your motorcar. Maybe she'll want to celebrate today's success with you."

"Miss Philips knows how to suit herself," Charles said crisply, not knowing what success there was, but tired of the staff trying to push him and Beth together.

"Right, boss," said his underling, "but here in Bhamjran she may realize she doesn't need to wait for a man to chase her."

Charles snorted through his nose, too aware of the desires pulsing deep inside him, desires a girl like Beth would have been appalled to hear about. He only wished he had the right to chase her, only wished he might deserve to be more than her friend.

Beth wasn't certain when she'd fallen asleep at her portable camp desk. The heat was drowsy—making and her copying dull—especially since the novelty of the demon-invented "scanning" machine had worn off. Some days, the draftsmen brought her interesting drawings to slide into Herrington's magic recording box, but this morning there had been nothing but dry descriptions on the preprinted forms. *Scrap of sandal leather found with Old Kingdom sherd, two meters from stone doorway.*

If she'd found the artifacts herself, Beth might have been excited, but she was stuck in this stuffy tent with the prohibited technology, hardly close enough to the action to hear the diggers' shouts.

This wasn't what she'd dreamed of doing when she'd bullied her way into coming to the site.

Somewhere in the distance jubilant cries rang out, but they did not penetrate her doze. She woke just a little at a camel's bray, but only enough to turn her head the other way. Her lackadaisical village schooling lay at fault. Well, that and her equally lackadaisical response to it. None of her siblings were as poorly read as she, and her older brother, Adrian, could be quite brilliant. Beth, on the sad other hand, wasn't qualified for more than babysitting paperwork.

That prospect unappealing, she slipped into a slow, thick dream in which a man with long blue-black hair swept it back and forth across her naked legs. Higher and higher he went, to her knees, her thighs, his silver eyes gleaming like mercury set aflame. *You're what I want,* he whispered against her mound. *You're the goddess I've been yearning for.* And she was a goddess, so lovely, so powerful she had only to crook her finger and he'd crawl panting up her body with his sex erect . . .

The sound of a loud throat-clearing yanked her up on her stool.

*Good Lord*, it was Lord Herrington, standing like a tall red-haired mountain in the formerly sealed tent door. Because of his atypical coloring, you couldn't tell he was a demon unless you looked at his eyes. They were the solid silver of all his kind, broken only by the jet-black shine of his round pupils. Those eyes had nearly hypnotized her when she first met him. Now, remembering the burning silver gaze from her dream, she was doubly mortified. Herrington was not a person she wanted to associate with anything like that.

Unlikely as it sounded, he was the father of her brother's wife, Roxanne. Humans and demons weren't supposed to be able to interbreed, but somehow he and Roxanne's mother had managed it. Beth being here at all, in Herrington's employ, was very much a favor to his son-in-law.

Thoroughly embarrassed, Beth peeled the recording sheet she'd been lying on from her sweaty cheek.

"Hm," Herrington said with an uncertain gesture of his right hand. "I think you've got a bit of ink on your chin."

"Hell." Beth licked the heel of her palm and scrubbed at it . . . until she realized she'd probably disgusted him. Yama were notoriously fastidious.

Fortunately, Herrington had grown accustomed to human ways. Something that might have been a smile tugged at his lips.

"I believe the stain is gone," he said.

"Lord Herrington!" she burst out. "I'm so sorry for falling asleep!"

"Not at all." He shifted uncomfortably at the passion of her cry. "I put you here because you're family, and you could be trusted with the machine. I should have realized a young, active human would find these duties dull."

Herrington thought of her as family? Herrington trusted her? Surprised and touched, Beth took a moment to shut her mouth.

"It's not really dull," she hastened to assure him. "Or only a little. And it's still much better than being home."

"Well." He rubbed his big, freckled hand across his mouth, and this time Beth really did think he was smiling. Evidently, his spirits were high tonight. "We must endeavor to ensure that remains the case. I was wondering . . ." He paused, the hesitation almost human shyness. "We have succeeded in clearing a route to the queen's chamber. I thought you might like to see the end to which all this paper leads."

"I'd love to," Beth exclaimed, "but I'm so behind!"

"Your work will keep," Herrington said, though the glance he cast around the stacks seemed dubious. He squared his shoulders as if bracing. "Tomorrow is another day, and this is worth seeing."

"Then I'd love to," Beth said more softly. "Really, really love to."

His face appeared to darken just a tiny bit. Beth supposed her effusion had embarrassed him. She couldn't doubt Herrington liked humans. His devotion to his daughter was unmistakable. Also unmistakable was that humans, especially those to whom he had personal ties, made him feel awkward. As much as Beth enjoyed traveling far from home, she couldn't imagine spending her whole life among a culture alien from her own. It must be nearly impossible for Herrington to relax, and perhaps he didn't unless he was alone.

Naturally it wouldn't do to let him know she was dissecting his character—and in this sympathetic way! Determined to keep her musings to herself, Beth pushed from her chair and shook out her bothersome long skirts. For the thousandth time, she wished she could have worn native dress. A muslin tunic and trousers would have been delightfully comfortable—if only her parents would have understood. She swept her hand around her hair, confirming that it was not in as frightful a state as it might have been. She was lucky it grew so straight. She could tie it back again as they walked.

"I'm ready," she said, pulling the draggled ribbon off her ponytail.

In answer, Lord Herrington offered her a bow that had *her* fighting awkwardness. Beth was not a woman anyone had to do honors for.

Leaving the confines of her tent to face the golden sweep of the desert was an actual physical shock. The Vharzovhin was an ocean made of sand. Dune after dune rippled to the seeming edge of the world, where the setting sun melted like crimson treacle into the horizon.

The other tents and structures of the excavation lay behind them, clattering with the hastened bustle that invariably met the loss of their working light. Diggers called to one another in at least three different dialects. Sand trucks rumbled, camels groaned in protest at being urged up or down, and behind it all—as if the absence of noise had more power than sound—the endless silence of the desert stretched.

"It's something, isn't it?" Herrington said, pausing for a moment to gaze over the great expanse with her.

"Yes," Beth agreed. "I can believe God is real when I look at this."

She flushed a little, recognizing what she'd said. Demons were . . . well, she wasn't certain, but atheists, she thought. Nor was the confession appropriate for an Ohramese. She was supposed to believe in God all the time, not just when she was here.

Herrington cleared his throat to break the brief silence. "If we're going to visit the queen's chamber, we had better grab a torch or two while we can."

"Electric torches?" Beth asked hopefully. "Oh, I love them!"

They were walking then, back through the busy anthill of the site, which she registered as being more animated than usual. The cook tent was halfway across the canvas village. Beth's shoulders tensed as she wondered if Charles would be there. Had his mood improved since morning? Would he ask her to ride home with him?

She was so intent on not betraying the direction of her thoughts that it took a moment for her to realize what she was seeing. Charles was *outside* the cook tent, where Herrington's demon water spigot was installed. Charles had stripped off his shirt and was dumping a bucket of water over his head. He didn't see her approaching, but she certainly saw him.

She had never seen him with his shirt off, had never been given a chance to admire the rippling muscles of his chest and belly, or the shading of darker hair on both. She stopped in her tracks, speechless with surprise. Charles wore native dress to cook in: a finely woven cotton tunic and loose trousers. The shirt was gone, as she'd already noted, and the trousers . . . Transparent from their soaking, the fabric clung to the strong round thrust of his bum, hanging from his narrow hipbones as if to tease her with the prospect of it falling off. He was a full tent-length away, but the curving weight of his sex was visible beneath the wet cotton.

It was *long*, she thought, and not a little thick—especially around the head.

She swallowed in reaction, her hands curling into fists as a heat worse than that caused by any daydream coiled between her legs.

"Ahem," said Herrington, the sound startling her. "I'm certain your mother would advise me to encourage you not to stare."

"Oh, Lord," said Beth and covered her face.

When Herrington turned to lead her forward, she was pretty sure he was grinning. Her only consolation was that Charles had not seen her ogling him.

"You won't tell him, will you?" she begged, and Herrington chuckled audibly.

To her relief, he had regained control of himself by the time they reached the active part of the site.

Hhamoun was large palace complex—a small city, really—from the period known as the Old Kingdom. Approximately two thousand years ago the complex had been swallowed in its entirety by a freak sandstorm, allowing its inhabitants time to flee but not to save their belongings. Now it was an archaeologist's dream come true, preserving a picture of a bygone era that was unmatched. During the preceding season, Herrington's team had uncovered a beautiful temple adorned with graceful alabaster statues. On its own, the temple was the find of a lifetime, but Herrington claimed to hold even higher hopes for the residence of the queen, where he'd been focusing his team this summer.

A sandy ramp led down into the partially exposed building, clear now except for a pair of burly guards, who nodded at Herrington. Some waterboy had left his empty goatskin lying at the top. At the bottom, a solid square of blackness loomed. Beth was no coward, but seeing that gaping mouth made her grateful for the torches they'd picked up.

"Watch your step," Herrington said, taking her arm as they descended.

She'd known his spirits were high, but it wasn't until he touched her that she felt the wound-up buzz of his energy. Her heart kicked a fraction faster. If Herrington was this stirred up, whatever his team had found was big.

"It's that good?" she asked, just a little breathlessly.

Herrington's mouth twitched on one side. "Wait and see."

There wasn't much to see at first, just a roughly square, sandy, compacted tunnel, stabilized by thick wooden ties. The air was close and musty, the shadows strange as their electric torches caught on irregularities in the excavated walls. Here and there they passed hints of doorways or building blocks, but Herrington had obviously known they didn't lead where he wished to go and hadn't instructed his workers to dig there. She'd heard whispers that he'd taken special pictures of the landscape from a flying car, but unless his demon camera could peer through dunes, she didn't know what good that would have done.

And then she could see a door that wasn't filled with sand, its lintel and frame constructed of black-veined gold marble.

"Here," said Herrington, his voice hushed but excited as he gestured her ahead of him. "Welcome to the Old Kingdom."

She hadn't known her heart could beat so hard. This was what she'd come to Bhamjran for, this blood-pumping glimpse of a forgotten world. Her kidskin boots scraped on the marble lintel. She swung her powerful Yamish torch up from the floor . . .

And promptly lost her breath.

"Heavens," she said when the musty air agreed to fill her lungs again. "I can scarcely believe it's real."

Though a layer of fine, sandy dust coated everything around her, she stood in a clearly recognizable bedchamber.

An ornate ebony couch, large enough to sleep four, stretched across the center of the room. One of its pillows lay on the carpeted floor, its bejeweled silk tassels hanging in a tangle. The covers on the couch—very fine dyed linen, from the looks of them—still bore the imprint of a female body, as if the long-ago sandstorm had interrupted the great queen's nap. A pair of elegant beaded sandals had tumbled under the couch's foot, suggesting there'd been no time to put them on. The leather looked desiccated but hardly two millennia old. In truth, the shoes were stylish enough that Beth wouldn't have quibbled to wear them herself.

She could see they had interested the other excavators, because fresh foot tracks led through the dust to them. Deciding it was safe to follow their example, Beth stepped farther inside.

What her light fell on next went beyond fashion: The most beautiful drinking cup she'd ever seen sat on an adjacent table. Big enough to be the Old Kingdom version of a loving cup, it was made of soft yellow gold and shaped like a pair of intertwined swans. The artistry of it awed her. The birds were so realistic, she could see the ruffling of each gold feather. Dried brown dregs stained the cup's bottom.

"I'm afraid to move," she said, her hand pressed to her mouth in wonder. "I don't want to break anything."

Herrington had come up beside her, his warmth and size a comfort in the dark. "The conservators have removed anything that looked too fragile. It's safe enough to walk around."

"But it looks as if the queen just stepped out! As if she drank from that wine cup mere hours ago!"

"Luckily for us, the sandstorm sealed that door as soundly as a tomb. Better, really, because so many burial sites have been looted. And there are no windows in this room—for defensive purposes, we think, from the records that were left behind. Apparently, Queen Tou had enemies."

"Queen Two?"

He spelled it for her. "We think that's how it's pronounced. Scholars have been able to link the Old Kingdom hieroglyphs to a modern dialect, but we don't know how much drift there's been in vocalizing sounds."

Beth was no linguist, just a stunned admirer. Feeling as if she were dreaming, she moved toward a painted wall. Its colors shone vividly beneath the dust. The paint followed the carvings: delicate, precise shapes worked into sandstone. She found the image of an egret, then a snake and a crocodile.

"Those pictures spell out a warning," Herrington said from behind her. " 'Let any man who breaks the sanctity of this chamber feel my eternal wrath.' "

The muscles along Beth's spine shuddered. "That sounds like a curse."

"I wouldn't worry. The desert broke the sanctity of this chamber long before we did." Herrington panned his own torch slowly across the writing. "Tou-Hhamoun was a powerful queen by all accounts, even allowing for official exaggeration. Bit of a mystery, actually. Scholars have been puzzling over it for years. She went from being an orphan, cast out by her tribe for theft, to supreme ruler of Upper Southland in a mere decade. She married thirty princes, each from powerful families. According to legend, they all begged to marry her."

He gestured toward a line of blue and gold hieroglyphs. "Here she says, 'My rule stretches four by forty,' whatever that means, 'and my rivals fear my'—*vigor*, I think that word is—'just as they fear my great armies.' I'm not sure who she intended to impress by writing this here, but that's what it says."

"Perhaps she read it to her husbands as a bedtime story."

"Perhaps," Herrington agreed, a smile in his voice. "Tomorrow the conservators will begin removing these artifacts. We need to stabilize them from the change in atmosphere. Eventually, I'm hoping your government will agree to return them here. Then visitors will be able to admire them in situ, as we do tonight."

"What a *wonderful* idea," Beth said, her eyes pricking with how deeply she meant the words. "Everyone should have this experience, especially the Bhamjrishi. This is their heritage, after all."

"Well, that's a ways down the road. My government will have to agree to the plan as well. The process would be technically complex. But Hhamoun could end up being a huge tourist draw. I doubt your secretary of the treasury will mind that."

He looked quietly satisfied by the prospect, and for the first time Beth saw him only as a person. Not demon, not diplomat, not even her in-law, but just a man with a dream that he was hoping to bring to pass.

It made her wish she had a dream herself, instead of simply wanting to escape the mundane life her family had planned for her.

"Thank you for bringing me here," she said, feeling more humble than she could express. "This is a night I won't soon forget."

Lord Herrington offered her a gentle, unconcealed smile. "I enjoy sharing my discoveries with those who can appreciate them." He tipped his head to the side, a definite glint of mischief entering his silver eyes. "Would you like to stay awhile on your own? Maybe commune with the spirit of Hhamoun's queen? I can wait for you outside."

"Oh, my," Beth breathed. "Yes, I would like that!"

Was it possible to communicate with the dead queen's spirit? Beth suspected Herrington didn't think so, but who knew?

While Herrington waited for her in the tunnel, she turned her torch's cone of light around the chamber. The furniture was exquisite, much of it bearing the heads and feet of animals. One table with lifelike antelope legs supported a long black wig on a stand, its countless tiny braids still shining with golden beads. The ghost of some sweet perfume tickled her nose. Beth shivered involuntarily. She was probably the first woman to see these objects since the queen had fled. Yama weren't as hidebound as Ohramese, but Herrington still only hired male diggers.

A soft noise, uncannily like a whisper, caused her to involuntarily yank her torch upward. *Falling sand,* Beth told herself, though she didn't see any. The ceiling was the same black-veined gold marble as the door and floor. Unlike those surfaces, the ceiling was coffered, the deep, stepped squares positively covered in hieroglyphs.

*What were you saying?* Beth wondered, the hairs behind her neck prickling. *Who were you warning to stay away?* She noticed a slender rod hanging from a nearly invisible eye hook not far from her. It seemed an odd object to leave dangling from the ceiling of this perfectly appointed space.

"Pull me," someone said right next to her ear.

Beth spun around while her heart beat like a mad creature trapped in her throat. The shadows wavered wildly, but no one was there.

"I'm imagining things," she whispered to herself.

*Pull me,* the walls murmured.

Beth bit her lip and stepped closer to the hanging rod. Her hand seemed to lift of its own accord.

*I really shouldn't do this,* she thought—even as she went up on tiptoe to grasp the thing.

Her fingers found polished wood with more carvings. With a prayer that her actions weren't going to bring the place crashing down, Beth gave the rod a gentle, experimental tug.

The testing pull was enough. A section of the ceiling came down as smoothly as if it were oiled, the marble block suspended by a silvery length of pipe. One small toggle switch was embedded within the metal—at least a switch was what Beth assumed it was. She glanced back over her shoulder toward the door. She ought to call to Herrington. He would want to know this was here.

*I am for you,* said the same voice she had imagined

she'd heard before. *Let any man who breaks the sanctity of this chamber feel my eternal wrath.*

Before her conscience could stop her, Beth flipped the switch.

The wall across from her, where the queen's warning was inscribed, rolled silently open.

Her head might have been floating, she felt so lifted out of her normal self. Herrington's interests forgotten, she moved forward like a sleepwalker. There was another chamber behind the wall: small, perfectly square, with dull black walls that absorbed her Yamish torch's light. As she stepped inside, a humming sensation swept over her skin. Some energy was radiating outward from the dark surfaces. Whatever it was felt delicious, like a cat twining around her limbs. The roof of this room was barely a foot above her head. She reached up to stroke the ceiling, and the moment her fingertips made contact, her insides melted with pleasure. It was as if she'd been tranquilized. She didn't even jump when the wall shut behind her.

Her mind turned off as her escape route closed. She had no other words for the phenomenon. She seemed unable to think, though images did drift dreamily through her mind.

She saw Tou within this room, but she didn't look like a queen. She was young, maybe fifteen, and she was crawling on her hands and knees, filthy and barely clothed, having scrabbled into this hole to escape the sun. Her palace didn't exist yet, even as a wish in her mind. She was all thirst, all hunger, all desperate drive to survive. Outcast that she was, she knew the drive was futile. If the desert didn't kill her now, it would soon.

Such was her state that she thought she was dreaming when the walls first spoke.

*Goddess,* they said. *You have returned.*

They belled inward to embrace her as if they were alive, turning to a tarlike liquid that was filled with stars.

And then it was Beth whom the walls embraced. A basso note rumbled through her bones, lower than the lowest horn ever blown. Colors and patterns flowered behind her eyes. She should have been frightened, but the capacity for that emotion had been drained from her. She felt more purely female than she ever had, desiring and desirable. As the walls pressed up against her, her body twitched and grew wet.

*Goddess,* murmured the chamber. *This is for you.*

Stars began to spin around her, celestial clockwork older than the sand. Stars couldn't tell time, of course, and yet Beth sensed these stars had been waiting for her, mindlessly patient down the centuries, hoping only to fulfill the purpose for which they'd been designed. That purpose was to make her better, to make her capable of birthing children who would survive the dark age ahead.

Odd sensations twanged through her nerves. She would have fallen had the clinging walls not cradled her upright. She breathed in stars and blackness, scented of cinnamon. The dark curled in teasing fingers between her legs, almost physical, almost causing a release. She reached to let the tickling deeper, her body straining to feel more of the sweet, slippery caress . . . until her every cell seemed to explode and reform itself.

Beth was on her knees, breathing in great, quick gulps, her torch fallen to the matte black floor. Her muscles trembled as she tried to throw off whatever had caused the strange vision. The door was open, not closed as she'd imagined, and the surfaces of the room were perfectly solid. Shaking, she fumbled for the torch, got to her feet and tottered out. Her legs felt odd, like someone else's legs rather than her own. The wall slid shut at her exit, the section of the ceiling that had descended now rising up with the faintest hiss.

She could not see a single crack to show where the stones had moved.

She was alone in the queen's chamber, so weakened by shock that the torch was nearly too heavy for her to hold. However long she'd been in the other room, her stay had not alerted Lord Herrington.

*That didn't just happen,* she told herself.

She looked up and found the slender wooden rod still hanging from its hook.

Every one of her siblings would have sworn this situation was typical: Tell Beth not to do something, and she was sure to leap straight into trouble. In this case, no one even had to tell her. She'd known instinctively not to pull that thing.

*I hallucinated what happened. I was dreaming about that demon and Charles, and being left alone in here must have been more than my nerves could take. I'm a simple, Ohramese girl who isn't used to foreign goings-on.*

Regardless of the cause of her experience, whether it was fear or ghosts or poisons lingering in the ancient air, her nerves compelled her to yank the whiplike rod from its holding place. Hardly able to bear touching it, she shoved it into a corner beneath a rug. One of Herrington's workers would find it eventually. Until they did, Beth didn't have to think about whatever she had or had not done.

# THREE

*Tou stumbled out of the secret chamber onto the sand, gasping for breath in the thick, baked air. Her knees gave way, pitching her forward onto a dune. Surprisingly, the sun felt good, calming the palsy that shook her limbs. She let herself roll onto her back to soak in the warmth, then tore off what shreds remained of her poorly made orphan's robes. She wanted nothing between her and the golden radiance—never mind how infernally hot it was.*

*She was alive. Better than alive. She was healing. She could feel the changes inside her, despite the recurrent tremors beneath her skin.*

*She laid one hand over her naked breast and cupped the other around her mound. Her nipple was sharp as stone, her pulse beating hard and steady between her legs. Never had she felt such a strong yearning to be filled. Oh, she'd been taken, once by a boy she'd thought cared for her and, later, by the judges of her tribe. The men who'd cast her out for stealing food had claimed the rape was part of her sentence, but Tou had known better. They'd forced her in secret, tying the tent flap against their wives' prying glances and gagging her so she couldn't scream. Then they'd banished* her *as a criminal.*

*Tou pushed herself upward until she sat. Her tremors were gone now, her thirst, even her fear. She watched a vulture circle overhead, probably the same that had followed her across the desert these last two days. From the way its spirals widened, she knew it was no longer interested in her. She wasn't easy prey anymore.*

*Ready to face what had happened, she looked back at the mouth of the buried chamber, the shadow of it black as the netherworld.*

*She fought a shiver.* But I'm a goddess now, *she thought, remembering what the voice had told her. Goddesses didn't cower at the past. Goddesses were meant to rule.*

I'll rule them, *she promised.* Before I'm done, I'll see every male in my tribe grovel.

*The vow swelled inside her as if the desire were more than mere ambition. She ran her hand down her naked body, feeling how smooth the skin of her belly was, how healthy and sensitive. The sun might never have burned her, her trek through the desert never weakened and starved her down. Gaunt no more, her flesh was as firm and sleek as the pampered daughter of a village chief. Within her intimate folds, her pleasure bud stood painfully engorged with blood. It wanted more than the gentle caresses she usually gave it, more than the soft release that should have satisfied a girl her age. Groaning with need, she pinched the bud between her longest finger and thumb.*

*Her response was a revelation. Pleasure exploded within her, not a climax but so close to one it caused her to cry out. The almost-release was torture. Tou had to work herself harder, had to squeeze and rub and grind that little organ as hard as she could. Juices ran down her strong, tensing thighs. Perhaps she should have been embarrassed, but it didn't matter where she was. Goddesses were different, apparently, and this goddess had to have a release or die.*

*Tou's second hand provided what she needed. With a moan of profound erotic agony, she thrust two fingers into her passage and immediately catapulted into orgasm.*

It was after midnight when Charles surrendered any hope for sleep. The desert night was cool, the breeze that wafted through his window pleasant, and the gauze-curtained bed on which he lay the most comfortable he'd known. Nor did the nocturnal murmurs of the city give any reason for his restlessness.

The *haveli* Herrington had bought for them to live in was a five-story merchant's mansion in the Old Quarter. Though the area wasn't completely residential—those who lived here still kept shops on their street level—it was one of the quietest in Bhamjran. This stemmed from so many of the great trading families having suffered financial losses when Queen Victoria brought the railroads in. The traders' fortunes had been made through camel caravans, and only those who'd adapted had been able to keep up their old luxuries. As a result, the narrow palaces on either side of Herrington's sat empty, though the privacy-loving demon probably preferred it that way. Charles himself hadn't given their abandoned state a second thought until this year.

Everything struck him differently with Beth here.

He punched his down-filled pillow and turned it to its cooler side, his body tightening at the thought of her. Other females wouldn't have changed the way they lived, but Beth was a relative innocent, despite her claims to the contrary. More to the point perhaps, she was an innocent both he and Herrington cared about.

Before Beth's arrival, the mansion had been a place to grab a meal or a shower bath. Charles and Herrington had each kept to their own floor, and to their own business. The house had always been spotless, of course; no Yama tolerated dirt or clutter, but it had all been very masculine and civilized. Beth's presence made the *haveli* feel uncannily like a home.

They ate together now, without their noses buried in newspapers, sometimes at a pretty table in the courtyard's shade. Herrington ordered flowers to decorate the mansion's fancy niches. Walls were painted rather than just repaired, and the number of Yamish conveniences multiplied. They had hot running water these days, electric lights, and an automated clothing sterilizer for whatever garments didn't need sending out. Charles knew the permits to keep these amenities in Bhamjran must have cost the moon, but Herrington acted as if he and Charles had always lived this way.

Herrington didn't say so, but Charles suspected Beth reminded him of his own half-demon daughter when she was Beth's age. Roxanne had kept her father at arm's length for a good long time, fearing—with some cause—that he would try to run her life. Today Herrington and Roxanne were close, but Beth must have been a reminder of old mistakes. Herrington knew Roxanne would no more tolerate him crowding Beth than she would tolerate him crowding her. He was obliged to be very canny in his quest to protect Beth *and* her sensibilities.

Despite how intimidating the autocratic Yama could be, Charles had to smile at the lengths to which he went to shield their new roommate. Though Herrington was no monk, with Beth in residence he no longer brought women here. The man who'd faced down empires snuck out like a boy instead.

The crunch of rubber tires on the street beneath Charles's window suggested his employer might be sneaking out tonight. Charles debated remaining where he was, but curiosity got the best of him. He'd heard rumors that the "Red Fox" had bagged himself a tigress this season, a leader of one of the Vharzovhin's mysterious mercenary tribes. Charles had never met a female chieftain, and even if Herrington's lovers weren't his concern, he couldn't resist the chance to see this one.

Throwing off his sheets, he crept to the deep-set window of his room. The *jali* screen that fronted it suggested these chambers had been designed to house males. Sandstone lacework extended over the opening to a height above his head, enabling him to see out without revealing his presence. Had he been a member of a harem, no one but his mistress would have been allowed to see his face. Finding that thought a bit too interesting, he kneeled on the window seat and peered down. There he saw his guess was correct. Herrington was stepping out of an electrified motorcar: a jeep, as he called it. Its headlights were the only illumination in the empty street.

As if she were a shadow herself, a tall, lean woman glided out of the darkness cast by the opposite row of homes. The auto's headlights lit her well. She wore trousers like a local, and her long over-robes were black. More black turbaned and veiled her head, a narrow slit between the wrappings all that bared her eyes. She was taller than Beth, her strides even less feminine. A leather strap secured an array of knives across her chest. When she pushed her sleeves farther up her arms, the wiry muscles that emerged suggested the wicked-looking weapons weren't just for show. Almost as barbaric were the stacks of golden rings that gleamed on her long fingers. They seemed calculated to draw attention to her knuckles, which were as battered as a pugilist's.

Stopping a foot from her paramour, the chieftain tugged her facial veiling down. The gesture bared features that were as hard and lean as the rest of her, not beautiful but dramatic. A tattoo formed of dark-blue dots followed the contours of one cheekbone—depicting some bird of prey, Charles thought. Above it, her eyes were narrowed to wary slits.

"Herrington," she said, her voice a cool challenge.

Herrington inclined his head. "I am honored you have come, Sahel."

Sahel laughed softly. "Does a demon know how to be honored?"

To Charles's surprise, the usually undemonstrative Yama took her face in his hands. His height and size made his partner seem smaller than she was. Charles couldn't help wondering if this was part of his appeal for her. Given how Sahel lived, she couldn't have been accustomed to meeting males this commanding.

Powerful or not, Herrington knew how to play suitor. His thumbs swept her cheeks gently. "Any man would be honored to spend time with you."

"You knew I couldn't resist your invitation."

"I dared to hope. Our last encounter did seem worth repeating to me."

The chieftain laughed again, just as dryly as before. "How polite you demons are! Kiss me, Lord Herrington. I feel the need for a reminder of why I'm not sorry I gave in."

Despite the icy fronts they liked to present, as a race the Yama were highly sexed. Herrington's response proved he was no exception. He kissed Sahel with a curse that let Charles know how much he wanted to devour her.

Charles should have moved away from the window then, should have given the couple their privacy, but the instant intensity of the embrace held him where he was.

There was more heat in that one kiss than he had ever seen his employer show. The pair looked ready to climb into each other, to damn possible watchers and do it in the street. Sahel was clawing at Herrington's shoulders and, though Charles's human eyes couldn't see it, her energy had to be running into him. Clearly affected, Herrington groaned and lifted Sahel, turning to press her body into the side of his open-roofed motorcar. Sahel's legs parted easily for his weight, her head falling back in mute surrender as he nipped her throat.

"Do it," she said, her voice a shade away from a moan. She caught the hand that had gripped her waist, urging it beneath the leather strap that sheathed her knives. Charles's breath stalled in his lungs as Herrington's hand disappeared into the folds of black robing above her heart. This was where her strongest pool of energy lay, the chakra most Yama liked to feed from.

"Take what you want from me," she said.

Herrington broke from her at the demand. Sahel frowned as he let her slide down the jeep onto her well-scuffed boots. Though she couldn't have had much experience with being thwarted, she didn't try to wrest away, probably because Herrington held her arms too tightly for her to succeed. He was breathing hard, his eyes glittering like jet as he took in her angry flush. She couldn't hide how much she wanted him, no more than Herrington could hide how much he longed to do as she asked.

Watching them, Charles's hands had tightened into sweaty fists. He couldn't have looked away to save his life, not when his darkest fantasy was so close to being acted out in front of him. A rim of silver was all that prevented Herrington's alien eyes from going black, and Charles knew very well what this signified.

The Yama was aroused but not out of control yet.

"I want to fuck you," Herrington said, his trademark demon coolness harshened to a rasp. "All night if you'll let me, with every scrap of power I have. If I draw off your energy now, you'll be too weak to stand up to that."

The chieftain tossed her head in anger, but Herrington did not relent. "I mean it, Sahel. Like it or not, you're only human. You'll never be as strong as I am."

"I should kill you for saying that. I should cut off your balls where you stand."

She sounded like she meant it, but Herrington grinned at her, an expression so human it startled. "I hope you won't, Sahel. I'd far rather put my balls at your service."

Sahel snorted, her anger turning to humor. "That's not all you'll put at my service, demon. That golden tongue of yours is useful, too."

She squirmed away from him, vaulting neatly into the passenger seat of his motorcar, where she waited like the queen she obviously thought she was for him to drive her where she wished to go. Herrington shook his head, but followed the unspoken order with a faint, lingering smile.

Clearly, he considered the cost to his pride worth paying for a night with her.

Charles closed his eyes as the electric engine hummed to life. He should have closed them sooner; should, in fact, have never watched at all. Now he was so hard he hurt, the blood beating hot and thick through his stiffened cock. His fist was close enough to touch it, but he forced his hand away. Bad enough he'd played the voyeur. He didn't have to reward himself for it.

*I need a shower,* he thought. *A long, icy one.*

The best bathing chamber was on the floor above. This was Beth's floor, though, thankfully, the bath wasn't next to her bedroom. As he padded up the servant's stairs to reach it, his erection bobbed inside his loose sleeping pants, seeming not to realize the castigation it was in for. Every step, every brush against the cotton thickened it. This shouldn't have felt so much like pleasure, but he couldn't deny it did.

With a tight shiver of arousal, he saw Sahel's hand again in his mind, dragging Herrington's to her heart. How many times as a boy had he seen some demon in an alley doing exactly that? How many times had he turned away, shuddering with relief that the human donor wasn't him? Now he wondered if his relief had been the birth of fascination. Had he secretly wished he'd had the courage to sell his soul to the enemy?

In those days, enemies were how they'd all thought of the Yama, despite Victoria's attempts to paint her benefactors as allies. Demons were smarter, stronger, richer—the poorest of them flush enough to buy the very essence of human life. Humans like Charles, who lived in the underbelly of the queen's empire, knew their continued existence depended on the demons' whims. They could crush his race any time they chose.

Humans were lucky the Yama weren't fond of battle—too messy, Charles supposed, not to mention uncivilized.

He pulled up short in the hallway and cursed himself. He'd walked too far, past the bathing chamber he'd meant to use to cool his raging blood. He stood outside Beth's bedroom, in front of her paneled door. His cock lurched higher inside his pants, the surge of heat so dizzying he had to brace his hands on her door frame.

God, he wanted her. Now. This instant. And he only wished he wanted her so he could bury his more shameful urges in desiring her. The truth was darker but too strong to deny. Charles didn't want a cure: He wanted to take her, to plunge his hardness inside her with that other lust riding him. He wanted to destroy her damned innocence, wanted her to be stained like him. He had no doubt the climax that would give him would be colossal.

*Lord,* he thought, *you are one sick human.*

Admitting it changed nothing. He wet his lips and stared at the door handle.

Maybe he would have moved away if he hadn't heard her; he was certainly ordering himself to go. But her cry carried to him, low and pained, and his hand couldn't help but reach for the knob and turn.

The moment he stepped into her chamber, his mouth went dry.

Herrington had given Beth the finest rooms in the *haveli,* those that had belonged to the former Bhamjrishi mistresses of this house. The walls were rich with murals, the molding gilded in arabesques. Her gauze-draped bed was massive, like a barge set sail on a carpet sea. A small Yamish nightlight glowed atop its headboard, a tiny, demonic beacon to his downfall.

That downfall was thrashing in the bed, caught up in some troubling dream. The sheet was tangled around her, shoved to her waist and half off her legs. This wouldn't have been fatal if Beth hadn't also torn off her night rail. The muslin lay in shreds around her, as if ripped by an animal.

Sweat enveloped his body in a burning wave. She was more beautiful than he'd dreamed. Her legs were endless: strong but unmistakably womanly. Worse, her hands were squeezed between her thighs, caught in the sheet and tight against her sex. She looked like she was touching herself through the linen, like she was trying to bring herself to release. Her head rolled on the pillow as if she were in pain.

"Please," she said, which caused his pulse to leap wildly. But she hadn't woken. She followed the word with a jumble of syllables that didn't sound like their native tongue.

Charles stumbled forward, hardly knowing what he meant to do. He touched her shoulder as his gaze strayed helplessly to her breasts. They were fuller than he expected, their curves enough to make his mouth water. Her nipples were dark and pointed, like ginger kissed with rouge.

"Beth," he said, his throat as tight and swollen as his cock. "Beth, wake up."

Her eyes flew open, but they weren't seeing him. In the soft glow of the nightlight, her pupils were black and huge.

"I can't do it," she said. "I can't give myself enough pleasure."

He groaned her name this time, a plea she ignored to resume her thrashing and whimpering. Charles could hardly stand beneath the terrible enticement that roared through him. He braced one arm on the mattress beside her head. Her eyes were closed again, making his battle both easier and harder.

"Beth." He took hold of the sheet where it draped her thighs, tugging it away from her clutched fingers. "Let me."

He pushed his hand beneath hers and instantly her legs flung wide. Her pubic curls were wet, her silky folds as hot as fire. His knees sagged onto the bed frame, utterly unable to hold him up. Despite his weakness, he couldn't stop what he was doing. Her clitoris was ripe and thick. He pressed it hard beneath the pad of his thumb, her juices making the digit slide.

Her weeping slit begged for the probing of his fingers.

She cried out hoarsely when he satisfied the mute request. Her body rolled, plainly liking his touch better than her own. Her hips jerked greedily toward his fingers, so greedily he could feel the tender stretch of her hymen against their tips.

The decent being he was trying to be bit his lip hard enough to bleed.

"No," he said to both of them, attempting to hold her safely down with his other hand. She was stronger than he expected, more determined. Her flesh tightened around him, a seduction more insidious than a siren's song.

"Please," she groaned. "Please, help me."

Not knowing what else to do, he crawled between her legs and put his mouth on her.

She came then, with a shudder like an earthquake.

"More," she pleaded, her thighs tightening on his ears until she nearly deafened him. "I need more."

He gave her more, and more and more, her taste bursting on his tongue, her clitoris so slick and swollen he thought he'd never tire of rolling it on his tongue. This was desire. This was need as strong as iron. Feeling like a sinner who'd been let into heaven by mistake, he ran his hands up her body to squeeze her breasts. The way she writhed at his caresses thrilled him to the bone. She came when he pulled her sharp little nipples and shivered when he licked her slit. Though he hadn't forgotten how she'd almost pierced her maidenhead, he couldn't help but curl his thumbs inside her—though only to the first knuckle.

That she liked enough to sob with need.

"Yes," she cried as he flicked his tongue against the very tip of her clitoris. "Oh, please, do that harder, too."

He sucked her strongly enough for her to shatter, her body bucking as it clutched dangerously on his thumbs. Charles knew he was adept at this, but she came longer than he'd known any woman to. Loving the reaction, he pushed her to go longer still. Her cries turned to pleasured whimpers and finally to long, soft sighs.

"One more," she murmured even as she took it.

Her hips shuddered once, twice, and then every muscle she had went limp.

He pulled from her, panting hard. She was sleeping now—or sleeping still, he supposed—this slumber deep and peaceful. One-tenth of her satisfaction would have suited him. He sat back on his heels and rubbed his aching jaw, his body shaking with unreleased tension. His prick was so aroused it felt like it was buzzing, and the front of his sleep pants stuck to his skin in a large wet patch. His cock had been dripping with excitement all this while, wishing it could share each and every one of her orgasms. It was white-hot now, a universe of lust embodied in a single rod.

The urge to rub it had his nails digging into his palms.

*Do it,* he thought, echoing Sahel. *Do it before your conscience gets the best of you.*

Her legs were splayed before him, her vulva glistening with her emissions. She smelled like sex incarnate, like an invitation to debauchery. Charles undid the tie that held his trouser flaps together, peeling the damp material from his skin. His scrotum was tight and throbbing, his shaft thrust high enough to bump his own body. He gritted his teeth, afraid to touch himself. He knew he shouldn't do this, knew it was breach of trust, but—perverse creature that he was—the knowledge only made him want it more.

*Do it,* he ordered. *Better this than what you really want.*

He fisted himself almost grimly, low and tight around his root. One stroke had him fighting back a moan of shock, had him clenching deep inside against the power of this pleasure. God, it was good to do this over her, to do this watching her. Every nerve he had seemed to coil and scream for relief, but he went as slowly as he could bear. He might never get another chance like this. He doubted she'd wake again tonight, not after he'd exhausted her. His cock thickened in his hand, hurrying toward release in spite of his wishes. Feeling how close he was getting, he knew he ought to grab a rag to spill into.

But that wasn't what he craved in his lustful heart. He crawled over her on his knees instead, trembling with anticipation, pointing the hard, pulsing head while her breasts rose and fell in sleeping innocence.

He knew exactly where he wanted his seed to go.

His hand moved faster, rougher, need overruling will. Images rose like monsters in his mind, driving him higher yet. He saw the Yama from the market, lounging like a pasha with his legs stretched out. Charles knelt on the sandy cobbles before his chair, and then he heard Sahel groan as she kissed Herrington. Some nightmare from his unconscious grabbed his hair and jerked it from behind. *Mine,* it said, hard and cold as steel. *Mine until you lose yourself to your desires.*

His fist made a slapping noise on his sweaty skin, a blur of desperate motion that whipped him to the edge and then over. Sensation burst like a star in his prick and thighs. He exploded over her nipples, long, white ribbons of ejaculate. The sight was so arousing to his twisted mind that he peaked again, moaning at the sweetness of the hard climax.

Charles knew how to pleasure himself, and he'd used the shadow side of his desires to strengthen his release before. In truth, he hardly knew how to avoid it. And yet in spite of that he'd never come as powerfully as this.

He looked down at Beth, *saw* her, sleeping like an angel spattered with his seed. Whatever needs her dream had stirred up, she hadn't deserved to be used this way. Despising himself, he swung off her body and out of the bed. The carpet was soft beneath his bare feet, his head as light as if he'd recovered from a long fever. He spied a rarely worn cotton glove lying near a chair and used it gently, softly, to wipe the evidence of his violation from her skin.

She shivered when he reached her nipple, a little, throaty sound breaking in her throat. He had to fight an urge to suck the tightening protrusion. To his dismay, his groin grew heavier at the thought. His guilt was powerless to stop his blood from surging. In fact, his guilt made it flow harder.

Unsettled by what this said about his character, he tugged the sheet over her. Evidently, living out the forbidden was even more addictive than fantasies.

# FOUR

Precise as all their kind, despite her quarter-human blood, Buttercup rang Pahndir's bell at exactly twelve o'clock.

Pahndir looked up from his desk and swore. He had forgotten he'd invited her, a lapse that was ironic, considering he'd spent months working up the courage to ask her here.

Fortunately, he was dressed and sitting in his office with the accounts. Unfortunately, he couldn't count on a servant admitting her. Noon was early enough that most of his employees remained abed. Knowing his heart was thumping far too fast, he did his best to compose his face. Royal Yama weren't supposed to get nervous.

*You're calm,* he told his reflection in the bull's-eye mirror hanging in the hall. *You're a gracious host who knows how to keep his feelings to himself.*

That patent falsity inspired a grimace. He was a gracious host who knew the closest thing he might have to a second mate was the very married woman on his threshold.

He wiped not-quite-dry palms on his yellow-and-sapphire tunic before he let her in. As was proper for Yama who were close in rank, he and Buttercup exchanged bows.

To his amusement—and, admittedly, to his pleasure—the formerly humble Buttercup was not too proud to goggle at her surroundings.

Marrying a prince could only change so much, it seemed.

"My," she breathed, craning her neck to admire the dome in his entryway. A painting of Shiva and Parvati bent around its curves, their explicitly entwined limbs lit by a hanging brass lantern. The flame that flickered inside was meant to remind clients of his house's name. Buttercup closed her mouth and looked back at him. "This place is everything I've heard."

"Then I hope you've heard good things."

He touched her arm to guide her down the corridor. She started slightly at the contact, but recovered with one of her gentle smiles. "I admit I've been surprised to hear people calling you Mr. Pahndir, considering this is The *Prince's* Flame."

"The house's name is a matter of marketing," he said. "The prince I used to be is dead."

They had reached the door to the parlor, where he realized he had nothing in readiness. "Forgive me, I—" He stopped himself midsentence. He couldn't say he had forgotten she was coming. That would have been rude. "Time got away from me. I'll ring someone to bring us hot water for brewing tea."

"Please don't be concerned," she said. "The wait will give me an opportunity to look around."

Knowing from experience that he'd only grow more awkward in her company if he didn't keep busy, Pahndir took the tea things from the sleepy servant to prepare the pot himself. He enjoyed coffee when he was alone, considering it one of the humans' more clever inventions, but for welcoming a guest of his own race into his residence for the first time, coffee simply didn't show appropriate respect.

Buttercup strolled the parlor as he measured and brewed, trailing her finger along the edges of his furniture.

Most Yama would have forced themselves to stillness, absolute self-control being their ideal, but Pahndir suspected she'd been cultivating human gestures, trying to connect with her heritage. They suited her, though she'd always be more mannered than a full member of that race.

His heart contracted as he watched her, stirring a wry amusement at his own fondness. It wasn't his people's way to pine, and nonetheless he didn't look away. Buttercup was as lovely as ever, slightly eccentric in her pale blue *salwar kameez*. The local-style silk tunic and trousers showed off her body's curves. She was rounder than the human woman from the marketplace; shorter, as well. The comparison put him strangely off balance. Buttercup would never fit the Yamish ideal, but to Pahndir's eye she was as succulent as a spring cherry.

Her obvious admiration for his place of business made him gladder than he should have been that he'd spared no expense.

"You think I'm insane, don't you?"

He hadn't meant to blurt out the question. He certainly regretted it when she turned to him in surprise.

"Why would I think that?"

"Because I'm running a brothel. Because if you and Cor hadn't saved me, I'd still be trapped in one myself."

She smiled, an expression he wasn't used to seeing on a Yamish face. "On the contrary, I don't find your choice odd at all. What better way to reclaim your power than to put yourself in charge of this? I know you treat your employees well."

"I frighten them. Not deliberately, but I do."

Her lashes lowered. Human blood notwithstanding, his confession had made her uncomfortable.

"Come," he said, deciding he'd better let this drop. "The tea is ready. Sit and tell me how your offspring are."

That topic made her laugh outright, a wonderful, sunny sound. The tea table was a traditional Yamish furnishing, built low to the ground in glossy black and gold lacquer.

Buttercup eased herself gracefully onto the matching brocade cushion.

"The twins are into everything, everywhere. Someone has to watch them every minute, or they turn the house upside down. Whenever they misbehave, Cor calls them *my* children. I swear, he makes me wish I were Bhamjrishi, with a harem of handsome husbands to keep them corralled."

The words were scarcely uttered before a flush washed across her face. She pressed her hands to her mouth. "Forgive me. I didn't mean to—"

"It doesn't matter," he clipped out before she could go on. "We both know who your harem's first volunteer would be."

"Pahndir." She reached across the table, not touching him but offering to. Pahndir stared pointedly at her hand until it drew back. Her eyes lowered then, and her hands folded in her lap. His coldness had shamed her for her sympathy. Despite his action being completely proper, that shamed him even more.

"You're very careful, aren't you?" he said.

"Careful?" Her head came up cautiously.

"Never to say things like that around me. Never to agree to meet me when I'm near my heat. I wager you know my sexual cycle better than I do."

"I doubt that," she said, her face still and serious. "I doubt anyone knows you that well."

Oh, she could cut a man to his knees with her human frankness. It was true no one knew him, true that she was his only real connection in the world. Pahndir set down his cup and rose. His feet took him to the window. Despite his crew of cleaners, its glass was hazed with sand-colored dust. Taller than the craftsmen who had fashioned it, Pahndir reached up to trace its peak. The ornate layers of stone were lobed like a lotus flower. Behind him, Buttercup spoke.

"If seeing me hurts you, I don't have to come."

He refused to look at her. He didn't want to know if her expression was as kind as her tone.

"I want to see you," he said stubbornly. "You're my friend."

"Yes," she said, and let out a near-silent sigh.

The sound goaded him into straightening his shoulders.

"We will have our tea," he said briskly, returning to the table. "You will tell me about your life, and I will listen."

Buttercup's mouth quirked in a tiny smile. "You remind me you are a prince after all."

He wondered if he ought to apologize for seeming to give her an order, then decided not.

"I *am* better," he said instead, knowing he had to give her this reassurance, no matter how personal it was. "Worlds away from the man I was when we first met at the pillow house. Then I hardly cared if I lived or died. Now I would mind not waking up tomorrow. Now it would bother me not to see what happens next."

She didn't have to work then to show her mixed heritage. Her eyes welled with tears, the refraction of the moisture calling a hint of alien blue into the silver.

"I am glad to hear it," she said, blinking the shine away. "You deserve as good a life as anyone."

The tears were enough to set his course. Pahndir refused to be pitiful. Somehow, some way, he needed to develop other interests.

---

Pahndir had never been to the Hhamoun site, though like everyone else in the city he was aware of it. With so few Yama in Bhamjran, some might have expected him to automatically seek out another of his race, but Welland Herrington—as the man called himself—didn't share Pahndir's royal class. He was *daimyo*, yes, but an aristocrat was not the social equal of a prince.

Since Pahndir planned to cadge himself an uninvited tour, he hoped Lord Herrington remembered that.

He drove his rented desert motorcar into the hive of

workers' tents, unused to the human vehicle but quick enough to figure it out. He often thought humans were brighter than his people gave them credit for. It hadn't taken the Ohramese long to repurpose the engine technology his emperor had granted them, though it went without saying that these primitive contraptions couldn't compare to aircars. Pahndir's teeth were nearly rattled out of his mouth by the time the first guards stopped him.

He used his title to get through them, and the even more effective expedient of a few gold sovereigns to grease their palms. That precious metal was the universal persuader. Once he'd breached the barrier of the guards, politeness was all the coin he needed to gain directions to his countryman.

He found Herrington supervising the removal of a long procession of padded artifacts from a tunnel. Floating pallets would have been safer for the purpose than human hands, but Pahndir supposed even famous diplomats couldn't get permission to use them here. Antigrav technology was a number of orders above electrical engines.

Pahndir parked his car behind a tent and proceeded the final distance in his impractical silk slippers. His clothing was considerably brighter than that of the dig's workers. Even Herrington was dressed in khaki like a Northerner. Given that Pahndir stood out like a peacock, it was no surprise when one of the diggers drew Herrington's attention to his approach.

A flash of irritation crossed the great man's face.

"Pahndir Shan," Pahndir said, offering his hand in the human way. Herrington accepted it blankly, his palm as dusty as the rest of him. His eyes didn't widen until the name sank in.

"*Prince* Pahndir Shan?"

"Yes," Pahndir confirmed. "Reports of my demise were premature."

Herrington glanced back at his workers, his longing to return to overseeing them as conspicuous as his sweaty brow. "My felicitations," he said, then cleared his throat. "To what do we owe the honor of your visit?"

The insult was small but deliberate. Strictly speaking, Herrington should have asked how he could be of service to a higher-ranking member of his kind. Insult aside, Herrington's reluctance to show Pahndir due respect was probably a blessing in disguise. Pahndir's interests were likelier to stay private if he pursued them under eyes less sharp than Yamish ones.

"Curiosity brings me," he said, his tone as smooth and bored as any prince could make it. If there was one thing he had practice at, it was ignoring slights to his dignity. "I've heard such astounding claims about the work you're doing. I'm wondering if you might spare some assistant to show me around."

*"Claims,"* Herrington repeated, bridling just a bit.

"Of course, if you wished to guide me yourself, I would not object."

Herrington had picked up a few human habits during his time with them, including the capacity to flush with annoyance. To judge by the red that washed up his cheeks, he didn't consider carting some pampered prince around his site the compliment Pahndir's words implied.

"I'd be delighted to spare an assistant," he said tightly. "I'm sure you'll find Professor Betters adequately informed."

"Most obliged," Pahndir drawled, careful not to betray his sense of victory. He offered Herrington a small but sufficient bow. "I am eager to see everything."

He *was* eager, though that had more to do with a pair of interesting young humans than any amount of old treasure.

Beth didn't know what was wrong with her, only that something was.

She'd overslept, which—ashamed as she was to admit it—wasn't unusual. Most days, Charles rapped on her door to get her up, since he was Mr. Punctuality. Either he'd forgotten to do it this morning, or she'd been sleeping too hard to hear.

She'd felt . . . different when she finally rolled out of bed; not bad but off-kilter. She remembered having a restless night, filled with strange dreams about the hidden chamber. In one, Queen Tou had been stretched out on her back on a dune and— Well, Beth considered the rest of the dream too personal to dwell on, especially since she'd been playing the part of Tou in it.

The whole thing was most peculiar. Beth's erotic dreams usually involved other people—usually Charles, to be truthful—but they'd never involved climax. Admittedly, she couldn't be held accountable for what her mind did after she fell asleep, but what truly disturbed her was how the dream lingered.

She always enjoyed the luxuries at the *haveli*. The Yama who'd invented the pulsating shower-bath should have been knighted. This morning, however, her time under the nozzles had been a near orgasmic experience, as if her nerves had been both sensitized and pulled closer to her skin. She'd felt ripe inside, bruised and achy, but in a disturbingly pleasant way. She'd begun eyeing the fancy Yamish attachments in a different light, wondering what they might be handy for besides getting clean.

The effect was enough to make even a healthy girl like her wonder what bee had buzzed into her brain, but that upset was nothing to what she felt after she'd been at work an hour and looked around.

She'd meant to sort through her backed-up tasks, to prioritize a *bit*. Without realizing she'd done it, she'd organized all her documents. Now neat stacks of drawings sat around her work tent, classified by sector and date. One pile was missing its associated forms. Another contained correspondence that needed to be copied to the local Ministry of Antiquities. Beth couldn't believe she'd accomplished all this in an hour, or that it had occurred to her to try. Work she'd expected would take a week now looked like it could be finished in a single day.

Shocked, she had to sit on her folding stool, her palm pressed to her pounding heart.

*This isn't right,* she thought. *My mind simply isn't this orderly.*

She was startled onto her feet by Professor Betters's voice outside her tent. Part of her job was handling inter-country mail, and the professor was as finicky as a demon about his letters getting out on time. Dry as dust they were, too. Beth doubted his colleagues at the university were waiting on the edge of their seats for them.

"This is just our copyist's tent," the professor was saying to someone. "There's really nothing of interest here."

A low murmur followed, after which Professor Betters and another man in bright silk robes ducked through her door. She was lucky she wasn't working on anything sensitive, because neither intruder did her the courtesy of asking leave to enter.

The instant she recognized the man in the silk she forgot her annoyance.

Her body clenched with a violence that made her gasp, as if a hot, steamy fist were closing on the flesh between her legs. Professor Betters's companion was the tall, dark demon from the marketplace. Mr. Pahndir stood near enough to touch, his long hair gleaming like black satin where it cascaded over his shoulders. He smelled too delicious for these close quarters, like spice and lemons and hot, hard male. Heat prickled up her muscles, from thighs to belly and breasts to face. Hard as it was to believe, the sensations were stronger than she'd felt in this morning's shower. Beth wanted to attack him, to tear off his fancy clothes and lick him all over. She could have "gone all night" just like the sari vendor said—night after night, for that matter.

The awareness swept over her in seconds, leading her to hope her little fit hadn't been noticed. She gave up that idea when she realized she couldn't tear her eyes from the demon's face. He was *so* beautiful up close, like a perfect statue carved from stone. His skin was the palest gold from living in the sun of Bhamjran, and his firm, exquisitely cut lips looked as soft as rose petals. When she met his eyes, virtually helpless not to, their shining silver color snapped momentarily black.

Whatever the cause of the reaction, it made her jump—as if a snake had flicked its tongue without warning.

The impression deepened when *his* tongue came out briefly to wet his mouth. The sight of its forked marking sent a shiver skipping down her spine. To Beth's dismay, a trickle of heated moisture overran her sex.

The subtle twitch that curved his mouth might have been his people's version of a smile.

"Bright in here," he observed.

Actually, it wasn't bright at all, unless you counted the sun streaming through the open door flap behind him. But perhaps that funny swelling of his pupils had caused the light to seem more intense than it was.

"This is Beth Something-or-Other," Professor Betters said impatiently. "She keeps our records in order."

"Beth Philips," she said, her voice both faint and hoarse.

Mr. Pahndir bowed as deeply as if she were a queen. "Pahndir Shan, at your service."

When he straightened, Beth couldn't help but notice how tall he was. She hardly ever had to look up to men.

Seeming perfectly self-possessed, the demon turned his now-normal eyes around her tent. "From the looks of things, you're good at your job."

There seemed little point in telling him today's display was an anomaly.

"Thank you," was all she got out.

"Tell me, Miss Philips," said the demon. "With all your responsibilities, do you get many chances to go to town?"

His hand was flattened casually on his chest as he spoke to her, his fingers just as long and flawless as the rest of him. His shoulders looked very broad beneath his sapphire-and-yellow robes. They weren't padded, either. Those were strong, lean muscles she saw under there.

"What?" she asked as Professor Betters muttered under his breath.

The demon's answer was as pleasant as if she weren't

acting like a half-wit. "I asked if you enjoyed visiting the city."

"I . . . live there," she said, doing her best not to gasp out the words.

"Do you?" His voice conveyed nothing but politeness, but unless the light was playing tricks on her, his eyes had gone a shade darker.

"In the Old Quarter. With Charles and Lord Herrington." Then, realizing that Charles was probably the person Mr. Pahndir wanted to track down, she added, "Charles works in the cook tent."

"Prince Pahndir," Professor Betters interrupted in a long-suffering tone, "if you're as determined as you seem to examine every corner of the dig, perhaps we should be moving on."

Prince Pahndir (apparently, she'd gotten the *mister* wrong) did not turn back to his guide. His eyes stayed on Beth as he offered her that nearly invisible smile and gracefully inclined his head.

"A pleasure," he said. "I do hope we'll meet again."

Beth found herself unable to say a word. She managed only a jerky nod, her gaze remaining on the tent flap long after it had fallen closed behind her visitors.

*Lord,* she thought. *Lord, Lord, Lord.*

Her shirtwaist was sticking to her back with perspiration, her sex throbbing and slippery with arousal. She was so stupefied by what had happened that she only just had the mental wherewithal to berate herself for being a tongue-tied twit.

She might wish she had the courage to pursue an adventure with a man like that, but, if nothing else, today's encounter had proved she wasn't close to brave enough.

*My, oh, my,* Pahndir thought as he and the professor stepped back onto the frying pan of the sand. His eyes watered at the light, his pupils still enlarged from their involuntary pleasure reaction.

That young human female packed a sensual wallop.

He was sorry to have made her nervous, but delighted that he could. His body hummed at the possibilities she presented. Now that he as good as knew where she lived, he'd be able to devise a plan to seduce her more carefully.

*She smells nice,* he thought, idly pleased by the fact. *Like soap and some warm, sweet spice.*

The misnamed Professor Betters sighed wearily.

"The latrines are that way," he said, only half sarcastically. "And if we continue past them, we'll reach a storage center for unassembled packing crates."

Amused, Pahndir turned his attention to his escort. To be fair to the pompous ass, for the last hour and three-quarters he'd guided Pahndir over every bump and shadow the dig possessed. Now, happily, Pahndir knew everything he'd come to discover.

"I believe I've taken enough of your time. If you could just point me toward the cook tent, we'll call it a day."

"The cook tent."

The professor's arms were crossed suspiciously. Pahndir put on his best approximation of a human smile.

"Oh, yes. There's nothing I like better when it's hot out than a nice cup of black coffee."

"I don't suppose you could spare me a cup of coffee," the Yama said.

The coffee was easier for Charles to spare than an answer, his mind having gone blank the moment the man stepped into his kitchen. Charles's undercooks were studiously not staring at their visitor. They were used to Herrington. Apart from his silver eyes, his appearance wasn't much more exotic than human Northerners. But a traditional-looking demon, in full eye-popping silk regalia, was a different matter. Mr. Pahndir looked every inch the prince some people whispered he was, from the curling toes of his slippers to the shining, midnight fall of his hair. He stood differently from other people, as if he assumed it would be an honor for anyone to breathe the same air. Charles wondered if he even knew he was doing it.

A man like that had probably been raised to think himself superior.

"What are you doing here?" Charles blurted out.

Mr. Pahndir picked up a coffee cup and waggled it. "Looking for caffeine. That lovely human drug?"

He was pretending not to know Charles, and Charles was more than willing to go along with that.

"Perhaps," Mr. Pahndir continued politely, "you'd be so kind as to bring the coffee out to the tables when you've had a chance to pour me some."

"Black?" Charles asked, his tongue as thick and slow as his brain.

"Oh, yes," agreed the Yama. "Black would be perfect."

Charles's hands were almost steady when he carried the tray to where Pahndir waited. If his face was hotter than it should have been, that could be blamed on the steamy atmosphere around the stoves. To his relief, when he came out, no one but the demon sat at the long tables. Charles set the coffee and a plate of biscuits in front of him. The Yama blinked at the cookies in mild surprise.

"What are you doing here?" Charles asked again.

"Hoping to find you," the Yama said.

"Because?"

The demon was silent for a few heartbeats.

"I am Pahndir Shan," he said at last, offering his hand. Charles shook it dazedly. The prince's palm was warm and smooth, his grip unusually firm. Demon strength must have been a challenge to rein in. "As you know, I am the owner of The Prince's Flame. You intrigued me when we met in the marketplace. I'm hoping I didn't say anything to inhibit you from using my services."

Charles only wished he had. His groin was feeling ominously heavy, though he didn't think he'd hardened yet. Just in case, he held the empty tray in front of his waist.

"You've come a long ways to recruit a client. Especially one who doesn't have deep pockets."

The Yama's face had been as still as a granite carving, but now it softened infinitesimally. "I'm looking for more than a client, though that need not concern you if you don't wish. I'm a good judge of character, Yamish and human. I believe you would find my house's services liberating, and I know I'd enjoy facilitating whatever healing influence they might have."

"Healing," Charles repeated with a bitter laugh.

"You might be surprised," the Yama said gently, "how much happier a man can be when he accepts his own desires."

For a second, more than their eyes connected. Knowledge seemed to darken the Yama's, secrets as bitter as his own. But what could this privileged, princely demon know of Charles's life? He couldn't absolve Charles. He couldn't understand. Charles shook his head at his own foolishness. "Mr. Pahndir—"

"Think about it," Mr. Pahndir said. "You have my word that I would look out for your interests as if they were my own, and considering how selfish my kind can be, that's more of a promise than you may realize."

"Mr. Pahndir—"

"No." He lifted his hand and came to his feet. "You don't need to answer. You'll be welcome at The Prince's Flame any time you wish."

*Just what I need,* Charles thought as he watched him leave. *A fresh dose of temptation to obsess over.*

He closed his eyes against the image of Mr. Pahndir's broad-shouldered back. Those silks weren't designed to hide a person's shape, and he hardly needed another reason to be aroused. It wasn't fair that this man attracted Charles on so many levels when he could hardly stand the pull Beth was exerting. He was hard behind the tray he held with white-knuckled fervor, as long and thick and stiff as Beth had ever gotten him.

It occurred to him that, with his talk of healing, Mr. Pahndir wouldn't have been wracked with guilt over pleasuring Beth while she slept. He wouldn't have been praying to every god he knew that she wouldn't figure out it hadn't been a dream. He'd have told her, Charles suspected. He'd have made a game of it that demanded a second round.

And maybe, just maybe, Beth would have preferred the demon's approach.

# FIVE

"You're avoiding me," Beth said as Charles walked past the ground-floor parlor's open pocket doors. She'd spoken on impulse, but guilt flared in his face for just a moment before he stopped.

It was late, nearly ten, and he was dressed to go out in a clean, pressed suit. He leaned against the door frame, natty as a song-and-dance man in a musical hall.

He quirked one fair brow at her. "I'm not avoiding you."

"You haven't been at dinner for the last two nights."

"I've been exhausted."

"Not too exhausted to prepare that cold soufflé for Herrington and me."

He shook his head and smiled. "You can out-argue anyone, can't you?"

Which wasn't, she noted, an answer to her charge. "Are you angry at me? Did I do something wrong?"

"Never." His smile shaded to wistfulness. He came inside the room and sat on her tufted footstool, his narrow hip bumping her crossed ankles beneath her skirt. The casualness of the contact reassured her more than his words. More than that, it warmed her, heart and soul and body, too, if she were honest. She let the book she'd been reading fall to her lap, happy to give him her attention.

"What's this?" Charles asked, laying his hand on the open page.

She'd been feeling calmer in the days following Prince Pahndir's visit to the dig. No inexplicable erotic dreams. No sudden attacks of lust. She'd been telling herself she'd imagined her reaction in the copy tent, but the sight of Charles's strong male hand stretched across the book had the same effect as something hot and long and silky pushed inside her sex. An electric lamp sat on the table beside her chair, a pretty fringed contrivance with a parchment shade. Its glow turned the hairs on Charles's fingers to tiny flaxen wires. Beth was wet in an instant. She had to fight not to rub her thighs together.

"My brain was hungry," she said, more colorfully than she'd planned.

"Your brain was hungry? That has to be a first."

The readiness of his laughter stung, despite it being justified. "We can't all be mental giants," she huffed.

"I'm only a mental giant compared to you. If you want to face off with a real one, you'll have to find my little brother, Max. He sent me another ten-page letter from that boarding school for geniuses. The little nut thinks I actually want a blow-by-blow description of his classes."

Charles was turning the heavy book around on her lap, a process that had an unsettling effect. Her thighs were tingling from the friction, her temperature soaring.

"Max adores you," she said, hoping he didn't notice the beads of sweat forming on her brow. "He only wants to share his interests with his big brother."

"I know that. I'm just not certain he realizes I don't understand half the things he writes. Speaking of which . . ." Now that the book was facing him, he closed it on his hand to read the cover. "*Queen Tou-Hhamoun and the Old Kingdom: Prevailing Theories on Her Rise to Power.* Now there's some light before-bedtime reading."

"It's Herrington's," Beth said defensively. "And it's not as dry as it sounds. Queen Tou was a seminal figure in developing the local tradition of matriarchal rule."

"A *seminal* figure." Charles pressed his lips together in amusement.

"That's what it says in the book!"

He grinned at her and dropped a teasing kiss to her nose. "Don't ever change, Beth. You are the best woman I'll ever know."

The compliment was as surprising as the kiss, a demonstration of fondness he'd never offered her before.

"You're leaving?" she asked, because he had opened the book again to her place and pushed to his feet.

"For a while." He smoothed a nascent crease from the front of his linen coat. "I want to stretch my legs and think."

He hadn't dressed in his freshest outfit merely to stretch his legs. He was going to see the demon. Beth knew that in a flash as clear as sunshine on an oasis. Prince Pahndir must have found Charles in the cook tent the other day. He must have convinced Charles he could afford the services of The Prince's Flame.

She sat back in her upholstered chair, angrier than she had any right to be.

Charles must have seen the tightening of her face. "I won't be long. No more than a couple hours."

A couple hours! Her hands gripped the edges of the heavy volume, tempted to tear the thing in two. Just how many of the prince's employees was Charles planning to enjoy?

"Do be careful," she said coolly. "This isn't the best-lit neighborhood at night."

He opened his mouth as if to ask what bee had flown into her bonnet, then shut it determinedly. Apparently, he knew he wouldn't like her answer. Instead, he nodded curtly and strode from the room.

*Damn him,* Beth fumed. *And damn that Prince Pahndir, too!*

She wagered Charles hadn't been tongue-tied when the brothel owner worked his golden wiles on him.

When she looked down at her lap, the spine to Herrington's book bore an inch-long tear. *Must have been bad leather,* she thought, temporarily distracted by the damage. She'd have to see if she could mend it. She didn't want Herrington thinking she couldn't be trusted with his library.

And on the topic of trust . . . She narrowed her gaze at the open parlor door, her lips pressed together with a mix of irritation and willfulness.

Charles really shouldn't be going out alone at this hour, not when he had a friend as willing as she was to watch his back.

Beth pinched some of Charles's clothing from the laundry room, knowing better than to venture out in a dress at night. Even in a matriarchal city, men would be men, especially when faced with a solitary female from a different culture than their own.

Charles's trousers were snug across her bottom and a bit too long. Other than that, the fit was fine. She kept her breasts from bobbling under his shirt by wrapping a length of bandage around her chest. *Like a mummy,* she thought humorously. She tied her auburn hair into a club. Suitably disguised, one of Herrington's electric torches finished her outfit. The metal tube was strong enough to serve as a weapon should she need one.

Though her preparations were as quick as she could make them, Charles was long gone by the time she crept out of the house. The powdery gold sand that coated every surface in the city proved her salvation. The imprint of Charles's Northern-style boots stood out distinctly. She had only to follow their trail, and he would lead her straight to the demon's den.

She grinned to herself at how easy it was. She hadn't had an adventure this outrageous in quite some time.

*I am brave,* she told herself, reveling in the freedom of the empty streets. The shadows didn't frighten her. Tonight, she was queen of all she surveyed.

Charles's trail of footprints ended a few streets south of the marketplace. Beth stood alone in front of The Prince's Flame, a noise like a drinking party pouring out of its windows. Noise aside, the brothel was a lovely yellow sandstone building, the facade so intricately carved it could have been made of lace. Small projecting balconies jutted from its front like decorations on a wedding cake. Though only three stories tall, Prince Pahndir's establishment stretched half a block before being separated from its neighbors by alleyways.

Those alleyways struck Beth as her best bet for sneaking in. They weren't lit, for one thing, and for another, no one was hanging out their windows.

She switched off her torch as she went to survey the closest one. The carving on the building's side provided plentiful handholds. When she tested them, dangling from one corbel like a monkey, they seemed substantial enough to hold her weight. All she needed was to pick a likely window and edge in.

She pursed her lips and looked up. The entire third floor was dark. One casement in the center appeared to be ajar.

Her stomach fluttered at the thought of climbing so high. *I can do this,* she told herself. She had, after all, been going places she wasn't supposed to since she could walk.

To her relief, the climb went quickly, her childhood escape-artist skills coming back to her. She wasn't seen or heard by the laughing guests, and though the hinges of her chosen window stuck at first, she was able to shove them apart wide enough to squirm through.

On level footing once more, she rolled her shoulders to relieve the strain she'd put on them. She found herself in a silent, nearly pitch-black room. She drew in a breath, let it out, and extricated Herrington's torch from the back of her filched trousers. Switching it on revealed her surroundings.

She was in an office . . . or thought she was. A blotter

sat on a hardwood desk, along with a decorative inkwell and a stand of newfangled silver ballpoint pens. Her confusion arose from the desk being only a foot high. No file cabinets or chairs were paired with it, just a few flat cushions and an unusual padded leather floor. Opposite the desk was a small indoor garden. Oddly shaped miniature pine trees grew from its mossy hills, and a little arching bridge allowed a winding path to cross a sand-filled stream. Beth had to smile when she looked at it. Herrington tended to decorate like a human. Here in the prince's garden, everything was so tiny, it could have been a play yard for Yamish dolls.

She was amusing herself by imagining the prince playing in it when an unfamiliar buzzing had her heart jerking like a thief's. The sound came from the direction of the door. It was followed by an ominous, and more recognizable, click.

*Damnation,* she thought, looking desperately around her even as the latch pressed down. These exotic furnishings were no help at all. She was caught red-handed with no bolt-hole.

Pahndir wasn't licensed to install thumbprint locks on his doors, but given his history (and his family) he hadn't hesitated to obtain them on the black market. What he hadn't expected was that his security would be this easy to breach.

The person who had done so froze when he keyed on the light.

"Well, well," he said, taking in the comically guilt-stricken figure in her too-big male clothes. Beth Philips had bound her breasts to disguise her sex. He remembered those breasts—their shape was burned into his brain—but the trousers revealed more curves than he recalled. With difficulty, he tore his eyes from them. The fact that she'd scaled his wall impressed him. A climb like that took both nerve and upper-body strength.

Rather than let his admiration show, he *tsk*ed at himself. "That will teach me to leave my window open to catch a breeze."

"I was worried about Charles," she said, her words tripping over each other in her haste to defend herself. "He came here alone."

"And because I'm such a big, bad demon, you decided it would be a good idea to break into my home?"

She bit her lip and lowered her eyes. Her lashes were so thick they should have belonged to a far more womanly woman.

"I'm sorry," she said. "This was very wrong of me."

Oh, she made him want to laugh, but he managed to control himself. "I imagine this show of remorse plays better to human parents."

"It isn't a show!" she exclaimed, her face going nicely pink. "I was worried about Charles. A little. And you *did* say you hoped to see me again."

Unable to resist, he crossed the room to her, cupping her cheek and letting her see the amusement gleaming in his eyes. At his touch, she went completely, warily still. Her pillowy cinnamon lips were parted for her quickened breaths. At once, he questioned whether touching her had been wise. He wore no gloves and energy rolled from her into his palm. Though the flow was not as strong as it would have been had he touched her heart, it was seductive nonetheless. Her human life, her passion and her youthful zest, beat in that softly luminous electric fluid. His cock thickened and lifted with what felt like little sparks shooting down its nerves.

Wondering how her hand would feel on him there was inescapable.

"As it happens," he said, his voice sliding unavoidably deeper, "I am glad to see you, if only to reassure you that your friend Charles is as safe as any customer can be. I came here with the express intent of watching over him."

"Watching over him?" she repeated, deliciously breathless.

Pahndir fought to hide his shudder of arousal. "You strike me as a female used to keeping secrets. I expect you wouldn't mind learning one of mine."

To his delight, she'd lost her powers of speech. She swallowed audibly and nodded.

"Have a seat." He gestured toward the embroidered cushion behind his desk. "I'll show you how I stay on top of everything at The Prince's Flame."

He sat next to her behind the strange low desk, his impossibly hard body pressed up against hers all along one side. His robes tonight were a striking gold-embroidered black. Within them he was oven-warm. Unaccountably, Beth found herself shivering.

To her dismay, Prince Pahndir was too sharp to miss the reaction—or to misinterpret its cause.

"It's good, isn't it?" he whispered. "That the two of us are so responsive to each other?"

Beth wasn't worldly enough to answer. Feeling as if she'd stepped into a more glamorous woman's life, she watched the prince press a piece of the ivory inlay on his desk. A hidden mechanism clicked, and a large section lifted and then tipped to show its reverse side. It revealed a square of dull gray metal in a sterling frame.

"Activate visual feed, room three," Prince Pahndir said.

The dull gray plate flickered to life.

"Oh!" Beth's scalp prickled with wonder. "It's a daguerreotype that moves!"

She leaned closer to the picture, barely noticing (and certainly not objecting) when her companion draped his arm around her back. Charles was in a bedroom, pacing back and forth along a flowered rug. He looked nervous, excited, and maybe a little grim. He stopped moving when the door opened. Two Yama entered: one male, one female. They were dark-haired and slender and as alike to Beth's eyes as twins.

"First cousins," Pahndir said as if he'd read her mind. "They prefer to see clients as a pair."

"But isn't that a little close to—I mean, I know our queen's first cousin once courted her, but—"

"Yes, we Yama find it shocking, too, maybe more than you do, for we know the dangers of inbreeding. I expect that's why they're here in Bhamjran, rather than safe at home. It isn't easy to want something even those who love you don't understand."

He was watching her with calm silver eyes, measuring her reaction.

"Do Yama love their children?" she asked.

An emotion tightened his face, so quick and slight she would have missed it if she hadn't been looking straight at him.

"Many do. They simply express it differently than humans."

His gaze fell to her mouth, as if he wanted to kiss her. The lust that had been plaguing her lately burst into renewed flame, like a match set to a pool of oil low in her abdomen. No doubt sensing this, Pahndir's pupils swelled.

"Do you want to watch with the sound on?" he asked softly.

"We can listen to what they say?"

"If you like, I can turn the volume high enough to hear their sweat plopping to the floor."

Beth glanced at the moving silver-framed display. Charles's jacket was gone. The Yamish courtesans were divesting him of his shirt, working together to pull it up his muscled torso and over his head. To know what they were saying would be a more serious invasion of Charles's privacy than she'd thought possible.

"Yes," she said, her throat as rough as if she'd swallowed gravel. "Please turn on the sound."

"Sound on," he said, and wrapped his hand around the fist she'd made.

His hold was probably meant to steady her, but her sex

seemed to be running out of her in warm gushes. It was impossible to pretend she was anything but excited.

Feeling the demons' hands on him was like being licked by fire. Charles's skin was hot everywhere they touched, his prick so stiff it might have been trying to rip through his trousers.

"My name is Donjen," said the male, his fingers hard and competent as he worked to free Charles's front placket. "My cousin's name is Darja. She doesn't speak much human, but she will have to be the one who feeds from you. She has more self-control than I do. Sometimes I get caught up in the pleasure and do not stop soon enough."

Charles gasped as his grossly thickened cock fell into Donjen's hands. This was more information than the state of his arousal needed. The darker part of Charles's nature, the part that would always revel in perversity, wanted to demand that Donjen take his cousin's place.

He didn't get a chance to do so. Charles's gasp became a choked-back cry as Donjen ran his hands up and down the sides of Charles's shaft. The caress was businesslike but wonderful.

"You are big," Donjen observed. "That is good. Both Darja and I like that."

Charles hadn't been certain he wanted to combine this act with sex, but now he was glad Mr. Pahndir had convinced him he'd be missing out if he refrained. He told himself he wasn't sorry he'd declined the demon's offer to do both deeds himself. His current arrangements were as inflaming as he could handle. As it was, chills of pleasure streaked out from his groin, so powerful he wasn't certain how much longer he could keep his feet.

He wasn't the only one burning up. Donjen's pupils were huge black pools as he stroked Charles, and Darja was rubbing her breasts across Charles's back like a cat in heat.

"Can you feel my energy?" Charles asked Donjen. "Does it transfer just from taking me in your hand?"

"It does," the male confirmed. "And I will feel it even more when Darja makes you come."

His cousin said something in their language, apparently urging Donjen to hurry things along.

"She wants your hot human shaft inside her," Donjen explained. "We had better move you to the bed."

They had to help him; his legs were that rubbery. Luckily, the bed was firm and low to the ground, a simple silk-sheeted mattress on an ebony platform. Darja threw off her pale pink robes as if she couldn't wait another second to be naked. She was pretty and delicate, her figure straight, her breasts barely there. She straddled Charles where he lay and flicked her straight dark hair behind her. As a *rohn*, she wasn't entitled to wear it long, and it hung only a little farther than her shoulders. Charles reached for her, wanting her to enjoy this, too, but Donjen caught his wrists and held them.

"No," he said. "Darja likes to prepare herself."

Charles could see she did. She moaned as she ran her hands over her slender body, pulling out her tiny nipples until they turned red. Her pubis had been depilated, probably by some sophisticated Yamish means. The skin was as smooth and glossy as the sheets on which she knelt. When she ran one finger between her labia, Donjen's hands tightened.

He was kneeling on the mattress above Charles's head, the only one of them still dressed. His erection pushed out the front of his loose blue robes, pulsing against them in excitement.

Helpless not to, Charles wondered if the cousins allowed themselves to have sex with each other. Maybe sharing clients was as close as they got.

"She will put her hand over your heart now," Donjen said. "You may feel a sensation of tugging at your breastbone."

Darja's hand was damp from stroking herself. She laid it flat across his chest and groaned softly.

Charles couldn't doubt this was a groan of ecstasy. She

clutched her breast with her other hand, the grip so tight her reddened nipple squeezed out between two knuckles. Donjen spoke to her in their language, a soothing procession of foreign syllables. Calming, Darja opened her eyes again. She looked down at Charles's rigid penis, and then into his eyes.

"Now," she said haltingly, "I take you."

Though he knew no human could overpower a Yama, instinct had him struggling against Donjen's hold. Charles hadn't registered much sensation when Darja touched his heart, but the moment her quivering passage pushed down his cock, he felt the energy she drew from him. Her wetness could not obscure it, or the involuntary jerks with which she undulated over him. It felt like she was pulling long ribbons of etheric force out of him—not only from his heart but from his cock. Once she'd sunk down all the way, she didn't seem to want to move except to grind around him. She began to sob, with pleasure perhaps, or from the emotions that twisted out of him through his aura.

"It burns her," Donjen said, his voice a little husky as he watched his cousin struggle with her desire. "Your energy burns her pussy when she covers you. You should thrust now. She needs to come very soon."

Charles didn't know what would happen if she didn't, but he rocked his hips up and into her. The movement reminded Darja there were more pleasures than simply engulfing him.

"Yes," she moaned, her head lolling back. "Human, come with me."

He was shooting toward it too fast to argue, even if he'd wanted to drag this out. Darja's sex seemed to have more muscles than a human woman's, and apparently she had control over all of them. She rippled over the thrusts he made into her, as deft as fingers stroking him.

With skills like that, she dragged him to the edge in half a minute, and looked just as close herself. This was fortunate, because Charles's teeth were too tightly gritted to warn her.

"Donjen!" she wailed, riding Charles hard and rough.

Her increase in speed undid him, the idea that she was desperate for release. Donjen's hands clenched on Charles's just as the orgasm seethed up his spine. The male's grip was so intense it would have been painful had Charles not been coming. Excited for a few more reasons than he needed, his energy swelled in a way he'd never known it to do before.

Both Yama cried out as it did. Darja's pussy clamped on his cock while Donjen's hips bucked wildly. They came with an abandon Yama rarely showed, and even in the midst of pleasure dread unfurled.

Charles was never going to forget this.

It took a moment beyond their shared explosion before Donjen released Charles's aching hands. Darja's slight weight sagged onto him soon after. She rubbed her cheek across his shoulder, possibly gathering a last few sips of his energy.

"Good," she purred. "Very, very good, human."

Her praise may have disturbed her cousin, because he lifted her away. Darja murmured a protest but did not resist. She looked drunk, her face streaked from weeping, her eyes an eerie solid black. Donjen had to hold her with her weight propped against his side.

Charles's eyes widened when he got a good look at him. Donjen hadn't simply come, he had come rivers. The wet spot on his robes extended all the way to his knees. If the Yama felt self-conscious over this, it didn't show. His alien face was as unreadable as a mask.

"Thank you, human," he said, offering him a crisp, cool bow. "You were a more than adequate partner."

They exited with no added formalities. Darja's head was resting on her cousin's shoulder, the pair more of a couple—despite the vaguely illicit nature of their bond—than a man like Charles could intrude on. The reminder that he'd never been part of a couple couldn't have been starker. Worse, their departure left him, whether he wished it or not, alone with his thoughts.

He'd finally done it, the act he'd craved and avoided much of his adult life. He didn't think he felt any different. Not more of a monster, not less. Pleasured, yes, but certainly not *liberated* the way Mr. Pahndir said.

Mostly he felt tired, as if he'd worked too many shifts back to back. While it was happening, the sex and the feeding had been incredible. Now he wished he could undo both.

Knowing he couldn't and too drained to rise, he flung his forearm across his eyes. He discovered the female Yama hadn't stolen all his tears. One squeezed out from beneath his eyelid and ran, warm as blood, down his temple.

# SIX

"Is Charles all right?" Beth asked as soon as her breath returned. "Maybe we should—"

At a loss, she stopped speaking. Going to Charles didn't seem the right suggestion. She knew he wouldn't want her there, and the precise nature of the prince's relationship with him was unclear. He'd said he wanted to watch over Charles, but would Pahndir ordinarily check on a client who seemed upset?

His quiet, watchful expression offered no clues.

"Your friend isn't ill," he said, "if that's what concerns you. He's simply fulfilled a craving he fought against for a long time. That can take adjusting to. Any other effects, he'll sleep off."

Beth twisted around on the cushion to face her host. Prince Pahndir's hands settled on her shoulders as if they were intimates. The move startled her, though he made no further advance. She wasn't used to being so close to a male she wasn't related to. This one's proximity posed a danger to her self-restraint, but she wanted to understand more than she wanted a safe distance.

"You're saying Charles has been wanting to feed a Yama with his energy."

Pahndir offered her a shrug so small she almost didn't see it. "Some humans enjoy the act more than others. I'm told it's an acquired taste: relaxing if you don't fight it, draining if you do. There are cosmetic effects, of course. Humans who feed Yama refine their looks."

His lean, hard face could have been an advertisement for that refinement, its planes and angles subtly different from a human male's.

"And your kind? Do they all enjoy our etheric force?"

Prince Pahndir's gaze fell to her throat, where she could feel her pulse throbbing. Was he trying to judge how aroused she'd become from watching Charles? He must have been, because his eyes returned to hers, darkened. This close, his irises were mesmerizing, like flames burning behind ice.

"I've never heard of a Yama who didn't enjoy a sip or two, though many fear the loss of control that comes with absorbing human emotions."

"It appeared as if . . ." Beth swallowed. "For your employees, feeding from Charles looked like an aphrodisiac."

"It is." Pahndir's elegant profile leaned toward her neck. "Do you know your smell changes when you blush? It grows just a whiff spicier."

This was too much for her. Overwhelmed, she put her hands on his chest and pushed, which was as useful as shoving at a cliff. Her traitorous body found her powerlessness exciting, making her next words come out ragged. "I'm not comfortable with you sniffing me."

"What if I were kissing you? Would that distract you enough not to mind?"

She shouldn't have licked her lips, but she couldn't help it. She was too hot, too soft and needy, and he was close enough to fan her face with his quickened breath. He smelled good, too, warm and spicy and very male.

"Just a kiss?" she asked softly.

Pahndir's silver eyes took on what she thought was a teasing gleam. "Perhaps you're right to be cautious. I'm certain if I kissed you, I would want more."

"Because watching Charles aroused you."

"Didn't it arouse you? I thought Donjen wasn't going to stop coming. Charles didn't even have to touch him to bring him off."

This reminder made her clench inside. "You liked watching the man more than the woman?"

She knew she shouldn't be encouraging this conversation. She knew it even more when his eyebrows slanted in amusement.

"Oh, Beth, I am going to enjoy shocking you."

Hearing him say her given name was enough to startle her. He ducked closer, ready to steal the kiss he'd offered earlier. Beth wanted it, but at the last second something stronger than desire had her drawing back.

Pahndir understood her reticence better than she did.

"I'm rushing you, aren't I?" He drew one hand down her front until it cupped her breast through Charles's shirt. "You want me as much as I want you, but I've pushed too fast."

She bit her lip against the shock of pleasure the gentle pressure of his palm inspired. Even through her bindings, he had to feel how hard her nipple was. "Maybe you could let me . . . do things to you."

*"Things?"*

"Maybe—" Helpless not to, she gave in to her urge to squirm her itch against the floor cushion. Her body felt like it was burning up, especially between her legs. "Maybe you could show me how you like to be touched."

He cursed in his own language, then covered her mouth with his. It was a swift, devastating kiss, his tongue curling in to claim her softness, his lips tugging hers to him. When he broke away, he blew out a hard, rough breath.

Those few seconds had her mouth buzzing.

"Why do your eyes go black like that?" she whispered. "What does it mean?"

He seemed startled by the question, taking a moment to answer. "My eyes go black when I'm very, *very* aroused."

Oh, he just made it worse and worse. She could barely squeeze her next question out. "You're aroused by me?"

"By you, sweet Beth. By the thought of your hands on me."

He lifted each one to kiss its palm, and then captured her mouth again. This time the kiss was deeper, longer. His arms came around her, drawing her to her knees and over his lap. She'd been kissed before and had enjoyed it, but those kisses had never turned her spine molten. His lips were satin on their surface and firm beneath. His hands moved slowly up and down her back, gentle but arousing.

The moment was unbearably intimate—the stroking of his tongue against hers, the closeness of his body. She sank into the pleasure, barely minding the vulnerability of her legs being spread apart around his thighs. Though the prince was silent, she couldn't keep her sighs inside. Moaning, she pushed her fingers through the night-dark silk of his hair.

The brush of skin on skin must have been too much. Pahndir pulled back with a quiet gasp. He cupped her breast again, looking down to where the peak pulsed wildly beneath the pad of his circling thumb. His tongue came out to bare its forked marking, and Beth immediately thought of places she wanted it.

It was embarrassing, really, how much she craved every part of him.

"Creation," he said, his voice a trifle husky on the demon curse. "I think we need to put our hands on each other."

"I want to touch you first," she insisted, not sure what she'd do if he touched her. The lift of Pahndir's brows reminded her that she was contradicting royalty. "I mean, if you wouldn't mind, Your Highness."

He let out an actual laugh, brief but unmistakable. "I only used my title to get past your employer. Pahndir will do for you. We'll make you the queen tonight. Nothing will happen that you don't wish."

His promise was enough to flush her from head to toe.
"That's what I'm afraid of," Beth confessed ruefully.

The fact that she'd made him laugh again was disturbing. Pahndir shouldn't have been this loose with her, this aroused. He'd brushed up against human energy before, casually and otherwise, but none of the paid companions with whom he'd performed his previous experiments had stirred him up half so much. He could have been two days from his heat, instead of two full weeks. Touching Beth had made his skin nearly crawl with pleasure, and kissing her . . .

That would have knocked him to his knees if he hadn't already been there. Her taste alone would have been enough to weaken him, but there had been more. Though her responses weren't without innocence, it was clear she'd wanted to kiss him back, and that she'd known how.

"You're frowning," she said.

Pahndir wiped the expression from his face. Disconcerting though his reactions were, their intensity was cause for hope. She'd made his eyes go black, and he definitely found her scent appealing: both indicators that a match was possible. After all his searching, he might have found a human who could give him the relief he craved. He wouldn't know for certain until his cycle peaked, but in the meantime, they could certainly enjoy themselves.

"I'm concerned," he said, the evasion as natural as drawing breath. "Despite your obvious daredevil streak—which, believe me, I'm grateful for—I don't wish to frighten you off."

"I'm afraid you'll have to work harder to do that. My sisters don't call me Fearless Philips for nothing."

He didn't fight the amusement that curved his lips, or the urge to tuck a lock of gilded auburn behind her ear. That the simple touch called color into her cheeks delighted him. Instantly addicted, his next demand was guaranteed to deepen it.

"Tell me what you know of Yamish sexuality."

"Well—" She fidgeted, and not just with nerves. The scent of her juices was enough to clench his jaw. "I know you're stronger than humans and, er, very controlled. And, generally speaking, humans and demons can't have children. I know you— That is, I assume you have essentially the same parts."

"Essentially." He cupped her beautiful warm face. "Have you ever seen a naked man?"

As he'd known it would, her skin flamed deliciously under his palm.

"Not completely naked, unless you count picture books. Are you volunteering to undress for me?"

He had to squelch another laugh at her hopefulness. With no wish to disappoint her, he rose and began unfastening his outer robes. Her eyes were avid, her hands pressed flat to her slender thighs. He dropped his outer garment, leaving only a tunic and lounging trousers made of thin gold silk. At that point, his arousal couldn't be hidden. Clearly fascinated, her gaze dipped to where his erection pushed out the cloth.

Pahndir expected her to find his body acceptable. Health and beauty were built into his genes. Still, Beth's reaction pleased him. He didn't think he'd ever seen quite her combination of avarice and awe.

"You touch me when I say," he warned her. "Not before."

"You're large," she said, her eyes refusing to move.

"I am in proportion to my height."

He'd only meant to be accurate, but the explanation caused her to laugh. The sound fluttered through him like butterflies. Wanting to be naked, and quickly, he made short work of pulling off the rest of his clothes. Her reaction to this was just as priceless.

"Oh," she said, her fingers to her mouth. She scooted across the leather floor to him on her knees, perhaps unaware of how provocative her position was.

Not that it mattered, he sternly told himself. He wasn't going to ask a neophyte to take him in her mouth.

When his cock jolted higher at the tantalizing thought, she almost touched him, pulling her hand back only at the last moment. Her big honey-brown eyes looked up at him in question. "You have no hair on your sex."

"We remove it. The women, too."

Evidently, she hadn't watched his employees closely enough to notice this. The omission flattered him . . . until he realized her attention had probably been on her friend. He didn't like the way that supposition felt, but before he could convince himself it was unimportant, she spoke again.

"You are larger than a human here," she said, indicating his scrotum.

Pahndir fought the urge to dig his nails into his palms. "It seems you didn't waste your time with those picture books."

"I memorized them," she confided with another laugh.

It was too unnerving, and too tempting, to have her sit before him like a supplicant. He returned to his knees in front of her, sitting on his heels to bring their heads level. "How good are you at keeping secrets?"

"Very." Her tone was sure, her face serious.

"I hope that's true, because I need to tell you another before we go further. I am larger than humans, and other Yama, too. Royals are different, Beth. Royals have extra needs."

"*Extra* needs?"

He took her hand and wrapped it gently around his balls, almost wincing at how good the contact felt. Possibly, the pleasure was addling him, because sharing a secret most of his own kind weren't privy to took shockingly little internal debate.

"Royals only ejaculate once a month, and only with partners who are biochemically compatible: those with whom we'd have strong children. We can have sex any time we like, but until we hit our heat, our orgasms are dry."

Her mouth had fallen open. "Once a— Are you in heat now?"

"Thank you for the flattering suggestion but, no, I'm not."

"Oh, God!" she exclaimed on a gust of air. "I feel like I am!"

Lust rolled through him in a hot, molasses wave. How could he behave as a respectable Yama should with a woman who said things like that? Speaking politely was a true struggle. "Would you like me to give you a release now?"

She shook herself, or maybe shuddered. "No," she said, her fingers shifting restlessly on his scrotum. "I think I trust your control more than mine."

No one, Yama or human, had ever said such a thing to him. His eyes pricked strangely. "You may safely enjoy yourself with me. I won't do anything you don't ask for."

She smiled as slow and sweet as a spring sunrise. "The way I feel, I'm afraid I'll ask for everything, and I'm not sure I'm ready to get it."

He did his best to hide his disappointment. No doubt she was a virgin, and not yet prepared to give the condition up.

"As you wish," he said, then jerked when her hand contracted on his testicles. She seemed to know she hadn't hurt him, because she repeated the testing squeeze. Though he wasn't as full as he'd be in a week or so, the pressure felt wonderful, her human energy warming him deep inside.

"Are you larger here because your seed is storing up?"

"In part," he said, his breath somewhat difficult to retrieve, and never mind his concentration. "Blood flows to those tissues when I'm aroused, so I'm slightly swollen and tender."

"Good tender or bad?"

"Good," he said, a fraction short of a gasp. Giving in to impulse, he shifted his knees wider. Her fingers had begun to play more surely over him, and his eyelids were sliding shut as if they were weighted. "All Yama like to have their balls massaged. It loosens us for later. Makes our ejaculations easier."

"I know about massages. They're my big sisters' favorite bribes for not tattling."

She must have paid them off many times. She was swiftly turning him into a puddle.

"I want to touch all of you," she murmured. "You look so smooth."

He managed to turn the groan he wished to utter into a grunt, much good as that did him. She took the sound as permission. Her hands shifted to his shaft, sliding over him up and down. She was cooing in admiration, but Pahndir could scarcely hear above the blood whooshing in his ears.

He thought of all the hands that had touched him, all the students who'd honed their erotic tricks on him when he'd been the Purple Crane's captive teaching tool. Whatever pleasure they'd brought, he'd always chained the emotions that hid deep in a Yama's soul. Now he wanted nothing more than to throw off those old constraints. He wanted to trust Beth, to simply be with her and enjoy.

But maybe these uncustomary inclinations came from her. Maybe they were seeping into him with her energy. He opened his eyes and found hers watching him anxiously.

"Is this right?" she asked. "Is this what you like?"

He put his hand over hers, guiding her to a smoother, harder stroke. She blushed when she felt the difference this brought to his reactions, how it heated his skin and caught at his breath. He was sitting on his heels, with her knees bracketing his. Their mingled scents perfumed the air. He thought he'd never seen a lovelier female, her human vibrancy preferable to any Yamish perfection. His eyes squeezed shut, just for a moment, when her thumb found a patch of sensitivity beneath his penis's head. Reluctant to miss a thing, he opened his eyes again.

She was biting her lower lip with the most endearing concentration he'd ever seen.

He had to kiss her then, had to lick that cushy surface and taste her once more. She moaned, her grip tightening painfully. When he drew back, her eyes were squeezed as tightly shut as his had been.

"Oh, God," she said, panting it. "I didn't know I could ache this badly."

The confession almost drove him mad. He forgot about not frightening her, about style or suaveness or anything but touching her. His hand was already opening her trousers, his weight already tipping her onto the leather meditation mat that formed his floor. "Let me bring you with me, Beth. It's better not to come alone. I'll only use my hand, I swear."

She squeaked out some protest that changed into a moan the moment his fingers reached the creamy slit of her sex. She felt like the human heaven as he explored, so wet, so hot, so responsive to his every touch. Her hands left his erection to clutch his back, her hips working frantically up at him.

When his thumb slid over the bursting bud of her clitoris, she uttered a strangled sound no Yama ever had.

"Sorry," she gasped even as her pelvis jerked in a hard climax. "Oh, please, do that again."

He wasn't going to disappoint her, or miss joining in. Yanking up her borrowed shirt, he shifted his hips to press his cock against her belly where the curve met her hipbone. That delight was eye-opening, her skin there melting soft. One of his legs had fallen between hers, and she was gripping it with both thighs. To be naked while she was dressed added one more coil to his excitement; power and vulnerability had always been equal stimulants for him. To experience both now gave him an almost giddy awareness of his freedom. He was no one's slave tonight. He didn't have to take orders.

Able to do as he pleased, he had just enough control to keep his fingers busy pleasing her—for which he counted himself lucky. She screamed out her second climax: softly, but she did.

*Oh, Fortune, could I get used to hearing that!* he thought. The burst of energy pulled him over—a good, deep orgasm, even if it was dry. Wanting another for them both, he rubbed her clitoris with even more direct intent, seeking out the brighter flare of life force where the little rod was most sensitive.

"Wait," she said, squirming wildly but not away. A second later, she shoved her hand between his abdomen and his shaft, pressing him against her skin. He wasn't giving her much room to fist him, but she was stroking him as best she could, her hand perfectly positioned to swallow up the head. The technique might not have been sophisticated, but it was intense, especially with the tiny chakras in her palm shooting lightning bolts. When she hit her peak, there was no way in the universe he could hold his own pleasure back.

His eyes just about crossed when he came that time.

He didn't realize he'd collapsed on top of her until she let out a muffled I-can't-breathe sound.

He pushed back from her at once, his hair falling around his torso in a long dark cloak. Pahndir couldn't remember the last time he'd done anything this inconsiderate to a lover. Worse, some of his horror must have shown in his expression, because she patted his arm.

"It's okay. Truly."

"It's unconscionable. I'm far too heavy to lie on a human female. I could have crushed your ribs!"

Beth laughed, which flustered him. "I'm not that fragile. I just needed air."

He was so unsettled, he shoved his hair back with both hands. "I'm usually more adept with women."

Beth blinked at that, which had him wondering if she doubted him. He certainly hadn't shown her his best techniques. But she shook her head at whatever she'd been thinking. "I suspect we were both a bit out of control tonight."

When her words sank in, they dumbfounded him. A sexually inexperienced human female thought *he'd* been out of control? Aghast, Pahndir watched her struggle to her feet to tuck her shirt back into her trousers. He wanted to convince her his control had never been better, except he wasn't sure he could convince himself.

Just looking up at her, he was well on his way toward wanting her again.

"Well," she said, standing over him. She looked awkward, which was probably his fault as well. "I suppose I should get out of here before Charles recovers. I don't want him thinking I spied on him, even if I did. Thank you for—" She hesitated, at a loss for the correct term. "Thank you for sharing that with me. Thank you for not being angry about me breaking into your home."

"I want to see you again," he blurted out.

Her face went as dark as a damson plum, and rightly so. The rawest pup of a Yamish suitor wouldn't have been so blunt.

"No, never mind," he said before she could utter whatever polite refusal she was scrambling for. "Let me call a car for you. I want to know you'll get safely home."

She rubbed a spot between her eyebrows, a human gesture of perplexity. He couldn't blame her. He was rather perplexed himself.

"That would be nice," she said with a crooked, if unsure smile. "I expect my legs are too shaky to leave the way I came in!"

# SEVEN

*Never mind. Never mind. Never mind.*

The phrase rolled through Beth's mind like an endless train, first in Pahndir's voice and then in hers.

Tonight was over. Done. And unlike the times she'd played silly board games with her older siblings, she couldn't throw a tantrum and retake her turn.

She would have retaken it in a minute, if only to enjoy the feel of Pahndir's hot, silken hardness in her palm again. She should have touched him more when she'd had the chance, should have caressed his face and those beautiful hands of his. Maybe just held him and stroked his hair.

That idea had her choking back a laugh. She could just imagine the icy prince letting her do that.

The irony of her thoughts did nothing to diminish her almost agonizing arousal. Knowing she shouldn't have been feeling it (she'd been pleased three times, after all) she tried not to wriggle too obviously on the leather seat. The prince's car was what Charles's younger brother, Max, would have called the cat's meow: a long, silver Daimler-Harris with a winged Victory on its prow. It rode so smoothly it put Charles's pride-and-joy rattletrap to shame. An older human in a chauffeur's cap was driving, his expression conveying as little interest in Beth as his employer's had at the end of their visit.

She'd never seen eyes go as flat and cool as Pahndir's had, and mere seconds after he'd declared he wanted to see her again. Had he recognized his own insanity? Or was it was hers that had put him off?

Evidently, her human energy could only interest him for so long.

She pressed a fist to her mouth and stared out the window, fighting to contain her inner turbulence. She must have lost her mind. Granted, most of tonight's activities weren't out of character for her—or not by much—but to throw herself at a man she barely knew, to beg him to pleasure her . . . that wasn't typical. Fearless Philips or not, apart from a little adventuring, she'd kept her beaus within bounds her mother would have approved of. She was, technically at least, still a "good" girl.

Of course, now she knew that was only true because she hadn't desired those other men as much as Pahndir.

Her groan of humiliation drew the driver's impassive gaze to her in the rearview mirror. While this was embarrassing, his opinion was the least of her concerns. She'd probably been absolutely awful compared to the sophisticated women the prince was accustomed to. Why, he'd had to put his hand on hers to show her how to stroke him, a titillating necessity at the time, but now just another reason to feel inadequate. She hadn't made him moan even once. She was reasonably certain men were supposed to, even Yamish ones.

And now that she'd mentioned moaning, what had he meant about Yamish royals going into heat? Would he be like a cat yowling in an alley? Helpless to turn her down? Desperate for the ejaculation he could only have once a month?

A fresh wave of arousal swelled at the idea. She really, *really* liked the sound of that.

"Hellfire," she muttered, and bit the side of her thumb.

None of this mattered. She was never going to see the prince again. She was going to behave herself for the rest of her natural life. She was going to ignore her impossibly aroused body and turn her eyes the other way when males walked by. Only then could she be certain not to mortify herself again.

The perfect cap to the evening came as she held her breath and tried to shut the *haveli*'s door silently behind her.

"Bit late for a walk," Herrington remarked.

The entry hall was dark, but she could just make out the hulking shape of him in the arch to the front parlor.

"You scared me," she said, her heart abruptly racing. "I couldn't sleep. I stepped out to get some air."

"I thought I heard a motorcar drop you off."

"Oh, no, that was a lost tourist looking for his hotel."

He stared at her, saying nothing, his demon eyes glittering coolly in a thin moonbeam. He was as bad as her mother for making a person worry that her lies were written on her face.

*Just stick to your story,* Beth advised herself.

"I took your torch," she said, pulling it out to show him. "The perfect weapon, should anyone have wanted to interfere with me."

He accepted it from her hand. "It seems that Charles has 'stepped out' as well."

"Has he?" Beth brushed a fallen lock of hair from her eyes. "Well, I'm sure he's fine. Charles is old enough to take care of himself."

"You're both my responsibility to keep safe."

"We *are* safe. Safe and happy and grateful for all you do. And now I really should get to bed. I don't want to oversleep tomorrow and be late for work."

Charles would have teased her for laying it on too thick, but Herrington simply turned his head to watch her climb the stairs tread by tread.

"Sleep well," he said, long after a human would have responded.

Knowing he'd see even in the dark, Beth nodded in answer and tried not to look as if she were running away from him.

Though it crossed her mind, she didn't have the nerve to ask what *he* was doing out so late. *Out* was where he had to have been. The great Herrington's boots had been caked from toe to ankle in desert sand.

Once she'd disappeared into the darkness, Herrington laughed softly.

How lowering was it that a twenty-something-year-old human had the power to hurt his feelings by lying to his face? The sting was a sign of how long he'd lived among Beth's kind. By contrast, the part of him that would always remain Yama admired her facile tongue. She was a smooth deceiver, cool as a cucumber. If he hadn't seen her get out of the motorcar with his own eyes, he'd have been tempted to believe every word.

She was fortunate his culture didn't believe in confronting others for deliberate lies. If they had, he'd have blistered her human hide. Herrington had been (and still was, on occasion) both diplomat and spy among her kind. The highest ranks of Avvar society had opened their homes to him. An invitation, however, was not the same as acceptance. Beth's parents were among the rare humans who simply treated Herrington as a man they liked. He'd promised to look out for their daughter, and he had no intention of letting her run wild until he'd approved of whoever her partner in wildness was.

But that was for later. For now, the tasteful crest that had gleamed on the expensive private auto's side was burned into his memory. After six seasons digging in Bhamjran, Herrington had built a good intelligence network. He'd make inquiries before he acted. As to that, he'd like to know what Charles was up to. Both the young people in his care were "acting dodgy," as the humans said.

Welland Herrington knew better than to let a trend like that go unchecked.

If one was a royal Yama, there were reasons for adding men to one's sexual bill of fare. Pahndir was contemplating them while staring blankly at the striped red satin walls of his brothel's long bedroom-floor corridor.

There was boredom, of course. No pampered royal was immune to that. Nor could the charm of variety be underestimated when one was bonded to a single female for life. But the primary reason royals ventured into playing with their own gender was their glands.

They had extras—three, to be precise. The common rabble weren't supposed to know about them, but when royals hit their heat, their body chemistry went haywire.

The two glands in their necks pumped a hormone known as kith into their saliva, which could then be passed with a kiss. Kith was a powerful aphrodisiac that heightened the sex drive of matched partners, ensuring that those Yama who were likeliest to have healthy offspring would be highly motivated to reproduce. Royal Yama sometimes needed help in that department, the duplication of their extensively adjusted and inbred genes depending on conditions being just so.

The third gland, the one that was foremost in Pahndir's mind tonight, was called the kingmaster. It piggybacked atop his prostate, and it, too, generated kith. When released inside a Yama's mate, through involuntary contractions that shot it up his urethra, the hormone made her as incapable of resisting sex as he was. Heat lasted five days, during which time the couple threw themselves into reaching climax as often as possible.

They might have done this even if they didn't have to. The orgasms royals had while under kith's influence were indescribably pleasurable. Pahndir held the opinion that this was fortunate. A female who wasn't so well rewarded for her efforts might not have wanted to engage in a carnal marathon that long.

Or so went the theorizing among genetic scientists.

The problem was—if you could consider anything that inspired such ecstasy a problem—the kingmaster gland was always sensitive, whether the male was in heat or not. As was the case for the human prostate, prolonged manipulation could produce climax. Fingers could be put to the task, or other creative toys. Some Yama, however—Pahndir among them—developed an affection for the feel of a man's erection running over it: living flesh, throbbing and jerking and taking its own pleasures. His wife had been understanding. A few of the threesomes Thallah had arranged were among his sweetest memories of her. His most painful, too. It was difficult for him to fathom how a woman of Thallah's generous spirit could have felt the need to end what they'd shared by taking her own life.

Pahndir closed his eyes and blew out a breath. He'd put that loss behind him. He'd had to, for the sake of his sanity. Thallah must have had her reasons, and if he'd been a part of them, he couldn't change that now. His only power was to change the shape his life took from here, or at least to try.

A door opened down the hall, reminding him where and who he was. A longtime customer flung her bright evening wrap around her shoulders and inclined her head to him.

"Very nice," she said. "As always."

He nodded back, not trusting his voice just then. She'd been with Samthan, a young man who offered her a bit more forçeful treatment than she got from her harem. Pahndir made a mental note to pass on the compliment. He believed in paying his employees with more than coin.

The corridor was quiet after the woman left, all his rooms being well soundproofed. The downstairs party had wound down as well. Pahndir glanced at the small silver *3* above the door he faced. He knew very well why he'd been woolgathering outside it, rather than going in.

Making a fool of himself once tonight was enough.

He lifted his fist to knock, then brought it down to his

side again. Would the human want to be checked on? A Yama wouldn't have, but—as his ineptitude with Beth had proved—his knowledge of what humans wanted might not be as accurate as he'd believed.

*To the Void with it,* he thought. One misstep did not a habit make. He wasn't going to let second-guessing himself paralyze him now. He knocked and turned the knob at the same time.

Charles looked at Pahndir when he entered but did not rise. He'd pulled the sheets to his waist, and his arm still lay across his forehead. Its shadow deepened the circles beneath his eyes, though even that couldn't dim his beauty. He looked doomed and lovely, a human angel dragged to earth by his own desires.

Pahndir stopped a foot from the rumpled bed.

"You've had a hard ride," he said, inviting a response but not demanding it.

Charles rolled his face toward the wall. "I'm fine. Just a little tired."

Pahndir wouldn't have pushed one of his own race, but for the human he bent his knees and sat on the bed's low edge. He touched Charles's shoulder lightly with the back of his hand. The human's skin was warm and damp, his muscles hard. Pahndir had time to feel the visceral jolt of that before the contact brought the young man's haunted gaze back to him.

"I hope you'll forgive my saying so," Pahndir said, "but you don't look fine."

Charles pressed his lips into a line. "I don't feel better. I thought maybe I could exorcize this need, but—God help me—as empty as it was, it felt so good."

"You have regrets."

The human shook his head in a half-denial. "I know I'd have done it some day. Eventually. Wanting to made me feel guilty enough."

"And why pay for the sin and not commit it? Except it isn't a sin unless you make it one. My people aren't the demons you call us. You can't give up your soul to us."

"I know that," Charles said, but his tone was uncertain.

"No one was harmed tonight. You brought your partners great pleasure."

Charles's mouth twisted. "I'm not sure they needed me for that."

"They may have. I don't know, or care to ask, what pleasures Donjen and Darja allow themselves on their own."

Charles shifted on the slippery sheets, apparently uncomfortable with the reminder of his reaction to the cousins' relationship. The sheet covered his groin, but Pahndir suspected he was experiencing a certain level of recovery. Though Pahndir wanted to capitalize on the response, he wasn't certain how. He was spared the effort when Charles spoke himself.

"I used to work in a place like this." He looked at Pahndir, daring him to disapprove, which he was hardly going to do.

"You and I have something in common then."

Charles seemed to think that over. "Are you sorry I didn't let you do the deed?"

"Are you?"

Charles pursed his lips wryly. "You Yama sure don't give anything away for free."

"And here I thought I was being especially forthcoming. I'll answer if you like." He drew a breath to pull his thoughts together, the expectation of honesty one he was not used to. "No, I'm not sorry, as it happens. I'm interested in you and, consequently, I prefer not to be associated in your mind with an event that caused you discomfort. Moreover, I know what it's like to be an unwilling partner. I don't want anyone, for any reason, to be an unwilling partner to me."

Charles's eyes narrowed. "What if I can't promise I'll ever be willing?"

"Then I can only hope my . . . excess of willingness will persuade you."

A smile ghosted across Charles's mouth. He seemed to

appreciate the delicacy of the answer. "You're all right, you know. For a prince."

"I am gratified to have your good opinion."

Had Charles been a Yama, Pahndir would have risen then. He'd supplied an end point to the conversation, truthful and yet indirect. But Charles wasn't a Yama, and Pahndir wasn't ready to go. He felt something gathering in the human, something hanging in balance.

Charles struggled up onto his elbows, his belly as flat and muscled as Pahndir's own. "Maybe I should have accepted your offer to feed from me yourself. Maybe I should have asked for everything I wanted."

The words went through him with a punch of adrenaline. Pahndir had suspected he was part of what Charles wanted, but to hear him say it . . . Charles's gaze was holding his, the shade he'd drawn over his private thoughts lifted enough for Pahndir to see the glimmer of a fire within.

Most astounding of all, Pahndir didn't think the glimmer was entirely lust.

That had his pulse tripping unavoidably over itself. Royal Yama didn't generally have the luxury of juggling lovers' affections. They found their mates, bonded, and if they took additional sexual partners, those relationships ran a distant second to the match their genes had selected. Bonded sex was simply too intense, too consuming for it to be otherwise.

Because of this, Pahndir wasn't prepared for the guilt that swept over him. He felt as if he were doing something underhanded by being drawn to this man when he'd so recently been thrashing on the floor with Beth. If Beth was sunlight, Charles was storm: two halves of one delectable repast. Pahndir couldn't deny he wanted to seduce them both, but he'd been thinking with his flesh alone. To his surprise, there was, in both these humans, the potential for true connection.

He couldn't imagine what the objects of his interest would think of his reluctance to choose between them.

Most humans were more conservative than Yama when it came to creative erotic arrangements.

*You'd be likelier to hit your target,* he chided himself, *if you weren't aiming for a million-mile-long shot.*

"Let me call for a meal," he said, deciding avoidance of the topic was his best strategy for now. "You need to replenish your energy. As a chef like you ought to know, everything looks better with a full stomach."

Charles touched the sleeve of Pahndir's robes before he could rise. "Thank you. You made this better than it might have been."

"Hmm. I believe I'll run out and quote you in all my ads."

Charles laughed aloud, not as easily as his friend, but easily enough. The pleasure of calling the reaction from him was sweeter than Pahndir would have guessed.

# EIGHT

*Being queen was no stroll along the river. Tou had miles of correspondence to dictate to the scribes, endless meetings with her advisers, and stacks of news to sort through from the provinces. As a formerly illiterate orphan, she reveled in the exercise of her intelligence. She loved being quicker, keener, and harder than those who would take advantage of their female liege. Still, administration was not the favorite of her queenly duties. Her favorite came after the sun had melted into the desert, after the torches of her palace were trimmed and lit.*

*She licked her lips like a temple cat as she strode down the well-guarded corridor toward her harem. She wore her thinnest pleated linen gown, the wrap of it around her modest, the transparency not at all. Some of the guards were hard-pressed not to stare at the curve of her beneath it. Their struggle plumped the folds between her thighs.*

*Tou was their ruler, yes, but she was also a woman men desired.*

*When she reached her goal, a wrestling match was*

*under way in the* zenana's *enclosed courtyard. The roar of watchers—that most primordial of male sounds—hit her ears before she stepped beneath the hammered bronze entryway. The heavy door stood open, waiting for her to free herself from her obligations and make her nightly selection of bed partners. Since her arrival was impossible to predict, her harem were entertaining themselves in the meantime.*

*Unseen as yet, Tou leaned against the doorway and grinned at them. A dozen men were clustered around the sand-filled fighting pit where two of their number strained for dominance. Most of the men were naked, the better to seduce her when she showed up, but some still wore the simple linen kilts of Hhamoun. Their skin gleamed with sweat and oil, the muscles beneath a sight to behold. Tou felt her nipples tighten with anticipation. These fine strong men were hers, every one, tribute from the tribes she'd conquered.*

*Tribute from the tribes I've conquered* so far, *she reminded herself.*

*They were chosen not just for their beauty but also for their health and stamina. The mysterious chamber around which she'd built her palace, the secret she would take with her to her grave, had magnified the strength of her person and her desires. Only the fittest slave could last a night with Hhamoun's glorious queen. Even five were sometimes challenged to keep up.*

*Some nights Tou feared she had a gaping hole inside her, a keyless lock no amount of sex could fill up.*

*She shook the pointless worry away. She was queen now, outcast no more, and that mattered more than anything. At the far side of the pit, opposite the door, Deir of the Jeru elbowed his companion. Both straightened from the smooth bronze railing at the sight of her. From there, news of her arrival spread around the courtyard in a murmurous wave. Soon even the pair who had been wrestling were on their feet. To her surprise, both were bloodied. Whatever had begun the fight must have been serious.*

*"Your Highness." Deir stepped forward, drawing her eyes to him. "You honor us with your presence."*

*He was the most confident of her harem, a natural leader who kept order in the* zenana*. He was also a creative lover, a frequent choice for her night's consorts. Now she frowned at him.*

*"My property has been harmed," she said, gesturing at the blood-streaked men.*

*"They are new, Your Highness. They thought they could win the right to be your choice tonight."*

*She turned to them. The larger of the two, a gold-skinned Southerner named Baal, fell to his knees and raised clasped hands. He must have taken an elbow to the eye. His left lid was swiftly swelling shut.*

*"Please, Your Highness," he said. "Alban and I only wish to serve you. You are so beautiful and we have been so many months without release. Our chiefs ordered us to refrain until you chose us to share your bed."*

*They must have obeyed, because the pain of their scrapes and bruises did not prevent their phalluses from lifting, thick and hard, between their muscled thighs. Both were hung like stallions, the equine impression heightened by the twitching of their sweaty skin. Arousal was always quick to rise inside her, and the pulsation of their large male organs was more than goad enough. Tou's body heated, thinking of the pleasure these two would give as they competed to outdo each other in her bed.*

*Sensing her thoughts, and deciding they didn't bode well for the rest of the harem, someone in the crowd of hopefuls groaned.*

*"You cannot mean to reward them for their arrogance," Deir said, his face both startled and aggrieved. "You choose here, not any of us."*

*"That is correct, Deir.* I *choose, for whatever reasons appeal to me."*

*Her tone was stern enough to remind him of his place. Deir shivered and bowed his head. Whatever his feelings at the reprimand, she noticed he had hardened, too. His cock thrust up against his snow-white kilt, lifting the material impressively. Indeed, as she turned her gaze around the room, she saw that all of the harem had reached full erection. To a man, their faces were flushed with their lust for her, muscles tense with restraint.*

*Tou was accustomed to them wanting her, but couldn't recall if she'd ever seen them all this fiercely aroused at once. The scent of them, the vibration of their longing through the musky air, wound her own desire to fever pitch. Fluid welled from her, hot and slick. She ached for their aching, her hunger so intense she feared it would swallow her.*

*No queen could afford a need as deep as this.*

*"Take these two to the bathing pool," she ordered Deir, hoping the harshness of her tone would be blamed on anger. "Bind any wounds that need it and escort them to my bedchamber. I'll choose the other three while you're occupied."*

*Deir's proud head bowed lower. Then, to her surprise, her favorite lover, the son of generations of chiefs, went down on one knee. When he spoke, his voice was low and rough.*

*"Your Highness," he said. "Beloved Tou-Hhamoun. You need not choose me, but can't you choose more of us? All of us would be honored to serve you more frequently."*

*Tou had been choosing five men a night for years. Five was enough to satisfy her, at least temporarily, without betraying what might be considered an unqueenly greed. When she looked around, however, she saw many heads nodding in agreement. She hadn't known her decision to restrict herself was so universally bemoaned.*

*"I have rescinded my order against self-pleasuring," she said. "Surely you are not all in such need."*

*"We would rather wait for you to choose us," Semna of*

*Saqqar answered softly. "Spilling inside your body is the ecstasy we all crave."*

*"You have been waiting? All of you? Without release?"*

*"We have been waiting," Deir confirmed, still kneeling on the floor with his erection standing out starkly. "We ache for you, my queen, but we prefer the honor of abstinence."*

*Her hand was to her throat, her pulse beating hard beneath her fingertips. What had she done to earn such loyalty? Moved by their offering, her need swelled large enough to drown the moon.*

*"I will take you then," she said hoarsely. "Tonight, all of you will come to me."*

*Beth opened her arms to them, her golden bracelets gleaming, her naked body trembling with the strength of her desire. They were lucky the bed was large. Every man who found a corner to crawl onto groaned with relief.*

*The ones who didn't knelt beside the low platform.*

*"Now," she said, her legs seeming to sprawl apart by themselves. "None of you need to wait."*

*A signal passed between the men, order amid the eagerness. The wrestler with the blackened eye found his place atop her first. Taking her at her word, he didn't wait to roll his hips forward, but kissed her as he speared her, slow and thick and powerful. Baal had indeed been hungry for this. As he reached full penetration, he expressed his pleasure in a groan that sounded more like pain.*

*"You are hot," he gasped. "As hot and sweet as they said you'd be."*

*The others helped him, a sea of arms and hands to maneuver their two joined bodies in the old rhythm. Beth couldn't doubt her harem enjoyed taking control in this unusual manner. Erections rubbed her from head to toe, all different shapes and sizes, all shuddering with passion and steam-hot blood. Mouths kissed her as she wriggled.*

*Fingers plucked her like a harp. Strong limbs braced her where she needed it. Her knees were crooked for her, her bottom tipped. She had the power to throw off the men, but their care for her felt too sweet. She moved only her pussy, only the muscles that surrounded her partner's increasingly rigid cock. The tight caress made him sob with pleasure, which shoved her pleasure past the edge.*

*She came without effort and brought Baal with her.*

*Another concubine replaced him, and another after that, each as fresh and eager as the one before. In truth, each man's efforts seemed to drive the next one to greater heights. She was filled and refilled with hot, sleek flesh. Those who had not had her began to pant with their struggle to keep their seed contained. Their cocks wept against her body where they couldn't resist rubbing, their hands growing slick with sweat. She teased one prick with her mouth until its owner begged her to stop.*

*"My queen," he pleaded. "Leave me hard to have my turn."*

*At last, only Deir remained unbedded. He was different tonight. His eyes were silver, not brown as she remembered. They burned into hers like crystals set aflame. One of the men moaned at the picture of desire he made. Deir was the largest of them all, the hardest, his cock so high and thick and red it barely seemed human. It dripped with excitement as he knelt before her, taking his place at last between her legs.*

*"I don't need help," he snapped to the others when they would have moved to him.*

*"Maybe* I *need help," she purred, her muscles slack from the pleasure she had enjoyed. She still wanted more, still wanted Deir—anger and all. She'd seen him in this state before, and knew he'd take her forcefully. Since the secret chamber had changed her, more force was almost always what she craved. She trailed her hands over her belly and onto her inner thighs, letting him see the sheen of the other men's seed on her.*

*As she'd hoped, rage flashed across his face. Though he*

*tried to hide it, Deir wanted her for himself. His hands felt like pincers where they wrapped her hipbones and heaved her up. She had to fling out her arms for balance, but he had no trouble supporting her. His night-dark hair spilled like a cape around them. With a grunt that might have been impatience, he notched himself to her gate.*

*The head of him was almost too broad to fit.*

*And then it did fit, pushed firmly into her body with the stubbornness of long-held lust.*

*"You're mine," he growled at her through gritted teeth. "The only help you'll ever need is mine."*

*Pahndir was right. Only when* his *shaft's ardent labors brought her to completion, did her body finally find peace.*

Beth jerked up in her chair with a startled cry. Damn it all to perdition. She'd fallen asleep at work again. And had another dream where she'd confused herself with Tou. The sensations she'd experienced had been so vivid she was still pulsing.

*Don't forget that bit at the end,* she told herself dourly. *Where you confused your favorite harem slave with Prince Pahndir.*

"Damn it!" She slapped her desk in anger at herself. A cracking sound unexpectedly met the blow, followed by the sturdy plank that topped the folding legs splintering in two.

"Memsahib!" said a frightened voice at her door.

She spun around in alarm. The dig's water boy stood there, the whites of his eyes showing. To her amazement, he had hidden one hand by his side and was making the two-horned sign against evil.

"Termites," she said. "Or the wood dried and split without my knowing it. This *is* the desert."

The water boy swallowed. "Memsahib should be careful what artifacts she handles. Objects at these digs can be cursed."

"I'm not cursed. The wood was dry! And I'm not a memsahib, just a miss."

"Yes, miss," said the boy. "Would miss like a drink?"

"I'd like one," said a voice behind him, "if you've got a cup to spare."

The voice belonged to Charles. His arrival seemed to relax the boy as much as it caused Beth to tighten up. But at least the water boy hadn't exacerbated her condition. She could console herself that she wasn't turning into an indiscriminate sex fiend.

That realization enabled her to pull herself together while Charles had his drink.

"What happened here?" he asked once their company was gone. He stared in bemusement at her broken desk. "Why did that water boy leave your tent like devils were after him?"

"He thought I— Oh, never mind. Sometimes the locals are too superstitious to take seriously."

He smiled, a slanted lift of his perfect mouth. To her gratitude, he didn't push. "I came to see if you wanted a ride home. It looks like you're finished with work for now."

She was actually a bit ahead, which made her feel less of a nitwit for her little nap.

*It was just a dream,* she told herself. *Just bits and bobs you put together from your subconscious. It doesn't matter how real it seemed.*

"Beth?" said Charles.

He seemed normal standing there. Smiling. Easy. Not like a person who'd engaged in his most-feared debauch the night before. If his looks had been improved by the encounter, she couldn't tell. If anything, he appeared tired, though only a friend would have noticed the tiny pulls of strain around his sea-blue eyes. Clearly, he was going to pretend his night at The Prince's Flame had never been.

"Do you want a ride?" he repeated. "It's been brought to my attention that I've been avoiding my dearest friend."

Being called his dearest friend was new, but rather than

question the compliment, Beth shook her head to clear her thoughts.

"Yes," she said. "A ride would be lovely."

The route to the city took them through a series of wadis: ancient river courses whose water had dried up. The sheer rock walls towered above them like the ramparts of an old castle. Beth knew Charles meant the trip to be a friendly gesture, but for the first few miles he didn't have a word to say.

*His secrets are too big,* she thought. *He doesn't know how to be a friend with all that locked inside.*

Between her strange experience in Queen Tou's chamber and following Charles to The Prince's Flame, Beth was beginning to know how he felt. Worst of all, the rumbling of the motorcar over the stony roadbed was almost more than the throbbing flesh between her legs could take.

She braced against the dash, trying not to be hypnotized by how smoothly Charles's hands worked the wheel. The side of his leg was a line of heat a finger's breadth away on the leather seat. What salary Charles hadn't spent on his natty clothes, he'd used to buy this boxy Model P. His "baby," as he called it, barely fit two passengers within its claustrophobic black confines.

Beth was used to ignoring the attraction he stirred in her when they rode in it, which they'd done many times. Tonight, though, her dream of Queen Tou's harem clung a bit too close. Every time Charles shifted his foot on the pedals, all Beth could think was how she longed to be riding his muscled thigh. She had memories of men's flesh now, even if they were fantasies. It would have felt so good to swing across his lap, to undo the fastening of his trousers, to ease out his thick, hard length, and—

"Are you wearing a new perfume?" he asked out of the blue.

They were turning onto the dusty paved road that would carry them to and through Bhamjran's Great North Gate.

The gate was part of the old Silk Road, where camel caravans had pulled over to be taxed. The smoothing out of the ride was welcome, but the idea that Charles could smell her undercut her relief.

"I'm not wearing perfume," she said.

"It must be your shampoo then. It smells nice. Like lemons and cinnamon."

Smelling of lemons and cinnamon was preferable to reeking of sexual need, but Beth remained confused. The only shampoo Herrington stocked at the *haveli* was scented with lavender. Then again, now might not be the best time to say so—or to mention that Pahndir smelled like lemons and spice to her.

Unbidden, one of Tou's memories (assuming the vivid dreams she'd been having could be true) slipped into her mind. The queen was watching the sun sink into the desert while comparing herself to a cat in heat, one that drew all the toms to her door. But that was crazy, because humans didn't go into heat, and even if they did, it wouldn't smell like fruit compote.

Of course, if it were possible, it might feel similar to what Beth was living through.

"It must be the shampoo," she agreed hastily.

Charles seemed not to hear her uneasiness. He looked at her and smiled. "This is nice, the two of us on the road again."

He reached over to pat her thigh. He'd done this a time or two before, but the touch had never affected her the way it did tonight. The instant his palm made contact, sensation shot through the muscle straight to her sex, hot and sharp and torturously good. She immediately wanted to shove his fingers inside her and writhe on them.

With a need like that stabbing through her, it was impossible not to make a sound.

Charles must have thought the muffled cry was a protest. He pulled his hand back like he'd been burned. "Forgive me, I didn't mean to—"

"It's all right, Charles. You have as much right to touch me as any man."

"In other words, not at all."

His face was steely with self-judgment, but Beth could hardly argue she was no angel without revealing what she'd done with Pahndir. That would have meant confessing she'd spied on Charles, which was the last thing he'd want to hear.

She squinted at the gate, whose sunset shadow they were passing under. The best course would be to encourage Charles to confide in her himself. She didn't have much time for that on the remaining drive. The Old Quarter where they lived wasn't far from here.

"Herrington was worried about you the other night," she tried casually.

"He needn't have been. But I expect I'll be staying closer to the mansion from now on."

"You didn't enjoy your walk?"

That was too leading. Charles shot her a look to say he knew what she was fishing for.

"Very well. I admit it: I'm prying into your personal affairs."

"Beth, when will you accept that there are things about me you simply don't need to know?"

"But I don't think it's healthy to keep secrets bottled up. And you might be surprised at what I'd understand."

"Beth."

Shaking his head, Charles turned the car into the *haveli*'s underground garage. It was a clever space whose rolling doors had been adapted to let Charles in with a button's push. Inside, where the Bhamjrishi were disinclined to leave any surface plain, the walls glittered with mosaics of river scenes: hippos wallowing in the shallows, palms swaying by the banks. Six autos could have parked here, but for the moment Charles's was the only one. He pulled his pride and joy into a slot decorated by the image of a bargeman poling with the current.

An unexpected shiver gripped Beth's nape. The bargeman wore the same knee-length white kilt as the harem men in her dream.

Lost in his own concerns, Charles turned off the humming engine and scrubbed at his face. Seeing him like that, so weary and bitter, Beth knew she wasn't going to be able to let their conversation drop.

"I'm aware that your life was difficult when you were young," she said. "That you saw things, maybe did things—"

"I was a whore," he interrupted sharply. "I sold myself to men at a top hat club."

He'd stolen her breath. A top hat club was a brothel for high-born males. Beth hadn't known that was how he'd survived, not in so many words.

"I'm sorry," she said when she could speak.

"Don't be. It kept me from starving, and now and then, when I had a client who took his time or was especially good-looking, I enjoyed my work."

For just an instant, an image flashed: Charles passionately kissing another man. Emotion coiled inside her, dark and forbidden and excited. The feeling couldn't erase her pity, but she also couldn't deny it was there.

"Are you expecting me to be disgusted?"

"I'm expecting you—" He must have heard the harshness of his tone. He forced his knuckles not to whiten on the wheel and tried again. "I'm expecting you to let sleeping dogs lie."

"You don't have to be ashamed of what you did to stay alive. Or that you didn't hate it all the time. I mean it, Charles. You can share this with me."

She honestly thought he wouldn't, not with the way he stared at her, as if no one—least of all she—could forgive his past. Then, for no reason she could understand, he gave in. He turned to her on the leather seat, his knee unavoidably bumping hers.

"One morning I woke up and my mother didn't," he said. "She'd finally succeeded in drinking herself to death. She left me with no education beyond how to be a whore, no food, no money, and whatever clothes I had on my back, which—at fifteen and growing—didn't last me long."

"What . . ." Beth cleared her throat. She knew she ought to match his matter-of-fact tone. "What about your father?"

Charles lifted his shoulders and let them fall. "I doubt she knew who he was. Some nameless customer who shot a bit straighter than the rest.

"The top hat club was a step up from what she did. They fed me, dressed me well enough to cater to the toffs. She'd have been proud of me . . . and then she'd have shaken me down for every coin I had; beaten me, if it took that."

"Not truly."

"Yes, truly. I know you think of parents as people who protect their children, but that's who she was, Beth. That's how the people we knew lived. She would have thought it was her right as the woman who gave birth to me. It's funny . . ."

Beth didn't seen how any of this could be funny, but he went on, his eyes lost to memories.

"She hated the demons. 'Stay away from those dirty demons,' she'd always say. She was old enough to remember a world before they came, to remember how Queen Victoria let the Yama settle their exiles in Avvar's slums, as payment for the technology they gave her. Most weren't even criminals that I could tell, just *rohn* who couldn't bootlick well enough not to be branded troublemakers in their own country. Their emperor sent them to us with gold in their pockets, so they wouldn't be a drain on our economy. He didn't realize he'd make them objects of envy. Those demons' stake was enough to set them up like princes in Harborside. Buy a little business, homes of their own. Every one of those exiles was richer, smarter, healthier, and a hell of a lot stronger than us humans.

"Victoria called us citizens and gave us gruel. Their emperor called them criminals and set them up for life. It's no wonder we hated them."

"You don't hate them now," Beth ventured. He couldn't. He worked for Herrington. Liked him. And as far as she could tell, the feeling was mutual.

Charles didn't answer directly. "One thing my mother never did was sell her energy to them. She might have earned more if she had, maybe moved up from working on the street. I doubt it would have saved her life, but she'd have looked better for her customers. 'We're humans,' she'd say. 'We don't sell our souls.' "

Did he think he'd sold his? "Charles, the Yama are only people, different from us but people nonetheless."

"Don't you think I know that?" He spat out the words, his face contorted with rage. "Don't you think I damn well know?"

His anger shoved her back against the car's tin door, her cheeks hot with a combination of embarrassment and hurt. Seeing it, his eyes closed briefly in remorse.

"I'm sorry." He brushed her face with his knuckles. "Look what I've done to the sweetest girl I know."

"If I'm the sweetest girl you know, we're both in trouble." She took his hand carefully. "Charles, you have to believe me. None of these things matter to—"

"No." He pulled away from her, opening the driver's-side door to swing his long legs out.

He was all business outside the motorcar, tugging out the electric cable that charged the engine, shoving it into the socket on the wall. Beth had heard that vehicles with Tesla coils, which sucked ambient energy out of the air, were more reliable, but Charles loved the Model P because it was what he could afford. Probably without knowing it, he stroked the cheap, shining hood.

In that moment, Beth could imagine how he must have looked to his customers when he was fifteen, a young man lovely enough to bring a burn to the eyes. Feeling as if one wrong step would forever ruin their friendship, she stepped cautiously out of the car. She left the bonnet between them, waiting for him to be ready to acknowledge her again. It took a minute, but at last he did.

He raised his eyes to her, the look in them heartbreakingly resigned. "I shouldn't have done that, shouldn't have burdened you with talk about my past."

*Yes, you should,* she thought helplessly. *Because I care enough to love you no matter what.*

# NINE

Charles didn't know if he was irritated or relieved that Beth didn't follow him from the garage. She let him stomp up the stairs alone, so hard with wanting her that every step was a punishment.

He slammed the door to his room behind him and held his head. *God.* Why did fighting with her arouse him? Why did everything arouse him, including blurting out his past? Something was stripping away his control, robbing him of the restraint he'd always been able to rely on. It had never mattered before that he loved her. He'd been in charge of his own urges.

He peeled off his tunic, the desire to strip and bathe uncontrollable. The front of his trousers was stretched taut over his huge erection, the finely woven cotton damp with sweat and other things. He pushed his hand down the firm, aching hump, biting back a groan at how good it felt. He wasn't going to remember how he'd masturbated onto Beth's breasts, wasn't going to fantasize about doing that and more. Knowing the vow was useless, he curled his fingers over his balls and squeezed. He'd die if he couldn't come soon, just plain die.

The click of the door latch nearly made him jump out of his skin. He couldn't turn. His erection was too big to miss. Besides which, he already knew who was sticking her head inside.

"Charles," Beth said, her voice so low and earnest it made his heart tighten. "Don't waste your life hating yourself."

He hissed out a curse she shouldn't have had to hear.

"Charles—"

"Leave me alone!"

His shout didn't scare her. Her light kid boots beat a tattoo across the floor. She was running to him instead of away. She hugged him from behind, pressing her face between his shoulder blades. He didn't think she'd ever touched him when his upper half was bare. Her cheek was warm, her arms stronger than he expected around his ribs. Clearly inspired by her closeness, his erection did its damnedest to lengthen.

*Shit,* he thought even as the betrayer inside him said, *Oh, God, yes.*

"I'm not going to let you do this," she said, her breath hot against his skin. "I'm not letting you push me away."

He should have been able to, but his heart mustn't have been in the effort, because her embrace seemed unbreakable. Even as he tried to get loose, she circled around to face him, her arms still twined around his waist.

Her chin lifted just a little to meet his eyes. "I'm not letting you think you're the only person in the world with desires."

His erection throbbed into the folds her skirts; half an inch of space all that kept her from feeling it. He wanted her to feel it, wanted to rub the bloody thing in her face. His entire body felt ready to catch on fire.

"You don't know what you're playing at," he growled.

"I'm not playing at anything. I'm your friend—your

dearest friend, according to you. Stop acting like I'm going to run screaming just because you're not the same as every other man I've known."

*I know how you taste,* he thought. *I put my face between your legs and sucked you to orgasm while you slept.*

"Charles!" She shook his shoulders at whatever anger or despair showed in his expression. "I need you to be my friend, too."

Something in him snapped like a piece of kindling. He wished she could count on him to be her friend. She deserved that and so much more. Instead, he kissed her, wrapping her tight against him to shove his tongue between her startled lips. The penetration was not the quick remonstration he meant to make it. Her mouth was a plump, ripe fruit that instantly enchanted him. He slid his hand up to steady the back of her head, almost moaning at the silken mass of her hair parting for his fingers. This was Beth's mouth, Beth's gorgeous, tender lips. He had to taste all of her, had to suck her tongue and nip her . . . and then he had to gasp for air.

"I'm not your friend," he snarled, and immediately kissed her again.

A sound broke in her throat. Suddenly, she was kissing him with equal fervor, pushing him backward until his legs hit his four-poster bed.

His heart leapt galvanically.

"Charles," she moaned. Her hands slid down his spine to close on his rear. She squeezed him there, hard. Her hold was more potent than any fantasy. She was pulling him toward her, forcing the painful swell of his erection into the soft notch of her thighs.

They were both as hot as if a ball of sunlight were burning there.

Charles didn't know how any man could have withstood her. He didn't give himself time to think, but ripped her shirtwaist straight down the front, just dug his fingers into the neck and pulled. Finding her bare beneath it, he cupped one breast up and fastened his mouth over her nipple. He was sucking her like he was starving before her buttons finished bouncing on the floor.

If she minded, it didn't show. She moaned again and writhed against him, her hungry little cries demolishing his sanity. Moaning himself, he switched to her other breast, digging his tongue around the hot, pebbled point. She was perfect: small but lush, her silky flesh just overfilling his palm. When he broke free to pant and look at her, he barely recognized her face.

She was flushed and dazed, her gilded hair fallen from its tie, her full lips swollen from the wildness of their kisses. She looked like she'd already spent the night in his arms.

"I'm going to take you," he warned, pulling the back of her skirt up in greedy wads. "If you don't stop me, I'm going to fornicate with you here and now."

"I can't stop you," she panted. "I don't want to."

He threw her onto the mattress and climbed over her.

"Charles," she said, low and shaking. He would have stopped at her tone of shock, but her hands were sliding down his bare torso to caress his groin. She moaned at the size of the bulge she found. "I saw you behind the cook tent. I saw you when you were wet from washing up."

He couldn't think clearly enough to figure out what she was confessing to. Her hand was on him, her thumb rubbing up and down the prominent ridge. He yanked her skirts up from the front this time. Her cambric drawers were damp, their lace-edged slit too loose to keep any part of him out. He cupped her curls, his longest finger sliding easily between the warm, slippery folds.

He might have been stroking a lightning bolt. She arched up at him violently. Cloth tore, loud in the evening hush. His cock was spilling into her hands before he realized she'd ripped the front of his trousers, not even bothering with the cord. Her fingers gripped his length and stroked, which made him feel like a brand was punching out of him from the inside.

"Stop me," he begged, but she only bit her lip and shook her head.

She was tugging him by his penis between her outspread thighs, aiming him toward her core. Maybe it was because it was *her* hand and—God knew—that excited him, but her fingers felt unusually warm and tingly on his shaft. It was extremely hard not to simply allow her to have her way.

"I need this," she whispered. "You don't know how much."

He'd wanted her too long to pull away, even if he knew she was going to be sorry afterward. He was so close to her now, too close. Helpless to resist, he ran his thumbs up her furrow and found her clit drenched in cream. The hood was slick as satin, perfect for working over the little rod. When he did, her body jumped like it had been shocked.

"Do that," she gasped. "Touch me there when you're inside of me."

And then she had him at her entrance, at that little mouth of hot, oiled flesh. It molded to his trembling crest, the tiny kiss an invitation he wasn't strong enough to ignore.

A raw sound of longing ripped from his throat. All those years of wanting her, of refusing to let himself even hope . . . The first thrust of his hips was like a convulsion, something his body did against his will. And then his will didn't matter. Her pussy felt better than any pleasure he'd ever known. No real woman could feel this good. She was so hot she could have burned him, so wet she squelched as he pushed in. He felt her barrier snap and just kept shoving.

He had to claim her or go mad.

"God," she gasped, her hands fisted in the small of his back. It was good they urged him onward, because his hips were hinging toward her, incapable of retreat. "Oh, God, keep going."

He cupped her bottom to tilt her to a better angle, then jerked his knee up the mattress to catch her beneath one thigh. This spread and bent her leg perfectly. Despite her virgin state, she took him like a dream, tight and creamy, her need as strong as his. The ease of his entry shocked him. It wasn't even twenty seconds, and his cock was nearly surrounded. He wrapped one hand around the headboard to increase his leverage.

Beth was beyond any such concern. She had thrown herself into his care with flattering abandon. Her head rolled back and forth on his pillow, eyes shut, lower lip caught between her teeth. Her cheeks were so red they appeared painted.

She was a million men's sex dream come to life.

"Look at me," he rasped before he pushed the final distance home.

Her extravagant lashes rose. She focused with an effort, her honey-brown irises so glazed he was mesmerized. He'd never seen a woman look like she wanted sex this much, nor guessed how incredibly arousing the sight could be. The skin of his cock hurt from its tightness. She licked the bruise she'd bitten in her lip. "I'm not hurt, Charles. I'm not afraid."

As if to prove it, she braced her hands on the headboard under his, the position lifting her sharp-tipped breasts. Her nipples were still shiny from his mouth, and his prick jerked inside her at the graphic sight.

"Do it hard," she said. "Please don't wait."

Her voice was as throaty as a stevedore. It didn't matter that he'd hate himself when this was over. No force on earth could have stopped him them.

Beth had to swallow back a scream of relief when he let his body do what they both wanted. Though she hadn't planned for this to happen, she didn't have a single doubt now that it had.

This was so much better than a dream, no matter how vivid. The slight soreness of his first penetration simply sharpened her pleasure. His hips felt like heaven shoving tight against hers, plunging the length of him inside her, over and over. He was sweating with his labors, gorgeous, mussed in a way she didn't think she'd seen him before. It felt so fundamentally *right* to have his heat and thickness moving inside her that she couldn't think of anything better than to be doing this with someone she cared about.

She was born for this, and so was he.

She wrapped him in one leg as he thrust hard and fast, then had to run her hand up his perspiring back. His skin was hot, his back muscles working deliciously. He was doing something wonderful with his hips, a steady, rolling motion she wished she had the experience to match.

Because she didn't, she touched him instead, dropping both arms from the headboard when she realized that despite his leanness he had the strength and skill to keep them perfectly in place. Free to caress him, she ran her hands over every inch of him she could reach. She loved his hardness, both where it was smooth and where it was rough with hair. The bunching of his upper arm, the one whose elbow he rested on, demanded that she admire it. That led her across his shoulders and down his neck. When she brushed his nipples, goose bumps broke out across his skin.

To her, his shiver was as good as a magic trick.

"Beth," he gasped. "You're going to make me come too soon."

That didn't seem like it mattered. Her hands were as greedy as the rest of her. But then he changed his position to put more weight on his knees, shafting her higher, longer, shifting his forearm to allow his finger and thumb to neatly squeeze her pleasure bud.

Lord, he really knew what he was doing. Her body *loved* the change, the parts he was focused on drinking in the new friction. She clutched his back, abruptly frantic for more. Pressure gathered between her legs, an ache as sweet as hunger before a feast. His hips began rolling faster, broken cries catching in his throat. The headboard squealed with how tightly his left hand was gripping it.

Something was happening to him, something big. His eyes squeezed shut, and the tendons in his neck corded. Instinct told her he was grinding his teeth against the closeness of his orgasm.

The sight of him straining to hold off for her made everything he did feel a thousand times more exciting. It was a repeat of her experience in the *haveli*'s shower, where her nerves seemed to multiply and draw closer to her skin. Each percussion of his cock was both a blessing and a torture. She needed release so badly she could scarcely breathe.

Betraying her inexperience didn't seem important. She flung her hips at him in desperation, at which he grunted and pounded in harder.

*Careful,* whispered some ghost of Tou. *You don't want to break your plaything.*

But Charles wasn't breaking. He was pistoning into her like a machine, his breath whining from him, his muscles standing out like they were carved from stone. The veins in his arms were popping like a wrestler's. Stirred beyond bearing, her pussy seemed to ripple over him of its own will.

"Lord," he gasped, feeling it. "Beth!"

The force he used then was exactly what she needed. She came with a gasp of astonished pleasure, and came and came until he hissed out a curse and yanked his penis awkwardly out of her.

He spurted against her belly half an instant later, long, hot fountain bursts of wetness, grinding his hips so brutally against her body that she feared he would hurt himself.

She came one more time before his hand unclamped stiffly from her clitoris.

"Shit," he said. He was on both his elbows above her, trembling, his silver-blond hair stuck to his forehead in wet, dark spikes. His fingers feathered the sides of her breasts, as if he had to touch her somehow. He shook his head disbelievingly. "Hell."

Beth touched his cheekbone in concern. "Are you all right?"

"Am *I* all right?" His laugh was rough. "I almost came inside you. I almost forgot to take any care of you at all."

"Oh," she said, her cheeks gone hot over how completely she had ignored that possible consequence.

Charles rolled off her onto his back, where he pressed one of the pillows over his face. "Beth, I am so sorry. I can never make this up to you."

"What are you talking about? I asked you to."

"Beth, you're not a virgin anymore."

"Well, I know that, but it's not like I'm going to have a husband or someone who'll mind . . . unless you're intending to write my parents and tell them."

He pushed the pillow off to give her a look.

"It doesn't matter," she insisted, annoyed and uncomfortably defensive at his attitude. "I wanted it to happen. I enjoyed it." At his continued stare, she folded her arms, a gesture that might have been more impressive if her shirtwaist hadn't been in tatters. Her nipples still felt as hard as stones. "I know I'm not experienced, but it seemed like you enjoyed it, too."

"Oh, I enjoyed it," Charles said grimly, then squeezed the bridge of his nose. "More than I should have, if you want the truth."

His muttered addendum wasn't precisely encouraging, or the way he flung himself from the bed to go to his washstand. With a house full of demon-style bathrooms, these old-fashioned accessories didn't get much use. To her surprise, Charles didn't clean up but returned with a soft, dampened cloth for her.

He sat on the edge of the bed to use it. Beth would have taken it from him, but he didn't let her squirm away. His strokes were gentle, his attention embarrassingly focused on her private parts.

Funny how she hadn't minded him doing all sorts of things to them a few minutes earlier.

"I was rough," he said, "so there's a little blood, but I don't think you need to worry."

"I'm *not* worried," she said, finally succeeding in catching his wrist. "There's supposed to be a little blood the first time. And you couldn't have been too rough, because I'm barely sore."

He didn't want to meet her eyes. He pulled the cloth

from her and balled it in his hand. It rested on his knee, making a wet spot on the trousers she'd torn open. She wanted to peel them completely off, to show him just how tender and thankful she felt toward him.

"Maybe we could try again," she said shyly. "I'm sure I'll get better as I go along."

Charles snorted and closed his eyes. "Beth, this is never, ever going to happen again."

Her shyness dissipated as anger rose. "And why is that?" she huffed. "Because you think I'm so much 'nicer' than you are?"

Unlike Pahndir, Charles had moaned for her, more than once and damn loudly. He wasn't allowed to act like this was a mistake he was going to forget the first chance he got. Beth filled her lungs and made up her mind.

"I followed you to Prince Pahndir's the other night. I saw what you did with those Yama. I thought it was as exciting as you did. In fact, I thought it was so exciting I . . . I let Prince Pahndir kiss me when you were done."

Charles's attention was on her now, the skin around his flattened lips gone white.

"You followed me," he repeated, his voice dangerously calm.

"And let the prince kiss me." More than kiss her, but there were limits to what even she was comfortable admitting.

"You stay away from him, Beth. That demon isn't anyone to play with." His hand was on her arm, too tight to easily shake off. "I mean it. You don't want to go down that road."

She was furious enough to wrench away from him. "Not that you have any rights over me, but I'm reasonably certain your concerns are moot. Pahndir didn't seem particularly interested in seeing me again."

Charles's pretty eyes narrowed. "*If* that's true, you ought to count yourself lucky."

What did he mean, *if* it was true? Did he think she was an idiot on top of everything else?

Rather than ask and have the suspicion confirmed, she strode to his wardrobe to steal a shirt.

"I'm leaving," she announced as she buttoned it over the ruins of her own. "I'm sure you have some guilt you'd like to wallow in."

He called her name before she stalked out, but for once she didn't feel like making peace with him.

After she left, Charles paced his chambers back and forth. Night had filled the mansion with shadows, but he didn't consider for a minute going down to eat.

Beth might have been in the dining room.

Her scent rose from his skin in waves. He stank from working at the site all day and then having sex with her. The salt of his sweat blended with her personal perfume. Normally fastidious, it drove him mad that he was reluctant to wash it off, especially since the combination was bringing him erect again—despite his cock stinging from the pounding he'd given it. Lord, he'd gone at her like a maniac, and had loved every blessed stroke. At least he couldn't worry she'd wanted it. She'd urged him on until he knew (no matter what she said) that he'd been downright rough with her.

That being so, could there be any doubt Prince Pahndir wanted her?

Beth had probably misinterpreted the prince's Yamish reserve. A man like Pahndir Shan wasn't going to let a spitfire like her slip through his fingers.

Charles stopped pacing and bit the side of his thumb. From what he'd seen, it didn't seem like Pahndir wanted Charles to slip away, either.

God, this was impossible. Did the demon honestly think he could seduce them both? Had he learned nothing about human mores when it came to people who *didn't* pay for their partners?

Charles sat on the chest of blankets at the foot of his rumpled bed, his breath going out of him in a shivering gust.

Beth had watched him at The Prince's Flame. She'd seen what it did to him to feed those demons. If anyone knew brothels had spyholes, Charles was that person. He'd fully expected the prince to watch, had even taken a twisted interest in the idea, but never in a million years had he expected Beth to stand as witness to his shame.

He wished he could have said he'd have walked away if he'd known. He wanted her again, right now. Wanted her hands on him. Wanted to spill inside her the way he'd come so close to doing that first time.

Most of all, though, he wanted the demon to watch.

"Fuck," he said, squeezing the bedpost so hard it creaked.

Why were confessions so easy for Beth? Why didn't she "wallow" in guilt, as she put it?

He wasn't sure if what he was doing now was wallowing. His emotions felt like they were battling each other: anger, horror, a sick relief that she didn't hate him. Twisted up with all that was some confused species of jealousy.

Beth had let Pahndir kiss her, and Pahndir hadn't tried to kiss Charles yet. Charles shouldn't have wanted him to. His life was tangled enough.

*I can't go back,* he thought. *I can't un-want what I've tasted.*

Unfortunately, what he'd tasted with Beth was an inferno that could burn a man to the ground.

# TEN

Prince Pahndir's visitor was unexpected, though perhaps he should have foreseen the call. The bell rang after noon, but Pahndir's valet, Biban, was still obliged to shake him out of bed.

Pahndir wasn't actually being lazy. He hadn't been unconscious for more than two hours. He'd been sleeping badly of late, his slumber broken by too-arousing dreams of his lovely humans, his thoughts racketing around in circles he didn't know how to stop.

He was generally better at seduction than he was proving with these two. At the least, he'd never had such trouble deciding what his next move should be. As the date of his heat approached, he grew less and less able to control either his hopes or his anxieties. He wasn't even certain he could bring the situation to a test this month, but if the answer was no, if Beth—or Charles, for that matter—couldn't trigger a full release from him . . .

Well, all he could say was someone had better hide the kitchen knives.

He could probably count on his valet to do it, if only to

keep the man who paid his salary alive. Biban was a young, brown-skinned Bhamjrishi with manners so punctilious Pahndir hadn't been able to break him of using his title. Biban had won the position because he'd seemed less fearful of working for a demon than the other candidates. He had a terrible burn scar on one side of his face, which Pahndir (accustomed to his own race's perfection) had initially found unnerving. Now he hardly noticed it. Though formerly poor as a mouse, Biban had proved an irreplaceable guide to all that was stylish in this city.

"I'm sorry, Your Highness," Biban apologized as Pahndir struggled up on his elbows. The silk sheets slipped down his chest with a crinkling hiss. "I wouldn't have woken you except the Yamish gentleman refused to leave until he saw you."

"Herrington," Pahndir repeated, the name having penetrated earlier.

"Yes, sir. He scolded the butler so harshly Artur was in tears. Should I not have interrupted you?"

Pahndir let his breath sigh out quietly, glad that his employees found one Yama more fearsome than him. "It's fine. Your waking me gives me the choice of saying yes or no myself."

"I know he doesn't outrank you," Biban said. "Though, him being a . . . one of your race, I'm not sure any of us would have the strength to toss him out."

Pahndir was so sleep-deprived he grinned at the thought of his servants piling on Herrington to drag him from the premises. It would be like teacup puppies trying to subdue a wolf. His muffled laugh startled Biban enough for the servant to jerk himself straighter. He knew his master liked to maintain face.

Pahndir dragged his palm down the chuckle, effectively stopping it. "Put Lord Herrington in the parlor. Tell him I'll be down as soon as I've washed and dressed. And bring him a coffee tray. Warm up some of those little cookies Serita makes with the chocolate bits."

"Sir?" Biban inquired, patently unwilling to bring someone who'd been so rude such a rich reward. Their cook Serita's sweets were legend in Bhamjran.

"If he's angry—which he is—he'll be too proud to eat them," Pahndir explained. "The smell will drive him insane."

"I see," said Biban, his own mouth twitching on the side opposite his scar. "And perhaps Your Highness could take a long time dressing."

"Perhaps I could," Pahndir agreed, for once perfectly attuned to an employee.

Pahndir descended almost an hour later, dressed in traditional silver overrobes with embroidered plum chrysanthemums. Herrington stood before one of the parlor windows with his hands clasped loosely behind his back. In his human jodhpurs, he looked like a general, ready to review his troops. He exhibited all the Yamish stillness Pahndir's friend Xishi hadn't bothered to employ.

Despite the propriety of his stance, Pahndir noticed an empty spot on the tray where a single cookie was missing.

"Good day," Pahndir said, though he knew Herrington was aware of his arrival and simply didn't care to turn right away. "I gather this isn't a social call."

He spoke to Herrington in their own language, his casual tone sufficiently insulting to ice over the great man's eyes.

"It is not," he confirmed crisply.

Herrington offered Pahndir no bow at all. Privately amused, Pahndir planted his rear on the hip-height table where the coffee and cookies sat. Taking his time, he poured himself a cup and balanced one of the fragrant biscuits on the saucer. The little sweet inspired a memory: the plate Charles had brought him in the dig's cook tent. Pahndir hadn't thanked him for it. He could have the other night, except Charles had been upset after his experience with Donjen and Darja. He'd been less so by the time Pahndir brought him food, but still very quiet. Now

Pahndir wondered if he'd get the chance to rectify his lapse.

More focused in the present, Herrington's gaze flicked to the tray with the barest hint of longing. He was rough-looking for a Yama, far more like a human with his red-headed coloring, and as broad and tall as a soldier. Pahndir understood why his staff would be reluctant to gainsay the man.

"You brought my butler to tears," he commented mildly over the rim of his porcelain cup. "Is it your intent to bully me as well? Or, I should say, to attempt to? It's hardly a feat to inspire a *human* to lose composure."

Herrington's mouth fished open at the bluntness of the slur, a mortifying shade of red creeping up his cheeks. With an obvious effort, he shut his jaw and forced his skin to pale again.

"My ward Beth Philips has been seen in your motorcar."

Pahndir set his cup and saucer on the carved table. "Your ward, is she? I wasn't aware she was a minor."

She wasn't, of course, and Herrington's lips pursed infinitesimally. "Beth is under my protection. As is one of your customers, Charles Watkins."

"Him, too?" Pahndir allowed his brows to rise a millimeter. "Well, The Prince's Flame is a popular gathering place for young men."

"I won't have you corrupting them!" Herrington exploded. "They are nice young humans. They don't need to be the objects of your games."

Pahndir had prepared for this accusation; Herrington couldn't know how unresolved their seduction was and would inevitably jump to conclusions. Because of his preparation, Pahndir didn't expect anger to surge up in him so strongly. He came to his feet and straightened his robes. His face was icy, but in another moment it might well grow as warm as Herrington's appeared to be.

"You insult me," he said, "and you insult your charges as well."

"You deny you have designs on them?"

"I deny nothing," Pahndir said with every drop of princely hauteur he had. "My so-called designs on them are my business, as their interest in me is theirs. They are adults, the pair of them, and more than capable of making their own decisions."

Herrington stepped right to him, his forefinger drilling into Pahndir's breastbone. "I know the sort of shenanigans royals get up to. You touch one hair on either of their heads—"

"You forget yourself," Pahndir cut him off, wrapping one hand around Herrington's poking finger to force it away.

Then, because asserting mere physical victory didn't quite satisfy, he let his aura swell as it hadn't since he'd lost his wife, and maybe as it hadn't in his life. His human staff aside, intimidating others in this primal Yamish fashion had never been his forte.

If it had, his family might not have been able to depose him so easily.

At the time, they'd barely broken a sweat getting rid of the embarrassment he'd been to them. Pahndir was surprised to discover how much control he had now. Naturally, Herrington's aura struggled against his. He was a man used to wielding power. Their battling wills had the air between them buzzing like enraged insects, a sensation that lifted all the hairs on Pahndir's arms. In the end, though, Pahndir's genetically superior energy subsumed the older man's. Herrington gasped and took a single involuntary step of retreat, rubbing his chest where Pahndir had prodded him with a spear of royal purple etheric force.

It was a measure of Herrington's control that he recovered within seconds. He bowed his head stiffly.

"Forgive me, Your Highness. I shouldn't have presumed."

His formal gesture of submission, however reluctant, allowed Pahndir's aura to recede. "I understand your position, Lord Herrington, but you shouldn't assume I esteem your young human friends any less than you do. I assure you, I am as likely to be hurt by my designs, as you describe them, as either of them is."

This unusual bit of honesty had Herrington's eyes rounding. As to that, it took Pahndir back a bit himself.

"It's not possible," he continued softly, "to protect those one cares about from all harm. I'm not certain it's even wise to try."

Herrington narrowed his gaze at Pahndir a moment longer, apparently hoping to bore into the truth of his thoughts. Pahndir gave him nothing, neither on his face nor in his energy. He'd bared his soul enough for one day.

"I see reports of your death weren't the only news that was exaggerated," Herrington said. "You seem to have more . . . personal authority than your family gave you credit for."

There was nothing to say to this. Thanks would have weakened Pahndir as much as admitting that his family's estimation of his leadership potential had been justified. Indeed, the only appropriate reaction was silence and a steady stare.

After half a minute, Herrington inclined his upper body in a genuine bow.

"I appreciate your attention to my concerns," he said coolly. "I will show myself out."

It was only after he'd done so that Pahndir let the sweat that had been gathering pop out on his brow.

The sun outside the brothel was headache brilliant, but Herrington ignored it. As soon as his boots reached the dusty street, he looked back at the deep-blue lacquered door to The Prince's Flame. His meeting with its owner had thrown him more off balance than he wanted to admit.

It had been decades since anyone had forced him to back down in a test of wills.

The reaction was instinctive, of course, bred into his genes like dominance in a pack of wolves. Any royal worth his blood, if he'd mustered up the nerve to try, could have elicited the same response from him. The surprise was that Pahndir Shan had mustered it.

A bicycle cab with a bright green awning tooted its brassy horn, reminding Herrington where he was. As he moved aside to let it pass, he thought he caught a glimpse of Sahel's tall, black-robed figure. He probably was mistaken, because whoever the woman was, she disappeared around a corner without a backward glance. Perhaps it had been another member of her tribe.

The thought of the hot-blooded chieftain warmed his groin pleasantly. Enjoying his own vitality, not to mention his good fortune in finding an inspiring bed partner this season, he stepped onto the pavement and began to walk. The city was alive with lunch crowds, businesswomen fitting in one more meeting over the meal, one more deal in a city that accommodated a million a day. Prince Pahndir seemed to have made a place for himself in Bhamjran, despite the handicap of his sex. Along with what he'd seen this morning, this revelation led Herrington to an inescapable conclusion.

The former head of the House of Shan wasn't the mentally defective weakling his family had tossed aside. Herrington had already been living among the humans when Pahndir's competency trial occurred, but he'd read reports of it through the Yamaweb, just as he'd read reports of Pahndir's subsequent "demise." The prince certainly wasn't paralyzed by grief these days. Instead, he was subtle, sly, and capable of disarming honesty. A dangerous Yama in any city, and one who excelled at a competitive and rather exotic job. In truth, Prince Pahndir was exactly the sort of man who'd appeal to a reckless monkey like Beth Philips.

The appeal he'd exert for Charles would be more complicated. Herrington wasn't unaware of the boy's background. He'd had him investigated soon after he'd found his daughter, Roxanne, who'd been taking care of Charles at the time.

Charles had survived things Herrington could barely conceive of. Poverty. Life on the street. Selling his body to his own gender for food. Though they'd never discussed it and, Fate willing, never would, Herrington respected Charles for pulling himself out of that. Now he was one of the most talented and hardworking employees Herrington had, a perfectionist in his kitchen realm. Herrington had watched him pine after Beth for years. Every time the two of them were together, Charles's feelings were obvious. Herrington had chosen not to interfere, judging that Charles's decision to keep his distance might indeed be appropriate.

Since they'd met the prince, however, the balance between his two charges seemed to be shifting. Pahndir's seduction had stirred them up, had muddied what had once been clear. Herrington didn't like muddy, nor did he see how whatever the royal Yama was intending could end well.

To his mind, Charles was better off leaving his past behind, and Beth . . .

Herrington felt a frown begin to tug his mouth as he sidestepped a water seller making a delivery. Herrington had friends in this town. Just because the prince had cowed him, temporarily, didn't mean Herrington couldn't squash him flat, should that turn out to be desirable.

An unexpected grin pulled his lips the opposite way. Herrington hoped he got a chance to eat another of those human cookies before he had to resort to that.

This must have been Pahndir's day for unexpected meetings with his countrymen. He was in his favorite restaurant down the street from The Prince's Flame, enjoying a leisurely version of the repast Northerners called "tea." He was alone, of course, but the solitude was agreeable. His corner table on the sidewalk terrace afforded him room to spread out with the *Daily News*. The service was attentive, and his view of passing traffic—foot and otherwise—was as colorful as any in Bhamjran.

The familiarity of it all relaxed him. This was becoming his home, even if the occasional Northern tourists did stop and drop their jaws when they saw him.

In his princely embroidered robes, Pahndir didn't resemble the humble gray-garbed *rohn* they were accustomed to. He imagined watching him being served by humans seemed as strange to them as if *he'd* seen a donkey climb onto a throne.

And speaking of donkeys . . . He smiled as one of these sturdy beasts clopped past the terrace, its saddlebags full to bursting with dried chilies. Its owner was coaxing it to continue plodding down the street.

"That's a good donkey," he said, catching Pahndir's eye and grinning. "Not much farther to the market now."

The small exchange startled Pahndir. The pepper seller had smiled at him as if he were anyone, had smiled because he was smiling, too. This said quite a bit about how relaxed and unguarded Pahndir had become.

The dangers of being unguarded were made crystal clear by the figure who stepped to the edge of his table umbrella's shade.

Muto Feng was average height for a royal: tall, in other words, but not as tall as Pahndir. His face was handsome and smooth and round, his body so well fed it verged on corpulence—an unusual trait among Yamishkind. Also unusual was his reputation for affability, a reputation only those who didn't know him gave the least credence to. Muto Feng was as affable as a cornered snake, as Pahndir had cause to know.

"Hullo, cuz," Muto said, affecting not just human language but human tones. "You look in need of company."

He sat without invitation, taking the second chair with a very unYamish grunt of satisfaction. His robes were an eye-searing acid yellow with avocado trim. Small, polished rubies gleamed in a swirling pattern over the green. Pahndir never wore jeweled clothes outdoors in the city. They asked too much restraint of Bhamjran's lighter-fingered residents. Unconcerned, Muto smoothed the cloth over his stocky belly, sniffed the spoon that had held Pahndir's clotted cream, grimaced, and set it down. The utensil investigation complete, he tilted his head to peer at Pahndir.

"You look much recovered from your ordeal."

Pahndir wondered if Muto meant the ordeal of losing his wife, being declared dead by his own family, or perhaps his six-year imprisonment as a sex slave in a pillow house. The answer hardly mattered, seeing as Muto's evil genius was behind the latter two of the three traumas. Without a doubt, Muto would have preferred Pahndir remain crippled by the depression Thallah's suicide had wrought.

"What do you want from me, Muto?"

"Tut-tut," Muto scolded, switching to the Yamish tongue as Pahndir had. "Can't a man express concern for a relative?"

"Not when he's you, he can't."

"I heard you'd been sprung from your . . . retirement by the Midarri prince and his charming quarter-human bride. I wanted to make certain you were adjusting to life in exile. From what I can see, you've done very well."

"You'll forgive me if I'm not overwhelmed by your felicitations. Spit it out, Muto. You've already stolen my inheritance. What more can you want from me?"

Yamish coolness flowed down Muto's features like ice water. Pahndir got the impression that this was his true face, that emotion was the illusion Muto had to force.

"Not that I admit to anything, you understand, but my father had no right to name you—an inferior first cousin—as head of my clan. Nor did you have any right to charm him into it."

Pahndir had charmed no one. He and Muto's father had simply shared an interest in early Yamish coins, over which they'd whiled a handful of amenable afternoons. He'd liked the old man, his uncle, but to this day, Pahndir didn't know what the elder Feng had seen in him that led him to select Pahndir as heir over his own son—no matter how underhanded that son was. Whatever quality he'd thought Pahndir possessed, no one else had observed it. This, however, seemed unlikely to soothe Muto now.

"I believe you addressed that injustice by encouraging

my family to fake my death," Pahndir said dryly, "thus enabling you to add the House of Shan to your holdings. So, again, I ask you, what do you want from me?"

"You are direct," Muto observed disapprovingly.

"You can answer, or you can go to the human hell."

Muto stared at him, unblinking as a basilisk. Pahndir felt his cousin probing his aura for weaknesses. His insides might have been quaking with fury, but luckily his energy sheath was impregnable. He had Herrington to thank for that, he supposed. There was nothing like a recent victory to shore up one's shields.

"Very well," Muto said at last. "Since you demand it, I will be frank. I want to know you've given up any idea of returning to Yamish lands. I want to know you cede all rights to leadership of your house or mine."

Pahndir was so shocked he couldn't speak for a few heartbeats. Could Muto honestly be afraid he'd try for those things? Muto had their empress in his pocket, and the emperor wasn't far from sharing the same lint-filled space. Muto had funneled so much gold into the imperial couple's purses through questionable business deals Pahndir doubted they'd know how to survive without it.

Struggling against an impulse to shake his head in disbelief, he laid his hands flat on the table. "The highest court in the Forbidden City awarded you those rights."

"True," said Muto, his eyes hooded. "But I want to know you cede them."

"How can I cede them more than you have forced me to? I cannot sign a contract to that effect, for you've had my family declare me both unsound and dead."

"You are obviously neither at the present."

"No thanks to you!" Pahndir spat out. One of the waiters had been walking toward them, perhaps to offer Muto a chance to order. Though the human couldn't understand Pahndir's words, the sound of his temper had him beating a quick retreat. Recalled to himself, Pahndir blew out a calming breath.

"How can I convince you I have no interest in reclaiming a house full of people who turned their backs on me? They chose you to lead them, and I wish them the joy of it."

If Muto heard the irony in this statement, he gave no sign of it. "I don't believe you," he said baldly. "No one walks away from that kind of power without a fight. Oh, your family's house is nothing, but mine . . . mine dines with emperors."

"I've made a life here," Pahndir said in exasperation, "as you yourself have noted. I'm not interested in dining with emperors."

Muto's eyes were slitted silver lines. "You can't deny you've been making new friends lately."

Pahndir's heart faltered. If Muto meant Beth or Charles . . . if he was thinking of hurting them to get back at him . . .

"What are you talking about?" he asked carefully.

Muto leaned across the table, his meaty hands fisted between the plates of curried eggs and scones. "I'm talking about Lord Welland Herrington, a Yama as famous among the humans as he is among our kind. He'd make a useful ally, don't you think? You've met with the great man twice now, and the second time he called on you."

Pahndir fought an urge to laugh hysterically. If Muto knew what that "call" had been about, he wouldn't have been concerned. "You've been spying on me," he said instead.

"Wouldn't you in my place?"

Pahndir had leaned forward when Muto did. Now he fell slowly back in his chair. Sweat had broken out in the small of his back, but he believed his face was impassive. How much had Muto's spy seen, and how far was Muto willing to go to get his way this time? Most royals considered it uncivilized to kill each other outright, preferring to watch their enemies suffer instead. And Pahndir did have powerful friends these days, honorable friends who would not betray him as his family had. Cor and Xishi Midarri had already foiled a number of Muto's plots. If something happened to Pahndir, questions would be raised.

"I have no words to convince you," Pahndir said, proud to hear how steady his voice sounded. "I've taken no action against you or yours, but if you want peace on this issue, you will have to find it within yourself."

Clearly, this answer didn't satisfy his cousin. Muto's lips pressed thinly together as he pushed his bulk to his feet with surprising grace.

"Time will tell," he said, his aura oozing royal arrogance as he looked down his nose at Pahndir. "And trust me when I tell you, cuz, I'm not willing to give you much of that."

# ELEVEN

Considering what had happened the last time Charles had patronized The Prince's Flame, he had to summon all his courage to return. Taking the afternoon off was another struggle. He didn't like missing work, but he wanted to ensure Beth couldn't follow him again. He needed another outlet for his desires, to counteract her increasing pull on him. He wasn't convinced he was ready for that outlet to be the prince, but at this point he was desperate.

Thoughts of Beth were haunting his every moment: her kiss, her cries, the feel of her softness around his cock. He'd grown hard more times than he could count thinking back on it. He had to save her from him somehow. If that meant throwing himself into the prince's web, so be it. He couldn't claim it would be torture. The lust-sweat flaming on his skin as he strode toward Pahndir's house prevented him from pretending that.

Given the state of his nerves, it was almost too much when the brothel's butler informed him Mr. Pahndir was not at home. Obviously, the universe was against him. Charles was destined to burn—and to drag his dearest friend into the fire with him. He was turning away, preparing to descend the curving sandstone steps, when a second male called after him.

"Mr. Watkins?" he said. "Are you Charles Watkins?"

Charles reversed direction to find a slim Bhamjrishi with a half-scarred face hovering at the door.

"I am," he said cautiously.

"Forgive me for hailing you so impetuously. I am Prince Pahndir's valet, Biban. His Highness has instructed us to make you welcome should you come by." Here, he glared at the butler, causing the larger man to shrink back from him. "Would you care to wait in the parlor? I'm sure His Highness won't be much longer."

This was all very flattering, but Charles didn't think he wanted to wait in that house without Pahndir there. "Where is Mr. Pahndir, er, His Highness?"

The valet hesitated, possibly having been left without instructions on how to answer this. "He is in the curry and teahouse down the street. I *believe* he is alone."

His emphasis obliged Charles to wonder how many seductions the valet thought his master had in the works. His feelings of flattery faded, replaced by a more familiar wry amusement.

"I'll be discreet," he assured the servant, and inquired which way he ought to walk.

In his haste to reach the restaurant once he'd spotted it, Charles nearly ran over a tall, black-robed woman who was slipping out of an alleyway. His apologies were perfunctory and, luckily, accepted without argument. The women of Bhamjran had been known to demand, in very decided terms, the respect they believed was due them. Relieved to have escaped a scene, Charles returned his attention to the sight of Pahndir rising from a table at the tea and curry house. He had no company that Charles could see.

His relief at that was swallowed by simple admiration.

Lord, the demon was something—that long black hair shining like a river down his back, those silver robes molding like a kiss to his athletic limbs. Pahndir threw a handful of bills beside his plate, his profile as perfect as an alabaster cameo. In that moment, Charles admitted he wanted the prince; not his employees, but the man himself. Nothing else would satisfy his baser urges. Nothing else would fulfill his need to cast himself into danger.

His body tightened as Pahndir turned toward him. Their eyes met and locked as they had a seeming lifetime ago in the marketplace. Pahndir's expression didn't change, though he hesitated slightly. Excitement streaked like champagne through Charles's veins. Pahndir stepped off the terrace onto the pavement, his long legs graceful and sure.

*Oh, yes,* Charles thought. *This is what I want.*

And then Pahndir turned to the left and walked away without a word.

Charles felt like he'd been slapped. Pahndir had seen him, had recognized him, and had given him the cut direct. So much for telling his employees to keep an eye out for him! Clearly, the prince had thought better of having anything to do with him.

The sting behind Charles's eyes warned him he needed to leave before he made an even bigger fool of himself. He gasped air back into his lungs and strode off in the opposite direction. Maybe he'd misunderstood. Maybe Pahndir didn't want to greet him in public. Maybe it would harm his reputation in some way Charles couldn't comprehend.

*Maybe you shouldn't care so damned much,* he lashed at himself.

He turned into an alley, the same one where he'd bumped into the woman. No wider from side to side than his arms could reach, it was empty of all but rubbish containers and a battered assortment of waiters' bicycles.

Feeling slightly nauseated, Charles pressed his hand to the painted brick, a cheery yellow that did nothing to improve his mood. He willed his muscles to steady. He was shaking with hurt, a breath away from having to choke back tears.

He'd been counting on Pahndir wanting him more than he realized.

"Charles," said a soft, surprisingly remorseful voice.

Charles's heart and stomach both turned over. The voice belonged to Pahndir. He'd come up the opposite end of the long alleyway, probably after using his demon speed to rush around the block. He put his hand on Charles's shoulder. His grip was warm, but it was the painted yellow wall that supported Charles.

"I'm sorry I ignored you back there," Pahndir said, his eyes as naked and pleading as Charles's were guarded. "I've discovered one of my relatives is having me watched, a Yama who doesn't wish me well. I didn't want him to suspect you meant anything to me."

Charles stared at him, then blinked and shook his head. In one short speech, Pahndir had altered his perceptions considerably. Charles had been thinking of Pahndir as a seducer, and not a person who might have problems of his own. He couldn't have said why, but the change made his blood rush more thickly into his groin.

"*I'm* sorry," he said. "Is there anything I can do to help?"

Pahndir's smile was slight but natural. "You might kiss me, if you've a mind to. I've had a hell of a day thus far."

Charles swallowed. This was what he wanted, more than he cared to admit, but it made him nervous nonetheless. Pahndir was asking him to take the next step, to choose rather than simply let himself be seduced.

"I'm not sure I can afford you," he said, the words inescapably breathless. "You must be more expensive than your employees."

Pahndir's soft curse was crude enough to blister the paint right off the alley walls.

"Creation take you," he said more mildly, once he was done with that. "I don't intend you to be my customer."

Charles's heart was lodged and pulsing in his throat. The

only part of his body that demanded as much attention was the ache between his legs. "What do you intend me to be?"

"My lover," Pahndir said, his hand flattened on the brick beside Charles's shoulder. "My friend, too, if that turns out to suit us both."

*What about Beth?* he wanted to ask. He couldn't bring himself to do it. The answer seemed too likely to stop whatever this was in its tracks. Charles didn't want to think about Beth and the prince right now, or about Beth and himself. He wasn't ready to confront the tangled fantasies in his head. He'd come to Pahndir to protect Beth from the sordidness of all that.

"I don't know what I can promise you," Charles said, almost dizzy with arousal. "I'm told I'm not the easiest person to be friends with."

Pahndir's elbow bent, bringing his face closer. Charles hadn't been with a man since he'd left the top hat club, and it was strange to be this close to one. Pahndir's lips were curved in a genuine smile, his breath scented with sweet spice. Chills ran up and down the front of Charles's thighs.

"You don't have to promise anything," Pahndir said. "Just let me show you what we could have."

Charles didn't consciously decide to move, but he found his hands on Pahndir's waist. The Yama was all muscle beneath the embroidered silk, lean and hard and so enticing to Charles's palms that he simply had to tighten his grip.

Pahndir shuddered when he did, then let out a nearly soundless laugh. His silken mouth brushed Charles's ear.

"I'm so hard I could scream," he whispered. "If you don't kiss me, I might explode."

His own cock lurched violently at the claim. He slid his hands up Pahndir's back, curling them over his shoulders from behind. The move brought them chest to pounding chest. Pahndir was a bit taller than he was, and harder, but he matched him well in breadth. Charles lifted his mouth and watched Pahndir close his eyes. Their lips touched, pressed, and then Pahndir's sleek, wet tongue slid slowly inside.

The Yama's moan of pleasure was almost too soft to hear. Charles had forgotten how hard a man's mouth could be, how direct and aggressive. They kissed without parting, their tongues stroking and parrying deliciously. It wasn't exactly a fight for dominance, but it was close. Pahndir's weight grew heavier as he pressed Charles into the wall. One of his thighs slid between Charles's legs, allowing the demon to brace his knee on the brick. The erection that burned through Pahndir's robes was large enough to widen Charles's eyes.

Suddenly too hot, his hands slid restlessly to Pahndir's rear. Great minds must have thought alike, because Pahndir was doing the same, his fingers digging insistently into the muscles to pull Charles forward. They were pressed together full length then, heat to heat and groin to groin. The intimacy of it felt as intense as sex. *Here's what you've done to me,* it said. *Here's what I've done to you.*

The city was going about its business at either end of the alley, but it seemed impossible to pull back from what was happening. Kissing Pahndir felt too good, too necessary. Charles rolled his hips, rubbing their cocks together just enough to let Pahndir know he liked the feel of them side by side. Pahndir appeared to enjoy the soft friction. His chest moved faster with his breathing a second before he broke away.

When he licked his lips, taking the taste of their kiss inside, Charles saw his tongue's dark marking.

"You're feeling my energy," Charles guessed huskily.

This time Pahndir's hips were the one to swivel. "That's not all I'm feeling."

"I can't feel you taking it."

Pahndir slid his longest finger to the center of Charles's chest, starting a delicate pulsing atop his breastbone. "Can you feel it now?"

Charles's breath came harder, his cock abruptly so stiff it hurt. He wasn't sure he could answer, but Pahndir must have felt the change in him. His eyes darkened, his pupils swelling as only a Yama's could. He spoke far lower and rougher than his race usually did.

"I want to take your energy, Charles. I wanted to before I saw Darja do it. I've wanted to ever since you brought me those cookies."

"Cookies?" Charles gasped, confused.

"When I came to you at the dig. You took the time to bring sweet biscuits with my coffee, though I imagine you didn't particularly want me there."

"Beth accuses me of trying to feed everyone."

He'd said the name he hadn't meant to say, but it didn't seem to upset Pahndir. His gaze didn't even flicker on Charles's. "It was a gesture of kindness, and we Yama take the smallest of those seriously."

A mesmerizing brilliance had overtaken Pahndir's irises, as if the control he exerted on his emotions had distilled them into a kind of fire.

"I'll have to be careful then," Charles said, reaching for flippancy but suspecting he was failing. "Make sure I really intend to be kind when I am."

"Yes," Pahndir agreed. "Otherwise, you may find it all too easy to earn my partiality."

Suddenly Pahndir's hand was spread across Charles's breastbone, his weight leaning behind it, effectively trapping Charles against the brick. Charles didn't think this was by accident. He thought Pahndir meant to demonstrate how strong he was. A surge of energy rushed up his body from the soles of his feet, the result of Pahndir drawing up his etheric force. The demon was doing it. He was really feeding from him. Charles's knees went weak and hot at the same time.

"This is what you want?" Pahndir asked, hushed and intimate. "Not my servants, but me?"

"Yes," Charles breathed, writhing helplessly against the wall. His various desires magnified each other, wreaking havoc on his restraint. "Oh, God, yes."

"I can't take much," Pahndir cautioned. "Not here." He

seemed to be struggling to control his breathing, his warning meant for both of them. More than anything, that pushed Charles over the edge.

"Don't stop," he said, putting his hand on top of the other man's.

"No," Pahndir agreed throatily, soaking up Charles's energy like another man might strong wine. "Not yet. Not yet." His beautiful, burning eyes slid shut for a long moment, his own body undulating so that his robes whispered over and away from Charles. "Infinity, I want to give you everything you want from me. I want to make you spill so many times you end up coming dry. There isn't one dirty thing you could want that I wouldn't wish to try."

Charles opened his mouth at this stunning declaration, but all that came out was a throaty sigh.

Pahndir didn't need an answer. He turned his hand and slid it down Charles's front, squeezing it between their bodies. The moment his fingers pushed over Charles's erection, Pahndir claimed his mouth again.

Charles squirmed with pleasure, losing all control of the encounter as the demon cupped and massaged him between the legs. Pahndir's mouth was avid and very skilled, but it couldn't capture Charles's attention like that lower hold. His hand was big, hard, his fingers longer than a human's and utterly fearless. Charles began to jerk like he was trying to fuck Pahndir's palm.

"Oh, God," he gasped, his head falling back against the brick with a little *thunk*.

Pahndir murmured praise in his own language. He was sinking to his knees, was working the straining buttons of Charles's Northern-style trousers.

"Oh, God," he repeated as his cock burst out into Pahndir's hands. Those long, hard fingers were running up and down him, tracing his distended veins, searching out his every pleasure spot. Sensation spiked through his balls as the Yama probed the ridge of flesh behind them with his finger pads. "Pahndir . . ."

He'd meant it as a warning. "Yes," the demon soothed. "I know what you want. I can drink from you here as well."

Pahndir ran his tongue around the tip of him, and Charles fought a moan. The extremity of his arousal seemed to have made him more sensitive. His skin tingled everywhere his energy rushed out to meet Pahndir's touch. Against his will, his nails were pricking holes through the silk that draped Pahndir's broad shoulders.

"I want this too much," Charles said, trying to be clearer. "I'm afraid I'll thrust too hard and gag you."

Pahndir steadied his shaft in one hand, his hold almost unbearably personal. "This is not a concern you need to have. Yama don't have the same reflexes that humans do."

Charles groaned even before Pahndir's mouth surrounded him. He was in an alley in broad daylight, his only protection from discovery a rubbish bin and a few shadows. A demon was going down on him, feeding from him, and that demon happened to be a male. Anyone who saw them would think they were depraved. Twisted creature that Charles was, there wasn't one part of this scenario he didn't find exciting—and that was before he discovered how incredibly good at this Pahndir was.

Charles shoved one wrist into his mouth to muffle his helpless cries—or maybe they were mewls, like a kitten being tortured. Pahndir was sucking his penis up and down—tight, strong pulls that threatened to turn him inside out. The Yama's throat closed on his crest with each downstroke, a strange but piquant caress. Charles almost stumbled when Pahndir shouldered his legs wider for more access. The prince's hand surrounded Charles's tightened balls, squeezing and rolling the tender sac with a pressure that flirted on the edge of pain. It hurt, but it felt good as well, helping him to last, helping him to savor every lick and swallow and pull.

Sweat rolled down him in the desert heat. When his nails unintentionally ripped through silk to draw blood, Pahndir made soothing noises against his cock. Charles forced his hands to relax, forced them to fork into Pahndir's hair and massage his scalp. Pahndir let out a muffled moan. Coupled with the noise of suckling, this almost sent Charles over the top.

"Lord," he groaned, his body jerking uncontrollably now. "When this is over, I am going to thank you like you won't believe."

Pahndir made a noise that sounded like approval. He strengthened and slowed his sucking at the same time. The hand that didn't cup Charles's balls was running up the back of his leg, soothing the cramp that threatened to tighten his muscles. Charles's scalp began to prickle, the ache in his groin rising. Pahndir's tongue was cushioning the lower side of his shaft, but it was also moving like a snake. Human tongues simply didn't do that, not so firmly, not so precisely, until the sweet spot beneath his glans felt like it was being hit repeatedly by a soft hammer.

As the orgasm tipped from *almost* to *there*, instincts too strong to fight took over. He shoved into Pahndir's mouth so hard the man couldn't help but grunt, no matter what reflexes he did or didn't have. Undeterred, Pahndir's tongue went into a rapid flutter as liquid heat exploded in Charles's loins. Charles let the climax go, let his hips buck and thrust uncontrollably. He wallowed in the waves of pleasure the way Beth said he had in guilt. Pahndir didn't make a sound, just tightened his hands and pressed his head closer. He was licking him like he tasted good, and those caresses felt so sweet Charles didn't get a chance to go completely soft.

He panted, sagging limply against the wall as Pahndir rose. When the Yama dragged the back of his hand across his glistening lips, a tiny afterspasm jolted Charles's cock.

"You bit your wrist," Pahndir observed, lifting Charles's arm to examine it.

Charles's eyelids could have been weighted with lead; it was that hard to keep them up. He looked at Pahndir's hands where they framed his forearm. Blood welled in the tooth marks, but the pain didn't register.

Pahndir's fingers were shaking a tiny bit.

"I was trying to be quiet," Charles said.

Pahndir's eyes slanted with amusement. "You honor me."

Charles touched his cheek, letting his fingers skate slowly down the lean hollow, watching the muted flush that bloomed on the other man's flawless skin. The flush could have been emotion, or a reaction to Charles's energy. Either way, Pahndir stilled beneath the caress, his humor gone as if a switch had flipped. In its place was a watchfulness that put a corresponding tightness in Charles's chest.

The tension in the prince's body was thick enough to taste. He'd shown more control than his male employee by not spilling along with Charles: a matter of pride as much as class, perhaps.

"That was something," Charles said softly. "I'm not certain I have the skills to thank you sufficiently."

Pahndir's eyes dropped gratifyingly to his mouth. The tip of his tongue came out briefly. "I suspect you're being modest, but in any case, I've always preferred enthusiasm to expertise."

His faintly suggestive tone encouraged Charles's *enthusiasm* to take on a renewed stiffness.

"May I walk you home?" he suggested, wanting to return the pleasure in more comfortable surroundings, and wanting just as much to experience more for himself. "We could continue this with more privacy."

Pahndir drew in a breath. He took so long to answer, Charles began to think he'd said something wrong. But he couldn't have mistaken how much Pahndir wanted this. The man's robes were standing out over his erection, which was larger than any he'd ever seen. Now that he had seen it, Charles could hardly tear his gaze from the way the thin material was vibrating.

He suspected he'd enjoy the challenge of accommodating it.

Sadly, Pahndir seemed to find his needs easier to ignore.

"Not today," he said at last. "Though I hope you'll ask again when the timing is better."

"The timing?"

Pahndir shook his head. "It's a personal matter, a royal quirk I'm not yet ready to put to the test."

"You can trust me," Charles said.

Pahndir kissed him gently on the mouth, his breath rushing out the slightest, flattering bit. "It isn't you I distrust, Charles. It's the cruel mistress both our races call Fate."

# TWELVE

Beth struggled to pull the buttons of her blouse together, but to no avail.

*Bloody poori and batata nu shak,* she cursed, these being her favorite Bhamjrishi foods. Her clothes had gotten tighter recently, but this was ridiculous. Beth was not a person who gained weight, no matter what she ate. Her three older sisters had been bemoaning that fact for years.

*Well, so what?* she told her half dressed reflection in the bedroom mirror. She didn't look bad, even if her long brown skirt was too snug to qualify as ladylike.

She shoved the offending garment down her legs and twisted from side to side. Without the waistband digging into her, she was no longer bulging but curvaceous—an adjective she'd long ago lost hope of ever applying to herself. Yes, it was strange that she'd turned curvaceous overnight, but who knew what effect Southern food could have? Deep-fried puff bread and spiced potatoes might be more powerful than people realized.

An image rose in her mind of Queen Tou's very queenly

figure striding down the corridor to her harem. Tou had been strong, but she'd also been a shapely woman, the sort men couldn't help drooling over, the sort who made them think of fathering children. Hadn't Tou noticed changes in her body after emerging from the black chamber? Wasn't it likelier that Beth's own venture into the room was affecting her?

"No," she said aloud, the sharpness of the denial echoing through her suite. She hadn't heard a peep from anyone about a secret chamber being discovered. It was still just possible that she'd imagined her experience there. Women's figures evolved as they grew older. That could be all this was.

She squeezed her breasts' new fullness between her hands. They'd evolved all right. Her nipples were deeply flushed, almost red, and they drew tight in the morning breeze. Their sensitivity reminded her of other changes she'd noticed. Swallowing back a knot of fear, she focused on the issue at hand. If her bosom got any bigger, she'd have to start wearing those newfangled Jeruvian brassieres.

"Then you will," she told herself. And while she was at it, why not get a whole new wardrobe? One that suited her tastes and comfort better than the clothes she'd come here with? Herrington paid her well enough to afford it. She was a grown woman—captain of her ship, and all that. Her parents' opinions didn't matter. Beth had slept with a man. The experience might not have ended ideally, but she wasn't a child anymore.

Surprised to find herself smiling (because, really, she ought to have been ashamed) she dug Charles's shirt out of the cupboard where she'd hidden it. She was glad she'd folded it neatly. It was big enough to wear, and it would cover up her skirt's poor fit. Fortunately, this was the weekend. Both Charles and Herrington would sleep in. She had plenty of time to do what she wanted before the men in her life figured out how to stop her.

Pahndir didn't remember if he'd dreamed of Beth or Charles, but when he woke he was grinding his hips against the mattress, so close to climax he truly couldn't stop himself until he came.

"Fuck," he groaned, the dry peak slicing through him in a hard, bright arc.

He only softened slightly when it was done—not unlike Charles when Pahndir had licked him clean.

He cursed again and flopped onto his back. The light that slitted through his heavy drapes implied that it was early morning. He doubted he'd slept three hours since locking up for the night. His body was exhausted, his lingering erection raw—which suggested the climax he'd woken to hadn't been his first.

He had five days left to his cycle's peak, five whole days before his royal hormones strangled him. Then even the questionable relief of masturbation would be denied. At that point, any easing of arousal could only come through a mate. No matter how many orgasms he gave himself, his excitement would rise but not recede, not for the five forsaken days it took heat madness to pass.

Pahndir shook his head at himself. He felt all too close to that state already. As much as he'd enjoyed being with Charles, he'd only succeeded in teasing himself.

"Shower," he told himself. "Shower and dress."

From the way his cock perked up at the prospect of being soaped, he'd been right to surrender any hope of going back to sleep.

A city like Bhamjran did business every day, but on the weekend it did it slowly. Pahndir felt slow himself as he ambled into the commercial quarter near his home. The day was bright, as always, the sun lending a sharpness to the humble beauty of the streets and shops. He didn't know where he was going, and he didn't care. He wanted to lose himself in human distractions, to forget his worries and simply be.

Again and again, he filled his aching lungs with the warming air.

*Let it go,* he told himself as he exhaled. Like it or not, his future would decide itself.

The fragrance of lemons and cinnamon rode the magic carpet of the breeze, the smell pleasant enough to lure him after it. He decided he'd find a café and have an early breakfast, something rich and filling and sweet. Except his feet weren't taking him in the direction of restaurants. They were taking him into narrower byways, until he finally reached the quarter known for clothiers. Weekend or not, Tailor's Row was busy, every shop supplemented by a bin of "bargain" offerings on its pavement. Here pedestrians could only walk in the street, which was barely wide enough for a donkey cart.

He stopped when he recognized a familiar figure hovering indecisively in front of Farouk & Assam's Sari Emporium. He hadn't been wandering aimlessly after all; he'd been following Beth's scent trail.

*Well,* he thought, *no sense fighting Fate if I've come to this.*

She didn't hear him as he walked up to her from behind.

"Beth," he said, and laid his hands on her shoulders.

She dropped her jaw as she turned and caught sight of him. "Mr. Pahndir!"

He couldn't resist cupping her face and stroking it, adoring the softness of her downy cheeks. He wanted to say her name again, but that seemed foolish. It felt so wonderful to be with her, exciting and relaxing at the same time.

"You look as if you could use some help," he said when she began to blush beneath his caresses.

"I . . . I was thinking of refreshing my wardrobe."

"Farouk and Assam's is a fine establishment. You couldn't choose better."

"Pahndir." She dropped her voice, despite the fact that no one was paying them any mind. "Are you following me?"

"No," he said, a half-truth at best. He had trailed her—just not deliberately. He smoothed her hair behind her ear, the shell of it glowing pink in the sunshine. "Thank you for using my name."

She laughed, and he didn't give a damn what had amused her. The sound warmed him too much to care. "It can't be a coincidence that you're here."

"Maybe it's destiny."

She stopped his hand before it could slide into the neck of her shirt: Charles's shirt, he realized from the faint scent that wafted off of it. The knowledge didn't help him behave more befittingly, instead stirring memories of other half-met desires. He licked his lips. Her breasts looked lovely from this angle: different, round and full and—

"Pahndir!" she said, a laughing scold this time. "If you're going to stare, why don't you come in and make yourself useful?"

She had his hand in hers, her fingers warm, and he followed her into the shop like a puppy tugged by a leash. The sari emporium was a cacophony of silk and cotton stacked floor to ceiling on overladen shelves. The place reeked of dye and incense, though the combination wasn't unpleasant. Two male attendants bustled out at their appearance. Without a second thought, Pahndir pulled four gold crescents from his pocket and slipped them into their palms.

"Bring things in her size," he said. "We'll want the fitting room to ourselves."

Beth widened her eyes at his order, but the attendants simply smiled and bowed. This was Bhamjran, the city that thought it had invented open-mindedness. Pahndir knew they must have handled this sort of request before.

"I need to be alone with you," he murmured as their guides turned and led the way through the teetering maze of cloth. "You've no idea how badly."

She almost tripped, and he caught her elbow, his cock

gone hard enough to stab through her plain brown skirt. He loved that he could fluster her this way, loved that he was going to be alone with her, loved that he was going to advise her on what to wear and she would obey.

*"Salwar kameez,"* he said to the attendants when they reached the back parlor that served as F&A's fitting room. "Saris would be too difficult for her to walk in."

He didn't watch to see them leave. His eyes were too busy savoring his companion's blushing confusion.

"You can undress now," he said softly. "Or have you forgotten that I stripped for you the other night?"

She fell back a step, her legs bumping a sapphire-silk settee. All the furniture was low and colorful, as rich as a parlor in a real Bhamjrishi home. Beth's heart was beating so hard he could see it pulsing in her throat. She had her hands crossed protectively over her breasts.

"I haven't forgotten," she said, and nearly killed him by wetting her lips.

"Are you shy then?" he asked, softer yet. "I'm sure the attendants will knock before they return."

"I . . . I've gained a little weight lately."

He laughed at her, unable to stop himself. A little weight would only make her more beautiful to him. "Let me see."

She bit her tempting lower lip and began undoing buttons, but after only two she stopped. "What exactly are you planning to do after I undress?"

"Look at you. Maybe touch you a little."

"Do you promise that's all you'll do?"

"On my honor. I realize going further in a public place would embarrass you. When you and I make love for the first time, I want you to be relaxed."

Her face turned as pink as poppies. "*When* we do . . ."

"When we do," he said firmly.

"So when I thought you didn't want to see me again, I was mistaken?"

He could scarcely believe she was serious. "Why on earth would you think that?"

"Because you were so curt when you sent me off in your car. You said—"

She squeaked as he stepped to her and covered her mouth with his. She was stunned only for a moment, after which she clutched his head and kissed him back eagerly. Oh, how he loved the sounds humans made when they were aroused. Beth's little moans were especially appealing, shooting like arrows straight to his groin. He found it almost impossible to lift his head again.

When he finally did, her fingers traced his mouth wonderingly.

"I'd have to be dead," he said, "before I stopped wanting you."

One of the attendants cleared his throat behind them. "I'll just leave these tunics and pants on the bench for you."

The bench was by the entrance, the pile of *salwar kameez* uninteresting at the moment. Pahndir's hands were on Beth's buttons before the heavy velvet curtain rustled closed again.

"Oh," he breathed, his palms cupping her exposed curves. She was indeed more bounteous. "Look at you."

He maintained one heartbeat of restraint, and then his mouth was on her nipple, his throat making hungry sounds without his consent. Truly, though, the most orthodox Yama could not have blamed him. Her skin was creamy and flushed with rose. It tasted like the scent that had led him after her. Crazed for her responses, he sucked her harder to make her bud more.

The shirt she'd borrowed from Charles hung open to bat his face, like a flag to a bull in rut. For the sake of his control, he suspected they were lucky the shirt was the only thing Charles's personal smell clung to. Had it covered any more of her, *marked* any more of her, Pahndir wasn't sure what he'd have done.

Royals could be very territorial.

"Pahndir," she gasped as he switched to stake his claim on the other breast. His mental powers weren't at their sharpest, but quite clearly, her nipples were sensitive. Her spine was arching, her hands pressing him closer. "I can't think straight when you do that."

He didn't want her to think. He wanted her to squirm and moan and grow so hot her juices would overflow her sex and perfume the air. She gratified the wish almost as soon as he had it. He groaned, tearing himself away because if he didn't do it now, he never would. He'd let matters go far enough as it was. He didn't remember moving, but he had one knee on the settee behind her and one hand smoothing the back of her thigh through her unattractive skirt. *Her* hands were buried in his hair as if she liked the feel of it.

Both of them were breathing hard enough to have been running for their lives.

"That's more than a 'little' touching," she panted.

He released her and straightened, but couldn't utter a word, his control too slim to waste energy on speech.

"Sit," she said, pointing to a tufted red armchair. "You're going to have to behave if you want to stay."

The thrust of her arm was as autocratic as any high-born Yama. Pahndir couldn't suppress the shudder that ran through him, the dark excitement at the unexpected shift in power. He didn't think she knew she was taking charge, or at the least she didn't know what that would do to him. He sat, his genitals so engorged it hurt to put weight on them.

He tried to keep the most salacious of his imaginings off his face. She was still nervous, watching him for a moment before she wriggled awkwardly from her clothes. The striptease was all the more effective for being unpracticed. He groaned aloud as her last undergarment dropped.

"No," he said when she would have covered herself. The little patch of hair between her legs enchanted him, the curves of her, the soft, embarrassed glow. She was perfectly tall, perfected rounded, her waist a strong inward dip that would have drawn a sigh from any race in the world. Every inch of Pahndir's skin was pulsing with desire. "Beth, you're so beautiful you steal my breath."

The intensity of his tone seemed to frighten her.

"You look as if you want to eat me up," she whispered.

He gripped the arms of the chair to prevent himself from doing exactly that. He wanted to taste her arousal enough to cry.

"Tell me a story," he said, literally hanging on by his fingernails. "Anything you like."

She smiled dreamily, and suddenly the power was hers again. "Oh, no. You're the mysterious demon prince. I think you ought to tell me one."

"I need distraction."

Her grin broadened. "Then I guess I'll have to offer you an incentive for the questions you answer."

Her sisters were right to call her the Fearless Philips. He watched her finger circle one nipple, which—unless his keen Yamish eyesight had forsaken him—bore a faint set of his tooth marks. He shivered, his desires pulling in two directions. To master or be mastered. To fuck or be fucked. Either one sounded blissful now. "What do you want to know?"

"Tell me why you look tired today."

The compassion in her voice pulled his gaze from her breasts. "An old family issue has reared its head."

"You have family?"

"I do. Or did you think I hatched from a serpent's egg?"

She returned the smile he hadn't known he wore. "You seem so independent I didn't think of you as having ties."

"I have one friend in all the world, and she's in love with and married to a man I owe my life."

He hadn't meant to say it, and wished he could take it back the instant tears welled in her eyes. She blinked them away as quickly as a Yama would have, but when she spoke her voice was all human, the emotion that shaded it as vibrant as the shelves of silk outside.

"I don't believe that's true. I'd be your friend in a heartbeat."

Her offer overcame him, until all he could do was hang his head and shake it hopelessly. Who but a human could be this unhesitating and sincere? And who but she could make his heart stop with emotion? His throat was immediately so thick he could not swallow.

"Tell me," she said, on her knees before him, her hands gently covering his where they clutched the chair. She seemed to have forgotten she was naked. "Tell me the whole story."

He sighed, the breath dropping from him like a weight he hadn't known he carried. He turned his hands beneath hers so he could rub his thumbs across her knuckles. Her skin was soft, her energy warm. With another tiny sigh, he released his hold. It would be enough of a challenge keeping his emotions controlled without absorbing hers.

"Once upon a time," he said, appropriating the human phrase with surprising ease, "I was married to a beautiful princess named Thallah . . ."

Beth knelt on the soft, patterned carpet, loving the excuse to stare at Pahndir this way. She listened, rapt, as he told her how he'd met his wife at a fancy party her parents had arranged to mark her sixteenth birthday. They'd held it in a lush green garden with ropes of pearls and diamonds dripping off the trees. To her, picturing it was better than a fairy tale.

"I was two and twenty," he said. "Far too old to dance attendance on a girl her age. I had not, however, found the black of my eye yet, and my parents were insisting I meet every possible candidate. The first time an adult royal male's eyes go black, it can only be for his genetic mate. As it turned out, Thallah was mine. She came to thank me for my present—a pair of antique gloves, as I recall—and I swear I thought my body had caught on fire. Laying eyes on her was like being struck by lightning bolts of lust. I remember taking at least thirty seconds to stutter, 'You're welcome.' "

"And she liked you, too?"

"She did, though Infinity knew why. She had other

princes after her, from better families, at least one of whom she could have matched closely enough. I was lucky she chose me. I'm what they call a solitary, and she was the only one for me.

"We waited three years to marry, until her parents thought she was old enough. By that time, my father had died unexpectedly, and I'd inherited leadership of my house. I was young for it, and while I had the intelligence to oversee the Shan businesses, I didn't know how to command respect. My various siblings and cousins circled me like sharks until Thallah put her foot down with them. She defended me. She watched my back against everyone."

Beth laid her cheek against his knee, trying to imagine him needing this. He seemed the quintessence of command to her, even with his hand falling to pet her hair.

She suspected he'd tried to stop touching her before. She was selfishly glad he'd forgotten to keep it up. She loved this sense of connection.

"Thallah and I were married fifteen years," he said. "I thought we were as happy and as close as any couple in the world. I thanked Fate every day I woke up beside her, for sending me a mate who suited me body and soul."

"And then?" Beth said, her hand curling protectively around his leg. She willed her touch to bring him nothing but comfort.

"And then," he said, "I returned one evening to our palace after a business trip. I was in a hurry. We had a party to attend that night, and I needed to shower and dress. I called out to her, didn't even stop to see her before I stepped into the bath. When I came out, I found her lying on our bed. She was dressed in a pale pink gown, which she knew was my favorite color for her to wear. Her hair was perfect, her jewels . . ." He shook his head, one fist rubbing his thigh. "She was dead, Beth. She'd taken pills, too many for it to have been an accident. She'd been lying there dead for hours."

His eyes were haunted, his pupils shrunken to pinpricks.

"Did she leave a note?"

He drew a ragged breath, pulling himself together. "She didn't, but it wouldn't have been expected. It's unusual for a Yama to commit suicide—disgraceful, to tell the truth. I suspect Thallah thought it would be crueler to explain why she killed herself."

"You think it was your fault? Pahndir, that can't be!"

He smiled at her, a sad little crooking of his lovely mouth. "It could be, Beth. Things happen in a marriage. You believe the other person doesn't mind, but maybe they do. I'm afraid I'll never know for sure."

"I don't believe it. If she loved you as you say she did—"

"But maybe she *didn't* love me as I thought. Maybe she grew tired of protecting me. I was . . . flawed. I didn't take her death well, to put it mildly. My family gave me a year to conquer my grief. When I couldn't, they had me declared legally incompetent."

Beth squinted up at him. "You mean 'incompetent' as in 'insane'?"

"Excessive grief is a form of insanity to my people."

He appeared so calm as he said this that she felt obliged to swallow her protests. This was his culture. Perhaps it wasn't her place to judge.

"Is that why you came to Bhamjran? Because you were thrown out by your family?"

He snorted through his nose. "I wasn't just thrown out. My behavior was so shocking they decided they'd better declare me dead before my taint rubbed off on the whole bloodline. Another of my cousins, Muto Feng, arranged for them to fake my death in an accident. Then he had me imprisoned in a pillow house, which is where—willingly or not—I became an expert in my current trade. I'd still be there if Cor Midarri hadn't broken me out."

"A pillow house?"

His eyes took on a gleam of wry humor. "For six long years I was a teaching tool. The madame used me to train her courtesans in pleasing royal males."

The air was abruptly thicker in Beth's lungs, a tiny tapping between her legs reminding her of the blood flowing to her sex. The words he'd said their first night together came back to her. "They needed to use you because royal Yama are different. Because only royals go into heat."

He'd taken her face in his hands, his thumbs stroking lines of warmth up her cheekbones. "Only royals go into heat, and only their genetic match can bring them to ejaculation. Or so I thought, until I met Xishi."

It was hard to be jealous with his silver eyes burning down at her. "Xishi?"

"The woman who eventually married Cor Midarri. She was one of the students. Unbeknownst to everyone, she's one-quarter human. I came when I was with her, truly came for the first time in the seven years since Thallah's death."

"That's why you want me? Because you think—" She swallowed, arousal blazing through her in a nipple-tightening wave. "Because you think a full-blooded human could help you spend?"

His hands slid down her face to her neck, the movement slow and sensual. His gaze dropped to the caress, each of his lashes iridescent and mink-black. "Not just any human: you. You call to me, Beth. To all of me. I would want you even if I didn't think you might be able to give me a full release."

She sat deeper on her heels, trying not to be stunned by what he'd revealed. She knew it wasn't common for Yama to be this frank. He let her search his eyes, seemingly patient while she decided what to make of his tale.

"You're older than I thought," she said, which maybe wasn't polite.

The skin around his eyes softened. "You know Yama live longer than humans."

"And age more slowly, yes." She put her hands over his, stilling them on her neck. "Do I remind you of her?"

"Of Xishi?"

She laughed dryly, seeing she'd set herself up very

neatly for that. "I meant Thallah. Because she was younger than you when you met."

He drew his hands away, resting them on his own thighs. "You don't remind me of either of them. Thallah was far more serious than you, and Xishi is far more sweet."

"Oh, thank you very much!"

"I'm not saying this correctly. You have . . . you have some of the qualities I admired in both of them, but you are your own flavor. Possibly you are too young for me—"

"I didn't say that," she protested, still laughing. "I'm twenty-four, the same age as Charles."

"I like hearing you laugh," he said as if he couldn't explain it any other way. "It makes me feel good inside."

For someone who liked her laugh, he looked awfully sad right now. That, however, hadn't dimmed his desire for her. His cock stood straight in his lap, the broad, damp head throbbing beneath his robes. His organ seemed bigger than before, taller than her hand, a prodigy of a phallus that made her insides squirm. She wasn't afraid the way she should have been. She wanted to touch him through the beautiful salmon silk, wanted to stroke him and lick him and do whatever he required to achieve his cure. She realized she felt *important*—which might not have been the best reason to become involved with a man.

It didn't seem any more appropriate to dwell on the fact that he'd certainly be strong enough to satisfy her mysterious new longings, or that going all night with him might be exactly what her body was crying for.

But she'd left the prince too long without a response. His face went from sad to stiff and dignified.

"I see you do not wish to explain your feelings. Please forgive me for pressing you."

"No," she said, touching his knee hastily. "You call to me, too, Pahndir. In more ways than I can count. I'd be honored to find out if I could . . . be what you hope."

"You don't have to be honored."

"Isn't it an honor, though? When people trust one another with their desires?"

Her hands slid up his thighs, preparing to part his robes and claim the object of her fantasies. Before she could, he clamped her wrists in his. The sudden change of mood surprised her. His grip was tight enough to hurt.

"Don't," he said as harshly as if he were human. "Touch me now, and I'll fuck you right on the floor. Touch me now, and I won't let you go for hours."

Her fingers curled against his thighs. His muscles were tense and hard here, and she longed to argue in the worst way.

"Trust me, Beth," he insisted. "You'll want to be alone with me for this."

She knew he was right, but her body was afire to have him now.

"Take me home then," she said as roughly as he had. "We'll do this as you wish."

The hot black lust that flashed across his eyes was almost reward enough for the delay.

# THIRTEEN

Beth couldn't tear her gaze from Pahndir's darkly handsome face, or her thoughts from the consummation that lay ahead. *He* arranged for the pile of untried clothes to be delivered to Herrington's mansion. *He* led her to the intersection where he hailed the electric cab. *He* told the bored female driver where to go. His presence of mind aside, Pahndir was breathing more deeply than normal, though not so deeply others would have noticed. No, all they would see was his cool demon face and eyes. His excitement was Beth's secret—Beth's delicious, sensual secret.

When he caught her watching him, his perfect, rose-colored lips went thin. "Stop looking at me like that."

She smiled and slid her hand under his, thrilling to the way his fingers immediately curled around hers.

His frown deepened. "I'm not making love to you in a cab."

He sounded like she could entice him to if she tried. Hugging the knowledge to her, she swiveled toward him and leaned her cheek against the seat's tobacco-scented leather.

She relaxed there, enjoying her body's anticipation, until she realized where the hansom was taking them.

"We're going to Herrington's house, to the *haveli*."

"You'll be missed, Beth. And you were right to remind me of your relative youth. I don't want Herrington to hunt you down and embarrass you."

"That's my concern, not yours!"

"Beth—"

"Damn you." She swept his hands from her shoulders, where they'd been trying to soothe her. "You're a beast to change your mind after what you said to me in that shop."

"Believe me, I'd rather do exactly as I threatened."

She slitted her eyes at him. "If you tell me this is for my own good, I swear I'll slap the words out of your mouth."

Her temper seemed to take him aback. "It's only a postponement. Until I'm certain we won't be found out."

Her body boiled with more than anger. He'd promised her fulfillment, and she bloody well wanted it. What's more, it was her right. She swung one leg across his lap, her grip at the top of his arms far less conciliatory than his had been. Though Pahndir gaped at her aggression, the advantage it gained her was debatable. The muscles she squeezed in her fury were hard enough—not to mention male enough—to goad her arousal infuriatingly higher.

"No," she growled at him through her clenching jaw. "No more waiting. You're not the only one who wants things, and you're not the only adult here."

The hansom rattled to a halt outside Herrington's tall town mansion. Pahndir shot a glance out the window and wet his lips. He seemed nervous, unsure of his own resolve. He was certainly aroused enough to be swayed. Beth could feel the evidence of that radiating heat between her parted thighs.

"You two getting out?" the female cabbie prompted. "Because I have to charge you for sitting here."

*What would Tou do in my place?* Beth asked herself. Not give up, she was convinced. No, Hhamoun's queen would demand she be satisfied.

"There's a plunge bath next to the garage," she said, her attitude as firm as Pahndir's was undecided. "It's big enough to swim in, and no one uses it but me. You could join me. Take your fill and then slip out with no one the wiser."

Pahndir's hands tightened on her waist as if tempted to pull her closer. "It'll be five days before I can take my fill of anyone."

A hot, wet quiver ran through her private folds. He had to mean his heat was five days away. A confidence that did seem oddly regal swelled in her breast. He was putting this off because he feared it would torment him, not just because he was protecting her. Knowing that, the kind thing would have been to respect his wishes, but Beth couldn't quite let the matter be.

"I want you inside me now," she said softly. "If you don't share that desire, I'll do my best to understand, but I don't want you contacting me again until you're ready to live up to your promises."

"But I like being with you."

The protest took her by surprise, and maybe him as well. He shook his shoulders and sat up straighter on the seat.

"I like being with you," he repeated more calmly, setting his face into sterner lines. "This isn't just about having sex."

His words turned her heart to mush. She would have agreed to any postponement then—and Tou's example be damned. Fortunately, she didn't have to, because he lifted her gently off him and handed the driver her fee. His movements were brisk as he pushed out the door and offered his hand to her.

"Come," he said. "I don't want us seen together here."

She didn't question why this concerned him more than it did her. She simply took his hand and grinned blindingly.

The plunge bath was a cavernous room, tiled from floor to ceiling in intricate blue-and-white patterns. Before

Herrington moved in, it had probably been lit with candles, but at present brilliant electric lights were rigged to its roof by wires. Bereft of windows, the bath took up all the space beneath the mansion that the garage did not. Its tiles were sparkling, so someone kept it clean, but it did indeed have the air of a little-used luxury.

Pahndir let Beth point him to the changing room. Despite his worldliness, he was glad for the privacy.

He needed time to wrestle his fears into submission.

Physically, he was more than ready to do this. Emotionally, not as much. Many times when he'd been a prisoner at the pillow house, Xishi had brought him into heat early. The idea that Beth could do the same concerned him. What if this encounter became the Test of Tests, and he discovered he couldn't truly come with her? Then again, if Beth could bring him into heat ahead of schedule, she ought to be able to inspire an ejaculation, too. Surely the universe wouldn't be so cruel as to give her one power and not the other.

Unconvinced that the universe harbored much kindness where he was concerned, Pahndir felt a bit of a wreck as he stepped naked into the main room. Beth was in the pool already. She stood facing him, her hands paddling lightly on the wavering surface. The water covered her breasts, deep enough to swim in but not to dive. Adrenaline flooded, tingling, through his veins as he descended the shallow steps. He had to use the brushed nickle handrail to pretend his shaky knees were firm. Chances were he was insane to be doing this, but—Creation help him—he wanted her.

Beth appeared to feel the same. Flatteringly dumbstruck, her gaze traveled his body from face to chest to pounding groin. There her attention stopped. Only the rising water level wrenched her eyes from his erection, until he longed to flush as deeply as she was.

He was in a position to know that humans and Yama were born with a similar range of genital sizes, the sole exception being royals. For good or ill, they were bigger, and became more so as their heats approached. Only the most skilled of princes could take a human woman without hurting her.

"I'll be gentle," he said, pushing through the water with his heart nearly choking him. "I know you're inexperienced."

She hardly seemed to hear him. As soon as he reached her, her hands settled on his chest above his nipples, her fingers wet and humming with energy. He stiffened when they kneaded restlessly into his flesh, the tiny movement affecting him as strongly as if she'd stroked lower things. Indeed, his "lower things" were jerking uncontrollably. When her lashes lifted, her eyes were dazed.

"Be as gentle as you want," she said. "Just don't make me wait anymore."

Her breathy voice destroyed him. He lifted her, felt her thighs part beneath the water to wrap his waist. He slipped one hand down to cup her bottom, and suddenly his tip was trembling at her gate.

He gasped at the sensation of that first contact, but she did more: She groaned and used the strength of her legs to pull herself down on him.

He had one brief moment to marvel at the ease with which he slid into her slick channel. After that, he was too inundated with pleasure to wonder who had been here before him. She was so warm around him, so snug and perfect and strong, her human energy seeping into every cell of his penis. She took all of him, tightly but without resistance, from thickened root to quivering crest, as if she had a Yama's ability to shift her sheath for extra-large partners. Large he was, his too-stretched skin on fire with sensitivity. It felt so good to be surrounded that he began to thrust almost at once, if only to convince himself these amazing sensations were real.

To his relief, her reaction to his movement was favorable.

"Oh, God," she moaned, her head falling back to trail her auburn hair across the water. "Oh, yes, I needed that so much."

"Smaller strokes," he said, fighting to keep his voice decently steady, gripping her hips to control them. "You don't want to lose your lubrication to the pool. We're going to be at this a while."

He wondered if he'd been too blunt for a human female. Her head came up and she blinked at him. But something made her smile. She leaned to him, winding her arms more securely around his neck. The simple but powerful gift of holding her naked washed over him.

"I don't think I can lose my lubrication," she confided. "My body keeps making more."

He swore in his own language, swore and began to shaft her the way he'd dreamed of since he'd first seen her in the market square.

He took her with a potency that awed her, though she'd known his kind was stronger than hers. The ease with which he brought them together, the sheer force he commanded with his very talented fingertips, thrilled her more than she had breath to say.

He didn't stop when he came like Charles had. He kept going and going, despite how many times she felt him stiffen in climax. She lost count of her own orgasms, though she knew they'd started kissing sometime after the fourth.

As clever as his mouth was, kissing him should have been a distraction, but after her too-short time with Charles she found herself motivated to pay attention to everything. Her nerve endings seemed to make a record of each caress, each thrust and squeeze and skin-ruffling sigh. She hadn't expected her sheath to be so sensitive. If other women liked this act half as much, she didn't see how they let their husbands leave the house. This sex business was amazing: a work of genius from a higher realm.

The best part might have been that her enjoyment spurred his higher—the effect, she supposed, of her orgasmic energy flaring over him.

Whatever the cause, each peak loosened him a little more, until he touched her as tenderly, as passionately as any woman could desire. His spine relaxed beneath her caresses, its movements both freer and more adamant. This was a change Beth couldn't pretend not to revel in. *Gentle* was definitely not what either of them needed. Lost to rapture, Pahndir's groans began to echo off the ceiling tiles.

"This feels so good," he moaned, one hand stroking down her back possessively. His hips rolled as smoothly as if they'd been oiled, his thighs apparently tireless. "I never want to stop taking you."

"It doesn't—" She gasped as he forged into her again. "It doesn't bother you that you can't spill?"

"I feel the relief of each orgasm, even if I'm not softening."

"And my energy?"

"Oh, yes," he agreed throatily, his head dipping to nip the bend between her neck and shoulder. "That might be the best part of all."

Talking about what he was feeling seemed to excite him more, maybe because his kind normally didn't express such things. Beth swore she felt his shaft grow harder, though logic should have said this was impossible.

"Fuck," he breathed, which seemed to confirm her impression. His fingers clamped on her bottom. "I need more leverage. I'm carrying you to the steps."

The water splashed as he laid her down, her breasts now rising above the waves their thrusting bodies were making. His gaze fell to her nipples, sharp as pebbles with her arousal. That and the change in pressure immediately made her arch. Her body did something she didn't think she had voluntary control over, her inner muscles stretching somehow, struggling to accommodate the bit more of him there was now.

She groaned as she felt him reach *all* the way into her. His cockhead struck some unsuspected sensitive spot deep inside, and it was like a gong had been rung. The sensations were softer, thicker than those he created farther out, and almost unbearably erotic. This was true penetration. This was being pierced to the core.

"Don't come," he cautioned, clearly feeling her tighten. "Hold off as long as you can and make this one really strong."

She'd thought all her orgasms had been strong, but of course he'd know better than she would. Unfortunately, the very idea of holding back made her wriggle hungrily.

"Breathe," he said, his silver eyes smiling. "Breathe through the tension and relax."

He seemed to know exactly what she was feeling, as if he'd reached into her mind and read it all. The suspicion stripped her defenses, until holding his gaze felt painfully intimate. She was in his hands, a newcomer to this act in which he was expert. As if emotion could flow in both directions through their energy, she sensed his gratitude for her trust, his banked excitement at her vulnerability. In many ways, he was a stranger and yet, in that moment, with their gazes locked together, he seemed as close to her as her own soul. His lips softened and curved fondly.

"When you go over, so will I," he promised. "If you make me wait long enough, you might hear me scream."

Oh, she wanted that, too much to laugh at the suggestion.

"Scream then," she whispered, rippling muscles she hadn't known she had to tug at him.

He went at her so hard then he should have hurt her, but the pounding felt good. Water surged up her body with his big, rolling movements, and she couldn't doubt where harem dances had come from. He was the dancer, she the extremely willing captive audience. He held her bottom, lifting it for the angle his cock desired, while his other hand cradled the back of her head. Despite his care, it was she who saved her skin from the friction of the concrete steps, her arms flinging out to grip the handrail and the marble coping with surprising strength.

The closer he drove her to culmination, the more that strength came to her aid, helping her to hold back the way he'd told her to. Her pleasure was a shining wire, coiling tighter and tighter on the verge of springing free.

She suspected she was hanging on that verge too long for him. He began to grunt with his thrusts, began to looked pained from his longing for release. She wished his release could include ejaculation, craving that burst of seed inside of her. Another part of her, the same that held her so triumphantly steady, reveled in his suffering. His veins were drawn on his temples in strong blue lines, his facial muscles twisting with the strain. He was trying to maintain his precious demon control, but it was unraveling before her eyes.

Her body bowed without warning, the orgasm like a beast breaking from a cage. It slammed out from her sex as he slammed in, hitting that ringing spot deep inside her. Just as he'd predicted, the burst of energy triggered his release. He didn't scream, but he shouted, hoarsely, pulling out one more time so he could shove back. Her hands were wrenched free of their mooring. Only he held her then, only he, with his hard, long cock convulsing forcefully.

And then it softened at long last, slowly, steadily, pulling a sigh from both of them. Her sexual muscles caressed it as it faded.

He had not spilled, but by Heaven he had relaxed.

"Beth," he said, and tipped her head to rest on his shoulder. He stood with her in the water. She didn't remember when he'd changed their positions. Had there been a moment's extra dizziness tipped into her lightheaded glow? Regardless, it felt lovely to hug him like a monkey climbing a tree.

It felt even lovelier to be hugged back.

He was breathing hard but not exhaustedly, holding her tight with him still inside. Though the water supported much of her weight, his control impressed her. She'd lost herself at the end. He'd been the one to keep her safe.

"Holy hell," whispered a voice behind her back.

It was Charles's whisper. He must have heard the noises they were making and come in from the garage to investigate. How much he'd seen only he knew.

Pahndir's head lifted from where he'd buried it in her

hair. Perhaps he'd been unable to recognize Charles from his voice alone. When he did see who it was, his sexual organ started to lengthen inside of her.

"Charles," he said, and the thing gave a little thump like a tail wagging.

The moment was a revelation, though perhaps it shouldn't have been. From the beginning, Beth had thought it probable the Yama was interested in Charles in a sexual way. To feel the evidence of that attraction swelling within her flesh erased any possible scrap of doubt. The bigger shock was her body's reaction.

She was excited. The flicker of her inner muscles, the resurgent wetness and rising ache could not be denied. She *liked* the idea that Pahndir wanted Charles.

By accident or intent, Pahndir had turned them so they could look up at Charles where he stood at the pool's wet edge. Charles's glare notwithstanding, Pahndir didn't loosen his embrace. She didn't think this was because her body hid his arousal. He seemed far more wary than embarrassed, though the continued stretching of his organ said it was happy to stay where it was.

Charles's eyes were stricken when they met hers. "What are you doing, Beth? I warned you to stay away from him."

"I know," Beth said softly. She squirmed a little in Pahndir's hold, less comfortable than he was with flaunting what they'd been doing. She wished the confidence she'd felt when she was alone with Pahndir would come back. Anything had seemed permissible to her then, as if the rules by which other people lived were simply suggestions.

That was then, though, and this was now. She pushed aside her insecurity. "The thing is, Charles, I'm not yours to warn. You made it clear you and I would never be intimate again."

"Again?" Pahndir's voice had an edge of sharpness. "You made love to him?" He turned his head to Charles. "*You're* the one who took her virginity?"

Charles flushed, the stain on his cheeks so much darker

than the one on Pahndir's. Anger beat behind the color, and guilt, and perhaps a shade of unwilling arousal. As Charles drew breath to speak, his eyes were so blue they snapped.

"Hey," Beth cut in, stopping him. "Nobody 'took' anything from me."

Pahndir ignored her in favor of continuing to berate Charles. "I thought such things meant something to your people. How could you be her first, and then say you'd never be with her again?"

"I was trying to protect her! And a fat lot of good that did with you seducing her as soon as my back was turned."

"Hey!" Beth said, louder this time. "I made my choices. *Me*. As I have every right to do."

Charles frowned at her and crossed his arms, patently unwilling to cede this point. "You had sex with him. In the pool."

Beth didn't see why this was worse than making love to him somewhere else, but Charles's deeply reddened face said it was.

"You could have made love to me in the pool, if it had occurred to you."

A quiet snort puffed against her ear, Pahndir's subtle demon laugh. The tiny movement shifted him inside her, reminding her how firmly, how fully, he was filling her. It occurred to her that he wasn't judging her for having been intimate with Charles. He'd been surprised, but his anger seemed mainly at the idea that Charles might have treated her disrespectfully. Now he held her (claimed her, some would say) but he wasn't trying to scare Charles away. Indeed, he was quite obviously stimulated by his presence. A door clicked open in her mind, spilling possibilities into her awareness that seemed as natural as breathing once she saw them.

Tou hadn't had any problem with this sort of arrangement.

She let her gaze slide down Charles's rigid body. He wore Northern clothes: trousers, a loose white shirt with the sleeves rolled up. The less-than-exotic garments could not disguise the bulge at his groin. He was aroused by what he'd witnessed, and twice as defensive on that account.

She knew her voice was going to be throaty even before she opened her mouth. "You could take me in the pool now, if you wanted. You could take us both."

"Yes, you could," Pahndir agreed.

Charles's jaw dropped, his breath rushing out in shock. "You're both crazy."

"We both like you," Beth said. "We'd enjoy pleasing you."

Pahndir gave her hip a little squeeze of support. Charles looked from one to the other, his formerly flushed face gone pale. She saw he was truly stunned by their offer. The muscles that formed his expression tightened. Anger rose into his eyes, but not before the deepest pain she'd ever seen sliced across his face. She didn't know if the pain was hurt or longing, but it was frighteningly powerful. He slashed his hand through the air and turned.

"I don't need this," he said, already striding toward the door. "The pair of you can go to hell."

Maybe she should have expected him to lash out, maybe any normal male would have, but his words stung nonetheless. Impatient, she dashed away the one small tear that had squeezed from her eye.

"Shh." Pahndir kissed the spot where it had been. "He's just afraid."

"Of me? Of us? Doesn't he know I'd never deliberately do anything to hurt him?"

Pahndir let her slide from him onto her feet. He was still hard, but that didn't seem to matter. "He's afraid of himself, Beth. Of how much he wants what you were offering."

"He thinks I'm a pervert."

Again, he gave that snorting laugh. "No, Beth. He thinks *he's* one." His hands came up to frame her face, his silver gaze even more intense than usual. His fingertips drew slow, drugging circles on the skin behind her ears.

"Tell me, love. Is the three of us together what you really want? Or are you trying to be nice to the hapless males?"

"You mean you truly wouldn't mind?"

His smile was crooked but unmistakable. "I'd count myself a lucky man twice over. I simply thought it would take more maneuvering to coax you into entertaining the idea."

She realized her mouth was hanging open when he kissed it gently shut. Maybe it shouldn't have, but hearing him admit that he'd been hoping to arrange a threesome unsettled her. Sensing her disquiet, he smoothed his thumbs over her wet eyebrows.

"Wanting you both doesn't lessen what I feel for you. Trust me, whether I'm lucky once over or twice, I appreciate how very fortunate either of those options is. I had . . ." He hesitated, suddenly awkward. "I had rather given up hope of experiencing such fondness toward anyone who would return the sentiment."

Beth's smile seemed to well up from her heart. She had more than a small suspicion that when a demon spoke of "fondness," the emotion was no light matter.

"I'm fond of you, too," she assured him. "Fond and intrigued and quite a bit lecherous."

He caught her hands beneath the water before they could find his sex. "You've had enough lechery for one day, especially since we've blown to shreds the idea of not being caught. I'll send you a message in a day or two."

"I'm sure I don't need that long to recover."

"You say that now, but I didn't hold myself in check the way I should have. You'll sing a different tune when your bruises bloom."

He had drawn her hands to his chest and was squeezing them lightly above his heart. His eyebrows were pushed together, offering the apology he'd almost voiced. Maybe demons didn't believe in them.

"I won't regret a single mark," she promised him.

His eyes darkened. That and the small contraction of his fingers revealed his pleasure at her words, a pleasure she sensed she didn't fully understand. He pulled her knuckles up for a kiss.

"Be well," he said, soft as smoke. "I shall count the hours until we meet again."

From the honeyed warmth that spread inside her, in strict defiance of her body's well-sated lassitude, Beth knew he wasn't going to be the only one counting.

# FOURTEEN

Pahndir fell into sleep with the relish of a drunkard falling into wine: deep, sweet, dreamless sleep. His needs weren't exhausted, but only because a prince's never were. They were content, rather, lulled like his worries into a patient state due to his ravishment of and by Beth. That this patient state might not last didn't matter. He had a chance. He had hope. He had a woman who'd embraced him with both tenderness and desire.

To expect Charles to drop as easily into his palm would have been greedy.

So he snuggled into his big, solitary bed as if it were all pillow and slept like the dead. The windows were open, their sheer silk hangings stirring in the soft night breeze. A dog barked in the distance and was hushed. At four in the morning, all but the most dedicated partygoers slumbered. Pahndir had sent his last customer home at three. As a result, no one saw the half-dozen shadows that swarmed silently up his wedding cake of a house. No one heard the faint scuffle of footsteps on the exquisitely carved stone of his balcony—or no one who'd admit to it. One by one, the shadows slipped inside without a whisper, each knowing what to do, each covered from head to toe in pure matte black. Only their eyes showed through their wrappings, scarcely glinting in what little light there was.

Four of the tall, whip-thin intruders circled his bed, leaving one to watch the windows and another to block the door to the inside hall. They didn't expect Pahndir's servants to interfere; they'd been assured all possible eyes had been bribed to turn blind. But they were professionals, and they'd done this sort of job before. They watched the entrances and exits because that was good form.

The tallest of the shadows, the most solid in musculature, lifted one finger and then tipped it down.

It was the signal they all had been waiting for.

Pahndir woke with a panicked lurch. He was being pressed into his mattress by four hard weights, his bedcovers smothering him around the neck and face. He struggled, tried to cry out, but the only noises he could make were muffled by the sheets. A fist backhanded him, as heavy and unforgiving as if it were made of iron. The strike simultaneously stunned him and woke him to the seriousness of the danger he was in.

Fury rose in a bitter wave. He wasn't going to die like this, wasn't going to let these assassins snuff out his light when his life was finally turning around. The universe could screw itself if this was what it had in mind for him. He called on his royal strength, tearing one hand through the covers like it had claws. With that arm free, he heaved a body off him so that it hit the wall with a crash.

He had an instant to wonder that his victim did not cry out. For that matter, someone on his staff should have come running.

"Aran," a voice hissed close to him. "Ether."

Pahndir knew what ether was, though not whether it could affect him. Yama had resistance to many human drugs. Preferring not to chance it, he threw himself toward the hissing voice, his attackers' apparent leader. His weight and momentum barreled both of them to the floor.

Like any prince, he'd been trained in hand-to-hand defense, but not like these fighters had been trained. These were street fighters, vicious and creative. Hissing Voice kneed him in the balls without a shred of mercy. Human or not, the force of the strike sent his breath wheezing out in eye-tearing pain.

An instant later, two more fists made his ears ring from either side, warning him he could not afford to nurse his previous injury. As he blocked his attackers' blows, he realized they were wearing heavy oxhide gloves with what felt like lead shot sewn into them. He was lucky they were human. Any Yama armed with those would have put him out. Angry, and not appreciably disabled yet, he ignored their continued pounding to wrap his hands around Hissing Voice's neck.

Which was when he noticed Hissing Voice was female.

"Back off or I'll kill her," he warned.

But he wasn't squeezing as determinedly as he should, as determinedly as he would have had she been a man. If she'd been a man, he'd have smashed her skull into the carpet and been done with it. The hesitation cost him more than he could afford.

"Now," she rasped through his hold, and someone—two someones, in fact—clapped a sickly sweet-smelling rag over his face.

He gasped, his body's instinctive response to losing its air supply. That first choking whiff was enough to turn his knees to water. He realized the heavy veiling his assailants had wrapped around their faces might serve a purpose besides disguise. Ether was a volatile liquid, quick to evaporate, but this rag was soaked, dripping with what seemed like a dose fit for ten humans.

He went limp, and Hissing Voice wriggled out from under him. The two who'd pressed the rag to his face kicked him forcefully onto his back, probably hard enough to break a human's ribs. Pahndir hoped they broke their toes on him. His arms flopped like a fish as he rolled, his fingers refusing to even twitch. He blinked in slow motion up at Hissing Voice, feeling consciousness inexorably drain from him.

In the meantime, he had an unpleasant epiphany. No one was coming to save him. Not his personal staff. Not his employees. They'd been paid off, most likely, or maybe just didn't care if someone so different from themselves lived or died.

"Good," Hissing Voice said, like an answer to his darkest thought. She was on her feet, looking down at him. Either she was very tall for a woman, or his perceptions had been distorted by the drug. Her black-turbaned head appeared miles away. "Prince Muto will be pleased he has not been harmed."

As Pahndir lost his futile struggle to remain awake, he had a feeling he wouldn't like the reason for that announcement.

# FIFTEEN

Beth woke the next morning from a beautifully sound night's sleep. Her body was warm and relaxed, birds were singing outside her window, and best of all Farouk & Assam's had delivered her package at the break of dawn. One of the servants had left it inside her sitting room. Delighted to have avoided a confrontation with Herrington, even if the reprieve was temporary, she ran a cursory eye over the bill before tearing through the brown paper wrappings.

Shaking out the clothes inside was better than opening a heap of presents on Winter Solstice morn. She was determined not to let thoughts of Charles spoil her buoyant mood. She'd tried to speak to him again last night, but he'd refused. Never mind what Pahndir said about him being afraid; it would have been embarrassing for them both if she'd pushed harder. What could she say, in any case? This wasn't the sort of situation etiquette manuals gave advice about.

*Leave it,* she told herself, the tightness in her chest warning her that she wasn't succeeding yet. She had to wait until Charles was ready to come around. She wouldn't let their friendship be destroyed by this. She just wouldn't.

That decided, she turned back to her new wardrobe. As luck would have it, the assistants at F&A had judged her figure to a *T*. Everything fit, and everything flattered. They'd even thought to include a handful of sleeveless, snug-fitting underblouses, which would serve her as well as any Jeruvian brassiere. Beth did a little houri dance in front of her mirror, imagining how very much she'd enjoy showing them off to Pahndir. She was ablaze to go to him that minute, though he'd still be abed.

Whatever else was wrong in her life, it was lovely to have an almost assuredly admiring man to wear things for. Beth could admire the clothes herself, of course, but sharing the pleasure was twice as fun. It was, in truth, nearly enough to make her forget her benefactor's likely response.

And then one of Herrington's stiff-backed male servants tapped and called through the door.

"'Scuse me, miss," he said when she cracked it open. She could tell from his face that the apology was strictly perfunctory. "Lord Herrington requests your presence in the breakfast room."

The breakfast room at the *haveli* gave Beth the "creeps," as Charles's slang-loving little brother, Max, referred to them. The walls above the dark wainscoting were covered in the iridescent eyes of real peacock tails, a unique decorating choice made by the previous owners. Considering the thousands of feathers it had required, Beth doubted they'd waited for the birds to lose them naturally. The fussy little chairs that slid under the dining table had been done in matching shades of blue and green. The rug was likewise blue, and the high oval ceiling shiny green with gold trim.

Sadly, Beth couldn't blame this atrocity on local taste. With the fashion for exotica that had lately infected her countrymen, the room could have been transferred in its entirety to Avvar and found itself perfectly at home.

Beth never ate breakfast here if she could help it, but

aesthetic repugnance would be no excuse for ignoring Herrington's "request."

"I'll be down directly," she assured the servant, then winced at her reflection in a nearby mirror. She was wearing her favorite of her new outfits, a matched tunic and trousers in pale yellow cotton that was embroidered with small white flowers. The top was light as air, the loose pyjama pants wonderfully easy to walk in. Beth looked nice, but hardly proper. Too bad the servant's stern delivery had warned her she'd better not delay long enough to change.

"Perdition take it," she muttered to herself. This threw a wrench in her hopes for slipping away to Pahndir. But maybe it was just as well. Although her body hummed with well-being, the prince had said he'd contact her in a day or two. Surely it was poor strategy to look too eager, even if she loathed the concept of playing games.

She sighed with resignation and smoothed her top. Might as well get this over with. She doubted Charles had spilled the beans about her and Pahndir in the pool, but maybe Herrington had seen the clothes arrive. Whether he had or hadn't, at least she'd be comfortable while he scolded her.

To her surprise, though not exactly to her relief, a scolding didn't seem to be her immediate destiny.

A couple sat with Herrington at one end of the large oval table, next to the remains of a chased silver coffee tray. Beth assumed the pair were married, though the woman was much younger than her tall, silver-haired husband. They were Northerners for certain, and prosperous ones. Beth could tell their clothing was custom tailored. The woman's extremely well-fitted bodice bared an expanse of bosom that would have made Beth jealous even a week ago. Now she simply observed the display and smiled.

It was small of her, she knew, but she didn't mind at all that the woman was perspiring, despite plying a native paddle fan rather vigorously. With her smooth dark hair and her hourglass figure, she was as pretty as an ad for soap.

Her husband slid his delicate chair back and rose for Beth, a courtesy she didn't expect from a male of his obvious status. She looked inquiringly at Herrington.

"Beth," he said, his tone indicating no awareness that her dress was any different than usual. "This is Hiram Hemsley, Ohram's minister of trade, and his wife, Eileen. They've come to tour Hhamoun and consider my proposal to establish an on-site museum. Minister Hemsley, Mrs. Hemsley, this is my assistant, Beth Philips."

Beth supposed she was an assistant, though Herrington made it sound as if her role was an important one. Unsure how to respond, she offered a nodding bow to each member of the couple, hoping this was appropriate. She'd never encountered a minister before except as a printed signature on banknotes.

"Beth sees every artifact we uncover," Herrington added misleadingly.

"How fascinating," Mrs. Hemsley cooed, her smile as prettily contrived as the rest of her. "And how *clever* of you to wear local dress. The minister and I fear we shall turn to puddles before this trip is through."

"Well, local dress is modest," Beth said, spreading the tunic to show how it covered the baggy trousers to beneath her knees.

"Perfectly modest," the minister agreed. "And very pretty."

The warmth of his voice surprised her as much as the warning squeeze he gave his wife's shoulder. This was an important man, but he was defending Beth from the whiff of disapproval his wife had given off. He resumed his seat and patted his spouse's hand.

"You must have quite the grasp of local history," he said.

Beth's throat threatened to spasm on a cough. "I . . . do find it interesting."

"Then you simply must share your theories," his wife

prompted. "Tell us who you think Queen Tou really was. Historians claim such terribly outrageous things."

If Mrs. Hemsley was trying to lure her into an intellectual display that her husband would find unattractive, she had the wrong female. Then again . . . Images from Beth's dreams of Tou rolled across her mind. Most weren't suitable for public airing, but they did lend an unexpected authority to her answer.

"I think Tou was an extraordinary woman who ruled during a period when men weren't used to obeying queens. I think she was a self-made woman, much as we have self-made men today. I think she overcame great hardships before she rose and, as a result, developed a sense of her own worth that no one could undermine. The accounts historians have passed down to us suggest she was ruthless, brilliant, and blessed with uncommon physical vigor. Such things may be exaggerated, but I suspect there's a grain of truth in the tales. I also suspect she was a woman with a feeling heart, or her harem could not have adored her half as much as they were reputed to."

Mrs. Hemsley's fan had stilled at her throat, giving Beth a chance to admire the large red ruby gleaming on her ring finger.

"Oh, yes, her *harem*," Mrs. Hemsley said with a tinkling, slightly scandalized laugh. "I suppose we're lucky our spinster queen hasn't taken it into her head to start one of those!"

"Queen Victoria has made decisions that are controversial," Beth said. "Who knows what people will say of her in a thousand years?"

"All the more reason to preserve the evidence as fully as possible," Herrington put in smoothly, seeing that Beth's last rejoinder had disconcerted both his guests. While the minister seemed more liberal than his wife, he was sworn to honor Victoria. "People should base their opinions on all the facts."

"Yes," Minister Hemsley said vaguely, as if he weren't

paying attention to what he was agreeing to. "Facts are useful things."

"As are assistants." Herrington turned his leonine head to Beth. "I was hoping you'd take Mrs. Hemsley around the city while the minister and I discuss business. Perhaps escort her to the Hotel Bhamjran? There's a festival today. The terrace should provide an excellent view of the elephants."

Mrs. Hemsley had been looking as dismayed as Beth at the prospect of spending the day together, but at the mention of elephants, she brightened. "Oh, let's do! Elephants are the most darling creatures!"

Beth turned her disbelieving stare to Herrington.

"You do know your way around," he said, bland and soft. "Apparently at any hour of the day or night."

So that's what this was about: keeping her out of trouble. She should have known, Yama being such masters of indirect assaults. She wished she could be petulant and refuse him, but she knew how important this proposed in situ museum was to Herrington. She liked the idea herself, which meant she also had an interest in getting pinch-minded Mrs. Hemsley out of the way.

None of this, however, meant she couldn't be a bit impish. She shifted her attention to Mrs. Hemsley with a devilish smile.

"We could stop at Jeweler's Alley along the way," she proposed, convinced the woman could do her husband's finances considerable damage there. "It's well worth seeing. You won't believe what Bhamjrishi artisans can do with twenty-four-karat gold."

"Oh," said Mrs. Hemsley, glancing unsurely at her husband. "I do love ethnic handicrafts."

Beth had the pleasure of watching the minister turn pale.

The pair engaged in a rapid-fire whispered "conversation," the sort husbands and wives excelled at, irrespective of their class. Herrington took the opportunity to pull Beth aside. For a moment, he regarded her with his unreadable silver eyes. It was hard to tell, even up close, but she thought he looked tired. She wondered if it had to do with wherever he'd been going when he stayed out all night. Even his kind had to rest sometimes.

"You answered her question about Tou well," he said. "I appreciate the steadiness with which you've been applying yourself to your job lately."

The last thing she'd expected was a compliment. Given who he was, the praise could have been a manipulation, though that didn't stop her cheeks from heating with pleasure.

"I'll take good care of Mrs. Hemsley," she promised.

"I didn't doubt that for a minute," Herrington assured her, but Beth thought perhaps he had.

Charles watched Beth lead the woman into the street through one of his suite's ornately screened windows. Herrington's guest was unknown to him; some diplomat's elite young wife, was his guess. Whoever she was, Beth wasn't cowed by her. She looked different in her new clothes, more confident. It didn't hurt that she topped the woman she was escorting by at least six inches—with or without her charge's platter-size straw hat.

Charles's amusement didn't quite reach his eyes. Beth had knocked on his door the night before, wanting to know if he'd like to have dinner out with her. She'd left when he refused to answer, which was no more than he deserved for sulking like a child. Herrington had been out until dawn, no doubt indulging untold demon depravities with his desert paramour. Charles had been awake to hear him return, his sleep having been fitful, to say the least.

*You're pathetic,* he told himself as he rolled his forehead on the cool carved sandstone of the *jali* screen. Evidently, he'd expected his fellow residents to hang around here and watch him brood. There wasn't even anything mysterious to brood upon. He knew exactly what was troubling him.

The people he cared about were supposed to hate him for his desires.

He'd built his adult life around the fear. He'd kept his secrets, crushed his cravings, all to fend off that seemingly inevitable rejection. And now his dearest friend had offered him his dearest wish as if it were nothing. Just, *Why don't you have sex with me and this dangerous demon in the pool? We both like you. Why shouldn't you?*

Charles pressed his fist to his heart as if he could stop the inconvenient organ from beating. They both liked him. They both *liked* him. What did that even mean? Did they still like him now that he'd told them to go to hell?

One thing he knew for certain: What he'd witnessed in that plunge bath hadn't been based on anything as tame as "liking." Fucking didn't describe it, or making love. They'd clung to each other like life preservers in a raging storm. Pahndir's face had been as readable as a human's. If he wasn't half in love with Beth, Charles would eat that diplomat's wife's hat.

What Beth felt in return, he didn't want to ponder on.

Except . . . if there was the slightest chance they might, someday, come to feel for him what they felt for each other, wasn't that a chance worth pursuing? Wouldn't it be blessing enough to turn his misbegotten life around? Charles had been loved—by his guardian, Roxanne, by his brother, Max, and maybe in her own way by Beth. He'd simply never had anyone look at him the way Pahndir looked at Beth—as if she were his very sun. There had been hope in the demon's expression: hope and affection and a sureness Charles didn't normally associate with love. Pahndir relished what he felt for Beth. He wasn't afraid of his emotions at all.

Charles fist had shifted to rubbing the bone that joined his ribs. Letting it drop, he turned away from the window.

If a demon had the courage to face his feelings, why couldn't Charles?

He grabbed his least rumpled linen coat and prepared to leave. There was really only one person he could talk to about this. Charles wasn't certain he'd be objective, but he didn't think he'd judge.

"Mr. Pahndir has left the city," the servant informed Charles. He was a portly, youngish Bhamjrishi male, but he was mustering a fair approximation of the disapproval Ohramese butlers were famous for. "The house is closed to customers."

"He's left?" Charles repeated, having a hard time believing it. "Just like that? No warning?"

He was standing on the grand front stoop of The Prince's Flame, his jacket slung over his shoulder, his shirt slightly damp with sweat. The butler shrugged airily.

"I believe he was called home on business."

"I wasn't aware the prince had business in his homeland."

"He's gone," the butler said more forcefully. "For an undisclosed period. There's no point in you coming here."

He began to shut the door, but Charles caught it. Something about the butler's manner, or maybe it was the effect of being disappointed after having screwed up his nerve, made him dig in his heels. "Surely he left some message to give to friends."

"I wouldn't know anything about Mr. Pahndir's *friends*."

This crossed the line from disapproval to insult, not only toward Charles but toward Pahndir himself. Charles stepped into the butler's face. The servant's sneer couldn't hide the fact that he was quailing. Beads of sweat were glistening on his brow.

"Look," Charles said in the hard, cold voice he'd learned on the street. "Why don't you call Mr. Pahndir's valet to speak to me?"

He remembered the more helpful, scar-faced servant from his last visit. Charles was pretty sure he could talk to him, man to man, and discover the real story.

"Mr. Biban is ill," the butler said primly, "and unavailable to converse."

"You're lying," Charles said.

"And you're deluded," the butler returned. "Now leave before I call the Watch."

Charles felt such an urge to pop him in the nose that it was a wonder his fist didn't shoot up by itself. The butler's budding jowls were quivering, his freshly shaven cheeks an unpleasant shade of brick. He looked like he *would* call the police, if only for the pleasure of tattling.

"Very well," Charles said after treating the man to a few more seconds of glowering. "When Mr. Pahndir returns, please inform him Charles Watkins called."

The butler drew breath as if preparing to spew more rudeness. Charles's lowered eyebrows made him think better of it.

"Fine," he snapped and wisely grabbed his chance to hastily slam the door.

Charles stared at it for a moment before scrubbing at his head.

This was a poser, sure as hell. What did Pahndir mean by leaving without a word? And why couldn't he have hired more polite servants? Was it all some crazy trick a human couldn't understand? Helpless to answer, he tramped back down the steps. He'd probably made a fool of himself, but he hardly cared.

Beth at the least deserved a farewell note.

Much, much later, Beth deposited Mrs. Hemsley and her numerous packages at the Ohramese embassy. She was gladder than she'd ever been for Bhamjran's abundance of electric cabs. After all that shopping, she didn't think she could have dragged her feet another step.

They hadn't even stopped for lunch to watch the elephants.

She slid her key into Herrington's front door with a

lovely sense of coming home. When this place had started striking her as home she wasn't sure, but she couldn't deny it did. The feeling made her want to find some way to stay here after digging season closed.

"Beth," Charles said from the parlor entrance as soon as she stepped in. "I need to speak to you."

She smiled at him; couldn't help it, no matter what was happening between them. Charles was as much "home" to her as any set of walls.

"If you've got something to eat in there, you can speak to me for hours."

He looked startled, then colored just a bit. "I did prepare a plate of sandwiches."

"Lord bless you!" she cried and hurried in. Practically starving, she ate two crustless triangles in quick succession. Nabbing a third and chewing slowly enough to notice it was tasty, she sat on a footstool to face Charles in the matching chair. Her mood sobered when she saw how serious he was.

"I have news," he said. "About Pahndir."

Beth's heart literally skipped a beat. She swallowed with difficulty. "What news?"

Charles leaned forward over his knees to gather both her cold hands in his. "I don't know how to tell you this, but he's left town."

"Left town?"

"For an 'undisclosed' amount of time, according to his butler."

Beth studied Charles's face, trying to read what he wasn't saying. He didn't seem to be gloating, just concerned for her. His fingers tightened on her hands with comforting naturalness.

"Beth, they've closed The Prince's Flame. It doesn't sound like he plans to come back soon."

"But . . . where would he go?"

"Home, apparently."

"He can't go home. He's been exiled."

*"Exiled?"* Charles looked like he wanted to ask a ques-

tion or two about that, but then he shook his head. "Maybe he's been pardoned. Maybe he was too elated to say goodbye before he left."

Beth pulled her hands from his and rose, though what she could do better standing she didn't know. "He can't be pardoned, Charles. Everyone thinks he's dead. His family staged an accident and had him secretly imprisoned in a pillow house. They betrayed him to save their own reputations when he couldn't get over grieving for his wife. The Yama think feeling too much emotion is a form of insanity. From what Pahndir told me, he wouldn't go back there even if he could."

Charles rubbed his hand across his mouth. Whatever he and Pahndir had talked about when they were on their own, it wasn't this.

"You're sure this isn't just a story he told you? Maybe to gain your sympathy?"

"Charles!" She'd been wadding her tunic on either side of her hips out of nervousness, but this made her let it go. "Don't try to turn Pahndir into someone you couldn't like simply because you'd be more comfortable if you weren't attracted to him."

His head snapped up at her bluntness. A moment later, he drew a breath and looked down. "All right," he said. "I admit concocting a story just to impress you doesn't sound in character, but how can we really know what Pahndir would do? You said yourself his culture is different."

She turned away toward the tall, peaked windows that overlooked the street. What did she know about Pahndir apart from what he'd told her? How could she be sure any of his actions were sincere?

*I know my heart,* she thought, *and I trust my instincts. They've never led me that far astray before.* What's more, she knew Charles liked Pahndir—in spite of himself, but he did. Charles was no easy man to cozen. He guarded himself too well for that.

"Charles," she said, "if you don't have faith in my judgment, please have some in your own. Whatever you think about . . . what we offered you yesterday, I know Pahndir has a certain amount of emotion invested in us both. He wouldn't leave without speaking to one of us."

"Perhaps he intends to send a note from wherever he is."

"He wouldn't *leave*," she reiterated, knowing Charles was trying to be reasonable and unsure if she had the right to tell him about Pahndir's approaching heat. "He has . . . strong incentives to remain close by. I think—" Her hands came up to her bosom and clenched together. "Charles, I don't want to believe it, but I think something must have happened to him."

Charles had risen behind her. Now he took her shoulders and turned her gently around. "What do you mean, you think something happened?"

Hearing the words repeated sent a chill through her heart. Beth tried not to let her chin tremble. "Yesterday, he said someone in his family had come to town, someone he regards as an enemy: another prince named Muto. Maybe he's behind Pahndir's abrupt departure."

Charles's bright blue eyes widened. "He mentioned that to me, too. He said someone who didn't wish him well had been watching him."

For whatever reason, the memory of Pahndir's remarks brought a wash of hectic color into Charles's face. Beth ignored the indecipherable pang tightening her throat. Her reaction to the bond between Charles and Pahndir was not remotely the issue now.

"I have to go to Herrington," she said. "He knows people. He can find out where Pahndir is."

"No." Charles caught her arm before she could more than lean toward the door.

"Charles, I know he'll be angry, but Pahndir's safety could be at stake."

"Beth, there isn't a single doubt in my mind that Herrington already knows you and the prince are involved. He'd consider it his duty to know. He takes protecting you seriously."

"But he never said . . . I mean, I thought he might suspect, but—"

"Trust me, Beth, he knows."

They stared at each other, the awful possibility Charles had been entertaining finally rising in her mind as well.

"Lord Herrington wouldn't hurt Pahndir."

"He might. He might not even think it was wrong. I don't know if you're aware of this, but he had Max abducted when he was little, as a ploy to get Roxanne to turn to him for help."

"Damn," Beth said and gnawed her lower lip until it hurt.

Charles rubbed her shoulders bracingly. "I could be wrong. Herrington might have nothing to do with whatever happened, and he might be perfectly willing to help. For now, though, I think it would be better if you went to someone else. Maybe one of Pahndir's friends has heard from him."

"He mentioned a woman," Beth said. "Xishi Midarri. She married a prince named Cor. He's the one who freed Pahndir from the pillow house. I got the impression they live in Bhamjran."

She also got the impression that Pahndir had been in love with Xishi, and possibly still was. Under those conditions, would Xishi or her husband want to hear from Pahndir's new lover?

"Charles," she said, nerves making it hard for her to meet his eyes, "I know the people in my life don't always feel they can rely on me. If I do something right, they have a tendency to be surprised. Maybe you feel the same way after the way I . . . went ahead and slept with Pahndir."

"Beth, that isn't my—"

"Please, let me finish. I need you to help me look for Pahndir. He might be in danger, and I'm not certain I can do this on my own."

"Beth." His grip on her shoulders tightened until she looked up. "I never intended to let you search on your own. You're my friend, and you always will be. As to that, Pahndir is sort of my friend as well."

He didn't seem terribly happy to be admitting this, but relief flooded Beth nonetheless.

"We'll start with the Midarris," Charles went on, his tone brisk and practical. "There can't be that many Yamish princes in this city. I expect we'll have no trouble finding them."

# SIXTEEN

His captor's name was Sahel.

They'd been on their seemingly endless camel trek into the desert for the remainder of the night and half of the next day before she and her comrades exchanged enough conversation for him to discover what to call his enemy. A few hours more gave him two additional names. Aran and Delilah were her lieutenants, if lawless desert chieftains could be said to have such things.

Sahel, by contrast, knew everything about Pahndir. How old he was. Where he'd been born. The fact that he'd been known to enjoy rather rough foreplay.

He supposed he shouldn't have been surprised by her informed state. Muto had been spying on him for years, probably long before Thallah's death.

Sahel knew his wife's name, too, which made Pahndir long quite passionately for a second opportunity to throttle her. The farther they rode from civilization and any chance of pursuit, the more talkative—and personal—she became.

Did he wonder if his wife had killed herself because of him? According to Sahel, he probably should, since he was such an easily defeated specimen of manhood. Maybe Thallah would have been happier with one of Sahel's harem. She could have enjoyed true submission from her partner without being obliged to shore him up in front of his family.

Pahndir's certainty that Thallah wouldn't have wanted her former kindnesses used against him enabled him not to be drawn into arguing. This, however, was the extent of his victories.

The women kept him bound to the jouncing saddle, his arms trussed behind his back with slim steel cables that had been braided over with leather strips. The leather he could have snapped, but the steel defeated him. An hour of struggling against his bonds had his arms screaming with pain from shoulder to wrist. Not struggling didn't greatly alleviate his discomfort, but it did provide less entertainment for Sahel.

She was determined to wrest that from him any way she could.

He lost any doubt of this at sunset. They'd been riding as fast as the camels would trot, without a halt, since he'd been abducted. He didn't know which part of the Vharzovhin they'd reached, because the landmarks were strange to him. Pahndir's body could survive a lot of abuse, but his leg now had a permanent cramp from hooking around the horn of the saddle, and his bare head ached from baking beneath the sun. He'd had no food, no water, and pride was all that had kept the aftereffects of the ether from causing him to throw up. Though obviously hardened to this kind of journey, Sahel and her crew were finally starting to look weary.

He could have cried when Sahel signaled for their little caravan to stop, though he managed not to outright fall off his camel when the beast knelt down.

Her lieutenants freed his wrists and poured him water

from the goatskin they'd been sipping from all along. His hands being too numb to lift the small tin cup, Sahel tipped it to his mouth herself.

She backhanded him when he neglected to say thank you.

"We have no man for you," she said, a comment his equally numb mind didn't follow. "Not like your wife used to let you have. No worries, though—our Delilah can compensate for that."

They shoved him onto his face in the dusty sand. They had stopped in the middle of nowhere. Nothing surrounded them but flat, cracked desert and the now multicolored sky. They were completely exposed and utterly alone. Free to be their own law, the lieutenants pulled down his trousers. Then one of them—Delilah, he presumed—raped him in the anus with a length of polished wood.

Shock only paralyzed him for a few heartbeats. He'd had no circulation in his arms, and very little in his legs until a few minutes earlier, but he still managed to fight hard enough that it took all six of the women to hold him down.

The struggle exhausted everything he had left. By the time they let him go and rolled him over onto his back, he barely had strength to blink. Once again, Sahel stood looking down at him.

She nudged his unaroused penis with the dusty toe of her boot. "How disappointing. We were told this sort of thing would get a rise out of you. Especially so close to your heat."

"At least he's big," Aran said. "The other demon didn't lie about that."

"Big is as big does," Sahel said. "We'll try again when we make camp tonight." She pushed his cock harder with her boot. "Nothing to say for yourself, demon?"

He swallowed, his still-parched throat a hot line of pain. "Nothing you want to hear."

She smiled at the first words he'd said all day. Her

turban's tail hid her face, but he read her amusement in the lines creasing her dark brown eyes.

"No worries," she said, apparently a favorite phrase of hers. "I know you demon males think you can't be broken, but I have all the time in the world to make you sing."

# SEVENTEEN

Beth and Charles didn't have any trouble locating the Midarris. In some ways, the city of Bhamjran was nothing but a big, gossipy village. The first market vendor they queried knew exactly where the "Prince of Silks" had his home.

"His firm makes beautiful fabrics," the stallkeeper assured them, probably assuming they were prospective customers. "As good as local stuff—and some of his products magically shed stains!"

The thought of magical, stain-shedding fabric had made Beth smile . . . until they were admitted into the Midarris' house. She'd been congratulating herself on being pretty Mrs. Hemsley's equal in looks. During their interminable shopping trip, she'd received as many surreptitious male smiles as the wife of the minister. Sitting across a parlor from Xishi Midarri set that smugness decisively to rest.

All Yama were attractive, and the woman Pahndir had impulsively confessed to regarding as his only friend was no exception. Her pale skin was perfect, her long black hair glossy enough to put her husband's silks to shame.

The flawless symmetry of her features had a sigh of helpless appreciation rising in Beth's breast.

But there was more than this to her beauty. Xishi Midarri possessed an extra spark of humor, of life, that Beth had never seen in a Yamish face. She was a *merry* demon. Beth could see it twinkling in her slanted silver eyes.

At the moment, those eyes looked concerned by the news Beth and Charles had brought about her friend. Her husband stood behind her chair, his hands laid lightly on her shoulders. He was also quite good looking, if a trifle stiff. It made Beth realize just how atypical of his people Pahndir was.

With a tiny furrow between her otherwise smooth, dark brows, Xishi twisted around and turned her face up to her husband. "Perhaps we should contact my grandmother."

"Fortune forbid," he said with a fervency that surprised Beth. "I'm not putting us any more in Xasha Huon's debt than I have to. She's already hinting that we should send the twins to visit her this winter. We may never see our offspring again."

"But if Pahndir truly is in trouble . . . If Muto has moved against him again . . ."

Cor cupped her worried face, his eyes so nakedly tender both Beth and Charles momentarily looked away. "I promise, love, I'm not ignoring that possibility. Just let me make some inquiries on my own before we take emergency measures."

He turned his gaze back to Beth and Charles, his face now as smooth as if emotion had never ruffled it. "In the meantime, uncomfortable though it may be, you two might consider turning to your employer. Welland Herrington has more contacts in this city than anyone."

Charles and Beth exchanged a wordless glance, after which Charles rose and bowed politely.

"Thank you for your help," he said, as carefully expressionless as the Yama. "We'll take your suggestion under advisement."

The beautiful Xishi showed them out with a promise to contact them the moment she heard anything.

"Hell," Charles said, when they were alone again in the street. "That didn't get us anywhere."

It was dusk, with a few brave stars beginning to appear above the city's minarets. Beth had a sudden and uncomfortable sense of time passing too quickly.

"We can't wait for them," she said, utterly sure of it. "The Midarris don't understand how urgent this could be. We have to do something now."

Charles stared at her—*into* her, it felt like. She hoped he wasn't going to try to soothe her or claim she was hysterical. Then he nodded curtly. "I agree. Right now, we . . . care about the prince more than anyone."

His words filled her with a thankfulness too deep for words. She put her hand on his arm and squeezed. "We could go back to Pahndir's house. Question more of the staff."

"Yes," Charles said, covering her hand with his. "I, for one, would like to find out how 'sick' Pahndir's valet is."

Charles parked his motorcar in front of The Prince's Flame. The brothel was lit up like a party in full swing, music and laughter drifting out in bursts from the bright windows.

"The cat's away," Beth said, echoing his thoughts.

Charles stepped out of the car and frowned. "From the sound of it, the mice are drinking the cat's champagne." He looked at Beth across the top of the car, wondering if she was prepared for what he meant to do. He braced his arms on the warm metal. "Look, Beth, if we're going to get information, I can't ask for it politely. I have to play this as hard as I can."

"I understand," she said. "We have to go in there like conquerors. We have to treat them like they're subjects and we're the queen."

"Exactly," he said, though her analogy pushed his brows together. "So if you don't want to watch what I—"

"One moment," she said, lifting her hand to cut him off. Her attention had been caught by an electric hansom that was parked across the street. The driver sat on the outside rearward seat, perusing a paper in the circle of the nearest lamppost's light. Possibly he was unaware that his usual source of nighttime fares was closed for business. He looked up from his reading as Beth approached.

"Pardon me," she said, "I'll give you two gold crescents if you'll loan me your whip."

The driver looked down to where the item stuck out of the ceremonial holder on the side of his cab. He had no horse to use it on, but many hansoms displayed whips as a reminder of the tradition from which they'd sprung.

"*Two* gold crescents?"

"Yes," Beth confirmed, holding them up. "And I'll give the whip back if you're still waiting when we return."

He handed it over without protest, though his expression conveyed very plainly his belief that she was mad.

Charles eyed the weapon warily. The lash end had to be six feet long. "What do you intend to do with that?"

"Anything I have to," was her answer.

*All right,* he thought and led the way up the brothel steps. He didn't bother with the knocker, but simply pounded on the wood with his fist. Half a minute later, his favorite butler in all the world opened it.

"*You,*" the man snarled in annoyance.

Charles punched him in the nose and sent him stumbling back onto his arse. It was a good, clean hit, and the butler started bleeding almost at once. Charles glanced into the nearby reception room, where it looked like Pahndir's employees were making serious inroads in his liquor supply. One of the women was dancing naked—and not very well—on top of an ottoman. None had yet noticed what was going on.

"Where is Mr. Biban?" he asked the butler.

The man drew breath as if to yell for help.

"I wouldn't," Charles said, pulling a handy little pocketknife from his trousers. "Just speak softly and answer my question."

"Mr. Biban is sick," the butler babbled, trying to scramble farther back on the slippery marble tiles of the entryway. "He's not even here anymore. He's gone home to be nursed by his family."

The butler was a ready liar but a bad one. Charles jerked him up by the collar and let the knife spring open just beneath the man's double chin. "Where is Mr. Biban?"

"We locked him in his room," the butler gasped, so frightened he couldn't get out more than a whisper. "He wouldn't promise to be quiet. We had no choice."

Charles didn't have to force the growl from his chest; he was that outraged on Pahndir's behalf. "Take me to him," he ordered, shoving the butler toward the stairs, "and I might let you keep your fingers."

"I'll keep an eye on them," Beth said, pulling his gaze back to her. She nodded at the still-oblivious party crowd. "We wouldn't want anyone calling the Watch."

Charles observed the businesslike way she was tapping the whip against her palm, and decided he felt perfectly comfortable letting her stand guard.

After a few more shoves and growls, the butler led him to the servants' wing.

The valet hadn't just been locked in his room; he'd also been beaten and tied to a chair. He was a small man, but as soon as Charles freed him, he sprang up and struck such a ringing slap across the butler's face that the man fell dazed to the floor. He also dropped the handkerchief he'd been holding to his bloodied nose.

"Bastard," the butler's former prisoner spat, plus a few things worse in his own language.

Charles had some difficulty pulling the valet away to the narrow bed. "Hush," he said. "I need you to calm down and tell me where Pahndir is."

"I don't know!" Biban cried, clearly still incensed with his colleague. His scars stood out pale against his angry face. "They sold him up the river like Judas goats. The finest, most generous employer in all of Bhamjran!"

Charles pushed his shoulders down until he sat. "Who did they sell him to?"

"To that fat demon prince, Muto. He said he'd give them a bonus if no one reported His Highness missing for a week. That's why they tied me up!" He struggled against Charles's hold to get at the butler, who was now weeping with guilt and fear.

"He promised us the brothel," the miserable man pleaded. "He said we could run it."

"He'd just as soon kill you, you idiot! Prince Pahndir was the only Yama we could trust." The valet began to weep himself then, his tears affecting Charles rather differently than the butler's had. "He saved us all, and now he's probably dead."

"He's *not* dead," Charles said firmly, despite being far from sure. "Yamish royals don't like to kill each other. They think it's uncivilized. We simply have to find out where he's been taken and get him back."

Biban stopped crying as if an angel had stepped into the room and promised him his heart's desire. The hope in his eyes made Charles want to wince.

"I don't know where he's been taken," the valet said. "But I think I can guess who was hired to capture him."

---

Beth had been cogitating during the ride from the Midarris' house. She didn't know how to help Pahndir, and she desperately wanted to. *What would Tou do?* she'd asked herself. *What would Tou do?*

She'd scarcely been aware of what Charles was saying when the cabman's whip called to her.

*I know how to use this,* she thought as she watched Pahndir's ingrate employees carouse around his best parlor. The knowledge came not from her mind but from her muscles—muscles that remembered training extensively with this and other tools of the soldiers' trade. She itched to put those skills to use tonight, her fingers caressing the familiar leather-encased handle.

It wasn't right that a man like Pahndir couldn't expect basic loyalty from his staff. These servants had no honor. Worse, they were incompetent. A perfect stranger had been standing in their entryway for at least ten minutes and they hadn't noticed yet.

A pretty male in a blue silk robe lifted his champagne into the brilliant light of the electrified chandelier.

"I'm empty!" he cried, laughing. "Someone fill me up!"

Beth didn't hesitate for anger or thought. She let the whip flick out as precisely as a cobra's strike. The tip wrapped the stem of the crystal flute and yanked it from the young man's grasp. The glass shattered against the wall where she flung it, leaving the courtesan to yelp and shake his fingers.

All the lovely young people stared at her.

"Turn off the music," she said, finding its happy, tinkling racket offensive. "Now!"

She brought the whip down, hitting nothing this time but creating a *crack* that sent the crowd scurrying back. One of the girls—not the naked one—had her head about her. She ran to the gramophone to shut it off.

"Backs to the walls," Beth demanded. "Hands on your heads where I can see them."

She felt inordinately satisfied when they obeyed.

"Wh-what do you want?" stammered a boy with a thick accent.

Beth narrowed her eyes so effectively he shuddered. "What I want is for every one of you to be ashamed of yourselves. Barring that, you're going to tell me everything you know about your employer's unexplained absence."

Charles had been so engrossed in talking to Biban that he hadn't noticed when silence fell downstairs. He returned to find Beth scowling fiercely at the nervous servants, all of whom had their fingers laced atop their heads.

Beth knew he was there without turning around.

"He was taken by desert mercenaries," she said. "Their leader is a woman with a blue tattoo of a hawk beside her left eye. One of the girls saw her scale the wall next to her window. She says the group rode in and out on camels."

This was consistent with Biban's hypothesis.

"Good," he said, trying to hide his shock at her behavior. Beth's sisters liked to call her fearless, but this seemed another order above that. The servants were literally shaking in their shoes. "I believe we've found out as much as we can here."

Beth nodded, but before she accompanied him to the door, she pointed the whip at Pahndir's cowering staff. At least half of them flinched back.

"Remember," she said in a hard, cool tone. "You call the Watch on us, and we call it back on you."

She left with him then, her posture tall and assured. The cabbie from whom she'd borrowed the whip was gone when they reached Charles's Model P, but Charles had the impression she wasn't sorry to be hanging on to her new toy. He opened the passenger door for her, then walked around to the driver's side.

He noticed she sagged a little when she sat back, rubbing her forehead as if it hurt.

"I can identify the head mercenary," he said, knowing he couldn't delay telling her no matter how he dreaded it. "Her name is Sahel. She's a famous chieftain hereabouts, and she's the person Herrington has been visiting at night. I've seen them together, and I know they're lovers, though I can't be certain he was involved in Prince Muto's plot."

"I think we have to assume he is," Beth said, which seemed to depress her as much as it did him. "Damnation. I really didn't want to believe this of him."

Charles turned to her on the narrow seat, his arm stretched along its back, his knees bumping over and between hers. It was dark in the car, and their positions were intimate. It felt good to be this close to her, even in the midst of a mess.

"I'm sorry," he said. "I don't know how we're going to find him. Sahel's tribe are nomads. They could be anywhere in the Vharzovhin."

He expected Beth to tell him he had nothing to be sorry for. She was silent instead, her thumb worrying the fullness of her lower lip. Finally, she looked up at him and sighed. "I think I can track Pahndir, but I need to explain a few things first . . ."

Charles sat silent after she finished, presumably stunned. Beth struggled not to bite her thumbnail. She'd been less nervous in that parlor with the whip.

"Let me be certain I understand this," he said slowly. "You think the spirit of Hhamoun's ancient queen is possessing you."

"It doesn't feel like feel like she's possessing me per se—more like I can tap in to her memories."

"Because of your experience in this mysterious secret chamber, which no one's found but you."

He sounded as if he wanted to disbelieve her, but not as if he did. Beth wished this hint of acceptance made her happy.

"I know it sounds crazy," she admitted. "I didn't want to believe it myself. I simply don't know how else to explain the changes I'm going through. My mind isn't working the way it did before, and my body . . ." She shook her head and fought a blush, not wanting to discuss those details.

"I know you've gained a little weight—which suits you, don't get me wrong. But that's no reason to jump to conclusions."

"Charles, I used that whip to pluck a champagne glass out of someone's hand. Do you honestly think I could have done that if I were my normal self?"

To her surprise, he cracked a grin. "I'm beginning to think I've underestimated what 'normal' is for you. That, however, doesn't mean I believe you can track Pahndir's scent across the desert like a hunting dog."

"He did it, Charles. He found me halfway across the city from his house."

The memory of their experience at the sari emporium caused her to wriggle on the seat in dismay. She was suddenly, painfully aware of Charles's body heat, of the hardness of his knees against hers and the shadow of his broad shoulders in the lamplight. She remembered how his lips had felt when he'd taken her, how silken they'd been as he'd licked and suckled at her breasts. Her sex heated and grew soft, its inner muscles twitching teasingly. She'd been convinced her and Pahndir's lengthy lovemaking in the pool would sate her for a good, long while. If she could want Charles now, in spite of her worries, that assumption was erroneous.

She looked away, embarrassed to have Charles know. "We have to try, unless you can think of something else?"

"No." He turned and put his hands on the steering wheel. He reached for the starter and activated it.

As the engine buzzed to life, she had a sudden vision of them trying to rattle across the deepest desert in the Model P. Much as Charles loved this car, it barely got them back and forth from the dig.

"I know," he said, putting his pride and joy into gear. "We're going to have to appropriate Herrington's jeep."

# EIGHTEEN

Pahndir's luck, such as it was, ran out the following night.

Sahel's "camp" was a small tent village that seemed too impermanent to call a town. A crumbling stone wall and bucket suggested the presence of a functioning well. Scrubby vegetation surrounded the nomadic dwellings. Pahndir imagined they looked much as they had millennia ago: the same thin floor cushions and guy ropes, the same camel regalia decorating the densely woven goat's hair walls. Sahel's harem had their own tent, near the penned-up goats. Pahndir didn't see the men at all, though Sahel's lieutenants, Aran and Delilah, immediately ducked beneath the dull black door flap.

Perhaps visitation rights came with their status.

He had no way to judge if the men would help him. Were they treated harshly or cosseted? Was being taken against one's will reserved for aliens like him? Sahel had mentioned her harem was submissive when she was taunting him about Thallah. Perhaps he'd do better to come up with whatever plan he could without hoping for aid from them. Certainly, some plan was going to be necessary. The chieftain wasn't showing signs of intending to let him go.

Soon after they'd reached the camp, Sahel and the other women gave him water and a little bread, then led him to a rough latrine. He didn't protest the lack of privacy. At the moment, there seemed no point. Used to being considerably cleaner than his current state, he wanted a Yamish-style shower and a bar of soap almost enough to cry.

Both appeared to be out of the question. He was staked facedown and naked, spread-eagled on a blanket not far from Sahel's small cook fire. Whatever the hardness of their nature, sadism wasn't a genuine calling for this tribe—a hobby, maybe, but no calling. One of the women beat his back and buttocks in desultory fashion while Sahel, the master of this little world, prepared coffee for perhaps a dozen of her fellow tribe members. The steam from the pot smelled good, strong and dark, just as he liked it.

Pahndir, of course, was not invited to partake from the tiny cups. He was shifted onto his now stinging back, restaked, and held by those same leather-wrapped steel cables. The stakes were the weak point in the arrangement. He was certain he could pull them up and escape if his captors left him unsupervised long enough. If that miracle happened, he'd only have to figure out where to run.

*East,* he thought, having observed that much from their two-day trek. He could walk the distance if he had to, but perhaps he'd get the chance to steal a camel. That would lessen the likelihood that he'd blunder into quicksand and disappear for good. He wondered if he'd been missed, or if Muto had somehow prevented that. Would Beth worry if she didn't hear from him? Would she care enough to raise an alarm? Was it even possible to find him where he was? He didn't think he ought to count on help from Cor and Xishi. One rescue in a lifetime was more than most people got.

A slim, oiled hand settled on his penis, hardly interrupting the dark currents of his thoughts. Apparently uninterested in dealing with him yet herself, Sahel had ordered one of the women to sit next to him on the blanket. He braced himself for more mockery, his body seeming too exhausted to perform for its audience.

And then the female fingers tightened and pulled.

Unexpected sparklers went off in his sexual nerves, the sensations so delicious, so intense, no amount of willpower could have staved off his hardening.

Conversation stopped as his penis lengthened . . . and lengthened . . . and grew so thick the woman who was stroking him could no longer close her fist. With every pull, he was swiftly reaching full royal size. Pahndir's scrotum began to throb, the deep, dull ache his body's way of complaining that it wanted emptying. His balls were heavy at this point in his cycle, stuffed with stored-up seed. With his involuntary reaction to being caressed, they also grew tender.

He knew his reprieve was over. He was in rut, full-blown, no turning back, and no chance for any but the most fleeting release. He'd be lucky to think straight, much less escape. He didn't have a single doubt that Sahel would be aware of this.

"Well," she said, her slightly hoarse voice bringing an end to the lull. "Maybe this demon *will* be some use to us. Widad, since you brought him up, I give you permission to take the first ride."

Widad took the first ride, and some other nameless woman took the second. They didn't remove their clothes beyond the necessary or bare their faces. Their human energy affected him but, thankfully, not as much as it might have. He wondered if his body had become keyed to prefer Beth and Charles. But it didn't seem wise to think about them now. Pahndir steeled himself against enjoying his captors' gyrations, grinding his teeth to fend off a dry climax. His arousal could only rise now and not recede. The less he gave in to it at this stage, the better his chance of maintaining a scrap of dignity during the next four or five days.

Naturally, Sahel wasn't interested in his dignity.

She had a little whip, the tail no longer than her hand,

which she began to ply against the soles of his feet. She had a finesse her women lacked, and a perceptible interest in the process. The snaps of pain cut through his self-control, twisting into his unwilling pleasure until, slowly but surely, that pleasure swelled.

He was truly helpless, as he'd never been in any game he'd played with Thallah. Sahel wouldn't hesitate to do him lasting damage, or to kill him if the situation called for it. Under ordinary circumstances, the idea wouldn't have excited him, but with his heat pushing him so hard, the fear and shame powered through his bloodstream like the strongest aphrodisiac. Though he throttled back a groan, no one, and certainly not Sahel, could have missed the heightening of his responses.

"Get off him," Sahel ordered his current partner. "I'm going to bring him to his peak."

She brought him by the simple expedient of lashing the whip against his balls while she worked her sex up and down his cock. The pain was exquisite, in every sense of the word. She brought him over and over, each orgasm a brief explosion of pleasure that turned instantly to frustration.

By the time she tired, he was bloody—and humiliated beyond bearing. He hated his male organ then, with a passion his kind shouldn't have been capable of feeling. If someone had freed his hands and given him a knife, he would have harmed himself. Sahel was simply being who she was: a woman who'd learned cruelty paid, a punisher for hire. His body's needs were what had betrayed him, yet again, and when he'd finally thought he might taste freedom.

He shouldn't have allowed himself to hope. He'd have been better off if he'd never met Beth or Charles. He'd have been better off if he were still a prisoner of the pillow house.

He rolled his head against the coarse blanket, knowing his rampaging hormones were partially responsible for his despair. This was heat madness, and he'd survived it many times. He would come out the other side, if he could just hold onto himself.

Sahel rose from him, her body leaving his still hard, still aching with desire. He bit his lip against begging her to return.

"Wash him," she said to the others, her voice slurred with enjoyment from their little interlude. "Bandage his balls if they need it. Demons heal more quickly than humans. I expect he'll be ready to entertain us again tomorrow."

Pahndir squeezed his eyes shut, not wanting to contemplate facing this again. He hadn't moved for the women when they'd taken him. He'd cried out in pleasure and in pain, but he hadn't thrust. Every instinct in his body had screamed for him to do it, but he'd refrained.

He held on to that: his only lifeline. If the angry pulsing of his cock were anything to go by, that lifeline wasn't going to take long to fray.

# NINETEEN

Provokingly, Herrington had taken the electric jeep. Charles and Beth had to wait until the next morning to steal it for themselves. Rousing before daylight, they crept together to the garage. After all that had happened, it seemed strange to be alone in it again.

"There's one good side to this," Beth said as she refilled the storage compartment's water tank.

Charles wedged a box of medical supplies behind a blanket and gave her a look. Beth didn't want to think about what the bandages were for. Ironically, it didn't bother her at all to lay her nice, long whip on top of everything. Grimacing, and determined to claim her silver lining, she forged on.

"If Herrington is involved in this kidnapping, we know they haven't taken Pahndir any farther than can be driven in a night."

"Which leaves us how many miles of desert to search?" He shut the boot quietly, then walked to where she frowned at him. His hand came up to stroke her cheek as he strove for a lighter tone. "I say, Miss Philips, you do look fetching in my clothes."

She'd borrowed his shirt and trousers again, in part because they were sturdy, and in part because she didn't want to ruin one of her new outfits. Charles's eyes were calm as they gazed into hers—not optimistic but steady. Beth thought about how she'd wanted to slip into his room last night, if only so she wouldn't be worrying alone. She wondered if he wished she'd come, and if he'd have wanted to offer her more than a hand to hold.

"Charles," she said, ignoring the fillip of inappropriate sexual heat. "We have to get Pahndir back."

"I know." He pulled her against him for a long moment, long enough for his warmth to seep into her. His hands tightened on her back and then released her. "Let's get going before the staff wakes up."

They got going but not very far at first. They had to drive to all three of Bhamjran's desert-facing gates before Beth picked up a whiff of Pahndir's spicy lemon scent.

With the sun rising behind them, the shadows of the city's palm trees stretched across the sand.

"You're sure it's him you're smelling?" Charles asked.

"I'm sure," Beth said and hoped he wouldn't ask how she knew. Pahndir's scent had tightened her nipples like they were being pulled, and her sex was liquid and warm. She hadn't expected this reaction when she'd volunteered to act as bloodhound, but, well, as long as it worked.

"That way," she said, pointing past the distant outline of Hhamoun.

They followed the scent as closely as possible, but there were places even Herrington's Tesla-powered demon vehicle couldn't go. Some dunes were simply too towering, and many wadis twisted like snakes without a hint of a road to promise a way through. Then they had to follow established, navigable tracks until they picked up the trail again. That could be a laborious process, involving driving back and forth and stopping dozens of times while Beth got out to sniff. She was ready to weep with frustration by the time the flaming ball of the sun reached its noon zenith.

"You're doing fine," Charles said, patting her knee. He wore a brimmed straw fedora, but it hadn't stopped his face from turning pink on top of its tan. The glare beat up at them from the sand as well as down from the sky. "Drink some water. Eat one of the sandwiches I packed. You'll find the trail again when you relax."

"You're so patient with me," she said, which made her want to cry even more.

Charles spread his hands and smiled crookedly. "All I have to do is drive. Anyway, if camels could get where they've taken Pahndir, so can this baby."

He patted the metal dash with masculine fondness. Beth wanted to kiss him, wanted to hold his lovely sunburned face and slide her tongue against his. Her body was tense with desire, the flesh between her legs heavy and swollen. Having him forge through those folds was what would relax her, having him push his smooth, hard cock high inside her sheath.

"What?" he asked when she wet her lips.

There was something wrong with her, there absolutely was. No woman should be obsessing about sex—and with another man—at a time like this.

"Nothing," she said, shaking herself. "You should drink some water, too."

Patience notwithstanding, Charles almost didn't believe it when they found the camp. There it was, though: tiny peaked black bumps sticking up on the shimmering horizon. Knowing better than to drive closer, in case there were sentinels, Charles turned the engine off and stared. He couldn't doubt the settlement was Sahel's. It was too great a stretch that Beth would find *any* people in this desolate sea of sand.

It seemed she hadn't been deluded. Something supernatural really had happened to her in the ruins of Tou's palace.

"Wait." He caught Beth's arm as she started to exit the car. "We need a plan."

"Charles," she groaned, and something about the sound struck him as odd.

Her face was flushed, which wasn't strange considering they'd been sweltering all day, but the color seemed more than sunburn. Her lips were swollen, despite being protected by the balm she'd applied. Their satiny curves were parted, and she was breathing faster than normal. Her pupils looked larger than normal, too, turning her honey eyes to molasses.

*She looks aroused,* he thought. *She looks like she did before we made love, almost desperate to be fucked.*

Blood surged uninvited to his groin, tightening his linen trousers against his cock. He knew the reaction was wrong; he shouldn't have been thinking of anything but Pahndir's safety. All the same, he hardened like Beth was the last woman in the world and he hadn't enjoyed relief in years. It was probably his imagination, but he thought he could smell *her*. His nostrils flared at the elusive scent. It smelled like she'd described Pahndir's: lemons and cinnamon.

*And sex,* he thought, the veins in his groin dilating in unison. *Don't forget that.*

Without thinking, his fingers fanned the skin at her wrist.

"Charles," she whispered.

He leaned in and kissed her with a low pained moan, a sound she sent back to him. Their tongues welcomed each other—wet, greedy, warm—and then she pushed back from him, panting.

"In case we don't make it," he rasped, because that explanation didn't sound as bad.

She touched his cheek, laying her palm and fingers gently against the skin. Her eyes were welling with emotion, the tears nearly spilling onto her lashes. He knew she was as glad as he was that they were acting like friends again.

Charles looked away, unable to hold her gaze. He'd be crying himself in a minute, and he was damned if he felt comfortable doing that. He cleared his throat. "I think I have a plan for how we could walk straight into that camp."

Beth drew her thumb along his jaw. "Does it involve me bringing my new whip?"

The hint of humor in her voice had his lips twitching. What other woman could have asked him that? As to that, what other woman could have stolen his heart so completely while making it feel like a privilege? She had the power to break him and seemed likely to do so eventually. Despite that knowledge, he'd never loved her as he did at that moment. Considering he'd been loving her damned hard for nearly a decade, that said something.

"It might involve bringing your new whip," he said, tapping her nose with a light finger. "In fact, it might involve you using it."

Beth prepared herself as well as she could. She and Charles slapped the worst of the dust off, and she'd combed and braided her windblown hair. Her new whip was tucked into the back of Charles's trousers. He'd stashed something in the boot of the jeep while she wasn't looking: a pair of brass "knuckle-dusters," as he called them. He slid his fingers into the holes, briefly examining the fit before dropping them into his right pocket. The motion looked like something he'd done before.

"You'd hit a woman with those?" Beth asked.

Charles was tucking his pocketknife into his boot. "I'd hit a puppy if it meant my life. Or yours." He straightened and shook his trouser leg back down. Beth couldn't help noticing he still looked natty. "Never underestimate your opponent and never hesitate. Either will get you killed faster than anything."

"You've been in fights before."

"They were a daily occurrence at one period in my life." He squeezed the ball of Beth's shoulder. "I'll have your back, Beth. Hell, I'd have your front if I thought a woman like Sahel would take any man seriously. Just look like you're willing to fight, and chances are you won't have to."

"Chances are."

His mouth slanted in amusement. "You said yourself you're stronger than you used to be. Plus, you have Tou's memories to help you. Just pretend you're the queen, and you'll have those women quailing the same as Pahndir's staff."

Beth doubted that, but she appreciated the attempt to bolster her confidence. She wished she knew how to call Tou to her like the spiritualists who worked the Street of Fortunes. Though she closed her eyes and thought of the queen, she experienced no tingle, no sense of otherworldly presence.

On the other hand, she did receive an awareness that Hhamoun's queen had been a world-class liar.

*Better than nothing,* she thought and rolled her tense shoulders. She was no slouch at lying herself.

She and Charles could have spared themselves the tramp across the sand from the motorcar to Sahel's camp. No guards had been posted on the perimeter. A goat looked up at their arrival, silvery green leaves trailing from its mouth, but that was the extent of the alarm they raised.

Charles pointed at the largest of the worn black tents. "I hear noise coming from in there."

The sound was a rising and falling murmur, reminiscent of an audience in a theater. The closer they walked to its source, the more Beth's body reacted. There was quite an assortment of scents in that primitive desert camp, but Pahndir's was thick in the air, seeming to drown out the rest. Her heart pounded harder, the surging of her blood to her most sensitive places making it difficult to breathe normally.

She caught Charles's hand a few feet from the entrance.

"He's in there," she whispered. "He's alive. I can feel him really strongly now."

The hold she took on Charles's fingers wasn't just to get his attention. It was tight, possessive, and probably a bit sexual. She let go, but not before his gaze flicked to the tips of her breasts. Though the glance lasted only a moment, it told her more than she needed to know just then.

Charles sensed what Pahndir's nearness had done to her.

"All right," he said, his voice carefully steady. "If he's alive, we have even more reason to give this ruse everything we've got."

He spread his palm against the small of her back. His touch was hot and sweaty but comforting. She'd already pulled out the whip and held it coiled in her right hand. She drew a breath and set her jaw.

*I am a goddess,* she told herself, echoing the message of Tou's black chamber. *I eat desert chieftains for breakfast.*

Charles lifted the tent's door for her, and she ducked through.

The interior was dark and stuffy, the only light coming from tiny rips in the goat-hair walls. Her eyes searched the dimness for Pahndir first. The choice wasn't strategic, but she couldn't help herself. When she found him, her heart gave a tremendous lurch, as if pushing a large enough volume of blood with a single beat could save them all.

Pahndir was very naked. He'd told her his people removed their body hair, but seeing him completely bared momentarily startled her. He'd been bound upright to a substantial wooden frame, his legs and arms spread wide. Slim strips of leather held his ankles and wrists secure. The position elongated the muscles of his upper body and bunched the ones in his legs, making him seem both more powerful and leaner. He reminded her of a pagan sacrifice: insurance that the rains would fall or the river rise. Thin red lines crossed his naked skin. Apparently, he'd been beaten to the edge of bleeding and left there. His eyes were shut, his face the hard, icy mask his kind were famous for. Only his hands revealed the strain he was under. They were fisted so tightly within his bonds that the veins at his wrists stood out.

The cause of his strain knelt before him, between his widely planted feet. She was sucking his erect penis, her head bobbing up and down the upper part of his shaft. She pulled all the way off him with each movement, baring the bulging, spit-shiny head.

The first time the fullness of his sex emerged, it was all Beth could do not to let her mouth hang wide. He was bigger than any drawing in a picture book, bigger than he'd been the night they watched Charles feed the Yamish courtesans with his energy. The woman couldn't take more than a third of him between her lips. One of her hands pumped his base with a seemingly steely grip, beneath which his balls swelled impressively. They, too, were scored by whip marks.

Beth knew she couldn't comprehend how much that must have hurt.

The mere thought caused every nerve, every muscle, every tender crease between her legs to contract, a reaction that thoroughly unnerved her. It wasn't pity—or not entirely. Fluid ran from her in a shocking rush. The evidence of Pahndir's suffering was arousing her. She wanted to soothe his pain more than she wanted her next breath, but she didn't precisely want that pain to stop.

The realization had barely finished rolling through her when Pahndir opened his eyes and looked straight at her. His pupils were large already, but the instant he recognized her, two shining wells of solid black overtook his eyes.

Her heart contracted in another galvanic beat.

"Well, isn't this a scene?" Beth drawled before he could speak and inadvertently ruin their plan. "I see why your women couldn't bear to stand guard and miss out on this."

She turned to the female who best matched Charles's description of the chieftain. Sahel had been watching her underling's performance with her arms crossed and her shoulder braced on one of the tent's supporting poles—the image of superior boredom. When Beth addressed her, a spark of temper lit the woman's cool, dark eyes.

"Who the hell are you?" Sahel demanded.

She pulled her veil down beneath her chin, which seemed to be a sort of challenge—as in, *All who see my face must die.* The chieftain had the hardest features Beth had ever seen on a woman—with cheekbones like blades and a jaw to match. In addition to the hawk tattoo beside her eye, her skin bore slender knifemark scars. Their rays formed a symmetrical crisscrossed pattern, and Beth knew she hadn't gotten them in a fight. They were deliberate: a proof of courage. Marked or not, Sahel was striking, even beautiful if one weren't afraid. Tou wouldn't have been afraid, of course; respectful, but not afraid.

"I'm Prince Muto's assistant," Beth said.

"His assistant." Sahel's disbelief was obvious.

"The term does cover a lot of territory."

"The prince wouldn't hire a human."

Sahel's objections were playing out so closely to Charles's predictions that her very doubts shored up Beth's nerve. "He hired you, didn't he? Not that it matters, seeing as I'm only half human. Perhaps Welland mentioned me? I'm Roxanne Herrington, his daughter."

Sahel couldn't quite pull off a demon's stony face. A muscle flickered beside her tattooed eye. That flicker told Beth that Herrington didn't know his lover had been hired to abduct his countryman, and that she wanted it to stay that way. The reaction also told her Charles's cover story was a good idea. Sahel thought of herself as above the ordinary run of human female. A half demon was more likely to intimidate her, thus rendering her less likely to force a fight Beth and Charles might not win. No matter what the secret chamber had done to her, these were hardened warriors they faced. With Pahndir bound, they were seriously outnumbered.

They were also seriously outarmed. No less than twenty mercenaries milled about the tent. Dagger hilts and other unidentified weapons gleamed among their black clothing—and that was in addition to the arsenal hanging on the walls. With an effort, Beth tore her eyes from the display.

"I've heard of you," Sahel admitted, her arms uncrossing reluctantly. "You're the half-demon Northerner who paints pictures."

"It sounds so flattering when you put it like that."

Sahel didn't return her smile. "Why are you here?"

"Just making sure you're treating Muto's special friend with appropriate severity. I must say, it doesn't seem as if you are. I know he's Yamish, but what kind of torturer can't bring a prisoner to tears?"

Three of the women stepped toward Beth at this insult, their expressions hot and threatening.

"I wouldn't," Beth said, caressing her whip with a fondness that wasn't feigned. "None of your hides have any value to me."

Sahel ordered them off with a small hand motion. She kept her narrowed gaze on Beth. "I suppose you think you can do better."

"Oh, I know I can."

Pahndir made a soft, involuntary sound, his first since she'd entered. Protest seemed to lie behind it, but at a stretch it could have been interpreted as a moan of longing. Beth didn't dare do more than glance at him from the corner of her eye. His body seemed tenser than it had been before, the muscles standing out like they'd been carved from stone. His sexual tormentor had moved away from him, more concerned with defending her leader than continuing to work on him. Left alone, his cock stood straight and unmoving, dusky, thick, the eye so dark it seemed unnatural.

Sahel was staring at Beth, clearly trying to gauge how seriously she needed to take her. For one such as the chieftain, to challenge Beth and lose would be intolerable. Beth allowed a faint smile to touch her lips as she waited for Sahel's verdict.

"You might enjoy the show," she coaxed softly.

The words were all the excuse Sahel needed not to press the issue immediately. She made a mocking *be my guest* gesture with one arm. Beth stepped forward . . . only to have two of the women move to block Charles.

"I don't tolerate men in my tent," Sahel explained.

"But Charles is *my* assistant. And very useful in this particular instance."

Sahel's lip curled in a sneer. "Prince Muto said this one liked men. The males of my harem know better than to settle for the attentions of the inferior sex."

"Do they? Locked up by themselves in that little tent with nothing to do all day? Perhaps you're right, but if it were me, I'd wonder."

It was the scene in Pahndir's parlor all over again. Beth's arm shot out almost before she'd registered that the mercenary was rushing her. The heel of her palm caught the attacker's chin, snapping her mouth shut and sending her stumbling back into a companion's arms. The woman spat blood and swore, the lightning swiftness of Beth's blow having caused her to bite her tongue.

Beth did her best to act like she did this sort of thing all the time—as opposed to having stunned the hell out of herself.

"Stop," Sahel barked, when another of her women prepared to charge. The chieftain crossed the tent to stand in front of Beth. She was taller than Beth by an inch or two, her eyes as flat and hard as stones. "I advise you not to try your demon tricks on me, daughter of Herrington. You'll find you're not so lucky against a seasoned warrior."

Sweat trickled down Beth's back as she schooled her face into an expression of mild humor. She knew she was treading a dangerous line. "I rarely rely on luck. At the moment, though, I'm more interested in carrying out my employer's charge. Do my assistant and I have your permission to proceed?"

Sahel lowered her brows in warning. "You do. Just see that you mind your tongue."

As she advanced across the large round tent, Beth could feel Charles's tension coiling. Some of that tension was arousal. His face was carefully empty, but she could see it in the way he walked, could smell it in the musky scent that mingled a bit too appealingly with Pahndir's. She and

Charles hadn't specifically discussed what they'd do after they'd talked their way past Sahel, though Muto's history with Pahndir suggested the prince's torture would be sexual. *We'll play it by ear,* was what Charles had said. Clearly, more lay behind that attitude than a wish to be practical. He might be ashamed of his erotic interests, but he wasn't running from them now. Two of Sahel's women nudged each other and nodded at Charles's crotch. Able to imagine what they must be ogling, the muscles of Beth's sex flexed hard.

The intensity of her need for both men frightened her. If they survived this, neither Charles nor Pahndir seemed likely to be safe from her.

Obliged to ignore that fact, she stopped in front of Pahndir. His lips were parted for his ragged breathing, the gauntness of his face hard to bear. He was in pain, and not only because of his heat. She reminded herself that his race had great recuperative powers, but it was difficult for her to stand this close and not rush to comfort him.

She tapped the coil of her whip in the opposite palm, as if considering where to start. "Stand behind him," she said to Charles, her voice as cool as she could make it. "I don't want that pretty face of yours to get lashed."

Charles obeyed without a word, the perfect dignified subordinate. Pahndir must have understood what was coming. His body began to move, a slow, helpless writhe against the smooth wood frame. He was like a cat trying to scratch its back, except she knew this particular cat would rather have remained still. He simply couldn't stop himself, any more than she could stop her nostrils from flaring at the rising sting of his scent.

Her borrowed trousers seemed to cup her pubis closer than clothing should.

"Yes," she murmured, too aware of the flooding heat between her legs. "You like the idea of being whipped by an expert."

She said the words as part of her role, but they caused a flush to sweep in a wave up Pahndir's throat and face. His muscle-ridged belly jerked. As clearly as if he'd said it, she knew it wasn't an expert he wanted whipping him, it was her: the woman he cared about and was attracted to. The knowledge disturbed her even as it titillated. To be learning this intimate thing about him now was unnerving. But she couldn't afford to be distracted. Despite the wariness he'd put on for Sahel, she could tell he knew she and Charles were here to rescue him. That he wasn't feeling betrayed was a great relief, though it could not ease her other hundred concerns.

To her dismay, Beth realized she'd been caressing the whip all this time. She felt a little too ready to use it, a little too hungry to cause him the pain she now suspected he'd enjoy.

She licked her lips, a nervous gesture she wished she could call back. Would Sahel let her get away without doing this? Beth truly wasn't certain she could trust herself, no matter what Charles advised about showing no weakness.

But it seemed Pahndir read her hesitation as easily as she did his arousal. He tossed his glorious black hair in scorn.

"I don't care who you are," he said, his voice as raw as if he'd been screaming. "You won't make me cry with that human toy."

He took the choice from her, forcing her to perform the very act she'd hoped to avoid. The realization hardened her resolve, made her speak as the emissary of his enemy actually might.

"I don't have to make you cry with this," she said. "I only have to get you ready to."

# TWENTY

Beth was here. She was *here*. And Charles was with her. The two people he most wanted to give a damn had come for him. He hadn't been abandoned by the world again after all. Such joy suffused Pahndir at their arrival, so strong, so fierce and irrational, that at first he hadn't recognized the truth.

Happiness wasn't the only powerful reaction humming through his bones. Pahndir's kith had begun to rise.

The instant Beth's golden eyes had met his across the tent, the swollen glands in his neck convulsed, flooding his mouth with the distinctive tart-sweet taste of his body's personal love philter. The influx dizzied him as much as the prospect of rescue.

Dizzy or not, he knew what the reaction meant. Beth could mate him. Beth could make him spill. If they kissed, his kith would flow to her, would seduce her, until she was as mindlessly wild to have and have and have him as he was to have her. After two long years of searching, he finally had his answer.

It was just his bad luck that the Universe chose this impossible moment to deliver his heart's desire.

His stinging, all-black eyes fell to the whip he had just obliged her to use on him. He'd known he had to push her to it; Sahel would not be satisfied with less, and all the same his body shuddered, wracked by unnatural lusts he could not suppress. Nothing could be more forbidden for a Yama than to lose control, unless it were to fall in love, which made having Beth be the one acting out this dark fantasy a good bit beyond too much. The circumstances couldn't quell his cravings: the danger, the unfriendly eyes. In truth, they were a stimulus. He did indeed want this enough to cry.

Beth's huge eyes took in the nuances of his expression, her own cheeks flushed with sensual heat. He hoped the humans couldn't see their color in the low light. He wanted her desire to be a secret for him alone—and not only because that was safer.

"Well?" Sahel said from a distance more than the stretch of the tent could account for. "Are you going to show us your skills or not?"

Beth's gaze slid to Charles and then returned to him.

"I am," she said, her voice touched by a hoarseness Pahndir suspected only he could hear.

She let her hands relax, and the whip uncoiled like a snake to trail on the floor. A shiver ripped down Pahndir's vertebrae, ending in a ghostly finger's touch beneath his tailbone. His kingmaster gland felt like it had tripled in size and sensitivity within the last minute, a hot, pulsing itch inside his rectum. The feeling was a familiar symptom of his heat, but with the liberation of his kith, his nerves were in overdrive. Pahndir had a second to fight the urge to grind the muscles of his rear against each other, to soothe that terrible burning. Before he could, Beth swung her arm and brought the whip alive.

He hadn't known what to expect of her technique, and probably hadn't cared, but the precision of the strike stole a gasp from him. The whip snapped the air a millimeter above his skin, licking it enough to sear him, though not enough to draw a single bead of blood. A moment later, the leather licked again, crossing the first mark to form a perfect X across his chest. His nipples tightened into points just above the ends of the two hot lines. The wounds the tribeswomen had inflicted felt like nothing compared to these; theirs were crude injuries, barely worth crying out over. But Beth found nerves that shot sensation to his sex in long lightning bolts, as if pain had always been designed to engender bliss, as if she had a secret road map to his body.

The effect was like alchemy. In the space of a few taut seconds, she'd transformed what Sahel's women had done to him, showing him the difference between what he wanted and what he had received. Though it made him shudder, he suspected he was about to get a better, truer version of what he desired than he'd ever known.

Without a pause, Beth set two neat Xs over his left thigh, then two matching ones over his right. Her eyes were hard and glittering, the eyes of a woman he'd never met before. She was breathing deeply, but not out of breath. Her lungs filled, her hard-tipped breasts expanding beneath Charles's shirt. The whip whistled yet again. This time the tail curled like a lover around his buttock. The skin there bloomed and pulsed with flame. She laid six stripes on either side of his arse in quick succession, her motions almost too quick to track. Seeing that, he was willing to believe she was half demon.

Then she stopped and stepped back.

A smattering of applause broke out from Sahel's women. Until he heard it, he didn't realize how completely Beth had decimated his restraint. He was struggling violently in his bonds, writhing as he gasped for air. The single sound that tore from his throat was dangerously close to a sob.

"There," she said. "That ought to have warmed you up for Charles."

He groaned, his dread and arousal not remotely a sham.

His dignity meant nothing then. He was on fire, inside and out. He wanted Charles's cock inside him, driving over and over his tormented kingmaster gland, wanted Charles's hips slapping the brands Beth had put on him. He wanted to be hurt as much as he wanted to be pleasured, wanted to be erased and remade with lust. Most of all, he wanted to be overwhelmed.

*Please,* he thought, biting his lip against begging aloud. *Please do it now.*

"Take him," Beth ordered Charles. "And, for God's sake, don't be nice."

When Charles had worked at the top hat club, he'd sometimes performed in front of customers, but none of those occasions had affected him like this. Lord in Heaven, he was *hard*, so stiff and hot he couldn't keep his hands from shaking as he unbuttoned the stretched front of his trousers and peeled the sweaty cloth apart. The role he was playing, the role *he'd* made up, had settled over his skin too easily. To be answering to Beth's orders, to be preparing to torment Pahndir at her behest, had his cock throbbing in agony.

The prince was at their mercy, very nearly broken by lust. The knowledge sizzled through his brain like a sexual drug.

Charles was fortunate he'd already taken advantage of the crowd's distraction to slip the pocketknife from his boot. He doubted his presence of mind was up to palming it now. Grimacing, he hooked both thumbs into his trousers and pushed the garment to his hips.

His cock bounced free from its constraints, heavy and alive. Voices murmured in admiration, but he ignored them to step closer to Pahndir. The heavy frame the prince was tied to gave Charles full access to his back. As if he sensed Charles approaching, muscles twitched beneath his smooth, pale gold skin. His narrow buttocks were knotted, heat rolling off his body as if from a fire. When Charles took hold of his cheeks to part them, a soft, pained sound broke from the prisoner.

Charles suspected it wasn't a reaction to the stripes Beth had put there.

"He's going to take him anally?" one of the desert women asked, startling Charles but hardly putting him off. She sounded more intrigued than horrified.

"Yes," Sahel said. "Muto tells me royals have an extra gland in their rear passage. When they're in heat, rubbing anything over it drives them mad, especially since they can't ejaculate without a proper mate."

This talk of heat and glands was news to Charles, but when he glanced at Beth, she didn't appear surprised. Looking genuinely autocratic, she motioned with her fingers for him to go on. Maybe she really did intend to make Pahndir cry. Maybe a demon's pride seemed a small price to pay for his freedom. Charles had no inclination to object, though that shamed him.

His marching orders clear, he continued pulling Pahndir's cheeks apart, finding the little opening tightly furled. Pahndir's hairlessness inspired a frisson of surprise, followed by a stronger shiver of interest. Lines of perspiration gleamed on the rounded, satiny flesh, joined by fresh ones even as he watched. Pahndir was nervous, but not from lack of desire.

He'd be dry, of course, and sweat wasn't lubrication enough. Charles would hurt him if he took him now, something Beth—in her inexperience—might or might not know. Discovering he'd rather not rip into him, even for the sake of verisimilitude, he went to his knees and drew his tongue up that warm furrow.

Pahndir bucked in shock, a moan of pleasure dragged unwilling from his heaving chest.

"My, my," Sahel said. "Isn't your assistant the considerate one?"

"We have our methods," Beth said just as dryly.

Charles continued licking until Pahndir was wet, until the Yama trembled with more eagerness than he could hide. Caught by a dark compulsion, he probed the puckered entrance with the tip of his tongue. Pahndir cursed in his own language. Then, using Pahndir's waist for support, Charles pulled himself up.

Pahndir was taller than Charles, but with his legs splayed the way they were, Charles's cock rose to exactly the right height. He discovered he could have forgone the tonguing. He was so excited his penile slit was weeping pre-ejaculate. All the same, he couldn't regret what he'd done. It was worth it to have stirred the prince so violently. Pahndir jerked when Charles pressed the head against his anus. Charles didn't give him a chance to fight, but pushed the flaring crest straight inside.

He wasn't certain which of them choked back a sound of bliss. Pahndir was hot and silky and tight, clutching him so snugly Charles was forced to penetrate him with extreme slowness. As gently as he thought he could get away with, he slid his hands up Pahndir's clenching arms, as if he were in need of a handhold. As soon as Charles got the chance, the pocketknife would be in the right position to cut his restraints—though Charles was hoping the chance wouldn't come too soon.

Right or wrong, taking Pahndir this way had to be one of the most intense pleasures Charles had ever felt. Knowing he needed to do it to save him—and that guilt was utterly pointless—he had waves of exultation crashing through his nerves. He wanted to store up each sensation, each sight and sound and smell. He didn't see how doing exactly what he wanted would ever be this wonderful and right again.

And then the sensitive tip of his cock hit a swelling he didn't expect, presumably the "extra" gland Sahel had mentioned. Charles had felt men's prostates before, but this was not the same. This was bigger, hotter, and quite obviously a potent trigger for delight.

Pahndir hissed in a breath as the rim of Charles's cock slid over the bump. That, apparently, made him want more of the same. His spine arched, the muscles gathering before he shoved back with his hips as hard as he could. The effort drove Charles more directly over the swollen gland, all the way across it instead of just to the edge. The pressure felt phenomenal to him, pure carnal enchantment against the upper curve of his glans. He had to clench his jaw against a too-swift rise of his own excitement. Pahndir might not be able to ejaculate, but Charles certainly could. He wouldn't look like much of a torturer's assistant if he shot his store in two strokes.

Though it was to all their benefit to convince Sahel this was real, Pahndir didn't appreciate Charles's pause. Grunting with frustration, he writhed backward again, unexpectedly driving Charles to the hilt. He only stayed there a moment. The full penetration had widened Pahndir's inner muscles enough to move freely. Obviously liking that, the prince was growling behind clenched teeth, working himself over Charles's cock as if he had some itch only the hardest friction could ease. His fervor left Charles at a loss for how to respond.

"Let him," Beth said, seeing his dilemma. "And thrust yourself if he stops. He'll be all the hotter for a few dry orgasms."

She'd moved closer than Charles realized, and had curled one hand over the tensing muscles between Pahndir's neck and his forcibly outstretched arm. Her eyes met Charles's, the air that connected them seeming to ripple like a heat mirage. Was this Pahndir's energy he was seeing? Was it theirs? And just how insane was it making their mutual victim?

Quite, it looked like. Pahndir's head dropped back with a louder groan, his Adam's apple straining. Charles wasn't the only one moved by his urgency. Beth's pupils were huge, her respiration shallow. The big wood frame creaked with Pahndir's desperate struggles to achieve release. The apparatus's legs were staked deeply into the ground, but Pahndir's agitation was testing their stability.

"I'm going to cup his balls," Beth said, though for whose benefit Charles didn't know.

He remembered the whip marks Sahel's women had left on Pahndir's scrotum, the exaggerated swelling a blind man could not have missed. Blood spurted harder into his cock.

"No," Pahndir breathed so softly it was as if the air itself whispered.

"Yes," Beth said, her smile curving half a second before Pahndir screamed.

He didn't mean to scream, but—Infinity help him—Beth couldn't know what she was doing by playing with his testicles. All Yama loved that, but royals especially. A good, deep massage loosened up the seed that accumulated over their cycles, and Beth's strong, slim fingers were really digging in. The sting of the healing whip marks only made it worse, the perfect blend of pain and pleasure—or, at least, perfect to him.

Pahndir shifted his weight in sensual anxiety. His balls were so fucking heavy, like someone had turned on a hose. He'd have no chance at all of holding back ejaculation, not if she slid her sex over him. The chemistry of her cream would trigger reactions no amount of self-control could stop. Sahel would know something wasn't right if he spilled his seed. He was supposed to suffer. That was the entertainment Muto had promised her. She'd probably kill them all if he—

The train of thought escaped him in a sudden deluge of bliss. Beth had put her second hand on his balls and was now squeezing him with both palms. His breath *whoosh*ed from him as his insides seemed to liquefy. Oh, fuck, she knew how to work him, her instincts superior to many women's years of practice. Her manipulations were so good, his muscles went too lax to thrust. Not that this did him much good: Per Beth's orders, Charles took up the job. He ran his thick erection over and over Pahndir's third kith gland, the thing so sensitive it was more than ready to make him come.

Pahndir was tired of fighting his arousal, exhausted from trying not to let it rise. His mind wanted more than anything to turn off. He pulled in air, seeking strength for his flagging determination, but it was too late. He was coming, dry but hard, the strong, tight spasms chasing up and down his genitals.

*More,* he thought. But the golden moment was gone. He'd shot up to the next plateau of frustration as if he'd never climaxed.

The logic his more primitive brain operated on said this wasn't right, not even remotely. Beth was so close to him, her breasts flattening on his chest, her panting mouth mere inches away. He yearned for her kiss so strongly he had to moan. He wanted to spill his kith down her throat, to share his madness and his esteem. That was how mating was supposed to be. Both partners were supposed to dive into the maelstrom.

When he licked his lips, she must have guessed what he was thinking.

"I can't," she breathed against his ear. "An enemy wouldn't kiss you."

He groaned, swallowing the kith himself so that the swimming in his head increased. She was right, though he couldn't quite remember why. He'd just have to wait for her sweet pussy, just have to pour his kith into her there. The thought inflamed him. His cock jolted longer, harder, until he wanted to bend in two from the pain. Sweat rolled down his chest and back in a steady stream.

"Bring him again," Beth said to Charles, loud enough for the others to hear. "He's almost where we want him."

Where they wanted him seemed to be completely out of his mind. Charles's pounding in his rectum intensified, squeezing the kith his kingmaster gland was so frantically producing into his seminal vesicles. Pahndir grunted as it tried to spurt from him. It wouldn't be able to until she took him, until she plunged her dripping sheath over his aching shaft. He could smell her overflowing with her own desire, the scent as heady as the strongest wine. He couldn't think of anything but that, couldn't want anything but to be inside of her.

Unless it was for Charles's hips to keep up their battering while he was there.

"Aren't you going to ride him?" asked a voice he couldn't recognize any longer. "We've heard demon cunts are as clever as human mouths."

He liked the voice then. It was urging his mate to do the very thing he wanted most. The prospect was enough to make him come again. He nearly did cry that time. The pleasure was too brief, too insubstantial. All it did was madden him. He forced his eyes open to meet those of his better half. The fire that flared behind her irises was dark and sweet.

"Beg me," she demanded, her voice as harsh as sandpaper. "Beg me to come onto you."

"Please," he groaned, unable to remember why he shouldn't.

"Please what?"

"Careful," cautioned the man who pumped so wonderfully into him from behind. "You don't want to get too distracted."

Pahndir dismissed that advice the way one would the buzzing of a fly. As long as the man kept moving, Pahndir wasn't going to regard a word he said.

"Please ride my cock," he ground out. "Please, goddess, ride me hard."

His mate wasn't listening to the man, either. Pahndir's words were the ones that spurred her. She undid her linen trousers and shoved them down. Luckily, the legs were wide enough to tug over her narrow boots. At the sight of her shapely limbs rising from the leather, he swallowed hard, drinking in lemon and cinnamon. The hem of the man's shirt hung over her pubis, but that was right. The three of them doing this together was right. He caught a flash of her gleaming slit before she slung her shapely, booted leg around his hip.

His cock was standing too high, shuddering flat against

his abdomen. Her slick, plump lips just glanced across the tip. The contact wasn't long enough to free the bursting pressure of his kith. His glans burned like coal, too swollen, too ready to explode.

"Please," he whispered, craving her wetness like a smothered man craved air. Something that might have been a tear rolled from the corner of his eye. "Please, please, please."

She seemed to welcome his desperation. Her fingers caught his shaft, pulling the pounding pole down to her. A moan tore from him as the juicy mouth of her sex cupped the distended knob. His kith shot out, a hard, concentrated burst like a miniature orgasm. His mate gasped in surprise, but a gasp was all she had time for. The madness took her almost instantly. She shoved herself down on him, fully, tightly, her muscles wet and rippling with hunger.

She ground her pleasure bud against him, but this was not required. With his kith inside her, every inch of her sheath became climactically sensitive. As soon as this became apparent, she began to undulate like a wild thing, avid to take in the pleasure everywhere she could.

A sob broke in his chest. Relief was the power behind it. Pleasure. Gratitude so deep it needed another name. The other man liked the sound. His hips churned harder into him from behind, offering more ecstasy, more hunger Pahndir could delight in. Streams of luscious human energy coursed into him with each surge, the exact vintage he'd been longing for. The man was tugging at the bonds that held Pahndir's wrists, though Pahndir couldn't imagine why.

When the man stopped and cursed, it might as well have been a foreign tongue.

"Shit," he said barely audible above the sounds Pahndir couldn't help making. "There's steel under these leather cords. My knife won't cut through it."

His mate ground her teeth together and gave her head a little shake, still trying foolishly to think. "What about the wood? Can you saw through that and free him?"

Pahndir didn't know why they cared. Who wanted to be free when there was such pleasure to be shared? He tightened his anus around the other's hard-driving cock, as thanks for the bliss he had already brought. The man had been saying something in a worried tone, but the words broke off as Pahndir's tricks made him forget himself. They were all shoving together then, harder, stronger, each slap of their bodies a delicious, reverberating blow.

The others' cries were music; better than caresses for his long frustrated lust. Release swelled inside him, thick, hot, like lava gathering beneath a slumbering volcano. He reached for the climax with all his might. Two years he'd waited. Two fucking years. His balls were so full they could not draw up, just lurch in and out in desperately eager pulses. His mate was fire around him, kith and cream trickling from her in a steady stream.

He snapped his hips so fast they must have been a blur.

"Oh, God," she said, high and thin, her fingernails biting into his back.

That tiny pain was nothing to the unbelievable discomfort in his genitals. He should have been going over. She was his mate. His friend. Every molecule of his being wanted to give itself to her. But maybe his body was too long out of practice. Groaning, he shifted the angle of his strokes to press a hotter energy spot inside of her, a swollen, coin-size patch beneath where her clitoris rooted. Despite his need, he rolled his hips with every ounce of skill he had. Her muscles moved over him like a Yama's, bringing him almost too much enjoyment to bear.

*Come,* he thought. *Please, love, come and bring me with you.*

She shivered and gasped and then she went over.

This was the explosion he'd been waiting for. Every vessel in his groin contracted at the blazing burst of etheric force. He needed no more kick to come than that, but suddenly the man went, too, driving so deep it felt like the force of his ejaculation would shoot out Pahndir's navel.

His own orgasm stuttered at the additional stimulation,

as if the very magnitude of the pleasure had confused his nerves. But it was right to have the man there. He was warm and kind and he fit them. He was another lovely piece of their biochemical puzzle. Pahndir tried to accept the addition, tried to will himself to keep coming. Before he had much time to worry, his sensations swelled more than twice as large. His cock convulsed from tip to root to balls, his stored-up seed erupting like it was indeed molten.

He roared with pleasure. *More,* said his delighted body. *Moremoremore.*

Wood splintered, then snapped to bits. The three of them tumbled to the ground in a pile, still fucking, still gasping for air and sanity.

Pahndir's hands were free, and that might have been the best thing of all. He poured himself into his mate with complete abandon, spilling, pumping, yanking her thigh up to wrap her close. The climax went on and on. He couldn't stop it, couldn't let go of her to save his life. He was reduced to less than an animal. All cock, all pleasure, all shooting seed and nerve and biological imperative. Into her and into her he worked his hips with all his strength. A puddle spread beneath her as he overflowed her sex with his white-hot spunk, and all he could think was that he wanted her to drown. Her spine arched hard as she came again, lifting both him and the sighing man behind him.

Her strength surprised him. Clearly, his mate was a woman to be reckoned with. She breathed a prayer to her human deity, after which his madness temporarily receded.

If coming like a volcano hadn't restored his cognitive power, he thought just maybe the rifle blast would have.

# TWENTY-ONE

"Stop!" Sahel ordered. "Stop, stop, stop!"

The sound of her shoving up the rifle's bolt to chamber the next round stood Beth's hair on end. The gun was a beautiful piece, dark oiled walnut with brass details. Surely a prized possession, the chieftain handled it with ease. Beth had a feeling the next time Sahel pulled the trigger, the bullet was going to rip a hole in more than the roof.

"You made him spend," Sahel accused, appearing to strain against an undignified impulse to stamp her foot. "You're not supposed to be able to do that."

"Well," Beth said, "at least I also made him cry. You can see the tracks on his face."

Sensing how fraught with danger this moment was, Beth tried to decide if she should squirm out from under Pahndir. Charles had already rolled off their pile, but Pahndir sprawled atop her, heavy as a corpse. Free or not, he didn't seem a good candidate for escape—unless she and Charles intended to drag him across the sand. Unbelievably, his shaft was still firm and full inside her, despite the veritable ocean of seed he'd spilled. His continued presence within her felt better than she could be easy with. He'd had the ejaculatory climax he'd been hoping for, and the handful *she'd* enjoyed had been nothing short of glorious.

That being so, shouldn't they both have been ready for a rest?

Sahel decided the issue by yanking Pahndir off Beth herself. Liberated from his weight, if not the distracting sight of his erection, Beth found sufficient coordination to pull on her pants. She was more than a tad embarrassed that she'd doffed them so readily. She'd gotten more involved in this pretense than she had planned.

Still holding Pahndir roughly up by one arm, Sahel swore as she observed the splintered ruins of his torture frame.

"You," she said to him, "are getting staked out on the ground again."

Pahndir was sagging in her grasp, his knees too uncertain to balance him. He gazed through the bedraggled curtain of his hair toward Charles, looking oddly feral in his disarray. Charles had set himself to rights the quickest of them all. He stood near one of the knife displays on the wall.

"Yes," he said in answer to some silent question Pahndir's eyes had asked.

With a sudden surge of excitement, Beth realized Pahndir was exaggerating his weakness. They were making their break right then, before Sahel figured out she had three enemies instead of one.

The prince spun into motion almost too fast for her eyes to follow, grabbing Sahel's rifle and breaking it—lock, stock, and blue-steel barrel—across his thigh. Chaos erupted in the tent as Sahel's warriors surged forward to quash this threat to their leader. Pahndir jabbed back with his elbow at Sahel, but his attempt to clip her jaw was stymied by the others.

"Here, Beth!" Charles called over the tumult. "Catch!"

She'd been gaping at the sight of Pahndir in full fighting

form, but Charles's shout jerked her out of it. As if they'd choreographed the move, Beth snatched the knife he'd tossed her out of the air. An exuberance that wasn't completely hers rose from her solar plexus, like a ball of heat expanding. Tou would have wanted a knife for each hand. Rather than ask Charles to toss her another, she filched one neatly from the weapons belt of the incautious tribeswoman who was charging her.

Not surprisingly, the next few minutes were a blur of violence and confusion.

Sahel's women came at Beth and she fought them off, sometimes with her daggers, sometimes with whatever body part was available to snap out at them. Being pummeled by women shocked her, for Sahel's warriors held nothing back. Nor were they above more traditional female tactics of gouging and pinching. Despite Tou's memories and Beth's mysteriously enhanced strength, she was soon bloodied and bruised. She wished she felt prepared to kill someone. That would have been easier than simply trying to defend herself. She could see she needed more practice drawing on Tou's ferocity if she was going to fight as well as the famous queen.

Her braid might have been her worst disadvantage. Beth was ready to lop it off herself the third time someone tried to swing her off her feet with it. Her neck wrenched from resisting, Beth drove the woman away with her knives . . . which gave someone else an opening to snake an arm around her neck from behind. Beth kicked back hard and heard bone snap, but the elbow choking her windpipe didn't ease at all.

*Boy,* she thought. These women didn't know the meaning of "cry uncle."

"We have you now," gloated one of the two tigresses who faced her. Their unrelenting assault made it impossible for Beth to turn her blades against the one behind her. She counted herself lucky that her strangler needed both arms to exert enough pressure.

And then, like magic, the throttling squeeze on her neck

was gone. Pahndir had plucked the woman off. He lifted her over his head and was tossing her like a log into a tent pole. Beth had a second to wonder if *she* was strong enough to do that, and then the wood cracked and bent in the middle as the body hit. When the woman fell to the ground, she joined three others who weren't moving.

Beth took advantage of the diversion to slice one of her attackers across the arm. She grimaced as blood spurted hot and coppery across her face. Some aspects of fighting she was never going to get used to.

"Sorry," Pahndir panted when Beth had a chance to glance his way. "Would have been here sooner. Not up to my normal strength."

She didn't have time to roll her eyes at that, because she'd spotted trouble on the other side of the tent. "Charles," she said, pointing.

He'd been backed into a corner by a crowd of women with sickle blades. Though most appeared worse for wear, they were overwhelming him with numbers. Looking far too tired for comfort, he was fending off their blows with an iron kettle.

"I'll get him," Pahndir said, pitching his voice for her ears alone. "See if you can shove over a second tent pole and slip out of here. Charles and I can cut our way out when the roof comes down."

"We have a car," she told him.

Pahndir's uncustomarily grimy face split into an equally uncustomary and blinding grin. He was off a second later, ducking and weaving on his way to the aid of Charles.

"I don't know why you'd rescue *him*," jeered a voice that spun her around. One of the veteran fighters faced her in a crouch, her face scored with the same crisscrossed scars as Sahel's.

"Yes," agreed her companion. "When I raped him with my wooden dildo, he fought like a little boy."

The inside of Beth's head went white and still. She felt Tou then, every ruthless memory, every protective instinct toward her men. It didn't in the least surprise her that

Sahel's harem had stayed hidden during this fight. Women without honor did not deserve to have their males defend them.

With the thought that these women really, really shouldn't have hurt *her* male, Beth ended the half a second she'd spent on the pause. Taking a page from Charles's book, she dropped one of her knives, grabbed a big iron skillet from beside the cook fire, and—in a single sweep—brained the two women hard enough to crumple them to the ground.

*That's more like it,* she thought, refusing to dwell on the fact that they weren't breathing. She didn't need to dilly-dally with the blasted blades; all she had to do was whack her enemies down.

With a quick glance to make sure Pahndir had reached Charles, she sidestepped her next would-be attackers and ran for what looked to be the nearest critical tent support. Her shoulder slammed into the pole at full speed, cracking it as her momentum carried her conveniently past it toward the closed door flap. A foreboding creaking circled the tent's structure.

Judging she had mere seconds to get out, she crouched and launched herself through the door as the tent collapsed. No one screamed (Sahel's women seemed immune to panic) but there was a satisfying bit of yelling. Deciding she might as well do what she could to head off pursuit, Beth hopped onto the top of the settling roof and swung with her big skillet at whatever wriggled and looked female.

She stopped when she heard Charles laugh.

He looked awful, his face distorted by goose eggs, his lip bleeding. He was on his feet, though, just like Pahndir. "I'll never again accuse you of not knowing what to do with a frying pan."

"Or a whip," Pahndir added sardonically.

Fresh tears leaked from his eyes in the outside light. The day was drawing to a close, but it still was too bright for him. He wore his own vivid embroidered robes, the silk extremely creased but recognizable. Sahel must have tucked his clothes away somewhere. As Beth absorbed the look of him dressed again, he wound one of the women's turbans around his head and face. Quick motions of his hands tucked his tangled black hair inside.

"Can't tolerate any sun at all," he explained. "It hurts the eyes when you're in heat."

His tone was matter of fact, but sensation tickled strongly between her legs. She was wet for him, beyond the wetness he'd already left. The realization that he remained in heat, that this wasn't over, coursed like flaming brandy over her skin. Oh, yes, she wanted more of what they'd shared, and she'd rather not wait for it. Her gaze dropped to the bobbing hummock that had reshaped his groin. Whatever showed in her face caused Pahndir to catch his breath. The sound was like catnip to her fresh desire. Beth looked into his jet-black eyes and took a step forward.

"Hey!" Charles snapped his fingers to recall them both to the present. "Some of those women are going to be waking up. We need to get to the jeep and ride the hell out of here."

"I'm driving," Charles announced before Pahndir could argue. He had no doubt the prince could operate this demon technology–inspired car, but the way he was devouring Beth with his eyes told Charles the prince's mind was not on practicalities.

Beth was no better. She was so busy mooning at Pahndir that she tripped over her own feet on their hurried journey back to the car. She would have pitched into the sand if Pahndir hadn't been quick enough to catch her.

Now the pair were holding hands. They slipped together into the dusty backseat of the jeep, leaving Charles to get in the front like their damned chauffeur.

There was no point whatsoever in the knot that was tying itself steadily bigger inside his chest. Given what he'd seen today, between the two of them, Charles knew he'd never be anything but a somewhat handy sexual third wheel.

"I'm so sorry we didn't find you sooner," Beth murmured to her lover. "I wish they hadn't been able to hurt you."

Pahndir shook his head as Charles scanned the landscape to make sure their tail was clear. "That's in the past now. The two of you turned my capture into something I'll be grateful for all my life."

"You fought so well," Beth breathed.

"So did you," Pahndir returned. "Like a warrior queen."

Charles turned the starter and suppressed a sigh. Neither of his passengers jumped when he gunned the engine and took off. Beth simply caught her balance by bracing both her hands on Pahndir's broad shoulders, an easy thing to do with their knees nestled so intimately together. Charles forced himself to tear his eyes from the sight of that in the rearview mirror.

"I suppose they didn't give you a chance to get away before we came," Beth went on. "Obviously, you were strong enough to free yourself."

"Strong enough, yes, but not fast enough to avoid having twenty knives flung into my back before I fled. I discovered I wanted to survive my escape."

"And why is that?" Beth's coquettish tone was not at all like her. Her face was turned up to Pahndir's like a flower soaking in the sun.

"I had things to live for. I had . . . hopes that were very precious to me."

"And now some of them have been fulfilled."

"Some." Pahndir cupped her chin. "The rest of my hopes are still aching."

*Oh, for Peter's sake,* Charles thought as Beth nuzzled Pahndir's palm. If they got any sappier, they were going to stick to the seat.

Oblivious to the danger, Pahndir tilted Beth's face back up. "I need to know, love: Was the story you told Sahel true? Are you half demon?"

"No!" she exclaimed. "I mean, I don't know. I don't think so. It's a *long* story."

Charles glanced at the mirror again and found Beth tracing Pahndir's mouth with her fingertips. Her emphasis on the word *long* had brought a grimace to the Yama's usually unrevealing face. Their gazes had locked together as if joined by a supernatural force.

"Maybe we don't need to talk right now," Pahndir said huskily.

"Maybe we don't," Beth agreed.

"Bloody hell," Charles muttered to himself as the sounds of wet, openmouthed kisses drifted to his unavoidably waiting ears. Both Beth and Pahndir were making throaty *mmm* noises, as if this were a feast and they'd been starving. When Charles heard clothing start to rustle, he'd had enough.

"So," he said loudly, trying and not quite succeeding to keep his eyes on the stretch of sand in front of the jouncing car. "How long does this 'heat' thing last?"

Pahndir broke free reluctantly, his chest rising and falling beneath Beth's caressing hands. "Four or five days. Under ideal conditions, we'd have sex continually during that time."

"Continually?" Beth asked, but not like she'd mind.

"Yes." Pahndir turned his head to meet Charles's eyes in the mirror. Seeing them solid black was like a kick to his gut, though exactly what the kick meant Charles could not have said. "It's hard for me to predict what heat will do to a human, but I'm afraid my kith has infected Beth."

"Your kith?" The electric jeep bumped over a rise Charles hadn't navigated carefully enough. The two lovebirds barely seemed disturbed.

"A hormone," Pahndir said, his darkened eyes back on Beth. "Royals secrete it in our saliva and pre-ejaculate. It acts as an aphrodisiac for mated partners."

Charles knew what hormones were. He'd read scientific journals on Yamish medicine—or as much of it as humans had access to. "Mating" he'd never heard of until the chieftain mentioned it. It sounded ominously permanent. He wondered if it explained the scent Beth had spoken of, but if it did, he didn't know why *he'd* be smelling it. The lemony-spicy fragrance wasn't his imagination, either. The pair were throwing it off like they'd swum in vats of perfume.

"Is your kith what I've been tasting?" Beth asked. "Maybe you should kiss me some more so I can be sure."

Pahndir didn't find her comment overly precious. He grabbed her shoulders and speared his tongue between her lips, pulling at her mouth until his cheeks hollowed. Kith was an aphrodisiac, all right. The prince looked like he was trying to swallow her whole.

That lasted for about a minute, after which Pahndir broke free again.

"Kisses aren't enough," he panted, though he'd been going at it pretty strong. "I need to— Oh, yes, untie your trousers. I'm dying to get my cock into you again."

Charles's eyebrows shot up his forehead. His passengers were changing positions, the prince moving hastily on top of Beth as she scooted down on the padded seat. Apparently, they were going to do this in front of him. Never mind that Pahndir was free, and putting on a show was no longer a strategic necessity. Beth's pants were yanked down her legs, and Pahndir's robes thrown open. To judge by Pahndir's gasp, her hands had just eased his prick out of his trousers.

"Can you come again?" she demanded. "Can you spill your seed into me?"

Charles bit back a curse that couldn't be aired in company.

"I can," Pahndir groaned. "Just move your hand to my balls, and you'll feel how heavy I still am." His body jerked as she performed this investigation. "Oh, yes, squeeze harder. Oh, that's perfect."

They writhed together in a tangle of arms and legs. Charles felt fresh sweat trickle down his skin. To make matters worse, the prince began murmuring to Beth with an expressiveness Charles wouldn't have thought his kind was capable of.

"Do you like it when I kiss your nipples?" he asked as Beth's long, naked legs climbed his sides. "Do you like it when I lick my kith over them? It makes them more sensitive, doesn't it? It makes you want me to suck them hard."

Beth moaned in answer, her back arching. The nipples in question were being offered to Pahndir's lips, the shirt she'd borrowed from Charles having been unbuttoned. Pahndir licked one lengthened peak, then sucked it greedily into his mouth. His effectiveness was impressive. When he released her first nipple to see to the second, the pebbled point was so red it glowed.

Charles's own nipples were itching, but Pahndir wasn't finished being vocal yet. His voice was hoarser than it had been in his imprisonment.

"What if I put the tip of my penis right against your pleasure bud? What if I spurted a little kith right there?"

He must have done it. Beth cried out like she'd been set on fire. She clutched at Pahndir in a panic.

"Put it inside me," she said. "Put it inside me *now*."

"I will," Pahndir promised. "I want to."

Pahndir's hand was between them, presumably teasing his penis tip over Beth's clitoris. Waves of heat crashed over Charles as Pahndir shifted that hand to brace against the door. His leverage assured, his hips contracted and thrust.

"Oh," Pahndir moaned, his eyes closing. "Infinity, you're tight. I have to take you hard now. I have to do it. Beth, please widen your thighs some more."

Beth couldn't speak. She was too busy thrashing and breaking out in little cries. The seat springs began to squeal like murdered cats. Pahndir seemed to be going at her with all his might, his face red and twisted with effort, his hips nothing but a blur.

Beth truly was stronger than a normal woman if she wasn't minding that.

"More," Pahndir pleaded. "Take it all. Take it all, Beth. Oh, yes, *yes*, that's it."

Charles punched the accelerator pedal with a bit more force than required. In doing so, he realized his own cock was strangling inside his clothes, the head trapped in a too-narrow crease beside the bending of his thigh. He tugged at the crotch seam, but that did no good.

"Hell," he said, forced to pull two buttons open before he could shift the pounding thing around. Though the release of pressure was welcome, it seemed to allow his cock to swell even more.

"Hell," he said again, in part because the lovebirds' moaning and thumping had increased. Did the two of them think he was made of stone? But they were probably too frantic to fuck to think, a possibility that didn't calm him at all. Nothing was going to calm him as long as they kept that up.

He was tempted to stick his hand back into his trousers and fist himself to climax. Beth and Pahndir certainly wouldn't notice. Unfortunately, someone had to pay attention to where they were going, unless they didn't mind him accidentally driving Herrington's motorcar into a ravine.

Considering Beth's and Pahndir's preoccupation, it really wasn't a surprise that—demon hearing notwithstanding—Charles was the only one to notice their pursuer.

---

The kith Pahndir had spurted over Beth's clitoris had made it swell and itch insanely. Of course, her entire vulva felt the same, and no matter how vigorously he pumped into her, he couldn't rub all of it at once.

Beth was too shy to ask for help until Pahndir dropped his head and rasped in her ear. "Want my hand on you?"

She meant to answer with a word, but all that came out was a pleading groan. Pahndir grinned, wedged his long-fingered hand between them, and squeezed every inch of her burning flesh against her pubic bone.

She orgasmed with a cry that should have mortified her, but her pleasure brought Pahndir's like an earthquake rolling up his spine. Her insides were so sensitive she could feel each individual jet of seed.

"Ohh," she sighed, her arms twining happily behind his neck. "Do that again."

Pahndir chuckled, his thrusts slowing but not stopped. He mustn't stop. They both needed this to go on and on.

And then Charles called back over the seat to them. "Hey, you two, save that for later. I think someone's coming after us."

Though Pahndir grumbled, he pushed off her. He squinted at the rear horizon and then stiffened. "That dust cloud is moving too fast to be camels. Someone's following us in a car."

His face was hard, his eyes backing off from their all-black state until a slender ring of silver showed. He began to straighten his clothing.

"You, too," he said, glancing at Beth. "I suspect that's Muto. You won't want to meet him undressed."

"Muto . . ." she murmured, thinking how ironic that the lie she'd told might be coming true.

She didn't have time to marvel. Though Charles had pushed the accelerator to the floor, their pursuer was gaining ground. The vehicle was still tiny, but Beth could see it was another demon-inspired jeep, and that it held two passengers. More troubling, a gun of some sort was mounted on its front bonnet.

"Damn," said Pahndir, his vision sharper than hers. "He has Sahel riding shotgun."

A distant banshee laugh confirmed this.

Something mechanical whirred behind her, drawing Beth's attention to the front of their car. A section of the metal dashboard was sliding back, revealing a tiny black and green moving screen—apparently a cousin to the one in Pahndir's desk at home. An odd, tinny voice issued out of it.

"Your vehicle is being targeted," it said. "Please take evasive action."

"Hard right!" Pahndir cried to Charles a second before

a ball of blazing white fire demolished the left corner of their rear bumper.

"Holy God," Charles gasped. "What the hell was that?"

Pahndir was lying on top of Beth, having forced her to the seat by flinging his body over hers. "That was a bolt from a plasma rifle. And, trust me, it's not approved for use in front of your race."

"Your vehicle is being targeted," the tinny voice repeated. "State your authorization and I'll drive for you."

"Ignore it," Pahndir snapped in response to Charles's confusion. "The autopilot is programmed to respond to Herrington's voice. Go right again, and floor that pedal."

"I am," Charles said as he spun the car sharply. "They're still gaining."

"Just do your best. They won't blow us up until they're closer. Muto must want to watch me die face-to-face."

"Sure about that?" Charles cut the wheel to the left as another fireball exploded to the right of them.

"I'm sure. As you can see, we're already in range."

"Fuck," said Charles.

"Your vehicle is being targeted—"

"Fuck, fuck, fuck."

Charles's curse drowned out the rest of the refrain. When Beth craned her head, Pahndir was frowning like he wished he could be swearing, too. He jerked when he saw her looking at him. His eyes were almost back to their normal silver.

"Do you have a knife left?" he asked.

Beth grabbed her remaining blade from the floor where she'd stashed it. "I hope you don't expect me to fall on it if we're caught."

"No." He braced as Charles hit a rise and all four wheels left the ground. They landed with a teeth-clacking thump. "I expect you to give it to me. Charles, when I give you the signal, I want you to hit the brakes."

"The brakes!" Beth and Charles exclaimed in unison.

Pahndir pried the dagger from her numb fingers. "I don't think Sahel can duck fast enough to prevent me from hitting her. Before I was married, I was a competitive knife thrower."

"Holy God," Charles said, apparently his special-occasion curse. His jaw was clenching, his eyes slitted on the landscape ahead. Despite his fear, Beth knew he was going to do exactly as Pahndir asked.

"That's almost close enough," Pahndir said. He clambered off her to crouch on the floor, facing the side of the jeep where Muto and Sahel's vehicle raced nearer.

Beth could see Muto now, at least in glimpses. This was the man who had twice paid for his cousin to be sent into captivity. He looked surprisingly ordinary, as portly as a human shopkeeper, though his robes were a blinding combination of orange and lime green. When he glanced over at Beth, she shivered, something in his expression fundamentally colder than the rest of his race. Unconcerned by the character of her companion, the chieftain laughed and swiveled the demon gun on its mounting.

"I should have taken that frying pan to *your* skull," Beth muttered, though in truth she might have. The veil end of Sahel's turban was fluttering behind her in a long black tail, and one-half of her face was clotted over with dried blood.

"Almost . . ." Pahndir said, and then, *"Now!"*

The jeep kept skidding forward across the sand even after Charles slammed the brakes, but the distance between the vehicles closed swiftly. Beth cried out as Sahel swung the plasma gun to retarget them. Cool as ice, Pahndir stood. Almost before Beth could comprehend that he'd thrown it, the pommel of the dagger sprouted from the center of Sahel's forehead. Pahndir had flung the blade with such deadly force that it had sunk through the bone. Killed in an instant, Sahel jerked backward like she'd been kicked. Muto mouthed a curse the wind tore away.

"Holy God," Beth breathed.

Charles seemed stupefied as well.

"Go, go, go!" Pahndir urged him, pushing her head down at the same time. "We can't outrun Muto, but at least he'll have trouble shooting *and* driving."

"Head for Hhamoun," Beth said, the idea coming to her as swiftly as that dagger must have come at Sahel.

"The cover would be useful," Pahndir agreed when Charles flashed a look at him. "And maybe someone will summon help."

Beth doubted that. Hhamoun wasn't far, but already the shadows were long enough that the site would be shutting down. Luckily, help from the diggers wasn't what she was hoping for.

"I'm taking over the driving," Pahndir announced. He grabbed the bar that was all the roof the jeep had and swung over the front seat. "Beth, keep your head down while I see if I can coax more speed out of this thing."

"Hell," Charles said, but he let the prince take his place as smoothly as possible. Muto had stopped to shove his dead partner out of the car, but the distance they'd gained wouldn't last.

As soon as Pahndir made it behind the wheel, he fumbled for something under the dash. "All right, where's that goddamned manual override?"

Under other circumstances, Beth would have laughed to hear this human curse from Pahndir. In this instance, however, she could only gasp in relief as the formerly quiet engine gave a roar and shot them forward.

"There," Pahndir said, looking downright smug. "Now we're both using human-restricted technology."

Whatever that meant, it seemed to have evened the velocity of the vehicles. Flames were shooting out from behind their jeep, not unlike the trail of a rocket. Pahndir's cousin wasn't falling back, but he wasn't closing the gap, either.

"Wow," Charles said. "You have got to show me how you did that."

Pahndir laughed, the sound so joyous it clenched her heart. Boy, would Tou have loved this man, and, boy, did Beth love him herself. She was going to tell him that the minute they got out of this. She was going to—

A *ping* against the metal of Pahndir's door cut the promise short.

"Shit," said Pahndir, the jeep swerving as he jerked. "He's shooting at us with a handgun."

Beth and Charles cried out in unison when they saw the spreading splotch of red on Pahndir's fine silk sleeve.

---

Refusing to give up the wheel despite his bullet wound, Pahndir drove like a demon of another sort to get them to Hhamoun ahead of Muto. As Beth expected, the place was empty when their headlamps swept over it. Ever since Tou's bedchamber had been cleared, perimeter guards had been reduced to a thin patrol.

"Kill the lights," she said. "Drive between the tents and park as close as you can to Tou's palace."

It was a sign of his exhaustion that the prince obeyed without question. Only when she demanded that he surrender his clothes to her did he protest.

"We don't have time for this," she said, physically yanking his outer robes down his arms. Weak from blood loss, he had collapsed beside the halted car. "I'm the strongest of us right now. Muto will be here any second. You have to let me lead him into the trap I've planned."

"He's got a gun, Beth."

"Which he's already shot you with." She balled her fist and shook it at him. "Don't make me knock you out."

As pale and shaky as Pahndir was, it wouldn't have taken more than a tap. How he'd managed not to keel over before this, she'd never know.

"Let her," Charles said, to her surprise. "If your cousin follows her thinking she's you, we'll have a chance to take him from behind."

Pahndir didn't seem strong enough to take anyone from any direction. Charles gave Beth a look that said he knew this. Reassured that her friend wouldn't let the prince kill himself protecting her, Beth ignored Pahndir's curses and drew his bloodied robes over her own clothes.

She began to run a breath before Muto's car slid to a halt, spraying sand. His headlights were extinguished, just like theirs had been. Charles held Pahndir hidden behind their jeep, out of Muto's line of sight. Beth prayed the moonlight would turn her into a good enough double for her beloved.

It seemed it did. She heard Muto running after her down the entry ramp to Tou's chamber, her hearing sharpened by the hush of the desert night. No doubt Muto could hear her, too. She could run as fast as she wanted without losing him. That was very fast, as it happened. She found she was more frightened now that she was alone, and the fear spurred her body to new limits. She pelted down the long tunnel, her heart thundering in her chest as if it were three times its normal size.

Muto's silence unnerved her. Shouldn't he be threatening all manner of awful things? Wasn't that what proper villains did? Even Sahel's women had taken time to mock her.

She had to slow as she ran deeper into the passage where the moonlight failed. The darkness was complete, a thick, black blanket before her eyes. She was thankful there were no turnoffs, and she needn't fear getting lost. She wished she could hear Pahndir or Charles trailing Muto, but it was probably better that she could not.

A second after she had the thought, she tripped headlong.

Luckily, only the heels of her hands were scraped. She scrambled up as fast as she could, realizing she'd fallen over the granite threshold to Tou's chamber. The sounds of Muto's pursuit sped up. She moved into the room, her hands waving before her to keep from bumping into anything. She hoped the Yama was as blind as she was and then remembered the space was empty. Herrington's crew had transferred all the goods out for preservation. All she had to do was find that damn ceiling hook.

*Help me, Tou,* she prayed. *Help me survive my enemies as you did yours.*

The answer came as waves of prickles across her skin.

"Pull me," hissed a whisper directly over her head.

Beth gathered her faith and jumped higher than she ever had in her life.

Her fingers caught the hook on her second try. She clung to it, her weight forcing the section of ceiling down. As soon as her feet touched ground, she fumbled for the toggle switch and slapped it. The quiet sound of the wall rolling open told her where to run. She stopped right on the track of the door, hoping the slab of stone wouldn't grind shut on her.

"I am for you," said the disembodied voice from her first visit. "Let any man who breaks the sanctity of this chamber feel my eternal wrath."

*That's what I'm counting on,* Beth thought.

The muscles of her heart pumped harder as she realized Prince Muto had found his way into the room after her. The sound of his scuffling footsteps and labored breathing were now coming from yards away.

"I knew you weren't going to give up your power," he said, the first words she'd heard from him. "I knew you were going to fight to hang on to it."

Beth said nothing, willing him to come toward the sound of her panting breaths. She gripped the sides of the doorway, her nerves wound to the snapping point.

This, naturally, was when whatever it was that haunted Tou's chamber shot her plan straight to hell.

# TWENTY-TWO

Behind her in the hidden room, small blue flames sprang to life on the matte black walls, as if some thick, flammable gelatin had been spread across them and set alight. As she and Muto gaped at each other in the eerie illumination, it was difficult to say which of them was more dismayed.

Or maybe not so difficult, seeing as Muto had a big silver pistol pointed straight at her.

The demon's mouth twitched like little shocks were going through the muscles. Against all expectations, the twitches turned into a laugh.

He sounded like he had some experience with the habit.

"Oh, my," he said, unshed tears of amusement glittering in his eyes. "I should have known my cousin would find another female to hide behind. Fortunately for me, I'm going to enjoy killing you as much as I did his wife."

"You killed his *wife*?" Beth's gasp was one of undiluted horror—not for herself but for Pahndir. She remembered the grief that had shadowed him at the clothier's. He'd blamed himself for Thallah's choice.

Faced with her expression, Muto laughed again. "Oh, if you could see yourself. Of course I killed her. Suicide isn't hard to fake, and I knew her loss would send him around the bend." One-handed, he cocked the hammer of his weapon and steadied its aim on her. "I must say, this encounter is even more delightful than the first. Just like a scene from a human novel. You make me wish I had a mustache to twirl."

Muto was moving closer as he spoke. Two yards. One. The muzzle of the silver gun looked black in the dancing light. Beth didn't dare step backward until he was nearer. She sensed the chamber's keenness to shut her up in it again, to add more enhancements to her body, to enjoy after all these years its version of company.

"You won't get away with this," she said, which she thought would please him.

It must have, because he giggled, a sound she never thought she'd hear a Yama make.

"I should probably threaten your virtue," he snickered, "though I doubt my randy cousin left you much of that."

Muto lifted the hand that didn't hold his gun toward her, undoubtedly intending a caress. Not about to miss her chance, Beth grabbed his wrist and heaved him into the chamber with every scrap of her unnatural strength.

Muto was so unprepared for her to do this that he nearly flew into the room's back wall. Sparks showered outward from where his head thunked as he stumbled.

The concussion seemed to wake the chamber up.

"Let any man," stammered its guardian spirit. "Let any man who invades the—" More sparks spat from the ceiling at its broken words, followed by a forking bolt of electricity. "You do not belong here. You are not our goddess!"

Muto had been stunned when he hit the wall, but now he sat up and shook his head. "What the—"

Beth's gaze went to the gun he'd dropped, which Muto was absently reaching for. She was close enough to grab it, but her time was up. Behind her, she could hear the door beginning to hiss shut.

Left without a choice, she turned and dove for the narrowing exit like a swimmer at the shallow end of a pool. Her form would have benefited from practice. She skidded to a halt halfway out. Cursing, she braced her hands outside the opening and wriggled frantically farther. Her hips were through the door, her legs . . .

"Stop," Muto shouted. "Stop right now!"

Beth's feet were losing their purchase. The floor behind her didn't feel as hard as it should, more like molten rubber than stone. Maybe the change hindered Muto, too. She expected him to grab her ankle any second, but he fired his gun instead. The shot ricocheted off the stone an inch from her foot. The door was nipping at her ankle, threatening to trap her there. She yanked as hard as she could, ripping a layer of leather off her boot to win freedom.

And then she was safe, alone in Tou's dark bedchamber with a seamless wall of granite between her and the enemy. Relief caused her limbs to shake so badly she could scarcely stand.

Her head swam with dizziness. Deep rumbling noises were rising inside the chamber. She heard the gun go off again, twice, but whatever Muto was yelling was indecipherable.

She didn't want to dwell on what the chamber was doing to him, didn't want to feel shame for consigning any living being to that.

*Oh, God,* she thought, imagining how furious the Yama must be. *Please let the door stay closed.*

Her hands were flattened to her chest in prayer when another person stumbled into the cavelike gloom.

"Beth," Charles panted. "I heard gunshots!"

"I'm all right," she said, then cleared her throat so she could be heard. "Muto's trapped in the secret room."

Practical genius that he was, Charles turned on the electric torch he must have stashed in the boot of Herrington's vehicle. He'd been waiting to turn it on until he was sure it wouldn't make her Muto's target. If she looked as bad as he did, it was little wonder that he'd worried. He was pale as milk in the strong white light.

"Beth," he said, and flung his arms around her.

It took a moment for her to realize he was crying. When she did, her heart squeezed tight.

"Shh," she said, deeply moved but disconcerted. Her oldest friend simply wasn't a weepy man. "He didn't shoot me. We're safe for now."

"I tried to stay right behind you, but you ran too fast."

"It's just as well you couldn't. Muto would have heard you, Charles. He would have shot you."

"He could have shot *you*!"

His tone was so aggrieved she had to fight a smile. "Pahndir was right. Muto wanted to kill him face-to-face, which, believe me, I had no intention of showing him."

That she had shown him her face she decided to keep to herself.

Charles hugged her tighter, his nose buried in her hair. "I can't lose you. I can't."

"You won't." She rubbed the shuddering plane of muscle between his shoulders. An echo of desire brushed her like a feather and flicked away. His warmth, his hold, steadied her as nothing else could have. Maybe it wasn't fair, but it felt wonderful to know she meant this much to him. She let her head rest against his shoulder a moment longer, then leaned back to stroke her knuckles down his tear-wet cheek. The faintest prick of stubble rasped her skin. "Where is Pahndir? I've discovered something he needs to know."

Charles's arms fell from her, a guardedness entering his expression. "He was too woozy from losing blood to come with me. I left him in the car. He said it had a communication device. He was going to signal Herrington for help."

Beth couldn't keep from pulling a face. Explaining this to their employer wasn't going to be fun. Then a worse thought had her hands flying to her mouth. "Oh, no! How are we going to break the news about Sahel?"

"It's already broken," Herrington said in his coolest tone. He was so angry he feared if he let one particle of fury escape his hold, he'd simply explode.

The idiot prince had explained a portion of the penny-dreadful tale on the way, having insisted that Herrington drag him—bullet wound and all—down the damned tunnel. Herrington had fully expected to be greeted with the slain bodies of his charges, but finding the pair alive had no positive effect whatsoever on his temper.

They were lucky he'd been close when Pahndir called, lucky he'd purchased a replacement vehicle so he could quarter the city in search of them. Most of all, they were lucky his nature was too evolved to turn the ire he felt over having been involved with Sahel onto them. He'd never thought the chieftain was a law-abiding citizen, but he'd also never thought her felonious tendencies would impinge on him.

Above all things, Herrington hated being wrong.

His face must have shown more than he wanted.

"We're sorry we stole your car!" Beth burst out.

"You're sorry you *stole my car*?" His rage swelled even hotter when she flinched back. "You should be sorry you didn't trust me! You should be sorry you didn't turn to me for help! Do you know what it did to me when you went missing?"

"You were seeing the chieftain," Charles said. "And you didn't want us seeing Pahndir. We thought you might have arranged for her to kidnap him."

"If I had, I wouldn't have *tortured* him!" Herrington roared.

"Herrington," Pahndir said, probably because Herrington was clenching the prince's good arm hard enough to cut off its blood supply.

Mortified by his lack of control, Herrington released

Pahndir. He shook his human-style frock coat back into place. "All I did was investigate him, and that's all I would have done once I saw he meant something to you. I would have helped you rescue him if you'd asked. Your safety—" He cleared his throat, hoping he wouldn't regret admitting this. "I value your lives more than arranging the world to suit me."

Beth was gawking at him, wide-eyed, as if this declaration took her by surprise.

"I feel *concern* for you," Herrington huffed.

Beth blinked at him, and then she smiled, and then she was striding toward him with an alarming glint of purpose in her human eyes. Sure enough, before he could gather himself to avoid it, she pulled him into an embrace. He truly didn't mean to, but his hand came up to cradle the back of her tangled hair. His emotions rose as she held him, a bit of her affection bleeding into his. Despite the blurring, he knew he cared about her then. For one thing, she was filthy enough to stink.

"We're sorry," she said, her arms tightening around him. "We'll never doubt you again."

"I *would* have kidnapped him," he muttered, "if I'd thought he meant you harm."

"I don't," Pahndir said. "I don't wish either of them anything but happiness."

*Either of them* was more than Herrington wanted to discuss right then, no more than he wanted to discuss how impassioned Pahndir was sounding. Composing his face, he set Beth firmly back from him.

"Now," he said, "why don't you tell me why that wall looks like it's filled with live wires."

Beth's head jerked around, her expression startled. The stone had gone partially translucent, revealing the obviously faulty circuitry it had hidden. Voltage was running amok through the metal maze. When Beth winced sheepishly at the sight, Herrington knew for certain he wouldn't like her answer.

"Er . . . There's a secret chamber behind that wall. I

think it's— That is, I'm relatively certain it's killing Muto, assuming it hasn't finished him off already."

Herrington fought not to rub the ache behind his forehead. "Why would you think it's doing that?"

"Because it doesn't like men?" She gnawed her lip. "We could open the door and check if you have a weapon. Muto was pretty bent on killing someone when I trapped him there."

Herrington stared at her, debating, then pulled his special-permit nine-millimeter automatic from the inside pocket of his coat. "Go ahead. If he's alive, I'll cover him."

"There's a hook that opens it," Beth said, pointing at the ceiling a few feet back.

She didn't get a chance to show him how she'd managed to reach it earlier. Without warning, the intermittent lightning that ran through the wall picked up speed and flared. A high-pitched whining set Herrington's teeth on edge. The sound took him back to his long-ago military training.

It reminded Pahndir of something, too. "Down!" the prince yelled half a second before the granite wall exploded.

Stone flew like shrapnel, filling the torchlit chamber with shards and dust. A weight slammed onto Herrington's back as he landed, driving the air from his lungs. Fearing the ceiling had collapsed, he was relieved to hear everyone coughing into the resulting cloud. His companions might be choking, but they weren't dead.

"Ow," Beth complained, between spasms. "You didn't all have to jump on me!"

In spite of himself, Herrington began to laugh. They had all leaped to cover her. Thanks to his slower human reflexes, Charles had ended up on top. He staggered off, his hair gray with dust, and helped Pahndir do the same. Their removal enabled Herrington to sit cross-legged on the floor.

He didn't bother trying to stand; his nerves were too shot for that. The fallen torch lay in the smoking rubble, allowing his archaeologist's eye to assess how much of his discovery remained intact. Most, from what he could see, though the wall that had exploded was a total loss. Behind the now gaping maw, Herrington saw nothing but broken rock and scorch marks. The chamber's involuntary inhabitant, and whatever else it had housed, had been obliterated as completely as if they'd never existed.

From what Herrington knew of Prince Muto, he'd have been annoyed to hear his big death scene had passed unremarked.

*No body to explain,* thought the purely Yamish part of his brain. It took a moment to consider the likelihood that the desert's creatures were performing a similar service for Sahel. Herrington made a note to keep an eye on her surviving tribe members, to ensure they didn't come after Beth or Charles for revenge.

"Well," he said above the ringing in his ears. "I believe this settles the question of showing mercy to Pahndir's cousin. Not to mention giving *you*"—he pinned Beth with his steeliest gaze—"plenty of time to fill in the holes in this story."

"Clearly," Pahndir said, "that chamber contained an artificial intelligence."

"Oh, clearly," Beth agreed, sharing an eye roll with Charles.

They sat around the polished table in Herrington's formal dining room, nursing cups of coffee beneath the sparkling, pony-size chandelier.

Beth wasn't ready to claim her boss had warmed up to her lover, but she'd noticed the meal he'd requested included enough red meat to build the blood cells of an army of wounded men. He'd loaned Pahndir a Northern-style shirt and trousers from his own supply. Beth would have said this was a ploy to prevent her from staring at Pahndir's chest, except he'd also ordered the butler to treat his bullet wound. At the least, Herrington seemed unable to shake his inbred deference for Pahndir's rank, a reaction she suspected the prince was happy to encourage.

Maybe it was her imagination; she only saw the phenomenon from the corner of her eye, but she could have sworn his aura flared with curls of royal purple when Herrington glanced at him.

Interestingly, Herrington looked away, shifting in his chair as if its seat had mysteriously grown harder.

"An AI is a kind of machine," he explained to her. "Its makers teach it to think for itself, after a fashion. They almost give it a personality. The one you stumbled into must have been an early genetic manipulator, from our people's previous golden age. It must have been designed to enhance human females, and it certainly explains how Tou made the mark she did. I don't know why the device took such a violent dislike to men, but perhaps over the centuries its code developed bugs."

Beth was going to develop bugs if he and Pahndir didn't start speaking plain Ohramese. "A machine can't explain how Tou's ghost came to me in my dreams."

"Oh, there wouldn't have been a ghost," Pahndir said, idly rubbing the shoulder of his bandaged arm.

"No, indeed," Herrington seconded. "Our ancestors were quite advanced. Our current scientists would weep buckets if they heard an ancient AI had been destroyed. Our forebears must have developed a technique for downloading memories. When Tou's played out in your dreams, they would have seemed very real."

Beth wasn't convinced this explanation accounted for everything, but Charles interrupted before she could say so.

"Wait a second." Charles pushed his cup and saucer away from him. "Are you saying this machine turned Beth into an early version of a Yama?"

"*Very* early."

"But then . . . that would mean your people come from ours."

"Exactly," Herrington said, nodding in satisfaction at

Charles's quick-wittedness. "There's always been the odd rumor that was the case, but nothing anyone dared repeat where they could be heard. You two shouldn't repeat it, either. No self-respecting Yama wants to think we evolved from a lesser race."

"Hey!" said Charles.

"Yes, I know," Herrington soothed. "You're not really lesser, just less advanced."

"Different," Pahndir said, his gaze coming to find Beth's.

As the black of his pupils swelled, she felt her pulse beat closer to her skin's surface. After all the uproar involved in rescuing him from Sahel, this was her first opportunity to think about what being mated to Pahndir meant.

*Intimate,* she thought. *And good.* As if the bond between them truly couldn't be broken.

On top of which, the crisp white cloth of his borrowed shirt looked extremely nice against his golden coloring. The bruises on his beautiful face were fading, and she remembered he'd walked to the table under his own power. Considering the significance of that caused steam to coil in her body. Yama did indeed heal quickly.

Pahndir must have sensed the drift of her thoughts. His eyes flicked downward, his lashes shuttering his feelings as he continued. "If we were convinced humans were that far behind us, we wouldn't work so hard at restricting our technology."

"As you wish," Herrington said. "Humans certainly have no shortage of curiosity—or the ability to get themselves into trouble."

That pointed remark tore Beth's gaze from Pahndir, but Herrington didn't have scolding her in mind. He rose from the table and looked down at her, his expression smooth but still conveying warmth.

"I expect you'll want to leave soon," he said. "You've had a scare, and Pahndir's been injured, but I doubt either of your bodies will give you much more reprieve. And, yes, before you ask, I know all about royals and their heats, though maybe not precisely the sort of heat that Beth has been experiencing. Why don't you use this time to make some clearheaded decisions while you're still able?"

Beth's cheeks flamed with embarrassment as Herrington headed for the door. Her accounts of entering Tou's chamber and its aftermath had been edited. Although she was relieved to have the secret off her chest, she really would have preferred he not read so accurately between the lines. Then Charles distracted her by rising, too, as if he intended to withdraw as well.

Herrington stopped him with a hard, cool look.

"Don't be a fool," he said. "I might not approve of what you three are up to, but I damn well know how much you want it."

It was uncomfortable to argue the value of taking risks with a man whose lover Charles had had a part in killing mere hours ago. He waited until Herrington was gone to turn to the other two. He and Pahndir had cuts and abrasions from the exploding wall, but Beth was unmarked, scrubbed and pink and practically shining in her pretty Bhamjrishi clothes.

That she had another side, one that wasn't as clean and sweet, made what he had to say harder. He'd been wrong to think her incapable of accepting him, just as he'd been wrong to think of Pahndir as nothing but a privileged prince. Now, with no one to blame but himself, it was too late to find out where either of those discoveries might lead.

Seeing something in his face, Beth drew breath to speak.

He lifted his hands, palms out, before she could steal his nerve. "You don't have to say it. I understand. You two are mated, or whatever the correct term is. And you care for each other. You don't need me crowding you."

"Charles!" Beth's protest was sharp. "Just because Pahndir and I share a bond doesn't mean we don't—" She looked helplessly at the prince. "We do, don't we? It was never just me you fell for. I'm not mistaken that you care about Charles, too?"

Despite Beth's claim, the look Pahndir gave her was proof enough that Charles was right. *Smoldering* didn't describe it. His nearly black eyes shone like stars reflected in pools of ink. Admiration for her infused them, and lust, and a thankfulness too deep to put words around.

"You're not mistaken," Pahndir said. "Or not about that."

"Then what am I mistaken about?" Hot color flew in her cheeks, which Pahndir could not resist stroking. His touch was so tender it made Charles ache.

"I had time to think, Beth, while I sat bleeding by that car. You saved my life—you and Charles. You restored my faith, and brought me immense pleasure. But if the three of us remain together the way I'd like, your life is never going to be what it was. Please consider long and hard before you walk away from the kind of marriage your family could accept, from the kind of marriage you could have with Charles."

"Marriage!" Beth and Charles cried in unified shock.

Pahndir's smile was wistful. "You love him, Beth, and he loves you. I could –" He hesitated, then pressed on despite the growing raggedness of his voice. "I believe I could love you both with all my heart. I believe it would be an honor the likes of which I never thought to know again, but I cannot deny you the chance to live a safer, simpler love with him."

"You'd give me up?" Beth appeared caught between hurt and wonder. She turned to Charles before Pahndir could respond. Charles's heart was thudding too fast. "And you? Do you think your life would be too complicated if you tried to live out your dreams? Do you think I'm a coward? Because you're both acting like one!"

"He is your kind," Pahndir said, spinning her back to him.

"Is he? Is he really? Does *my kind* even exist anymore?" Beth was wild and angry . . . and maybe a bit afraid. "You heard Herrington. He's doesn't know what's happened to me. None of you know exactly what that machine did."

Pahndir refused to be distracted from his point. "You already love Charles. You've been friends for years. You can't be sure what you feel for me. Neither of you can."

Charles heard Pahndir's unspoken plea as if it were his own, and, truthfully, it was. *Say you love me,* his stubborn expression begged. *Make me believe you do.* Charles himself was ready to demand Pahndir elaborate on that bit about Beth "already" loving him. His mouth opened on a breath, but no words emerged.

He didn't dare let them. His idiocy level was high enough—besides which, Pahndir seemed to be enmeshed in his own crisis.

Beth had her fingers pressed to her lips. "Is this about your wife? Is this about Thallah?"

Pahndir shoved from the table and turned away, his fist pressed to his mouth at the impossibility of controlling his emotions the way he wished. He flinched when Beth scraped back her chair to lay one hand on his back. The table stood between Charles and the couple, but he felt as if he were willing Beth to ease Pahndir's pain. Charles knew he loved Pahndir then. He knew it because he longed for Pahndir's happiness as intensely as he ever had for his own.

"She did love you," Beth said softly.

"You can't know that."

"I can." She gripped his hunched shoulder. "She did love you, and she didn't kill herself. Before he died, Muto bragged to me that he faked her suicide. She didn't want to leave you. She thought you were a good husband."

A long, raw cry ripped from Pahndir's throat, an animal wail of pain. His head rocked back and then forward. Beth wrapped her arms around him from behind. Charles's body urged him to join her, but he couldn't move.

"I'm sorry," she said. "Maybe I shouldn't have told you like that. I know this is a private matter between you and Thallah, but you have to know I love you, too. Getting to know you better might add to the reasons, but it won't change the fact."

Overcome, Pahndir covered his face. "I can't do this," he groaned, but caught her arm when she would have pulled away. "No. Don't leave. Just . . . don't make me talk."

Beth kissed his shoulder and, with her cheek remaining pressed against him, turned her head to Charles. Her eyes were bright with sympathetic tears, but when they met his, they gleamed even brighter. Charles realized he had a death grip on the door handle, where he'd frozen on the brink of flight.

What, he wondered, did Beth see in his face that made her tears well higher for him?

*Please*, she mouthed: just that, and nothing more, so that he had to guess what she was asking for.

Was he a fool, the way Herrington said? Was he a coward, the way Beth did? These two people desired him, cared for him, and might come to care more. Did it matter that their bodies had bound them together in a way his could not? They were, in their separate ways, his darkest and his brightest dreams come true. More than that, they were themselves: complicated and complicating but very worth knowing. Surely Charles had the courage to believe they might love him as much as they seemed prepared to love each other.

He gripped the handle of the door until his knuckles ached. Then he let it go. He was walking: one stride, two, around the long mahogany table. His knees were quicksand, his jaw clamped tight. He stopped a foot from where Pahndir was bowed over. The prince had his arms wrapped around his stomach, as if Beth's hold alone could not provide comfort.

*Do you want me to stay?* Charles tried to ask. The words wouldn't squeeze past the awful pounding of his heart.

Pahndir's damp, hot fingers caught his wrist in an iron grip. "Yes," he said, rough but firm. "I want you to come with us."

# TWENTY-THREE

During the cab ride to The Prince's Flame, Charles and Beth enlightened Pahndir as to what had happened at his home. The defection of his servants seemed no more than he expected, and he took it in with grave calm. He'd already absorbed so many shocks, Beth supposed he couldn't be rattled by one more—even if it had been in his nature to react that way.

Standing straight and tall on the stoop, he smoothed his shirtfront and pulled the cord that rang the bell.

"We shall see who's here," he said. "And I'll decide what needs to be done."

Pahndir's valet, Biban, opened the door.

"Your Highness," the Bhamjrishi whispered, his dark eyes filling with emotion at the miracle in front of him.

For a moment, Pahndir simply met his gaze. "You have been loyal," he said at last. "And you were the only one. I am dismissing the others and making you my manager. If you think any are worth rehiring, that will be your choice."

It was a princely gesture, not to mention a shrewd

revenge. The very servants who had tied Biban to a chair would now be obliged to curry favor with him.

Biban did his best to lift his jaw off the floor. "I sent them home," he admitted. "I didn't want them here if you returned."

A breathtaking smile transformed Pahndir's face. "If you got them to obey you, I see my trust in you is well placed."

"Are you hungry?" Biban asked, standing back as the trio filed into the entryway. "My mother taught me to cook simple things."

"We have eaten," Pahndir said, "but if you would bring some claret and glasses to my chamber, I would be grateful."

They bowed to each other, Biban deeply and Pahndir only with his head. Despite the disparity in the gestures, Beth suspected the respect they had exchanged was equal.

"Come," Pahndir said, waving Beth and Charles after him while Biban disappeared on his errand.

He led them three flights up the long staircase, to the floor where his antique brass lantern burned beneath the cavorting deities of the dome's mural. Beth and Charles had no difficulty keeping up, for Pahndir's steps could only be called trudging. His interaction with Biban seemed to have sapped the last of his energy.

He opened the door for them when they reached his private quarters. Curious, Beth stepped inside. Given Pahndir's exotic wardrobe, the rooms weren't what she expected. They were light and airy—white, for the most part, with pale, sky-blue walls. A long gilt-framed painting of an elephant parade was all the art she saw. The furniture looked comfortable, but there wasn't a lot of it. His bed was a large four-poster, his windows hung with billows of sheer white gauze.

*Here,* she thought, *is the sense of freedom he must have done without for years.*

"I'm tired," he said, and to Beth it sounded like a confession.

"Why don't you change into your own clothes," Charles suggested. "Beth and I will wait for the wine."

It seemed the right thing to say. Pahndir nodded, almost as he had to Biban, and disappeared into his large closet. Though the circumstances were somber, Beth found herself smiling.

Charles lifted an inquiring brow.

"I was thinking you know more about men than I do."

"And for more reasons than just being one." The quirk of Charles's mouth was irresistible. Knowing he could joke about his past eased the awkwardness between them. This was fortunate, because Pahndir didn't seem to be coming out of his closet. Biban arrived with the wine and poured three glasses, leaving Pahndir's guests to settle into pale striped armchairs in his sitting room.

"He has to mourn his wife again," Charles said.

"Yes," Beth agreed. She set her delicate goblet on a white-marble tabletop. "I'm glad we don't have to mourn him."

He looked at her, possibly surprised by her acknowledgment that both of them would have felt the loss of Pahndir, that both of them had a right to. She hoped Charles understood how deeply she believed that.

Silence fell, and then, "Is this really what you want?" he asked. "You're not just feeling sorry for me?"

She didn't stop to think. She slid onto his lap and kissed him, deeply, softly, until their arms wound around each other and their bodies flushed. The ridge of Charles's erection grew until it brushed her bottom, present but not pushing.

He pulled back from her slowly. "All right," he said, his eyes decided now. "I won't be a coward about this."

Beth traced his face from temple to jaw, going gently where bruises bloomed. "I shouldn't have called you that. I just want you to accept yourself as you are, the way Pahndir and I do. I can't force you to, but it's what I want for you."

"When did you become so wise?"

Beth laughed as he pretended to bite the heel of her palm. "Maybe I'm not wise. Maybe I'm just greedy."

"Maybe Tou is greedy."

Beth shook her head and smiled. "She's not inside me, just her memories. It's me who's discovering I'd like to recreate a few of them for myself."

Charles's hands slid flat down her back, pulling her a little harder against him. "I heard she had a harem."

"Indeed, she did!"

His eyes turned speculative. "You make me wonder if two men will be enough for you."

"Two men I love will be. Two men to love is better than anything I dared hope for."

"*You're* better than I dared hope for," Charles whispered back.

Beth broke into another hushed chuckle. "That may be, but Pahndir certainly provides you with one or two accessories I can't offer!"

He blushed, then kissed her, an edge and force to the action that hadn't been there before. Her underthings dampened with a swiftness that startled her.

They jumped apart when Pahndir appeared at the door, though he didn't seem to see anything wrong in, or really to even notice, what they'd been doing.

"I am well," he said, giving it the air of an announcement.

Beth's eyes widened. He wore a long black robe that was a perfect match for the silky fan of his loose, combed hair. He was the image of Yamish elegance, all the trouble smoothed from his features, all the redness cleared from his silver eyes. His response to the news of Thallah's murder had been so understandable that it hadn't occurred to her he might not be fine. But perhaps, as a Yama, he wasn't supposed to react at all. Perhaps he was remembering how vulnerable grief had made him before.

"We're glad you're well," she said, then threw her caution aside. "Hell, Pahndir, Charles and I don't care if you're upset. *We* don't think there's anything wrong with it."

He looked at his bare feet and snorted out a quiet laugh. When he lifted his head, his eyes were black. The sight was more potent than she could have guessed. In one lurching heartbeat, every drop of her lust raced back. She couldn't help wriggling on Charles's lap.

"I'm *very* well," Pahndir said in a different tone. His hands slid down his hips, drawing their attention to the swift and sizable developments at his groin. "Perhaps you'd like to help me prove it . . ."

---

He'd said goodbye to Thallah in that closet, to the person she really was: a woman who'd loved her life, a woman who'd loved him to the very end. He'd felt empty when the private storm was over, and calmer than he'd ever been.

Then, with a single, unexpected laugh, his heat filled him up again.

He couldn't remember the hot, hard thrust of it having been so welcome before. He'd been a young man with Thallah, eager but green. Now he took nothing for granted. Now he luxuriated in the urgent ache of his cock and balls, in the pulsing pressure of every one of his three kith glands.

His heart expanded as he took in both Beth and Charles. He had two of them to spend his passion on—two lovely, loyal, wonderfully warm humans. His eyes stung with how close he felt to loving them. Maybe he was there already. Maybe the only place to go from here was to love them more.

"Come to me," he said huskily, his arms opening. "I want to pleasure both of you. I want to do everything I couldn't while Sahel was watching."

"I want us to pleasure *her*," Charles burst out, his pupils swollen with the fantasy he was confessing to.

He was a vision with that lust-struck look in his sea blue eyes, a rich dessert Pahndir was looking forward to savoring. His tongue came out unthinkingly to lick his lips. Charles fought a shudder as his forked marking showed, the reaction every bit as delicious as Pahndir's anticipation of tasting him. Beth bit her lip and inhaled sharply, her attention drawn from one man to the other. Her heat appeared to have rushed back as strongly as Pahndir's. Between the three of them, the atmosphere in his chambers had gone syrupy with desire.

"Oh, yes," Pahndir said, his approval coming out a purr. "Do let us pleasure her."

Pahndir kissed Beth, his claiming of her mouth both delicate and insistent. The now-familiar taste of his kith set her lips atingle. She moaned, and his tongue slid deeper, wetter. Her arms seemed to lift themselves, allowing her hands to stroke and play among the cool and heavy silk of his hair.

She shivered when Charles succeeded in slipping her Bhamjrishi trousers down her legs. Crouching behind her, he eased off her slippers and gently planted her feet wider.

"Don't close your thighs," he said.

The soft-spoken order sent a lash of liquid heat whipping through her sex. Pahndir groaned at the scent of it.

Their lips parted, ending the kiss for now. Pahndir removed her arms from around his neck, but only so Charles could peel her tunic over her head. Charles undid her braid as well, twist by twist, his fingers combing through it until it fell in auburn ripples down her arms and back.

Pahndir waited, breathing with deliberate deepness, tense with his need not to wait at all.

"You now," she said once she was naked.

He untied the belt of his robe and let the garment fall, baring the tall, muscled grace that was his body. The sight of his fading whip marks, marks *she'd* placed on his skin, caused her breath to catch. Pahndir's eyes grew hotter at the sound. He knew what she was thinking. He traced the X she'd scored on his chest with a fingertip.

"I still bear your brand," he said softly. "I wonder if you know how much I treasure it."

She should have been shocked, but the air in her lungs had turned to fire. She spoke with an effort. "If you wish, when it heals, I'll give you another."

"Perhaps I'll mark you. You might enjoy a good spanking."

Behind her, Charles made a small, pained noise that trailed out just long enough to qualify as a moan. Beth and Pahndir quivered together to realize they weren't the only ones aroused by the idea.

"Of course, no one needs a spanking now," Pahndir said with a tiny devilish slant to his mouth. He rubbed the unmarked plane of his abdomen, where his well-defined muscles filled the lower legs of the whip marks. Beth's gaze followed the invitation. She loved that he was shaved, that no part of him was hidden. His erection thrust aggressively before him, the skin around its thickness satiny smooth, the skin that covered it as red as ripe berries. The head was large and shiny, the small dark slit issuing a slender line of fluid.

"Let me lick you," she whispered.

He inclined his head in princely acceptance and helped her kneel on the area rug. For Beth, the view from there was even better.

She took just the tip of him into her mouth, sucking up his juices, laving that melting silkiness round and round with her tongue. His kith was even richer here than in his mouth. As she absorbed it, her blood seemed to seethe with heat, her pulse beating wildly inside her thickened sex. The noises Pahndir made, so deep, so appreciative, overcame any hesitation she might have felt in her inexperience with this act.

"Take her," Pahndir said to Charles, when he could stop moaning long enough to speak. "Take her while she sucks me in her mouth."

Charles knelt behind her, naked now as well, his hard,

lean body pressing warmth up against her spine. She moaned herself as the head of his penis searched through her folds and nudged her opening. Her entrance found, Charles surged inward, gasping at the pleasure of her creamy flesh parting for that most responsive of male organs. He was thick and hard, long enough to make her writhe when he was fully in. His hands slid up her undulating torso to cup her breasts. He held them up, offering them to Pahndir with the nipples squeezed long and red between his knuckles.

Her head fell back with boneless yearning, onto Charles's broad shoulder. This left Pahndir to follow the suggestion Charles was so blatantly making. Pahndir steadied his shaft beneath the flaring girdle, between his thumb and two fingers. Gasping, he rubbed the slowly dripping crown around each nipple, spreading the shine of his kith across both of them. He grew firmer with every pass, breathing harder, more ragged, until neither of them could bear more torment.

Beth cried out and ducked her head to swallow him just as Charles's fingers reclaimed the beaded tips of her breasts. He pulled them out, stretching them, rolling them, causing licks of electric feeling to race down her nerves. He'd begun to thrust inside her, slow and strong, and Beth found herself imitating his rhythm to sink down and up Pahndir's shaft.

"Oh, yes," Pahndir sighed, his hips cocking forward to intensify her suction. "Oh, yes, make your lips pull tight."

His fingers were in her hair, massaging delicious circles into her scalp. Beth was almost hypnotized by pleasure: giving it, receiving it, feeling it more than triple with the three of them. She fisted one hand at the bottom of Pahndir's shaft and wrapped the other around his testicles. Their heft radiated fire into her palm.

"Oh," Pahndir said. "Oh, *Beth*."

But for once his balls weren't where he wanted the pressure most.

"There's a spot," he panted, the strong, corded muscles

of his thighs jerking. "Beneath the slit of my penis. Where your tongue is. Yes, there. Put your thumb there while your mouth is still on me. Put your thumb there and rub a nice, hard circle."

The groan he rewarded her with was unforgettable: tortured and grateful at the same time. His entire body tensed and relaxed in waves. Even his toes were curling into the floor.

"God," Charles rasped from beside her ear. "I think I want to know about that spot, too."

Since he was craning over her shoulder, Beth removed the crest from her mouth and showed him. The area she'd been pressing was duskier than the rest of his glans, along with being slightly raised. Charles looked at her, read her smile, and took Pahndir's leaping erection out of her hand. Beth watched his lips slide over the fat red bulb with her heart pounding.

Charles seemed to understand the trick of what she'd been doing. Pahndir groaned just as loudly at being sucked and rubbed by him.

"What is it?" Beth asked, unable to wrest her eyes away from Charles's mouth. "Why does having that spot stimulated feel so good?"

Much of her enjoyment in asking the question lay in knowing Pahndir would try to answer. Yama weren't supposed to be rendered speechless by sensual bliss.

"It's—" Pahndir inhaled a desperate gasp for air. "It's called the princes' flagellum. The little whip. It . . . fuck . . . It's an extra organ only royals have." His buttocks contracted, shoving him harder against Charles's tongue. "After a bonded couple have been together for a while, it . . . uncoils from inside his penis, and . . ." His chest heaved violently again. "It hooks onto a receptor the woman has inside her womb. It's . . . an aid to conception."

"And pleasurable," Beth observed, her sheath contracting in a hard, tight knot around Charles's slowly gliding cock. Charles's breath hissed inward as if that felt good to him.

"Very pleasurable," Pahndir panted. "Maybe too pleasurable right now."

With his loudest groan yet, he withdrew from Charles's sucking mouth. Flames seemed to glow behind the glittering black expanse of his eyes. His cock was every bit as big as it had been after she whipped him.

Beth wanted to lick it all over again.

"Lean back," Pahndir ordered Charles. "Keep her on top of you. I've been forgetting this is about us pleasuring her."

Beth laughed, because everything had been a pleasure for her.

She didn't laugh for long. Charles leaned cautiously back with her spine pressed to his front. He remained inside her but not as deeply, and the change in position spread her legs wide around his thighs. This left her unusually exposed. Her knees were bent, the throbbing flesh that had concealed her secrets stretched and opened for Pahndir's eyes. The air cooled the copious wetness outside but not within.

With a throaty growl of appreciation, Pahndir leaned toward her, sliding his palms up the length of her torso. When he crossed her breasts, he gave them an extra squeeze. He caressed her there just long enough to make her squirm.

"I hope you don't mind my saying this," he said somewhat breathlessly, "but I'm very glad the ancient Yama preferred voluptuous women."

Beth couldn't have objected even if she wanted to. She'd been robbed of speech the way Pahndir hadn't. Charles's cock felt so thick and hot inside her it could have been Pahndir's. The way they were lying, he couldn't really thrust. The best they could manage was to grind together a few inches. Beth tried to do this as Pahndir began crawling back down her front, his lips and teeth nipping tender flesh as he went.

"I don't think you need to worry about how the gene chamber changed you," he murmured against her navel.

"From my perspective, all your responses seem quite healthy."

His eyes rolled up to hers, glinting with mischief. She would have pinched him if Charles hadn't captured her hands right then. He stretched her arms out to either side, trapping them on top of his on the floor. The sense that she was spread out like a feast, helpless to do anything but wait to be eaten, had her whimpering.

"Almost," Pahndir whispered, his breath ruffling her pubic hair. "I'm almost where you want me."

And then he was there, licking up her juicy folds, teasing her with the uncommon strength and agility of his tongue. The pressure he could exert with the action was astonishing. Charles had to grab her hips to keep her from accidentally twitching off his cock. He twitched himself when Pahndir licked the part of his shaft that stretched outside of her. They both felt so good, so absolutely what her body needed, that she could scarcely wait to go over. When Pahndir finally surrounded and sucked her with all his mouth, she shattered with a loud, hoarse cry.

Charles grunted, his shaft jerking in reaction to her contractions. Pahndir tortured them a few heartbeats longer before lifting his head.

"If you want to spill, Charles," he said, his voice strained to the breaking point, "I suggest you do it soon. I need to get inside her pussy, and once I do, I very much doubt I'll be able to pull out for a long, long time."

Beth groaned at this implicit promise, but Charles had enough brain left for other concerns.

"I can't spill inside her. She might—"

"She's not fertile now," Pahndir interrupted. "Believe me, I'd be able to read that in her energy."

"Oh, God," Charles said and then cut loose.

He'd been able to thrust, after all. He'd simply been teasing her. His hips heaved off the floor and into her—hard, long jabs that, with every penetration, pushed his cock's sleek swollen head over the sweetest cushion of sensitivity at the front of her sheath. She could tell he was doing it on purpose; he was gripping her hips to keep the angle firm. Pahndir's mouth returned to her clitoris, his hands to her shaking breasts.

Taken all together, it was too much. She clutched his head, and sensation exploded through her body, intense enough to frighten her. This orgasm was life itself, as necessary as breathing. Charles shouted and drove in hard. She came as he did, her wetness pouring out of her with his.

To her shock, she couldn't stop it from spurting. Neither of the men would stop moving in and on her. Every exhalation became a sigh as they drew her uncontrolled climax out. Pahndir especially drank in the repeated bursts of energy.

Moved by his old fixation for feeding demons, Charles shuddered—against her, inside her—when he heard how loudly Pahndir was panting, when he saw how swiftly lust was darkening his face. Their combined etheric force couldn't help but affect the Yama. Unable to come yet himself, he shook with need by the time he moved over them. He kissed Beth, then Charles, then pulled her carefully off Charles's spent body.

His strength made lifting her onto him effortless.

They were standing, or Pahndir was, and she was hooking her ankles together behind his hard, narrow hips. His long, dextrous hands were beneath her bottom, his shining eyes locked on hers. Those eyes weren't hiding. They were speaking to her. They were telling her what she meant to him without holding back.

"I've fallen in love with you," he said.

His saying the words stole her breath. "You have?" she asked when she recovered.

He nodded seriously. "I think it started the first time I saw you. You were so alive, laughing with Charles in the marketplace. Every chance I had to be with you, I fell deeper. By the time you rescued me, I was lost."

"That could have been gratitude."

His hands caressed her bottom. He appeared to be considering how to counter her argument. Amazingly, she wanted him to start thrusting. Despite the flooding climax she'd had with Charles (which embarrassed her a little now) her need was rising again.

"I was grateful," he admitted. "But my feelings aren't confused. It was having *you* rescue me that meant so much, having you and Charles care enough to find out if I needed you." His lips softened in a barely visible smile. "Getting to know you better might add to the reasons I love you, but it won't change the fact."

They'd spoken so softly Beth wasn't certain Charles had heard. Whether he had or not, he sat up on the floor with a groan. She'd never seen him look more like a fallen angel, though at the moment he was not a miserable one. When he rubbed one hand up and down his chest, the gesture caught both her and Pahndir's gaze. Even sated, even wet with both their emissions, Charles's penis appeared heavy.

"Better carry her to the bed," Charles said. "Even you'll get tired of taking her standing up."

"Will you join us?" Pahndir asked, the question slightly hesitant. "Will you help me pleasure her some more?"

Charles flashed a grin Beth didn't often see. "I will," he said. "Just don't count on me not pleasuring you, too."

Pahndir looked at him, the men's gazes locking just as Pahndir's had with Beth's. The prince's lungs went in and out faster. "I trust that's not an empty threat."

Charles's eyes slanted and gleamed. "You sound a trifle hoarse, Your Highness. Are you sure you don't like threats?"

Pahndir's hot, steely flesh thumped inside of her.

"The bed," Beth reminded. "I think I need you again."

Pahndir's gaze returned to her, his grip tightening on her cheeks. She wasn't lying about needing him. Clearly, he hadn't exaggerated how much sex mates liked to have during heat. She ached for him to move inside her, for him to spill and spill again. Even more, though, she ached for him to throw off the last of his self-control. After everything they'd been through to reach this moment, she saw no reason why all their desires shouldn't have a chance to be met.

"I want him to take you," she said, "while you take me. I want him to push his cock inside you with my cream on his skin."

That was enough to do it. Pahndir growled, took two long strides, and tumbled with her onto his big white bed. Already shafting her before they landed, he groaned when Charles climbed up behind him and grabbed his hips.

"Slow down," Charles said. "Give me a chance to get in."

"Hurry," Pahndir pleaded, his head flung back.

Charles parted him and pushed, and Pahndir's body abruptly twisted like an eel, his spine as flexible as a cat's. Apparently, Charles had no trouble finding the gland that wanted to be rubbed. Pahndir was making noises, loud ones, but they didn't seem to be words.

"Like that?" Charles panted as he thrust. "Do you like feeling her on me?"

"Yes," Pahndir gasped, though he hardly had to. Beth and Charles had trouble hanging on while he bucked and writhed. "It burns so good. Oh, please, go faster."

Charles went faster, increasing the force with which Pahndir bumped into her. It was exactly what she needed, and maybe more. Her breath whined from her, one hand clutching either of the men's arms. She came so hard that Pahndir shuddered in the backwash.

"Again," he said, his hips rolling into her like lightning.

Again it was, and this time he convulsed with her. Luckily, Charles had the foresight to hold his own peak off.

"More?" he suggested once the prince settled.

"Oh, yes," Pahndir sighed, his pace already picking up again. "Oh, thank you. That's *soo* lovely. Infinity help me, I don't think I've ever felt anything as good as the two of you!"

Beth didn't think she had, either. She lost count of how many wrenching climaxes the men gave her. When her body finally needed a rest, the only break she wanted was to crawl over both her sweethearts and kiss and lick every inch of them.

# TWENTY-FOUR

They were animals, the pair of them, and Charles loved every minute of rolling around the bed and just about everywhere else in Pahndir's rooms with them. It felt like a privilege to watch them fuck, though admittedly he spent more of the next three days sleeping than they did. To rest with their arms and legs flung around him, to wake to the grunts and groans of them making love, to watch the last scraps of Beth's shyness or Pahndir's reserve unravel, was an undeniable delight.

Everything Charles offered was a welcome contribution to the expiation of their lust. Nothing forbidden. Nothing too much. Driven beyond any limits he thought he had, he took them both more times than he could count, in every way he could think of—and still he didn't wear out their desire for him. More than once, they dragged him from slumber with the sweet, hot greed of their mouths and hands.

The first time Pahndir took him with his immense cock, Beth had held Charles's face and stared into his eyes. He'd felt more naked than he ever had—his excitement bared to her, his secret thoughts—and yet he wouldn't have drawn away to save his life. The shame he used to feel for his own desires seemed less substantial than gossamer. When Pahndir took *Beth* that way, Charles couldn't resist sliding into her pussy. She'd moaned for both of them then, her body trapped between their mutual labors, until tears of pleasure bathed her cheeks.

That memory he would have bottled, but there were plenty more where that came from.

Beth's and Pahndir's heat aroused him when any other human would have been worn out. Midway through the second day, Pahndir had to call for a balm to soothe the stinging skin of Charles's shaft. Of course, how inspiring they all found the process of applying the ointment rather undercut its purpose.

Somewhere in the middle of all that coupling, Charles became aware that they were building something far deeper, far stronger, than a sexual friendship. For lack of a better term, they were having a romance.

They fed each other food like sweethearts, and soaped each other in the shower bath. When they couldn't keep their eyelids open a second longer, they took turns being the one to get snuggled in the middle for their naps. The others both told him they loved him, with almost identical shyness, as if they feared they wouldn't be believed. Perhaps they were right. Charles certainly found the assurances sweet to hear.

"One more," Pahndir finally said on the evening of the fourth day. "One more climax and I'll be done."

Charles had just finished taking Beth. She was still bent forward at the waist over the back of a small sofa, trying to catch her breath. Charles had filled her so well and fucked her so hard that when he pulled out, the imprint of his erection seemed to remain. Her insides hummed with satisfaction as she rested her cheek on her folded arms.

"Stay there," Pahndir said, his palm curving gently around her bottom. "I want to take you just like he did."

The gruffness of his voice told her this idea did something for him. Beth was agreeable. Her very well-pleasured body liked the position: the pressure of it, the way the men bent their broad, hard chests around her. She liked it even better when Charles flopped onto the couch beneath her and offered her a hand to hold. Over these last few days, she'd discovered she enjoyed having a grip on something when she came. Pahndir and Charles could make her peak so hard that holding on was a necessity.

"One more enough for you?" Charles asked her.

"Ye-es," she said, the answer unexpectedly broken by Pahndir kneeing her legs wider. She always felt more vulnerable when he did that.

"I'll make it enough," Pahndir growled as he delivered one eye-opening smack to her right buttock.

"Oh, God," she gasped, because the sting had gone through her in an oddly erotic way. Maybe there would be more to explore during their next heat. When Pahndir began to push his thickness inside her, her muscles twitched with unexpected energy.

"Oh, *God*," Pahndir echoed an octave deeper. "He got you so fucking wet. Charles, your seed is all over me."

This must have been a good thing, because she felt the already formidable stiffness of his cock increase, pushing deliciously against every one of her extremely sensitized interior nerves. Though the pleasure this brought her was intense, Pahndir also slid his hand around so he could finger her clitoris.

Sensation streaked through her like demon's fire.

"His semen *is* silky," she agreed breathily, working her hips the way she'd learned Pahndir liked, making sure every inch of his erection knew how much she loved it. "I expect it makes it easier to move, you being so big."

Pahndir groaned, his lips against the back of her neck. "It isn't just that I'm big. His seed is mixed with your essence. It makes me . . ." His teeth pressed into her skin as he thrust harder. "His seed makes me want to soak up every drop. It makes me want to flood you with my own."

Charles kneeled up on the couch at this, his eyes wider.

A moment later, Beth was past speaking, despite how much she'd discovered the men liked her to comment on whatever they were doing. Pahndir was going faster and faster, and her body actually needed it. Her climax tightened, heated, *reached* for culmination like sparks building higher to jump a wire. Pahndir bit her shoulder and her head flung back. She smelled the coppery scent of her own blood, her hands gripping Charles's until the pressure must have hurt.

"Go ahead," she heard him pant. "Go ahead and scream."

She did scream, coming in great, hot rockets of feeling as Pahndir slammed into her so hard her feet left the floor.

He was coming, too, crying hoarsely as his climax propelled the last of his ejaculate into her. There was more than she expected, as if he'd been saving up this last packet of desire. Like fireworks. Like the final overwhelming burst of thunder.

The seed inside her overflowed and rolled down her thighs.

"Beth," Pahndir sighed, a song in her name, and then, "Charles." One hand left her hip to weakly stroke the face of her dearest friend. Peace rolled through her as sweet as the orgasm.

Charles began to laugh, for once in better shape than them. "You're going to fall over, Pahndir. Let me help you both to the bed."

He helped them, and they curled up together with Beth in the middle, which she had to admit was her favorite place. She felt deliciously safe, just a girl again, being protected by her men. Then again, defending her men with a frying pan hadn't been bad, either.

"I need to wash up," she said drowsily.

Charles and Pahndir hitched their legs over hers simultaneously. Evidently, neither wanted her to rise. "Later," Charles said, "after you've rested."

"I stink."

Charles sniggered. "You both smell like fruit salad."

Pahndir lifted his head from the pillow at least an inch. "You can smell our essences?"

His surprise turned Beth to him. "Isn't he supposed to?"

"I wouldn't think so," Pahndir mused. "Another Yama wouldn't be able to, not unless the scent belonged to his mate, though I admit I don't know everything there is to know about the human nose."

"Maybe mine is special."

Pahndir snorted at Charles's smugness. "Maybe it is."

The prince's eyelids were at half-mast, his lashes black over his silver eyes. He almost seemed a different person. His face was utterly relaxed, younger and at ease. To Beth, he looked no more than a blink from sleep.

"Pahndir?" she said, not quite ready for this wonderful experience to be over.

"Mm?"

"Earlier, at Herrington's when we were arguing, you spoke as if you expected Charles and me to get married."

Pahndir rubbed his face deeper into the pillow. "It's what I want. Why should Charles settle for less?"

Beth abruptly came more awake. "It's what you want?"

"Mmph," Pahndir grunted, lazily draping his upper arm over her stomach. "You could marry both of us, if you liked. Polygamy is legal in Bhamjran, though only for women. Not fair, I suppose, but there's probably some city somewhere where it's only allowed for men."

Beth wriggled up on her elbows. The time it took her to do this was all the time it took Pahndir to succumb to unconsciousness. She gritted her teeth in frustration. Should she shake his shoulder to discover if he'd meant what she thought by this?

"Don't look at me," Charles said, his eyes alight with humor. "I can't tell if that was a proposal or just Pahndir keeping you informed."

"But he might have proposed to you, as well!"

Charles closed his eyes and grinned. "My first," he sighed, ignoring the punch she drove into his arm. "I believe I'll have to sleep on it."

They all slept, but Pahndir was the first to wake. His head, or maybe his heart, was too full to remain at rest.

He was standing on the tiny stone balcony in his bedroom, gazing out over the night-dark city, when Beth came to him. There was just room enough for her beside him, her left arm warming his right as she braced her hands on the balustrade. She'd wrapped one of his robes around her nakedness. It smelled of all of them—of Pahndir and Beth and Charles. He liked that more than he could explain, his very bones filling with comfort.

"I thought I'd sleep for days," she said. "Charles is out like a stone."

He stroked her hair down her back, loving its silky length, loving the abandon its looseness lent to her looks. When she gave a little shiver of pleasure, he turned so that his spine was pressed to the railing, so that he could look into her wonderful human face. "I was out here thinking I can't be sorry for anything I went through if it brought me here. This place, *you*, feel more like home than The Forbidden City ever did."

She leaned her head against his shoulder as if she'd always had a spot to rest there. Her emotion touched his awareness like a faint perfume. The hope she felt was a tuning fork to his own. *Marry me,* he thought. *Marry me and Charles.*

"Can we really do this?" she asked. "Can this truly work?"

"I think it can, but I think we'll have to be careful."

"I'm afraid for Charles," she confessed.

"I think we both know—" He faltered, then found the courage to be frank with her. "We love him enough, Beth, enough to be patient while the knowledge of what we feel becomes real for him. That's all that's lacking: for him to know, for sure, that we don't love him less."

"And physically? We exhausted him, Pahndir. I know he didn't complain, but what if we—"

"We won't. I'll take him to my private doctor tomorrow. I'll have to bribe the hell out of him, but whatever Yamish science can do to support his human constitution, Charles will have the benefit of. Fortune willing, someday he'll exhaust us."

"He'd like that," Beth said with a soft, rough laugh. "And Lord knows what he'd come up with."

He pulled her into his arms, her slight weight settling peacefully against his chest. He loved the way her head fit perfectly beneath his chin.

"I have to ask you one more thing," she said. "About Xishi. I want to know if you're still in love with her."

The question was inevitable, he supposed. He let her push back far enough to meet his eyes. "You seem to think I'm rather profligate with my affections."

"I'm serious."

"Very well. I'll answer as best I can. Xishi was, and is, a dear friend to me. There were times when I feared I loved her, but looking back, I don't think I ever was more than fond. My body made choices for me, but so did my heart. You fit all of me, Beth, and in a certain way, so does Charles. Even if Xishi had been free to be my mate, I doubt I could have experienced the depth of regard and rightness I feel for the two of you."

She gazed at him a moment longer and then nodded. "Good."

"Good? I bare my cold demon heart to you, and all you can say is 'good'?"

She laughed, her arms squeezing tighter around his

waist. "You fit all of me, too. Oh, and please don't ask me to share you with anyone but Charles."

"Wouldn't dream of it," he said, his heart lifting giddily at her possessiveness. "My queen should be able to keep all her men to herself."

# EPILOGUE

The marriage took place six months later in the courtyard of a hotel owned by a Yama who'd once been a famous dancing boy. Lush white roses had tumbled up the columns of the surrounding galleries, with pink ones carpeting the path to a bright silk awning beneath which the traditional Bhamjrishi ceremony had been held. Wine had flowed and guests had gotten silly and, to Beth's happy, excited eyes, everything had been wonderful.

This was due in part to none of Pahndir's relatives being invited. Interestingly, a number of Prince Muto's servants, now bereft of their mysteriously vanished leader, showed up to request to enter into service with Pahndir. Apparently, their years with his ruthless cousin led them to reassess the benefits of Pahndir's gentler managerial style.

It was no surprise to Beth that *her* family showed up in full force. They'd been nonplussed by her unusual union, but categorically unwilling to miss out, considering that their old friend Charles was part of it, and that Beth's other fiancé was footing their travel costs.

As a result of Pahndir's generosity, every one of her nieces and nephews had overrun the charming hotel. They'd taken pretty Xishi Midarri's toddlers under their, well, "wing" wasn't quite the right word—more like their evil influence. With precious little coaching, the two adorable Yamish boys had proved able to produce shrieks of delight as ear-piercing as any human child's. Xishi's repeated apologies had embarrassed Beth, though Pahndir's old flame had also wished Beth well with a sincerity that brought tears burning to her eyes.

"I'm so happy my old friend has found you and Charles," she'd said. "The two of you are everything I could have hoped for him."

Touching though such scenes were, Beth was twice as thankful to have retreated with her husbands to Pahndir's new mansion.

*Her* new mansion, actually. According to local custom, the residence was considered Pahndir's dowry gift to her. Because the evening was as soft and balmy as a kitten's purr, the three of them were sprawled on cushioned lounge chairs in the rooftop garden, watching the Indypt River roll past their private wharf below. Charles's small sailboat was tied up beside it. According to him, this was his wedding present to both of them, though neither Beth nor Pahndir dared step inside the secondhand *felucca* until Charles learned to navigate a bit better. Above his new acquisition, the sky was a deep azure, the clouds streaked in shades of tangerine and scarlet by the setting sun. Enjoying the weather as much as they were, tiny black bats wheeled over the river's palms, saving them the trouble of swatting insects.

Beth thought the quiet was delicious, and her companions the best of all. They'd pulled their chairs side by side, their hands close enough to stretch out and touch.

As if his thoughts were unfurling along similar lines, Pahndir heaved a melodic and unYamish sigh. "Your parents weren't as horrified as I expected."

Beth had enough energy to smile. "I think my brother, Adrian, broke them in when he married Herrington's daughter. Roxanne isn't just half Yamish, she's also a bawdy painter."

"I liked her," Pahndir said. "She reminded me of you."

"Well, that would explain some things. Charles had an awful crush on her when he was her ward."

"Oh, Lord," Charles groaned from Pahndir's other side. "Don't be trotting out those old stories."

"Your younger brother is quite intelligent," Pahndir offered, willing to change the topic for his sake.

"Max is a genius," Beth and Charles chimed in unison.

This seemed to be Pahndir's signal to reach out for both their hands. For a long, quiet moment, Beth simply enjoyed the intimate twining of their fingers.

"The wedding feast was nice," Charles put in, "though I think my crew makes better *korma*."

"Good thing you'll be running your own restaurant soon," Pahndir said.

"Good thing Biban is working out so well as your manager, and you'll have plenty of time to help me start it up."

Beth stifled her laughter. While Pahndir claimed he wanted to be a silent partner in Charles's new venture, Charles was insisting he wanted his advice. Beth had no idea how the two perfectionists were going to rub along if Charles succeeded in involving him. She was, however, looking forward to encouraging them to work out any disagreements in bed with her.

"Herrington gave me a wedding present," she announced on her own behalf. "He's promoting me."

"Is he?" Pahndir said, giving Charles a look to say their discussion of his restaurant could be tabled for later. "It's well deserved, I'm sure."

Beth had to snicker to herself at that. Pahndir hadn't known her before Tou's chamber turned her into Miss Efficiency.

"He's still calling me his assistant," she said out loud, "but he's going to let me out of the copy tent. He says my—ahem—unique perspective on Queen Tou should prove helpful in developing the site as a museum. Plus, I think he likes having someone to hand off the diplomats' wives to."

"You do have your charming side," Pahndir said.

"Hah!" Charles barked. "Beth thinks all her sides are charming."

"They are," she said, sweetly batting her eyes, "or you seemed to think so when you were kissing them last night."

"Speaking of Herrington," Pahndir said before Charles could toss out a comeback. "He and I had a chat after the ceremony."

"A chat?" Beth asked, alerted to his tension by the sudden stiffness of his fingers.

"Nothing bad," Pahndir assured her as Charles rolled to face him, too. "But possibly important for all of us. Herrington explained his theory of how he'd impregnated Roxanne's mother, who—as you know—was human. He said she'd had intercourse with a human immediately before having it with him, and he believed there might be some enzyme in human semen that prepared her to be fertilized by Yamish seed."

Beth discovered she was sitting up without remembering when she'd done so. "We've done that before, more than once, and I haven't gotten pregnant yet."

"Yes, we have." Pahndir hesitated. "The problem is we don't know how human you are. Or how Yamish. Between Charles and I, we might well get you with child."

"You said you knew when I was fertile from reading my energy."

"I do. Except—" Pahndir sat higher, swinging his legs around to face her. "You remember what I told you about the princes' flagellum? How it's an aid to conception for royals? I've noticed . . ." He cleared his throat. "I've noticed mine has been sensitive with both of you. I believe I may hit that stage of my development soon. If I do, it's possible that I—with Charles's help—could make you pregnant no matter where in your cycle you are."

Pahndir's face was very carefully blank, but Beth was

getting better at reading his emotions even when he tried to conceal them. Her guess was that he was a little afraid to want children, but some part of him truly did.

"Your flagellum never emerged with Thallah?" she asked.

Pahndir shook his head. "Some bonded couples never experience the phenomenon, which doesn't happen every time anyway. I suspect it's the three of us together that's speeding up the process for me now. Given that Charles can smell our bonding scents, he may be a kind of biochemical mate for us, perhaps a necessary catalyst. You know I've . . . always liked the feel of his seed."

"Among other things," Charles added with a grin. Obviously more at ease with this topic than Pahndir, he clambered onto Pahndir's lounge chair and hugged the Yama from behind. His chin fit perfectly next to Pahndir's ear. "I like kids, in case you were wondering. I never thought I'd have them, but I was pretty good with Max when he was little."

"I like them, too," Beth said. "Even monsters like your friend Xishi's twins. And you do have all these new servants. What better way to keep them busy than chasing after a few offspring?"

"So we're . . . agreed?" Pahndir said, though if anything he sounded more nervous than before.

Beth leaned forward to kiss his lips. "We're agreed that having children is a possibility, which we'll revisit in a year or two."

The breath Pahndir had been holding gusted out. "A year or two sounds civilized."

Beth tried to restrain her amusement at his relief, but Charles wasn't quite as tactful.

"What would you do," he teased, "if Beth had a child and then there were *three* people for you to love?"

"Faint with proper Yamish horror?" Pahndir suggested.

Beth didn't believe for an instant that their prince wouldn't open his heart to a child and more. Even now, he was hugging Charles's crossed arms closer to his chest, his facc tilted to the twilight, his eyes closed with rare pleasure.

Her gaze met Charles's over Pahndir's head, joy filling the air between them like a ringing note. This was what she'd hoped their marriage would be: a perfection of imperfections, a knot they would unravel with an endless feeling of gratitude. She loved that Charles's knowing smile was a match for hers.

Both the humans had noticed Pahndir wasn't even trying to hide his happiness.

Turn the page for a preview of the next book
in the Upyr series from

EMMA HOLLY

# Devil at Midnight

Available November 2010
from Berkley Sensation!

# 1460

Despite the cool autumn breeze that blew off nearby Lac Léman, sweat ran down Christian's muscles in steady streams, soaking his padded gambeson and causing it to itch like Hades against his skin. He had been training his father's men since morning. He was young for the responsibility—maybe too young—but Gregori Durand preferred to leave his own flesh and blood in charge. Since Christian was his only living son, that meant the honor was his.

Though currently engaged in blocking a downward cut from a six-foot blade, Christian caught sight of trouble from the corner of his eye.

"Hold," he said to his training partner.

"Gladly," William laughed, allowing the blunted tip of his weapon to drop to the bailey dirt.

They fought in chain mail rather than plate armor, plate being more expensive to repair. Conveniently, depending on your point of view, the iron-ringed hauberks were no lighter than forged steel. Added to that, the two-handed swords they swung were twice as heavy as normal blades.

The reason for this was simple. Stamina in battle spelled the difference between life and death. If they used more weight during practice, normal weapons felt easier. To gain that advantage, today they suffered. Though William was larger than Christian, his face was just as red and sweaty beneath his helm.

"Left arm!" Christian called to Charles, who was struggling ineffectually against a taller veteran.

*"Merde,"* Charles cursed. The soles of his boots slipped in the dirt as he went down flat.

With a happy chortle, Hans—the veteran—pressed the axe-head of his halberd into Charles's mail-clad chest. Charles's orange hair—the bane of his existence, according to him—had straggled from beneath his coif to plaster his face.

"He is stronger than me," Charles said as Christian came to stand over him. "And Christ knows how many stone."

"You would not notice if you remembered you had two arms. In any case, you are faster than he is. Why did you let him close with you that way?"

"We have been at this for hours," Charles complained. "Forgive me if I grew weary."

"Battles do not halt because you are weary," Hans and Christian chimed in, in unison.

Laughing, Hans offered his felled opponent a hand up. The numerous scars that seamed his cheeks made his grin a fierce thing to see.

"Walk until you catch your wind," Christian said to Charles. "Then go work with the pell."

Charles groaned, because the pell was a hacking post and—while not as dangerous as combat—it was one of the more grueling exercises he could be set to.

"Left arm strikes only," Christian clarified. "I shall tell you when you may cease."

*"I shall tell you when you may cease,"* Charles repeated in mincing tones, but Christian knew he would obey.

Charles only pretended to be contumacious. When the need arose, he always fought valiantly.

"You stay with me," Christian said to Hans, which wiped the grin from the warrior's face. "Charles did not give you enough of a challenge."

"Ha!" Hans barked, recovering his humor. "The day you challenge me is the day I retire." With his hands spread wide on his halberd's shaft, he brought up the weapon and began to circle. At forty and a few years of age, he was built like an old prize bull. Even through his chain mail chausses, Christian saw his thigh muscles bulge. "Do your worst, stripling."

"Christian," someone hissed through the continuing clatter of mock combat. "Your father comes to the yard."

Christian lowered his sword and turned. His father was indeed entering the bailey of their fortified hillside house. Like his son, Gregori Durand was swarthy from his mingled French and Italian blood—a common enough mixture here in Switzerland. Thanks to his departed mother, who had been a Habsburg by-blow, Christian was a mite taller than his father but far less broad. In contrast to his offspring's litheness, Christian's bearlike sire walked as if each step ought to shake the ground.

Today he dangled a writhing burlap sack from one meaty hand.

The frightened yelps that issued from it had Christian's stomach sinking like a stone.

*"Scheisse,"* Hans muttered beside him. "He found Lucy."

Knowing there could be no delaying this confrontation, Christian closed the distance between him and his father. Gregori's expression was, as always, icy. His father never showed his temper by losing it.

"Would you care to explain this?" he asked coolly.

"She is but a hound," Christian said, striving for equal calm even as his heart thudded in his chest. At this point, any pretense of continuing to practice ceased. The men were all turned to him and his father, not drawing closer but watching. Whether by accident or design, the five who most often fought in Christian's *Rotte* stood nearest. Hans was the exception among his silent supporters. Hans served in whatever group needed him.

Wanting to prove he was worthy of their espousal, Christian squared his shoulders. "I thought the vineyard owner's children might like to play with her."

"I gave you an order," his father said. "Are you saying you cannot obey me any better than this dog?"

"She is still young, Father. She did not mean to ruin your hunt."

"What she meant does not matter. She acted without discipline, and she cost me my prey. The other dogs did not fail me the way she did."

The other dogs lacked Lucy's spirit—and her love for humans. She was smart and playful and brought out the boy in men who had earned their keep killing strangers for more years than Christian had drawn breath. Lucy had slept on one or another of the mercenaries' pallets since she was a puppy, had shared their food and sent them into gales of laughter over her antics. Christian did not know a single member of their household who had not slipped her a treat or two.

Except his father, of course. His father had no love for any creature that Christian knew.

"I will take the whipping," Christian said. "This is my fault for letting the men make a pet of her."

His father stared at him, his eyes as black as wet stones. The back of Christian's neck tightened. Too late, he saw he should not have offered this.

"You will take the whipping," his father repeated, his face gone blank.

Not knowing what else to say, Christian bowed his head in submission.

"Very well," said his father. His hand gestured toward the men. "Hans, tie him to the pell."

The veteran soldier cursed too softly to make out which

saint he was blaspheming. He did not, however, hesitate to lead Christian off. All of them knew better than to stand against their commander, for each other's sake as well as their own. Christian did not resist his mail tunic and shirt being stripped from him, nor did he protest when his best friend Michael was ordered to wield the single-strand rawhide lash. This was simply another in the endless series of tests his father was forever requiring them to pass. *Whip your friend. Kill this dog. Grovel until your knees grind down.* The reward was never approval, but just living another day. Christian even understood why his father did it. This world was a hard and bloodthirsty place. Only those who commanded fealty could survive.

Hans's motions were brisk as he bound Christian's wrists together with a thick hemp cord. Christian hugged the pell, the hacked wood post a support he would be grateful for soon enough.

"Ready?" Michael asked, the single kindness he would permit himself to give.

Christian nodded and clenched his jaw.

His father ordered him to take twenty strokes, and Michael's strong right arm ensured they were hard enough to suit the elder Durand's tastes. Once destined to become a monk, Christian's golden-haired friend grunted with the force it took to break Christian's skin. Luckily, Michael's aim was precise. The leather stayed on his back and shoulders and away from kidneys and spine. This whipping would neither kill him nor leave a disabling scar. Christian would live to earn other ones.

His breath whined through his teeth by the fifteenth lash, his body jerking helplessly at the pain. Christian tried to contain any other noises, not only because they would betray weakness to his father, but because the evidence of his suffering would distress his friend. Though Michael was a few years older than Christian, his heart would never be as hard. Keeping silent was a luxury Christian fought for. Salty sweat stung his wounds like acid as Michael was obliged to cross stripes he had already made.

"Nineteen," he counted, his voice ringing out as if he, too, were being struck.

Then he brought the last blow down.

Christian's back was throbbing, the fiery heat of the lashes like snakes writhing on his skin. He flinched when the blood from one rolled into the next.

"Water," someone said quietly. A moment later, a bucket of blessed coolness was poured on him.

Hans cut his wrists free, gripping Christian's elbow just long enough to help him lock his buckling knees and stand. The scarred old warrior's face was angry, but only if you looked closely. Nostrils flaring, Hans stepped away and stood at attention as soon as Christian faced his father. Christian was shaky, but his head was high. He blinked until the sweat cleared from his vision.

To his amazement, his father laughed.

"I give you this, son," he said, almost sounding pleased. "You are no swooning lad."

Christian had one shocked heartbeat to enjoy this rare piece of praise. His father's expression sobered as he once again lifted Lucy's sack. He thrust it squirming in Christian's direction with his usual flinty look.

"Now," he said. "Kill the dog."

Afterward, Christian sat in the dirt with Lucy cradled in his lap. She was . . . She *had been* a short-haired hound, white with liver-colored splotches. Her once perpetually wagging tail hung limp, her body cooling under his petting hands.

Christian's eyes were dry. If he had cried even as a child, he could not remember it.

"We will take her," Philippe said. "Matthaus and I will bury her outside the walls under a nice tree."

"Bury her deep." Christian's instruction was distant but steady. "Else, some animal will dig her up."

"We will," Philippe promised, easing Lucy's slight weight from him. He glanced back over his shoulder to where Matthaus waited, slim and tall . . . or perhaps his gaze scanned the shadowed archway where Christian's father might again emerge.

Christian found it difficult to care. Other hands helped him up, careful to support him without touching his bleeding back. Christian's eyes met Michael's. His friend's face was tight and angry over the beating he had been forced to inflict. Christian suddenly felt exhausted, as if he could drop where he stood and never get up again.

"Be not troubled," he said to Michael. "No one else could have whipped me as well as you."

Michael snorted out a bitter laugh, then cleared the gawking servants from the bailey entrance with a sharp command.

"Find Cook," he snapped. "The young master's wounds need tending."

The staff scurried away even as the men half-carried, half-dragged their *young master* in. Gregori Durand's fortress was a thick-walled square built around a large courtyard. His men-at-arms slept on the upper floors, three or four to a chamber close to the weapons stores. They had never been attacked at home, but they all knew it might happen. No one could doubt they had rivals among the area's mercenary bands.

In these parts, war still brought in more gold than wine.

Christian was one of few with a private room, a narrow, stone-lined chamber with a single window—monklike quarters, at best. The two most massive of the men, Hans and William, laid him on his bed facedown. Despite their care, Christian hissed with pain as the muscles of his back shifted.

"St. Sebastian's balls," Hans swore darkly. "If your father weren't such a good commander . . ."

He was, though, sharp as a Venetian dagger on the battlefield and off. Gregori Durand found them contracts and got them paid, not always an easy matter when the merchant they had been escorting decided he would rather spend their fee on a new mistress.

"It's fine," Christian mumbled into his mattress. "I shall sleep in tomorrow."

Only Michael stayed while Cook came to clean his wounds and dress them in bandages. He sat on the bed after she had finished, not touching Christian but probably wanting to. Ferocious though he was in battle, Michael had a tender heart—and a tendency toward guilt left over from his former failed calling.

"I am sorry," he said now.

"You had to whip me," Christian said. "If you had not, Father would have demanded worse penance."

"No. I am sorry your sacrifice failed to save Lucy."

Christian's hands curled into themselves. "She was just a dog. I should not have let you men get attached to her."

"Stop."

Michael's order was sharp. Christian rolled onto his side to look up at him. His friend's lean, ascetic face was flushed with intensity. "Do not turn into him, Christian. Your father is no better than a beast. In truth, he has less soul than that dog you killed."

"Do you want me to weep for her?" Christian asked, hard with scorn. "Do you think that would change anything?"

"I want you to feel. Or pray. Anything human." Michael covered his clenched hand. "Your mother would not want you to grow cold like this."

Against his will, Christian's gaze slid to the wooden crucifix that hung on his wall. This and a small gold ring were all that remained of the woman who had brought him into this world. He had been seven when she died in childbed, trying to birth the third of his brothers who had not lived. He still remembered his father saying *good riddance to weak stock*. A burn flashed across his eyes, but he tightened his jaw swiftly.

"Let her pray for me," he said. "Let her look down from heaven and pray for me."

Christian tugged his hand back, and Michael rose. He paused, seeming as if he would speak further. But the one-time monk could not bring himself to preach. As he put it, his flesh had always been too weak to counsel others to holiness. Instead, his breath sighed out of him and he left.

Christian knew he had disappointed his friend. He also knew he could not have responded any other way. He wanted to survive, wanted to protect the men who relied on him. If that meant hardening his heart, so be it. From what he could see, God and the saints were a capricious lot anyway.

He rolled onto his face again, ordering his fists to relax. His right hand stroked the coarse wool blanket on which he lay, fingers petting it until he recognized what he did. Pain seized his rib cage worse than any scourge. He could feel Lucy's fur again beneath his fingers, could see her eyes turned trustingly up to his. She had thought herself safe up until the instant he snapped her neck. She had thought herself safe with him.

The first sob tore from him, so harsh and strange he barely knew what it was. Tears came with it and he could not stop them, though he fought hard enough. He could scarcely breathe through the fit of sorrow, the violence of it taking him aback.

Stupid, to cry for a dog. Stupid and pointless.

His sole consolation was that no one was there to see.

Grace was on her feet, standing on the grass-clad stage beneath the magical movie screen. She felt as if her cells were going to explode. Never had she felt more called to action—or more helpless. Considering her recently ended life, that was no small claim.

"I should be there," she said, so sure of it her voice vibrated. "You said he was my *friend*. I should be there to comfort him."

Her tuxedoed guide came toward her down the broad aisle steps, his expression smooth and unreadable. "These events happened long ago."

"You said you could do things for me, if I allowed it. I'm willing to be sent to him."

"I can't send you like you think, Grace, not as a person."

"But you *can* send me."

He glanced at the screen where the young man named Christian lay racked with grief on his narrow bed. "I can send you after a fashion. If that's what you truly wish."

"I promise you, it is."

He looked at her, considering. "I didn't expect you to ask this. There are . . . limitations on this sort of thing. Time will stretch but not indefinitely."

"I accept the limits. Don't you want me to help him?"

She knew she had to convince him. She'd never had a friend that she could remember, not one she'd been allowed to keep. Dead or not, she wanted to know this one.

Michael smiled, slowly, sweetly, his face abruptly so lovely that it hurt to look at it. "I would like you to help him, yes."

His words had power. This place she'd ended up in—the emerald grass, the plush red seats, the flickering screen—melted around her like colored sugar left in the rain. For just a moment she was frightened like the old days.

*Holy cow!* she thought.

And then her feet found solid ground again.

# *Kissing Midnight*

THE FIRST BOOK IN THE FITZ CLARE CHRONICLES
BY *USA TODAY* BESTSELLING AUTHOR

# EMMA HOLLY

Edmund Fitz Clare has been keeping secrets he can't afford to expose. Not to the orphans he's adopted. Not to the lovely young woman he's been yearning after for years, Estelle Berenger. He's an *upyr*—a shape-shifting vampire—desperate to redeem past misdeeds.

But deep in the heart of London a vampire war is brewing, a conflict that threatens to throw Edmund and Estelle together—and to turn his beloved human family against him...

penguin.com

M413T0209

DON'T MISS THE SECOND BOOK IN THE FITZ CLARE CHRONICLES TRILOGY BY *USA TODAY* BESTSELLING AUTHOR

# Emma Holly

# BREAKING MIDNIGHT

Edmund Fitz Clare has been kidnapped by rebellious *upyr* who are determined to create a new world order. It's up to his family and his lover to find him.

penguin.com

M438T0609

# Emma Holly

# *Strange Attractions*

When high-school dropout and unrepentant heartbreaker Charity Wills is offered a chance to attend college for free, she jumps at it. There's just one little catch...

She must travel to the estate of a reclusive physicist with an ingenious mind for sex games. Now, with Eric Berne, her sexy "keeper" lending a hand, Charity's education is about to begin—and it's beyond anything her wildest dreams ever allowed.

"EMMA HOLLY'S GIFT FOR SENSUAL DETAIL IS ABSOLUTELY STUNNING!"
—Susan Sizemore

penguin.com

M104T0907